STORMY SEAS

Forcing her eyes closed, Leana clenched her arms around her knees, trying to will herself not to think such sinful thoughts about the rogue pirate slumbering next to her.

I must go to sleep, she kept forcing herself to think. And then her eyes jerked open widely when the ship pitched with the thundering of a massive wave, causing Brandon to flop over on his other side, facing the back side of her. Leana swallowed hard, drowning in raging passion when Brandon's arm draped over her and his hand rested on her chest. A sensual tremor engulfed her when she became aware of his hot breath on her neck.

And when she felt the hard frame of his body fit into hers, she closed he in frustration. She coul im.

But Brandon was t to let Leana know that . .

BELOVED EMBRACE

CASSIE EDWARDS

ZEBRA BOOKS
KENSINGTON PUBLISHING CORP.

ZEBRA BOOKS

are published by

Kensington Publishing Corp.
475 Park Avenue South
New York, NY 10016

First printing: August 1987

Printed in the United States of America

*For Dee Hansen of Gardena, California,
first a reader, then a fan,
then a dear, close friend.*

—CASSIE EDWARDS

Sing me a sweet, low song of night
    Before the moon is risen,
A song that tells of the stars' delight
    Escaped from day's bright prison,
A song that croons with the cricket's voice.
    That sleeps with the shadowed trees,
A song that shall bid my heart rejoice
    At its tender mysteries!
And then when the song is ended, love,
    Bend down your head unto me,
Whisper the word that was born above
    Ere the moon had swayed the sea;
Ere the oldest star began to shine,
    Or the farthest sun to burn,—
The oldest of words, O heart of mine,
    Yet newest, and sweet to learn.

—HILDEGARDE HAWTHORNE

Chapter One

Scotland . . . 1818 . . .

Gray dawn was breaking. The six-hundred-ton galleon, *Erebus,* eased closer to shore, rail-lined with pirates. *Erebus* was a great, glistening mound of black, almost a sea animal, perhaps a whale, breathing its way through the water, the hull tuned to the motion of the sea . . . alive *to* the sea. It was of a full-rigged design with plenty of canvas in the sail plan, built of superb oak and copper fastenings. It had been built in Vijcaya for the Indies trade and carried eleven guns in each broadside, and Long Tom cannons made of brass were emplaced amidship and on her fo'c'slehead. She was sharp as a wedge below the waterline and flew a black flag on her mainmast with a big white *E* on its foreground.

Cyril Dalton stepped up to the rail on this, his largest conquered vessel, as his crew of pirates made space for him. He stood proudly erect beside the ship's main cannon, which was massive and bronze with twin decorative dolphins riding its massive tube.

Cyril was a commanding figure with his great beak of nose dominating his sun-bronzed face that sported a pencil-thin mustache, framed by coal-black hair tied into a long pigtail down his back. A bright gold religious medal hung around his neck and loops of gold earrings hung from each of his earlobes.

He was dressed in an elegant, brocaded waistcoat, bright red breeches, wide-topped high boots, a brace of pistols in his belt, and a cutlass at his right side.

Lifting his brass telescope, he let his eye scan the land, his heart anxious to see the girl whom he had made his wife a year ago this exact date. Though fifteen and he then thirty, Amelia had stolen his heart and he had married her, keeping her legally as his own, yet knowing that the sea would steal him away from her more oft than not.

But a year being gone he had not planned. It was his business transaction in New York that had delayed him. Had she waited? Was her love that true that a full year apart had not weakened her vows spoken aloud to him?

"Aye," he whispered to himself. "She waited. I promised her many trinkets of wealth upon my return. Ah, how the gold will shine in her violet eyes."

As the ship's white sails fluttered in the soft breeze, Cyril watched as Port Alvin of Scotland's Inner Hebrides drew closer. It was as quiet as the morning sun. The neat slated houses were still slumbering behind darkened windows and the village church steeple rose tall and serene, mirroring itself in the becalmed waters of the Sea of the Hebrides.

Mist was on both the mountains and sea. The risen but still veiled sun gave the eastern sky the cold glow of stone-ground iron. Flecks of white could be seen against rock-torn turf as hardy blackface sheep spilled across the distant hillside.

"Sir, are we just about there?" A young male's voice broke through the silence, edged with that sort of cracked huskiness that came with changing from a boy into a man.

Cyril dropped his telescope from his eye and looked down upon a lad who had just stepped to his side, seeing how he was now almost as tall as himself, that of being six foot, and the lad was only the mere age of eleven.

Slipping his telescope into his waistband, Cyril hesitated at first, then slid an arm about Brandon Seton's lean, yet firming shoulder. "Aye, lad," he said, nodding. "'Ere we be. You're soon to meet me wife." He winked at Brandon. "But I'll have none of yer flirtin', lad. Amelia *is* closer to yer age than mine."

"Sir, I have no eyes for the ladies," Brandon laughed. "Not *yet,* that is."

The mention of ladies reminded Brandon of his mother, and guilt splashed through him for having enjoyed being away from home this past year. But only a few weeks out to sea and he had known that he had been born to be a part *of* that sea and had come to even idolize, instead of hate, the man who had given him that opportunity, though the man had abducted him and had even received *ransom* paid *for* the abduction, to have Brandon returned to his family.

Cyril chuckled, tightening his hold on Brandon, seeing that the rugged life of a pirate this past year, the toil and endurance demanded *of* a pirate, had begun to develop Brandon at once into a man. Though still such a youth, there were traces of his soon being ruggedly handsome. He was bronzed by the sun; his shoulder-length hair, drawn back and tied by leather strings, was now even sun-bleached out to a reddish-blond color.

Brandon's eyes were dark and he was dressed in soft black boots, black leather breeches, with a red sash around his waist, and a loose white cambric shirt opened to the waist.

At Brandon's left side he wore a short saber, called a *manchette*, held within a leather scabbard, a gift to Brandon when he had shown that he had accepted his fate of being a part of Cyril's pirate crew, now even being so willingly.

"And how are you farin', lad?" Cyril asked thickly, his brow furrowing in remembrances of how Brandon happened to be on his ship, the *Erebus*. With thoughts of returning the kidnapped lad after ransom had been paid, it had been something special in Brandon that had changed Cyril's mind, even after the ransom *had* been paid by Brandon's affluent New York father.

It had been while Cyril had been awaiting receipt of the ransom money that he had seen how Brandon had picked up the skills of handling a ship so quickly, and showing a love *for* it. So impressed, Cyril hadn't returned Brandon home. And after a while, seeing that Brandon had accepted his new lot in life, Cyril had begun to treat him as a son.

To Cyril's relief, Brandon hadn't taken long to return the admiration in kind for Cyril, and now all was well in the world for them both. They shared not only the love of the sea, but pirating as well. . . .

Brandon proudly placed his hand on his manchette. "I'm just fine, sir," he said, smiling over at Cyril. "This past year has been the most exciting of my life, thanks to you."

12

"You hunger for adventure, eh?"

"I live and breathe for it, sir."

"No regrets, laddie?"

"Only a few."

"Eh?"

"My parents. My parents must believe that I'm dead," Brandon said, his dark eyes taking on a faraway cast as he turned his gaze back toward land. "But I understand why we've never been able to contact them. If I would, it would most surely lead the authorities right back to you."

"And you don't want that, Brandon? It *was* I who abducted you . . . took you from yer true family."

Brandon's head jerked around. His jaw was set firmly; his dark eyes were flashing. "Sir, I would never let anything happen to you," he said flatly. "Though a pirate, I respect you."

"Those words melt my 'art, they do," Cyril said, dropping his arm down and away from Brandon. He then leaned against the ship's rail. "Brandon, I think it's time you quit calling me *sir*. Call me Cyril. Only boys call me sir. You have developed into quite a man. For that, I am proud." He cleared his throat. "Cyril will do. Aye. Call me Cyril." Having always hungered for a son, Cyril would have preferred to be called father, but he knew that could never be. He hadn't gained that sort of respect from Brandon.

"It would honor me to address you by your name," Brandon said, half-hoarsely. "Thank you, Cyril."

Cyril smiled and nodded.

English by birth, Cyril had been a merchant seaman by trade until he had decided to seek buried treasure in the Bahamas. Having failed to find the treasure and down on

13

his luck, he had turned to piracy. Operating all over, he and his crew plundered cargoes of many ships, attacked and took slaves, then gave them the choice to serve and share equally in the work and the booty with him, or be set free.

A pirate who roved the seas, he and his crew had accumulated a record of activity and seizures and had chosen Scotland's Inner Hebrides for one of their private hideaways. It was a place to return to for rest and leisure before another adventure at sea. It was there that Cyril had met and married his only love, and now he was only but a few heartbeats away from holding her in his arms again. . . .

The drag of the anchor was felt, and anchored too far offshore to run out a plank, longboats were lowered, and Cyril and Brandon were soon on land. In the first light of a Scottish morning they walked on past the wharves and into the heart of the village that sprawled back of the wharves in pleasant disarray, the cobblestone street lined and brightened by flowers.

Chimney pots were clustered on slanting tile roofs above serpentine streets. The tracery of wrought-iron gates framed glimpses of peaceful courtyards that belonged to houses standing and sighing in the sea breeze.

Hurrying their pace, moving on to the outer edge of the village, where a small cottage retreat awaited Cyril's return, the sun found jewels in the dew-drenched bracken and glittered green and gold in Irish-twined vines and in trees planted a century earlier by Scottish lairds.

"This is a lovely land," Brandon remarked, inhaling the moist sweet air, sea-seasoned, moor-scented. "So *quaint.* Nothing like New York. I can see why you chose it as your retreat."

Brandon's gaze traveled along the rocky shore where they were now walking, and settled on a huge castle. He laughed softly and nodded toward the castle. "Though I would have thought you would have chosen a castle instead of a cottage for display of your captured prizes from your many voyages," he added.

"My best prize of all awaits me, lad, in that yonder cottage," Cyril said, smiling. "Me *wife.*"

"I see," Brandon chuckled. Then his face grew serious. "You did make mention of another hideaway. Is that where you keep your jewels? You never say much about it."

Cyril patted Brandon fondly on the back. "Nor will I now," he said. "When the time is right you will even be *taken* there."

"Is it because you do not yet trust me?" Brandon pouted, showing the not quite yet mature side to his nature.

"Trust?" Cyril said, forking his eyebrows. "I do not even wager on who I can or cannot trust. One has to win it."

"And . . . I . . . haven't yet, Cyril?"

"Time will tell. But, aye, I think that you have nothing to worry about, lad. But we haven't been back in New York waters again since your abduction. Which will you choose when we *do* return? Your life of the sea? Or will you return to that of the land?"

"You already know the answer to that," Brandon grumbled. "But if proof is what you will need . . . proof is what you will *get.*"

Cyril saw the determination etched across Brandon's

15

handsome face and could hear it in his voice and he already had his answer, but he wouldn't tell Brandon that no true proof of loyalty was needed. It was best for Brandon to prove it to himself. For that reason only did Cyril change the subject as they continued making their way toward the small cottage that faced the sea, alone on a high bluff.

"So you think a castle would be a proper home for a pirate, eh?" Cyril said, cupping a hand over his eyes to shut the glare of the morning sun from them as he looked toward the castle.

Brandon lifted a shoulder in a casual shrug. "It would do in a pinch," he mused, his eyes twinkling dark as he looked over at Cyril.

Cyril's head jerked around and his eyes locked with Brandon's. "In a pinch?" he said, roaring with laughter. Then he sobered and gestured with a sweep of a hand toward the castle. "Lad, you do not know whose castle you are belittling."

Again Brandon shrugged. "No. I do not," he said softly. "Should I?"

"Being from America? No. S'pose not. But let me tell you a bit about that castle, lad," Cyril said, again absorbing the great structure of stone beyond, on the rocky shore. "It was the fortress seat of the MacDonald lairds, who ruled under Norwegian and later Scottish kings until the strong, sly Campbell laird of the eighteenth-century empire."

He nodded toward the flock of sheep on the hillside close to the castle. "See the sheep?" he said. "The money-hungry lairds found sheep more profitable than men and evicted thousands of crofters from farms their families had worked for generations. This was back

16

during the time of the old clan system, when the laird was chief as well as landlord and often kin to the small tenants who pastured their flocks on clan lands. After the defeat of Bonny Prince Charlie in 1746, the old society collapsed. The rush for money replaced feelings and gave rise to new-style lairds, among them many outsiders."

Cyril paused at a white picket fence, letting his eyes feast on the cottage and what awaited inside it. He was anxious, hopeful. "Some of these lairds drove crofters from the ancestral land when sheep were reckoned more profitable than peasants," he added. "But they were wrong. And before long the Dunyveg Castle stood vacant, as did most of the village of Port Alvin. That's why I felt safe to establish a retreat here, to come here when in this part of the Atlantic. There is no law here. Everyone is their *own* law."

"Seems peaceful enough," Brandon said, looking over his shoulder toward the village and in awe as to how quiet it was, now realizing that it seemed to be a hideaway for more than Cyril and his pirates. All sorts of outlaws surely made up the population.

Cyril opened the gate and stepped inside the fence. "Lad, let me go to 'er first," he said. "After we've made our proper hellos, you can come in and meet my bonny lassie."

A flush rose to Brandon's cheeks, remembering having seen intimate embraces of his parents that had been meant to be private. "I understand," he said, smiling awkwardly. He began walking away, toward the rocky ledge that dropped many feet downward into lapping waves. "I'll be over there until you're ready to introduce me."

Brandon stooped and picked up several pebbles and be-

17

gan tossing them downward into the water as he stepped up to the ledge. Out of the corner of his eye, he saw Cyril go to the door of the cottage. He tensed when he saw the door open, wondering why Cyril didn't embrace the lady at the door, or go on into the cottage *with* her, yet then he saw why. Upon closer examination he knew this lady couldn't be Amelia. This lady was elderly. Amelia was known to be young . . . beautiful . . . ravishing. . . .

Cyril clasped his hand onto his belted pistol, his heart lurching when Amelia's aging Aunt Maudie stood at the cottage door, her wrinkled face void of a smile and with fear in her eyes. Had something happened to Amelia?

Not waiting to ask, not even giving Maudie a civil hello, Cyril brushed on past her and into a sun-brightened living room filled with plushly upholstered furniture of a bright flowered pattern.

Only silence greeted Cyril. He rushed into one bedroom and then another, seeing no signs that would reveal that Amelia even lived there, *ever*.

"Cyril . . ." Maudie said from behind him. "She's gone, Cyril. She *and* her baby."

Cyril swung around, his face inflamed with color, his stomach churning with the knowing. He took one wide step and clutched his fingers onto Maudie's thin shoulders, feeling bone through her plain cotton dress, more than flesh. Her gaunt face had paled, blending with the gray of her hair coiled into a tight bun atop her head.

"Where is she?" he stormed. "And you said that she had taken her child. *What* child? Maudie, if you value your life, you'll tell me."

"Please release me, Cyril," Maudie said, trembling. "Then I'll tell you. I'll tell you as much as I can."

Cyril dropped his hands down away from her, his gray

18

eyes wavering. "I didn't mean to hurt you," he said thickly. "But findin' 'er gone has half crazed me. I had . . . half . . . suspected it. But I hadn't wanted it to be. I know how long I've been gone."

"Go into the living room and sit down and I'll serve you some tea while we talk," Maudie said softly, placing a hand to Cyril's elbow, trying to urge him from the bedroom.

Cyril turned and boldly faced her, knocking her hand away. "Maudie, tea is the last thing I want," he said flatly. "Now tell me. Where's Amelia?"

Maudie began to wring her bony hands, her eyes apologetic as she looked up at Cyril from her five-foot height. "I don't know, Cyril," she murmured. "All I know is that as soon as her child . . . *your* child . . . was born to her and she and the baby were strong enough for traveling, she boarded a ship for America. That's all I know, Cyril."

Cyril kneaded his brow, his gut twisting, the hurt was so severe. "My . . . child . . . ?" he said hoarsely. "Amelia gave birth to my child . . . and . . . then left for America?"

Rage engulfed him. He again clasped onto Maudie's shoulders. "Damn it, Maudie, why would she do that?" he shouted. "Why?"

Maudie winced. "She said she couldn't let her daughter be raised on an island of outlaws . . . by a pirate father," she whined. "She said she'd prefer her daughter be raised in total poverty than by a . . . father . . . who was a pirate."

"A daughter . . . ?" Cyril gasped, slowly lowering his hands to his sides. "I have . . . a daughter . . . I'll never see?"

19

He walked from the room and from the cottage, his head hung. He had known that Amelia hadn't liked the fact that he was a pirate, had even tried to talk him into retiring. Had she waited just awhile longer, he would have granted her that wish. He had planned to enjoy his craft for possibly one more year and then . . .

But now all was changed for him. He would be a pirate until he died! The sea . . . being a pirate . . . would never betray him!

"Cyril? Sir?" Brandon said, hurrying to Cyril's side when seeing him leaving the cottage in such a strange, withdrawn state, and so soon after having just entered.

Cyril only half heard Brandon as he headed back toward the village. He had lost not only a wife, but also a daughter. He couldn't understand how Amelia could do this to him. Why hadn't she waited and at least talked it over with him?

But instead she had deserted him as though he had never meant anything to her at all. He felt used . . . miserably used. . . .

"Cyril, what's happened?" Brandon asked, matching Cyril's wide, hurried steps with his own, proud of his taller height. "Amelia's not dead, is she, Cyril?"

"No, but better if she were," Cyril growled, his face dark as thunder, his rage was so intense.

"What . . . do you . . . mean . . . ?" Brandon asked, lifting an eyebrow quizzically.

"She's gone, lad," Cyril said hoarsely. "And she's even taken my child away from me so that I'll never see 'er."

Brandon's eyes widened. "Child?" he said. "You never made mention before of being a father."

Cyril glared over at Brandon. "I didn't know that I

20

was," he said. "Amelia gave birth while I was gone. A daughter. She's taken my daughter away to America, yet I know not where. I'll never even *see* 'er, Brandon. Me own flesh and blood."

Cyril raised a fist and looked up into the heavens. "May Amelia be cursed forever for what she's done to me," he snarled.

"I'm so sorry, Cyril," Brandon said, swallowing hard.

"Not as sorry as Amelia'll be if I ever catch up with 'er," Cyril growled. "And I *will*. One day I will, lad. She'll wish she hadn't thought our daughter too good to be raised by a pirate father."

"Why would she?" Brandon asked. "Amelia knew you were a pirate when she married you, didn't she?"

"Aye, that she did," Cyril sighed. "But she married me because her father urged her to *and* with hopes of reformin' me."

Cyril stopped and gestured with a full sweep of a hand toward the distant green hills. "When I first saw Amelia she had come down from those hills, a wee lassie she was, ah, so innocent, trailing along after her father, who had come to the village for a month's supply of household items," he said thickly. "It was 'er father who introduced us. *Glad* he was to marry 'er off, to even a *pirate*. One less mouth for him to feed."

Cyril lowered his eyes. "A delight she was in *and* out of bed, though only fifteen," he mumbled, flashes of remembrances of silken thighs and budding breasts flooding his memory. "And now she's *gone*."

Straightening his shoulders and firming his jaw, Cyril placed an arm about Brandon's shoulders. "Come with me to the village. Let us find us a pub and open it. Share several tankards of ale with me, Brandon," he snapped.

21

"Today we make you into a *real* man. You'll learn to hold your liquor, *and* you've already learned this day to be wary of women. We won't be lettin' any female do to you what my Amelia has done to me, will we? Don't ever give a wench your name. Then yer 'art will be spared the ache mine is feelin'."

"Yes, sir," Brandon mumbled.

"And after we get damn drunk, let's leave this wretched place behind for*ever*," Cyril stormed. "It's the *Big Thicket* for us, Brandon. Let's journey on to *Texas!*"

Cyril then chuckled. "Lad, I've just proven my trust in you," he said. "I've just let you know where my main hideaway is."

Brandon's eyes brightened. "In Texas?" he gulped. "Where the Comanche Indians take scalps for not even a reason?"

Cyril roared with laughter. "Aye, lad," he said. "That's Texas all right. Comanches. Mexicans. And beautiful women if you can find 'em. The type of women you bed then *leave*."

Then Cyril sobered. He placed his face into Brandon's. "Always remember, lad," he growled. "Women are for beddin'. *Not* marryin'."

Brandon's face suffused with color. "Yes, sir," he gulped. "I'll try and remember that."

Cyril patted Brandon's back. "Aye, you do that," he said dryly. "And you'll be 'appier for it."

Chapter Two

Fifteen Years Later . . .
1833 . . . New York City . . .

Leana Rutherford was not so deeply engrossed in her needlepoint that she wasn't aware of eyes on her, silently studying her. This only added to her displeasure of her boring pastime of sewing, realizing that her stepbrother, Matthew, was again amusing himself by watching her.

Leana now wished that she hadn't worn her new silk dress with its daring low-swept bodice. She could feel Matthew's eyes warming her flesh where her breasts now formed a cleavage, something of which she had only recently become proud. Becoming a full-fledged woman had fascinated her. It had even become something to show off, so proud she was of her new, womanly curves. But not to her twenty-three-year-old stepbrother!

Anger rose inside Leana, knowing to expect more than mere silence from him at any moment now. Whenever he could find her alone, he added torment upon torment by pursuing her affections. It had been after she had begun blossoming fully into a woman at her age now of sixteen that this had begun. Each day Matthew was becoming more demanding, yet only when alone with her.

Up to now, Leana had been able to handle Matthew. But she knew that before long she would have to go to her stepfather, Parker Seton, and demand that he talk to his bothersome son!

Leana would have done this sooner, but she hadn't wanted to paint an ugly picture of her stepfather's only surviving son to him, especially after having lost his other son so tragically those many years ago.

Parker Seton had never truly gotten over the fact that though he had paid a ransom as had been required of him, his son, Brandon, had not been returned as promised by the heartless pirates. And not only had Parker lost a son because of the evil doings of the pirates, but also a wife. Her heart had not taken the shock of losing her oldest child.

It had been four years later that Leana had been introduced into the Seton family when her mother, Margaret Rutherford, had become Parker Seton's second wife. And though Leana's true father had been dead for many years now, having died in a massive fire when she was five, she still retained her father's name of Rutherford.

Though he loved Leana dearly, Parker Seton hadn't taken time from his business affairs to legally adopt her.

But that seemed to matter not, except that Matthew Seton felt that the name difference gave him the excuse needed to toy with the thought of seducing the beautiful young thing who slept under his same roof, and who was not of his blood kin. . . .

24

Pricking her finger because of her annoyed state, Leana emitted a soft uttering of discomfort and placed the bleeding fingertip to her lips.

"Ah, I see I've come just in time," Matthew announced as he marched on into the sitting room. He dropped to a knee before Leana and took her finger from her mouth. "Let me do the honors, Leana."

Before he could get her finger to his own lips, Leana had it jerked away from him. "Stop that," she hissed, glowering at Matthew as he gave her a whimsical smile. "If not for you I wouldn't have pricked my finger. Why must you persist at watching me as though . . . as though . . . I were a prized filly on display?"

Matthew straightened his back and rose to his full six-foot height. "Ah, but to my estimation you *are*," he teased, his dark eyes dancing. "But one not yet petted by a man. Now, my dear, if *I* were that man—"

"Oh, you!" Leana interrupted, flustered. She knew that her cheeks were red because they were scalding her clear to her bones. Though handsome Matthew was, with his dark shock of hair groomed neatly to his shirt collar, and a face so handsome all women stared openly at him, and even magnificently built with muscles rippling at his shoulders and thighs, he stirred her heart all right, but only into a silent loathing.

He was not only egotistical, he was a bore. And every time he chanced a touch of her, she would only grow cold inside, as though a winter wind had touched her all *over*.

Even now, dressed in an expensive maroon velvet frock coat, satin cravat, and tight fawn breeches, Matthew couldn't draw a look of admiration from Leana. Instead, she gathered her needlework together and slammed it on a table beside her chair and rose quickly to her feet.

"I find this room a bit too crowded to my liking," she spat, walking in a huff toward the door. "If anyone should ask, I've gone to the privacy of my bedroom."

In a swish of skirt and petticoats, she turned and gave Matthew a sour glance. "At least while there you don't dare to bother me," she said icily. "Matt, if you ever so much as open my bedroom door, I will go immediately to your father."

In this room of gilt chairs and velveteen settees, lace curtains, and flowers arranged in vases on many oak tables, Matthew thought Leana to be even more beautiful and enticing. Her face was oval, with ivory skin and wide ocean-blue eyes. Her luscious lips were ripe and full, her body supple and slender, yet already fully bosomed.

Soft and shining, her coal-black hair hung long and free to her waist and appeared to hold a cast of blue within it with the morning sun so vividly brightening the room.

"My, my, aren't we a mite touchy this morning," Matthew laughed, removing a thin cheroot from a gold-encrusted cigar case. After casually lighting it he hurried after Leana, who had rushed on out of the room. He fell in step beside her before she reached the grand staircase that led to the second floor of this mansion in Manhattan.

"I wouldn't be in such a hurry to isolate yourself in your bedroom," Matthew said dryly, taking puffs from his cigar. "Father sent me to tell you that he will be in the sitting room shortly after he first has a talk with your mother in privacy. He wishes an audience with you, Leana."

Leana stopped short. She turned on a heel and looked up at Matthew, suspicious. "Is this a new ploy of yours,

26

Matt, to keep me with you longer?" she said vehemently. "If so, it's not going to work."

Whipping her skirt around, she took a quick step away from him but was stopped when he was again beside her, grabbing her wrist.

"Damn it, Leana," he growled. "Why must you always be so supicious of me?"

Leana laughed sarcastically. "Ha! You can ask that?" she said. Then she frowned darkly up at him. "Unhand Me, Matt. I've had enough of your games this morning. Won't you ever give up?"

"I'm serious, Leana," Matthew sighed, dropping his hand down and away from her. "Father did send me to tell you that he wanted to talk to you. He asked that I see to it that you are in the sitting room. He will be there soon."

Leana rubbed her aching wrist, always having realized just how strong Matthew was, and wondered, if he should ever truly decide to take full advantage of her, would she be able to stop him?

She swallowed hard, knowing that, yes, she must talk with Parker, and soon. Matthew must be stopped before it was too late.

"What does he want to talk about?" she said coldly, lifting her chin haughtily. She would not let Matthew see that she was the least bit afraid of him. That would only add fuel to the fire where he was concerned.

"That's for him to say," Matthew said, taking his cigar from between his lips. "So you see, you'd best return to the sitting room."

He leaned into her face. "And I promise to behave," he chuckled.

"Only because you know that Father will be here

shortly," Leana hissed, then stormed away from Matthew and back into the sitting room.

She paced the floor, waiting. She ignored Matthew as he came back into the room. She didn't even look his way, relieved that he was a man of his word at this moment, for he was leaving her alone.

But when heavier footsteps entered the room, Leana turned on a heel and smiled toward Parker Seton, again taken by his magnificent physique and good looks, though he was now in his late fifties.

Parker's dark eyes were the same as Matthew's, but his hair was not. It was the color of carrots. His facial features were strong, his jaw was squared and determined, his nose quite perfectly straight. He was always dressed impeccably in the best woolen suits, and his leather shoes were always polished to such a luster as to see oneself in them, as though they were a mirror.

This day he wore no smile, and Leana could see worry heavy in his eyes.

Parker went to Leana and embraced her. "Honey, how are you this morning?" he said in his deep, resonant voice. "I hope I haven't detained you from something else you may have had planned for yourself."

Leana returned the hug, always relishing the strong feel of his arms and his manly smells of after-shave and cigars. In him she had found a father, as she knew that he had felt for her as a daughter. He made her feel safe, even peacefully happy.

"No," she murmured. "I have nothing planned. I always have time for you, Father."

He stepped back away from her and held her at arm's length. "Good," he said thickly. "We have much to talk about."

28

Leana felt a strange pulling at her heart, hearing such an odd, withdrawn tone to his voice. It was as though he were carrying the burden of the world on his shoulders. But he *had* the world in the palm of his *hands*. He had everything. Wealth, power, a wife who loved him, and everything else that could make a man content and feel secure with life. What could have changed for him? Visibly, it all seemed the same. . . .

"What is it, Father?" Leana murmured, now letting him urge her down into a chair. "Has something happened?"

Parker eased into a chair across from Leana. "There's to be a change in our lifestyle, Leana," he said, clasping his hands together on his lap. "I've been planning it for some time now but just haven't told you or your mother. I didn't want to worry you."

Leana glanced over at Matthew, seeing a small smile lifting his lips. Something cold touched her heart, realizing that only he had been taken into Parker's confidence. Was her stepfather suddenly disenchanted with his wife? Was he going to cast her and her daughter from the fold? But no. There had been no signs of this. It had to be something else.

Focusing her full attention again on Parker, Leana leaned forward. "What is it that you haven't told me?" she said dryly. "Have you . . . have you already spoken with mother about it? Matthew did say something about you speaking to Mother this morning in private."

Parker nodded. He casually crossed his legs. "Yes," he said. "She knows. And she seems to be taking the news well enough." He cleared his throat nervously and began drumming the fingers of one hand on a knee. "And I think even you may accept what I'm about to say.

29

Perhaps you will even see some excitement to the idea."

Leana sighed. She flipped her hair back from her shoulders. "Father, I cannot say unless you *tell* me," she sighed.

"Leana, we're going to make a move," Parker blurted, watching her closely for her reaction. She had become as important, if not more so, than Matthew. She had come along just in time, to take the place of Brandon. She would always be special to him because of this. She had been a blessing when blessings had been stolen from him, as well as his heart.

"A move?" Leana said in an almost whisper. "Do you mean we are all leaving New York?"

"For now it will be only myself and Matthew," he said hoarsely.

Leana's insides splashed cold. She stiffened. "What do you mean, only you . . . and . . . Matthew?" she dared to ask. "What about me and . . . and . . . Mother?"

"You will be taken care of properly in my absence," Parker said, his eyes wavering.

"Oh, I see," Leana said dryly, setting her lips firmly. Had she been wrong about him? Had he never truly loved her at all? Had he just been playacting with her *and* her mother? Perhaps there was even another woman. . . .

"No, you don't," Parker said. He went to Leana and took her hands and eased her up from the chair, to stand before him. "Matthew and I must go ahead of you and your mother because we must first get settled. I will then send for you both. But it may take a full year, perhaps even longer, for the proper preparations before we can send for you."

Leana frowned up at Parker. "Will you truly send for

us?" she said coldly. "Or is this a way to rid yourself of us? Father, please tell me I am wrong. You wouldn't do that, would you? You wouldn't abandon us?"

Parker's face paled. He now understood how this had all sounded to Leana. In a rush he grabbed her into his embrace and tightly hugged her. "Oh, honey," he murmured into her ear. "You don't think I could ever abandon you or your mother, do you?"

"I don't know what to think," Leana said, drawing away from him to look defiantly up into his eyes. "Perhaps you could tell me exactly what you and Matt have planned. Where do you plan to go? And why? I thought things were going so smoothly here. You're the president of the largest bank in New York City. Everyone admires you so. Has something happened to change that?"

Parker turned his eyes away from her. He went to the liquor cabinet and poured himself a shot of whiskey. "What I have planned to do has much to do with many things," he grumbled. "I had planned to make a move many years ago, after Brandon's abduction. When I saw that he wasn't going to be returned to us, I had wanted to run and hide *then*. I wanted to get away from this city that had managed to steal my son away from me."

He turned and stared at Leana. "But I couldn't," he blurted. "I always had hopes that Brandon would still be alive . . . could, somehow, come home on his own. I clung to that hope. But it's time for me to accept life as it is. Brandon is dead. There's no need to wait any longer. I must get away. Soon. And far away, Leana. As far away as I can."

"But, where . . . ?" Leana persisted, going to him,

placing a hand on his arm. "And I want to go with you. I don't want to have to stay behind like some helpless ninny."

"You and your mother *must* stay behind," Parker said, frowning down at her. "Matthew and I are going to be traveling to the frontier, to the primitive land called Texas. It is a new land. It will be a new life."

"Texas?" Leana gasped, taking a wide step away from Parker. "But Indians are there. And crazed Mexicans. I've read about it. The Comanches strike everywhere without warning and with a terrifying vindictiveness. They are burning homesteads, leaving charred and mutilated bodies behind. Father, surely you aren't serious about going there."

"Texas is a land of wealth and adventure," Parker said, refilling his glass with more whiskey. He took a quick swallow, then placed the glass down on a table. He couldn't tell Leana and her mother *nor* Matthew that he also saw Texas as a place to hide. He couldn't tell them even why he had the *need* to hide. Only he knew.

But soon many would know. Hopefully Leana and her mother would be spared the embarrassment of knowing. If he could hide them away in the church rectory until he could send for them . . . ?

"Texas is for those who dream of independence," Leana argued. "Why would you need any of these things? You have your wealth here. You have as much independence as a person needs to survive. Or is it the adventure that you need, Father? If so, I'm afraid you may find more than you bargain for if you travel to that untamed territory."

"Mexico has promised four thousand acres of free land to anyone with a family who will settle on the land, provided he and his family are Catholic or will join the Catholic Church," Parker argued back. "By going there, I will amass much more wealth, and since we are a family of Catholics, I see no reason not to take the Mexicans up on their offer."

"But Father . . ." Leana said softly, worrying so about his decision, thinking that if he would go, she may never see him again.

"The Mexicans hope to seek, through an influx of settlers, to check the Indians who dominate the huge province," Parker stated flatly. "It is the remote section of Texas, bordering the land called the *Big Thicket*, that I have chosen to bargain for with the Mexicans. If luck is with me and Matthew, we will have a *rancho* built in less than a year's time and then we can send for you and your mother. But first Matthew and I must have the chance to tame the savage wilderness, to make it *safe* for you women."

Leana sank down into a chair, feeling as though her world was tumbling around her. "So mother and I will be staying here? At the house? Until you send for us?" she asked softly, pleading with her eyes up at her stepfather. She already missed him and he wasn't yet gone.

Then she glanced over at Matthew, seeing the only light at the end of the tunnel with this decision of change for the family. Matthew would no longer be around to torment her. At least she had that for which to be grateful.

Parker turned his back to Leana, not wanting to give her the opportunity to see his eyes, for fear she would see so much in them that he didn't want to reveal to her. He went to a window and drew aside the lacy curtain and looked out upon a busy thoroughfare, the huge buildings

33

already crowding out residences. He felt choked at times and welcomed the chance to leave.

"No, Leana, you won't be staying here," he said thickly. "It wouldn't be safe for two women to live without a man in the house." He again couldn't tell her the absolute truth. He had to hide them away from the truth that would soon be disclosed upon his absence from the bank. Now if only he could make it sound valid . . . this way he had chosen to keep them from finding out!

Leana rose quickly from the chair and, in a rustle of skirt and petticoats, went to Parker's side. She clasped anxiously onto his arm. "Father, what are you saying?" she gasped. "Where would mother and I stay? This is our home. We know nothing *but* this house as our home."

With his heavy brows knitted together, Parker slowly turned his gaze to meet Leana's hurtful, questioning stare. He lifted a heavy hand and patted hers fondly, reassuringly. "Honey, you will be staying in the rectory with Father Bailey," he said softly. "I can think of no better place for you and your mother."

"Father Bailey . . . ?" Leana said, her eyes wide with wonder.

"Yes. And you are to go there soon," Parker nodded. "And once there, you will be isolated from all that you know. It is a necessary evil to this plan of mine."

Leana gasped; she paled even more. "Isolate? Do you mean I . . . I could not even see my friends? I could not entertain?" she barely whispered.

"A rectory is not the proper place for entertaining, would you say?" Parker said, finding this harder than he had anticipated. He had forgotten Leana's spirited makeup, her restlessness. Could she stay hidden away

34

from those who would question her about her step-father's sudden disappearance? She must. God, she must!

"No," she murmured, lowering her eyes. "It is not. But I will miss it all so much."

"I will make it all up to you, Leana," Parker said, drawing her into his arms, tightly embracing her. "Just be patient. When I leave this city, it is best that you and your mother stay quietly at the rectory. Women without men are so . . . so vulnerable. Do you understand?"

Leana circled her fingers into tight fists as they lay against his chest. "I think so," she murmured. "But it will be so hard, Father. So hard. I only . . . only recently developed *into* a woman. I had planned to enjoy socializing . . . well, you know what I mean."

Parker chuckled. He held her away from him and let his eyes move slowly over her, admiring her newly acquired curves. "Yes, honey," he said. "I understand. But you won't waste away to an old woman in the short time Matthew and I will be gone." He glanced over at Matthew. "Will she, Matt? Wouldn't you say that she will be just as pretty in, let's say, one or two years from now?"

Matthew, who had remained silent the last several minutes, stepped up beside Leana. He gave her a look that only she understood, a look of hidden, lustful desire. It made an involuntary shiver engulf her.

"Yes, I would say Leana will even be *more* lovely," he said thickly. "Time enhances beauty."

Parker forked his eyebrows and kneaded his chin as he studied Matthew, hearing more in his words than was intended? Then he shrugged doubts aside. "Something else I failed to tell you, Leana," he said. "When I do send for you and your mother, Father Bailey will be ac-

35

companying you on your sea voyage to Texas. I will be paying his way in return for looking after you. He says that many lives are in need of God out in the wilderness. He is anxious to go there."

"You made mention of a *Big Thicket*, Father," Leana said, clasping her hands together behind her, now letting herself see the excitement in what lay ahead of her. At first, fear had robbed her of any other feelings. But the more she thought of herself going to Texas one day, the more she liked the challenge *of* the adventure.

"What is the Big Thicket?" she added.

Parker again turned his back on Leana and gazed from the window. "It is a wilderness that the Indians call the *Big Woods*. The white man gave it the name the *Big Thicket*," he said quietly. "It's land that lies between the Sabine River on the east and the Brazos River on the west. It is land of swamps and bogs, forest and savannas, sand hills and floodplains that lie in close proximity. It's a big thicket of dark and mysterious forests and wild creatures, of ghostly visions. There are legends of ghosts and visits from the dead, and of buried Spanish gold, and phosphorescent balls of fire. There is even talk of it being the denning-up ground of an assortment of desperadoes."

Leana hugged herself, suddenly feeling cold. "And you . . . wish . . . to settle close by there?" she said, her eyes wide. "Father, surely there is a much better place for our new home. Surely none of us will ever be safe there. You may not even get a house built before . . ."

She bit her lower lip, unable to say the words that she felt. But she did feel that perhaps her father would never be able to send for her and her mother. The chances were that he would not even live *long* enough to.

"Father, it's as though you are settling near the Big Thicket because *you* have a need to hide," she said in a strain. "Why is that?"

Paling, Parker turned around in a jerk and looked down at Leana. "I have explained enough to you about my choice of land," he said thickly. "Please accept it, Leana. I have thought long and hard about it. This is what I think is best for the family."

"But . . . ghosts . . . desperadoes?" Leana said, visibly shuddering. "Isn't it enough that you will be going to a savage wilderness of Indians? Why must you settle so close to . . . to . . . a place that offers even more dangers?"

"Leana, I have made my choice," Parker said flatly. "And that is all that I have to say about it."

Leana watched as he lumbered from the room, leaving her alone with Matthew, in an awkward silence.

Matthew went to her and cupped her chin in a hand. "Leana, I don't know what you're worrying about," he chuckled. "I'll be there to protect you, won't I?"

Leana's gaze moved slowly upward. She was feeling his eyes undress her and knew that she had more to fear than the Indians once she had also traveled to Texas.

Then she stiffened her spine and sparks of fire appeared in her eyes. "I don't need you for anything now, nor will I when in Texas," she hissed, jerking away from him. "And, Matt, remember what I'm about to say. When I do arrive to Texas and you ever so much as lay a hand on me, it won't be the Indians nor the desperadoes you will have to fear."

She leaned up into his face. "Matt, I would shoot you first. . . ."

Chapter Three

Two years later . . . 1835 . . .

It had been a week of wild extremes in which the pirate ship *Erebus* was first swept backward by headwinds and then lay becalmed in quiet waters for endless hours, and was then lashed by storms.

Though known by most seamen as a superstition of the sea, the seventh wave in the turmoil of a gale was said to be the worst, the one that does the most damage. But on that one savage evening in the Atlantic, the worst waves seemed to be coming at the *Erebus* in a strange, new sequence . . . not every seventh, but in random groups of *threes*. As the monstrous swells crested and thundered toward the *Erebus*, each one was capable of swamping, capsizing, or destroying the craft.

But when the storm had finally worn itself out and became as only a whisper of a breeze, the *Erebus* was found to be partially disabled and was forced to limp close to New York moorage for repairs.

Dawn found the pirate vessel clutched in the clammy

grip of a fog so thick it was barely possible to see the ship's bow from the stern. Brandon Seton was on the main deck, pacing in a cottony world all his own, aware of other creatures only through the cries of unseen gulls and the hammerings of the crew making the needed repairs.

Haste was needed. Once the fog lifted, the dangers in these waters were worse than any storm at sea. Too many knew too well the identity of this pirate ship. It was this menacing vessel that had ravaged these very waters for the past fifteen, even twenty years. . . .

But Brandon had other reasons but to worry about where the *Erebus* was anchored to cause his brow to knit and a tugging at his heart. Though he and the crew of the *Erebus* had been in these New York waters many times since that day he was abducted those many years ago, the ship had never before dropped anchor, tempting him as it was tempting him now.

Now as never before he felt the need to see his parents and his brother Matthew. It was like a wound festering inside him, this guilt he felt for having never tried before to see his parents since his abduction.

But he had chosen the alluring life of a free, unrestrained outlaw . . . an outlaw of the sea. Not only would he place his idol Cyril Dalton's life in jeopardy, but even now himself. He was now on the list of wanted men as well. . . .

"So you are torn, are ye, Brandon?"

Brandon turned with a start. Cyril's voice had cut through the fog like a knife, making him now even feel guilty for wanting to leave the ship to go in search of his family. His loyalty was now to Cyril, not a family who even now surely thought Brandon to be dead.

Brandon and Cyril had gone to hell and back together while riding this pirate ship. No one could ever replace the times Brandon had shared with this man he so admired. Cyril was a man of dedication to his craft. And he was a respecter of man. Never had he tortured those he had taken captive. Those who wished to be set free had been set out in longboats, left in awe of the pirate whose name was synonymous with fear. . . .

"Cyril?" Brandon said in a strain as Cyril stepped out of the fog and to Brandon's side. "I didn't know you were there. How long *were* you?"

With gray threads now weaving through his black hair and wrinkles creasing his commanding face, Cyril placed an arm about Brandon's shoulder. "Long enough, lad," he said thickly. "Long enough." His brow furrowed. "I was readin' yer thoughts, Brandon. I know what ye be needin' to do. And I understand. You even have me blessing." He nodded toward a longboat. "Row ashore, lad. You'll never have peace o' mind if you don't."

"But what if the authorities . . . ?"

"You'll have to decide yer fate once you reach shore, lad."

"And how can I have such a power as that?"

"You'll have to make a choice as to whether you just see your family from afar, or go to them and let them see that you are still alive."

Brandon placed a hand on his manchette, aye, truly torn. "If I do see them, I fear that I will have to embrace them," he said hoarsely. "How could I not?"

Cyril lifted a shoulder into a casual shrug, though his insides were anything but relaxed. He knew what Brandon must do . . . deny himself the pleasure of reaching out for comfort of a mother's arms. Even a handshake with his father was something that had to be denied. Both these things would seal Brandon's fate, and also Cyril's. . . .

Cyril had to believe that Brandon was stronger than Brandon was at this moment giving himself credit for. He silently observed this man whom he had raised as though he were his own son.

Brandon had developed into a powerfully built man, now even taller than Cyril, and Cyril could boast of being six feet tall. As Cyril had wagered, Brandon had grown into a ruggedly handsome man, his skin burned bronze; his hair, which was drawn back from his face and tied by a leather string, was burned reddish-golden.

Brandon's dark eyes were almost fathomless, his thoughts so often kept to himself. In his pirate attire of full-sleeved white cambric shirt unbuttoned to his waist, revealing his powerful, lightly furred chest, and tight black leather breeches, revealing muscled thighs, he was the epitome of virility.

Cyril smiled to himself, realizing that Brandon had left a trail of broken hearts behind him, having always remembered Cyril's warning that women were for beddin', not marryin'.

But now it was not a woman in the throes of wanting to be seduced by Brandon, but his family doing the seducing. And Cyril knew that it had to be Brandon who would have to make the decision as to whether or not he *or* his family would be the victor. . . .

"Lad, go ashore," Cyril finally answered. "Then do as yer 'art guides."

Brandon squinted his eyes, trying to see into and through the fog, where the shoreline of New York City lay. Still he could only see a wall of white. "But what if the fog should raise while I am gone?" he worried aloud.

"If the ship is mended, we will take 'er farther out to sea," Cyril said, setting his lips into a narrow line. "You will then have to use yer skills and muscles to find us, lad." He dropped his arm down away from Brandon. "But we won't go far. I don't want to test yer abilities too much. I don't want to lose ye, lad."

"Then you truly do understand why I must do this thing?" Brandon asked, yet seeing concern in Cyril's pale gray eyes, this enough to know what Cyril would rather Brandon do. Brandon admired Cyril even more now, realizing that Cyril was ready to risk everything just to let Brandon test his feelings about the past, challenged by the future. . . .

Cyril patted Brandon on the shoulder. "You don't need anyone's approval or understanding," he said thickly. "You're yer own man now with decisions to be made regarding yerself. You don't have to answer to me now, as you haven't at all in the past. Once aboard the *Erebus*, you became your own person, lad, even from that first moment, though you were at that time known to be my captive. I saw in you strength . . . knowledge of the sea . . . never before seen in a lad of such a young age. Even then, before you even knew yerself, I knew that yer future was with me and the sea. Yer decision to stay with me was not only guided by my decision to keep you, but by yerself, when love for the sea became stronger than that for yer family."

"And now?" Brandon said thickly, his eyes wavering. "How do you think it will be? Once I see my family—"

"*If* you do," Cyril said, nodding. "Remember, lad. You may feel it best not to see them." He motioned toward the longboat with a sweep of his right hand. "Take the boat.

42

Go ashore. Now. The fog is only a momentary shield for the *Erebus*. Make haste, lad. My 'art will be on hold until yer return."

Brandon's pulse raced. It felt as though something heavy was at the pit of his stomach, his anxiousness was now so severe. He looked down at his clothes, knowing that they alone could reveal that he was not an ordinary businessman roaming the streets of the city. He was a pirate in appearance. Anyone could tell that. He must change into ordinary street clothes, those which he saved for such occasions as playing another identity in other cities, when wanting to remain incognito, where pirates were hung when recognized.

"Aye, I shall make haste," he blurted. Then he was compelled to throw his arms about Cyril in a fond embrace, that which he seldom did for fear of what the crew might think of these two pirates who were almost inseparable.

But in the cover of the fog, such fondness could be shared without criticism, and all the well for Brandon, for he felt nothing but warmth and gratitude at this moment for the man whom he loved, and wanted to be able to show it!

"I shan't be long, Cyril," Brandon said softly, then turned and rushed away into the fog and below deck, to change his clothes.

Cyril's heart pounded against his ribs. He clasped his hands onto the ship's rail so tightly that his knuckles were white, so fearing the next few hours. If he lost Brandon, he would lose a part of himself. He felt as though he should go with Brandon, be there to protect him if need be, but he had to remind himself that Brandon was now a man, even more so than Cyril was himself, for Brandon was young . . . strong . . . and quick on his feet. He needed no protection from anyone.

Except from, perhaps, his . . . family . . . ?

Filled with gloom, Cyril stood alone and listened for Brandon's departure, then tensed when he heard the longboat being lowered into the water. Now all he could do was wait. . . .

Upon his first landing, Brandon had moved quietly along the cobblestones of South Street Seaport, where ships were docked in the East River, veiled in the still lingering mist of fog. He had found a horse and buggy for lease and was now traveling down Schermerhorn Row, going north, and then traveled on past towering buildings until he made a turn on Second Avenue, where he began looking for the house in which he had been born and raised until he was ten.

But the farther he traveled, the colder he grew inside. Most residential houses had been razed and had been replaced by new brick buildings, all of which were now being used for commercial purposes. Through the fog he could make out a restaurant, bookstore, retail shops for clothing, and an art shop.

Open food stalls now replaced some of the houses, the smells almost mind-boggling and appetite-tempting.

But food was the last thing on Brandon's mind. He now knew that the house that once was the Seton family's proud mansion was no longer in existence, and he had to wonder about the family themselves. Where were they? Why had his father sold out, when all along his father had sworn to never let the city eat up his property with ugly buildings that had no personality.

"But apparently he did. And it seems that *I'm* fifteen years too late," Brandon whispered harshly to himself.

Snapping the horse's reins, he rode onward. He knew where he could find the answers. He would go to his father's bank. But he had to be careful. He had already decided that he would only view his family from afar. Seeing them was all that was important to him. The time for embracing had long since past. They had surely given up on him long ago and it would serve no purpose now to reveal himself to them, for he would not stay once he did.

He also knew that it would only add insult to injury if they knew that he hadn't only died, but had chosen a life of piracy over them. And there was the chance that he would be turned over to the authorities by someone needing the glory for having done such a deed.

Brandon would not take that chance. No matter what he found out at the bank, he knew to remain dead to his family. . . .

Seeing a trace of morning sun trying to break through the fog, Brandon tensed. He knew that he didn't have all that much time. . . .

He traveled the cobblestone streets, weaving his way around other buggies, stately carriages, and lone horsemen. The city had fully awakened. The doors of the buildings had been thrown widely open, beckoning customers toward them.

And when Brandon caught sight of the grand old building that housed his father's bank, he felt a knot of remorse entangling his insides. He now knew how much he had missed his father, even more so his mother.

As for Matthew, Brandon could honestly confess to himself that he hadn't spent that much time in wonder over his younger brother. Matthew had been a thorn in

45

Brandon's side from the time he had been able to walk and talk. Matthew had been spoiled and mean, to the point that Brandon had almost hated him.

Brandon had to wonder what adulthood had done for Matthew. But he could just imagine. Surely Matthew was arrogant . . . probably even a womanizer.

"He probably even keeps count of the ones he succeeds in seducing," Brandon laughed to himself. "Probably even notches his gun with each conquest."

Then he grew somber as he drew the horse to a halt alongside the sidewalk. With a trembling in his knees that Brandon was not accustomed to, never having been plagued by cowardice, he reined the horse to a hitching post, then stepped up to the bank and tried to compose himself before entering the wide double doors which reflected him in their shining glass windows.

Taking a slow look at himself out of his pirate attire, Brandon hardly recognized himself. He was dressed impeccably in a beige frock coat, a satin cravat at his throat.

His breeches were of a fawn color and clung to him as though they had been poured onto him, and his brown leather shoes shone from a fresh waxing.

Having removed the leather string from his hair, Brandon had brushed it to hang neatly to his shoulders, and in his eyes he could see an anxiousness, that which usually only reserved for when seeking out the pleasures of a lady.

"God," he whispered, brushing his fingers through his hair. "I've got to get hold of myself. I'll give myself away, for sure."

Understanding the dangers only too well, Brandon knew that he had come this far and could not turn back.

If only it would have been simpler for him! If only he could have seen his mother in the window of the stately mansion of which she had been so proud! If only he could have seen his father leaving this house for his morning duties at the bank! Then Brandon could have returned to the ship, victorious.

But not now. He had to find out answers and be damned with the dangers. Being a pirate, he had taken many chances. This was only one more to be faced. . . .

Sucking in his breath and walking straight-shouldered, he stepped on into the bank. He saw many eyes focus on him from behind the windows where the clerks waited for new customers. Brandon stopped long enough to study each face, yet saw nothing familiar about any of them. But it had been fifteen years, hadn't it?

Then his gaze began moving slowly on around the room and settled on the closed door that had always led to his father's private office. His heart began to pound as his gaze lowered and began to read the name engraved in gold on a wooden plaque attached to the door. And then his heart became encircled by a strange coldness when seeing that it was not his father's name, but instead, someone else's.

Taking a step backward, Brandon emitted a low gasp. He jumped when a soft hand touched one of his and he found green eyes looking studiously up at him from a delicate lady of perhaps fifty years of age.

"Young man, may I be of some help to you?" the lady asked, smiling warmly up at Brandon, displaying a straight line of white teeth. "You seem at a loss as to what you wish to do. Do you wish to make a deposit? Or withdrawal? Or do you wish to speak to someone about a loan?"

"I have business with Parker Seton," Brandon found himself blurting. His eyebrows forked when he saw a sudden look of distaste encompass what was only moments ago a gentle face on the lady.

"You have come to speak with Parker Seton?" the lady said, lifting her chin, her eyes now flashing angrily back at Brandon.

"Yes," Brandon dared to say, knowing to see his father face-to-face could be disastrous from the very moment of discovery. But he had no choice. It seemed to him that his family had suddenly disappeared from the face of the earth! And he had to know why, and *where*, if answers *could* be given to him.

The lady began walking away from Brandon, yet looked at him over her shoulder. "Come this way, young man," she said. "I will show you to the proper person for which to speak business with. You see, Parker Seton is no longer with us."

The words seemed to sting Brandon as though a dozen bees were swarming over him, sticking their stingers into his flesh. Now he knew that his father *wasn't* at the bank. The thing to find out next was *why*. But he had to be cautious. No one could know who he was. He had to playact as never before. . . .

The lady opened the door that Brandon was so familiar with. How many times had he come and gone from that door? If he would close his eyes, he could even feel that he was that ten-year-old boy again, ready to go inside to talk over the troubles of the day with his father. He had even pretended that he *was* his father at times, the voice of authority at the bank. He had even dreamed of following in his father's footsteps when he was older.

But that had all changed, once at sea. Ah, how

48

wonderful it had felt, that feeling of freedom, that aloofness with the rest of the world that came with riding the waves. . . .

"Well, young man?" a booming voice spoke, shaking Brandon from his reverie. "What is it that I can help you with this day?"

Brandon cleared his throat nervously, as he also did his thoughts of yesterday, and found himself staring down at a face quite familiar to him on a tiny form of a man slouched behind a great oak desk. Brandon paled when seeing his father's partner . . . a partner always to Brandon's disliking. He was even uglier in his older age, his gray hair groping his thin face like fingers, his thick nose spreading and flaring with each of his heavy breaths.

"Uh, sir," Brandon said quietly, feeling uncomfortable under the close scrutiny of the paling blue eyes of Joseph Chauncey. Was Joseph recognizing him, seeing him, though fifteen years older? "I've come to complete a business transaction begun with Parker Seton. May I please speak with him? He is more familiar to my affairs than you, a mere stranger."

"How long ago did you begin this, eh, transaction with Parker Seton?" Joseph asked, leaning forward with his elbows on his desk and his fingertips together. His eyes were twinkling, as though he was enjoying this cat-and-mouse game, seeming anxious to catch Brandon in a lie.

"Does that matter?" Brandon asked, stiffening his spine, disliking Joseph even more now than before.

"Seems so," Joseph chuckled, again easing back against the plushness of his leather chair. He began stacking papers into a neat pile, yet never taking his eyes off Brandon. "If you would say you had transacted business with Parker, let's say, last year, I would even then say that you are mistaken."

Brandon's eyes wavered. "And why is that, sir?" he dared to ask, his lean fingers loosening the cravat at his neck, almost choking from it and emotions now swimming around inside him. Something was quite amiss here. He wasn't sure now if he even wanted to know what. . . .

"Parker Seton has been gone two full years now," Joseph growled, placing the neatly stacked papers aside. "And he'd better stay gone. If I got my hands on him, I'd . . ."

Joseph stopped in midsentence as his face took on a red cast. "Uh, I spoke out of turn, sir," he apologized. "Now, if you would be so kind to take a chair, I will assist you since Parker Seton is no longer here to do so."

Brandon had had enough of beating around the bush. He leaned his hands down onto the desk and lowered his face into Joseph's. "I won't do business with anyone but Parker Seton," he growled. "Now. Tell me. Where can I find him?"

Joseph stirred in his chair. "Sir, I have no idea where he is," he said dryly. "He just up and disappeared one day." He snapped his fingers. "Just like that. He and his family were gone." He emitted a low snarl. "And not only that, half the money of the *bank*."

Brandon jumped as though he had been shot. He stepped back away from the desk, disbelieving what he had just heard. "Are you saying . . . that . . . Parker Seton . . . embezzled the bank's money and then left town with his family?" he gasped.

"Yes. Seemed he wasn't rich enough to suit him. He became greedy. Parker embezzled the money and left

50

town with his *new* family," Joseph corrected, lighting a cigar, thrusting it hard into his mouth. "Yep. His new family. The first wife died almost as soon as her son was abducted. Her heart. Poor woman. Her heart just wouldn't hold up under the pressure. But lucky for her. Had she lived to see what Parker had done? It'd killed her for sure."

Brandon's brains seemed scrambled; his eyesight had become strangely fuzzy. Too much had been revealed too quickly, and most of it shocking. His father had turned into a crook. His mother had died? And his father had . . . remarried . . . ?

Joseph lifted an eyebrow quizzically. "Young man, are you all right?" he asked. "You seem a mite pale. Was it something I said?"

Brandon kneaded his brow, his insides feeling empty. If his mother had died, wasn't he at fault for not having gone back to her? Yet hadn't Joseph said that she had died almost at the same time he had been abducted? She had been dead when the ransom had been paid . . . ?

"Do you know where Mrs. Seton is buried?" Brandon suddenly blurted, his voice sounding thick, almost inaudible.

"Why, certainly," Joseph said, squinting his eyes as he further studied Brandon. "But why would you want to know?"

"I was lucky enough to make her acquaintance at one time in the past," Brandon said, almost choking on the words.

"Oh, I see," Joseph said, kneading his chin contemplatingly. "I guess she was an impressive one, she was. I always felt drawn to liking her." He wrote an address on a piece of paper and slipped it into Brandon's hand. "Go there. You will find her grave. And light a candle for me in the church, son."

Without even a thanks, Brandon rushed from the bank, his eyes filled with tears that he had refused to shed for many years now. Boarding the buggy, he only barely was aware of the lifting fog. All that he could think about was the grave . . . his mother's name on a gravestone. Oh, how the knowing hurt. And where could his father have disappeared to? Who had he married?

Traveling the streets, Brandon finally found the Catholic church that he had always known as a child. He reined the horse and fled on inside the church, eager to see Father Bailey again.

But when he found that Father Bailey had recently, in fact, only a day ago, left for a long sea voyage, he had only the grave to visit, and then he would become a part of the sea again himself.

Hurrying on outside to the back of the church, where many gravestones rose like pale ghosts from the ground, he searched until he found the proper one. Dropping to his knees, he wept over the mound of dirt under which lay his beloved mother.

"I'm sorry, Mother," he sobbed, feeling a boy again, only wishing his mother were alive to comfort him in his sorrow. "Had I known, I would have come sooner."

He said a few silent prayers, but when the sun began beating down onto the back of his bowed head, he was alerted to the real things of life, that which waited too close to New York's moorage.

"Christ," he gasped, looking up into the clearing heavens. "I must get back to the ship. What if it's already too late . . . ?"

Breathless, he ran to the buggy and whipped it in and

out of the hustle and bustle of traffic and back to the docks. He paid for the services of the buggy, then hurried to his longboat and began rowing, seeing the many white sails furled out on all the ships leaving the harbor. He had to beat them to the *Erebus*. If it was spotted, it would be doomed.

He turned his head and looked over his shoulder, seeing the sails of the *Erebus* becoming filled. He was now close enough to see Cyril waving at him, and knew that all was well, except in Brandon's heart. . . .

Chapter Four

Leana stood at the ship's rail, worrying about the silence of the ship, *Jasmine,* on which she was now traveling, along with her mother and Father Bailey. The wind had deserted the schooner altogether and it had lain becalmed for hours. There had been mention made of pirates in these waters and she knew the dangers of staying in one place too long.

Restless, feeling the heat of the sun on her head free of any sort of a bonnet and where her silk dress dipped low at her bodice, she looked down into the water, envying the porpoises that were torpedoing past the ship, leaving ghostly phosphorescent trails.

Then her eyes followed another movement. Pale ghosts in the stern light's glow, gulls searched the wake for edibles thrown over the side.

"Leana," a weak voice spoke from beside her. "Father Bailey is worse this morning. I'm worrying so. We've only just begun the journey. Without proper doctoring, he may not survive our voyage to Texas."

Leana's eyes widened in horror with such a thought.

She glanced over at her mother, Margaret Seton, seeing that even her mother was still much too pale, as she had been since the very first movement of the ship. "But, Mother, surely it will pass," she murmured. "It's surely only motion sickness, as it has been even for *you*."

In her mother she could see an older mirroring of herself in the blue of her mother's eyes and the darkness of her hair. Her mother's tiny waistline was becoming to a lady her age of forty, yet she hid her other asset, the magnificent swells of her breasts, behind a high-necked dress, too dark even for Leana's liking.

But Leana had to think that her mother had worn such a dress because her mother had been told by her husband to behave anonymously while on the voyage, had even, strange as it seemed, urged her to use the name that her first husband had given her.

It was as though Parker Seton *still* had something to hide. But neither Leana *nor* her mother understood what, or why this change in her mother's name while on board this ship. If they had been face-to-face, Leana would have questioned her stepfather about these strange orders.

But having only been given instructions as to how to handle this voyage by way of letter, she had no other choice but to comply. She had wondered if it all went back to the time when Brandon had been kidnapped. The name Seton was well known to many. If it became known that Margaret Seton and her daughter were traveling alone on the high seas, might pirates take advantage of this knowing and again command a large ransom from the prosperous Parker Seton? A second time would surely kill him.

Yes, surely this was the reason for anonymity. It was the only thing that made any sense.

"It is more than motion sickness," Margaret still worried aloud. "Father Bailey seems . . . seems to have fallen into some sort of unconsciousness. He doesn't know me this morning, Leana. You'd best go to him. I will instruct the captain of the ship of his worsening health. There must be something that can be done."

Leana began walking hurriedly away, with her mother following alongside her. "If need be," she stated flatly, "the ship will have to dock at the closest port. If Father Bailey is that ill, a doctor must be summoned for him."

"Yes. You are right," Margaret nodded. "Do hurry on, Leana. I will now go and speak to the captain."

Leana nodded and hurried below deck. She traveled the narrow, dark corridor that took her to the cabin at the far end. Remembering that her mother had said that Father Bailey was unconscious, she didn't stop to knock. Barely breathing, she opened the door and tiptoed inside, into a dimly lighted cabin. A whale oil lamp fluttered golden light down upon a face ashen in color where Father Bailey slept soundly on a bunk beside the outside wall.

Hearing a strange rattling with each of Father Bailey's drawn breaths, Leana tensed, having heard about the death rattles. Was he this ill? Was . . . he . . . going to die?

This tore at Leana's heart, having grown so close to this special man these past two years while living with him in the church rectory. He had done everything in his power to protect, even entertain, Leana and her mother during their awkward time of separation from the rest of the Seton family.

And now this was the way he was to be repaid for all of his kindnesses? He was ill, possibly dying, before getting to spread his gospel in the land of Texas, the thing that had begun to matter most to him?

Leana moved to her knees beside the bunk and placed a hand to Father Bailey's fevered brow. "How can God let this happen to you?" she quietly sobbed. "You've always been so kind and generous. You've not a selfish bone in your body."

The rattles continued as he breathed. Leana sank a cloth into a basin of cool water and wrung the excess out, then began gently rubbing the dampened cloth across his brow, then his cheeks. He had become sick so suddenly and his face showed what the fever had done to him. His cheeks were sunken and gaunt, his eyes had sunk back into his sockets, his lips were flaking from dryness. His sparse gray hair was wet ringlets circling his face; a gold cross hung from about his neck against his flat chest, where a blanket was drawn up to rest beneath the pits of his arms.

"It has to be some sort of strange fever," Leana whispered. "I now know that it has nothing to do with motion sickness. One doesn't get this sick." She half moaned. "Oh, what shall I do? I feel so . . . so . . . helpless."

Determined, she dropped the cloth back into the water and rushed from the cabin back to topdeck and began looking for her mother and the captain. She would demand that the captain stop at the next available port for a doctor.

Then Leana's gaze was drawn to the sea. She stopped abruptly and her heart began a happy hammering when seeing a ship on the horizon. It was as though a silent prayer had been answered. A ship meant possible medical assistance. Perhaps a physician traveled the ship and could come aboard and see what could be . . . *must* be done . . . for Father Bailey.

But remembering the lack of the wind, her heart sank. How could the ship travel any faster than the ship Leana was on? Without wind, the sails were useless.

A creaking of rope and a flutter of sail above her made Leana look quickly upward. And when she felt the lift of her hair from her shoulders, she knew that perhaps another prayer had been answered. The wind was now blowing, filling the sails! There was hope after all!

Running to the *Jasmine*'s rail, she leaned against it and began waving toward the other ship.

Then her eagerness faded into a numbness. The approaching ship bore a black flag, that which was not welcomed by anyone who happened along it while on the high seas. Oh, God, it . . . was . . . a ship . . . of pirates . . . !

Swallowing hard, she again began her search for her mother and the ship's captain. But this time for another reason. She had to spread the word, though she knew that this ship's crew had surely spotted the devil ship that was now much, much too close. It was obvious that with the scurry and scrambling of the crew, they were preparing for possible battle. . . .

Cyril was sweeping the horizon with his telescope, Brandon at his side. And then he spotted the white sails against the brilliant blue sky in the distance. His blood began pumping hot through his veins, as it always did upon discovery of a possible *prize*. It had been too long. He had fought off the urge of capture for too long now.

But no longer. He must again feel the victor, for the

time had come to seriously think of placing the pirating days behind him.

His gut twisted, thinking that he would have even done so fifteen years ago had his wife not deserted him. But because she had, he had had the need to work the hurt from his system, not knowing that it would take forever. . . .

Cyril chuckled low. "Do you see 'er, lad?" he said, dropping the telescope from his eye, handing it toward Brandon. "Take a look. Wouldn't you say that yonder ship needs some excitement? Don't you think that it lies much too calmly in these waters? It's surely the Mexicans flying a different flag, meant as a disguise, yet carrying many a weapon. Don't you think so, lad? If they transport these weapons on to Mexico, they'll only be used against the American settlers who've settled close to Mexico, in Texas. You know the threat is real!"

Brandon took the telescope and looked toward the fluttering sails on the far ship, not able to deny the fact that he also hungered for the fight. He knew that once they reached Texas, more than likely it would be the last of his pirating days. He had prepared himself for the change by learning the art of horseback riding. He had even gone looking at the land, wondering which would most fit his needs.

But the influx of settlers had chased him back into the Big Thicket for security, always fearing being recognized.

Would . . . that . . . ever change? He did want a normal way of life one day. But could a woman ever be a part of that life? He was always haunted by Cyril's tormented words, that of no trust for a woman . . . any woman, ever. . . .

"Aye, I see her. I'd bet it is the damn Mexicans,"

Brandon nodded, handing the telescope back to Cyril. "Do you say we fire on her? Or do we sail on past?"

Cyril's eyebrows arched; his gray eyes were dancing. "We warn 'er first," he mocked. "We must be fair, eh, lad?"

Brandon smiled back at Cyril. "Aye, we must be fair," he said amusedly.

"The fight is what you need, Brandon," Cyril said, clasping onto Brandon's taut shoulders. "It'll be a way of gettin' yer mind off New York and what you found there." He laughed hoarsely. "Seems yer father took to piratin', but in another way, eh?"

Brandon's brow furrowed; his back straightened. "It is not what my father did that bothers me so," he said quietly. "It is the grave that I had to kneel beside. My mother. She's been dead for so long now and I didn't even know."

"Aye," Cyril said, turning from Brandon, again peering toward the ship that they were soon to board. "And it is my fault, lad?"

"No," Brandon said sullenly. "It is neither of our faults. To have gone sooner would have been disastrous for us both. You know that."

Brandon cleared his throat of the knot paining him there. "It was best that it happened the way that it did," he said. "But I do have to wonder where my father has disappeared to. And my brother Matthew. But it is a foolish wonder. I shall for certain never see them again."

He nodded toward the awaiting ship. "Cyril, let's go and have our fun," he suggested, placing his hand on the manchette at his side. "It's been too long. Aye, too long."

Cyril's eyes were agleam when he turned on a heel and began shouting out orders to his pirate crew. And glad for

60

the return of the wind to his ship's sails, he watched the distant ship grow closer . . . closer. . . .

"Shoot 'er a warning shot across the bow!" Cyril shouted, drawing his cutlass, waving it in the air. "If she fires back, give 'er hell!"

The cannon shot boomed out, causing even the *Erebus* to shudder from the jolt. Brandon watched as the cannonball whizzed across the neighboring ship's bow. And when the fire was answered by cannons firing back at the *Erebus,* there was then a series of more cannon bursts from the *Erebus,* filling the sky with smoke so black, day seemed to suddenly turn to night. And as the *Erebus* drew even closer to the other ship, stinkpot jars which had been hoisted up to the masthead, rigged on halyards, were tossed over onto the other ship's deck, starting fires in several places.

"I think we've got 'er," Cyril shouted, waving his cutlass. "Move closer! It's time to board 'er!"

Black, thick smoke swirled over the other ship's deck, its crew panic-driven to put the fires out. The helmsman at the tiller of the *Erebus* sailed right up on the ship, underneath the scrolled and fancifully decorated aftercastle overhang. Sharp-fluked grapnel hooks with light lines attached to them were thrown up to catch along the aftercastle molding; the pirates then scrambled onto the other ship, which bore the name of *Jasmine* painted on its hull, musket and pistol fire ringing in the air.

When the firing was done and all was mutely silent, Brandon began walking along the deck of the ship, inspecting the bodies, seeing if any were still alive, in need of medical assistance, while the defeated crew that hadn't been slain looked angrily on. Brandon was numb from the discovery! This wasn't a Mexican ship at all! It was a full American crew. A mistake had been made, and he regretted it, though Cyril seemed not to.

"All's well up here," Cyril shouted, ignoring the look of horror on Brandon's face. "Brandon, go check below deck. See if there are any cowards hidden there. If so, bring them up here. I'll check out the hold of the ship. We have ourselves quite a prize here, wouldn't you say? All signs lead me to believe that though this is not a Mexican ship, it carries riches . . . riches that are now ours, fairly fought for and won."

Still momentarily numbed by the discovery, and seeing Cyril as he remembered him as the powerful pirate he had been those many years ago, and understanding why Cyril needed this sort of escape from his worries, Brandon tried to accept what had already happened this day, yet vowing it would be the *last*. From now on, the ships would be carefully scrutinized before being fired upon. Brandon himself would see to that!

Brandon withdrew a pistol from his gunbelt and began moving stealthily down the companionway, each step taking him farther into a smoky dungeon, it seemed. He coughed, he rubbed his eyes, yet moved on through the narrow corridor. His plan was to start with the cabin at the far end of the corridor and make his way back to the companionway, searching along the way. He had to wonder if there were any women aboard this ship, but had to think that there were. This was a passenger ship. He had to believe that he would find many women huddling behind these closed doors that reached out on both sides of him.

This was another part of pirating that he didn't like. . . . Though most ships sought out were Mexican ships carrying weapons as their cargo, there were usually

62

ladies on board. The capturing of helpless ladies bothered him sorely. Most were enjoyed by the pirate crew before being left at a port to find their own way back home without money, husband, and most usually respect for their bodies that had been ravaged.

Brandon was proud to be able to say that he had not been a part of such ravagings. He had refrained from taking a lady by force, having enough colorful ladies at each port to satisfy his manly cravings *willingly*. He had even refrained from joining in with the shooting of these ship's crews, except when it was to protect his very own life.

He knew that both these things had disappointed Cyril, yet then again, Cyril had shown hidden admiration for these traits of Brandon's, realizing that the first ten years of Brandon's life had molded his personality, having been taught the evils of murder . . . and . . . rape by his father after Brandon had reached the age of teaching the good and bad of what life had to offer.

Having now reached the far end of the corridor, thankful that the smoke was thinning as fresh air from top deck made its way downward, Brandon moved his free hand toward the latch of the door on his first cabin to search. Tense, he slowly opened the door and peered inside, then dropped his pistol to his side when seeing a man lying lifeless beneath blankets on a bunk against the far wall.

Gingerly stepping on inside, looking cautiously from side to side for the possibilities of someone hiding, waiting to jump out at him, he made his way on across the cabin and took a better look at the unconscious man. He was jolted by recognition when looking down upon the face of the man. Though the man was old and bleached pale by sickness, Brandon couldn't help but recognize the features of Father Bailey! How could he not know him? Father Bailey had spent much time with Brandon in Brandon's youth! Father Bailey had taught him everything there was to know about being a Catholic! Even that of being a *man!* He had taught him much about life, even more than Brandon's own father had had time for.

Dropping to a knee, suddenly a boy again, forgetting the havoc wreaked on top deck of which he had been a part, Brandon knelt close to Father Bailey, having never thought to suspect that this was the ship that Father Bailey would be on.

"Father Bailey," he said, placing a hand to Father Bailey's cheek.

Brandon drew his hand quickly away, a tremble coursing through him, when having felt the complete coldness of Father Bailey's skin. "Lord," he gasped. "He's dead."

The knowing tore at Brandon's heart, feeling at first responsible, then realizing that this man who lay before him had been dead much longer than even before that first shot had been fired from the cannon on the *Erebus*. He had apparently died from natural causes. Not from the battle.

Tears splashed from Brandon's eyes as he slowly drew the blanket up and over Father Bailey's face, feeling the loss, wishing it weren't so. Father Bailey had been the last link to Brandon's past now that Brandon didn't know where his father and brother had traveled. And now even Father Bailey was gone from him.

But he knew that life for himself must go on. He rose to his full height and lumbered from the cabin, then again poised his pistol in front of him as he stepped up to the next cabin's door and slowly opened it. His eyebrows forked when seeing two beautiful ladies embraced, clinging, their eyes wild as they watched him enter. His gaze raced over them, seeing that one was young, and the other perhaps in her early forties.

Mother and daughter, he presumed, and guilt plagued him as it always did when seeing women in distress, that from his own doings.

Upon closer examination as he stepped closer, seeing the fine details of the younger lady beneath the soft glow of the whale oil lamp burning beside her, he found her to be intriguingly beautiful, the most ravishing lady he had yet to lay eyes upon.

His loins did a slow aching, his heart began a dangerous pounding, something no other lady had ever caused before at first notice of her. His eyes took in the soft blue of her eyes, the sleek, satiny blackness of her hair which hung to her waist, and the perfect oval of her face, pink with fear.

Unable to control himself from looking farther, he found her heaving breasts to be quite magnificent in proportion, and her waist so tiny, if he wrapped his hands about her, he could surely place his fingertips together behind her!

Her chin was held high, daring him to move closer, and though her eyes were soft in color, they now flamed in anger back at him.

A slow smile lifted Brandon's lips, liking fire in a lady, and thinking this particular lady was the first whom he desired to, indeed, ravage!

"Who are you?" Leana hissed, yet already knowing the answer. This man standing before her, more handsome than any other man ever seen before, had to be one of the marauding pirates from the devil ship that had taken over the ship on which she had hoped to reach Texas. Now would she ever? She didn't even want to think of her fate now, *or* her mother's. Perhaps it was a blessing, even, that Father Bailey had already died. He would be spared the wrath of the evil pirates!

"My name matters not," Brandon said dryly, having to remind himself of the duties that lay ahead of him. These were the first of the survivors below deck. He had the task of rounding them all up to force them to the upperdeck.

But in the lovely lady's presence it was hard for Brandon to remember anything. He felt like a schoolboy, eagerly awaiting that first kiss from a pretty girl.

Brandon gave Leana a roguish smile. "But later I will see to it that you will tell me *your* name."

"And it will be I who will refuse to tell you," Leana said icily.

Margaret stood trembling. She began to worry about Leana's snappish remarks, thinking this might cause the pirates to treat them even more badly than already planned. "Leana, please be quiet," she whispered, yet not quietly enough so that Brandon didn't catch the name.

"Leana is it?" Brandon chuckled. "Aye, you would have a captivating name to match your, shall I say, colorful personality and lovely face."

"A pirate who knows the art of flattery?" Leana hissed, doubling a fist to her side. "But, yes, I am sure you have had plenty of practice. Just how many women have you captured and ravaged, sir? Or do you even bother to keep count?"

Though Brandon was enjoying this bantering, he knew that it had to be brought to an abrupt halt. Cyril was not the sort to want to linger on a captured ship for long. The exchanges of captured booty and prisoners were usually made in only a matter of moments, escape necessary before another ship might happen along to spot the ship responsible for leaving another to drift lifelessly along, having been turned into a ghost ship.

Brandon took a quick step forward and latched his hand onto Leana's arm, just touching her sent a spiraling of heat to his brain. "Go to topdeck, Leana," he flatly ordered. "And also your mother." He gave Leana a sideways glance. "This is your mother, I gather."

"And should you even care?" Leana snapped, following alongside him as he led her from the cabin. "Isn't one lady the same as another with a pirate? Or do you sort the young from the old and have your fun with the prettiest?"

Brandon ignored her, knowing already what he had planned for Leana. It would be the first time, ever, for him to take a prisoner for himself, alone, on the *Erebus*. But there was too much about Leana that was causing his heart to thump wildly inside him to not pursue these feelings further. With someone like her the words of warning spoken to him by Cyril could be so easily cast aside. . . .

"Just do as you are told and quit questioning me as to what I shall or shall *not* do," Brandon said dryly, now releasing his hold on her as the corridor was reached. He nodded toward the closed door that led into the next cabin. "Tell me. Who is in there?" His gaze traveled from one door to another and another. "And who are in the others? Are there men? Or are there only women?"

"Ha!" Leana laughed sarcastically, lifting her chin even higher. "I refuse to tell you anything. Just let you find out yourself. Who knows? A pistol might be awaiting you." She laughed bitterly. "You deserve much more than merely to be shot, though. You should be made to suffer an agonizing, slow death for being what you are."

Her eyes wavered as she looked toward the companionway. "Just how many were killed on topdeck?"

She then glowered up at Brandon. "You're inhuman. How could you attack a ship of innocent people and kill and maim?"

Her eyes traveled over him, again seeing how handsome he was, seeing even a gentleness in his eyes and in the smile that he had given her earlier. There was even something about him that was familiar, yet she couldn't put her finger on it. But she was very aware of how his dark eyes were disturbing her. Had she met him under different circumstances, she could gladly accept the nervous beat of her heart while standing so close to him. She could even understand the coil of desire that was drawing more tightly inside her.

But this was a pirate. She couldn't let herself feel anything for him but hate and disgust. She should only loathe him, not be letting her mind wander to what it might be like to be kissed by his sensually full lips, or to be touched by his strong, bronzed hands. How exciting it would even be to be held by him, or even to share a bed with him, enabling her to explore the taut, muscular length of his body. How exhilarating to have found a man whose very presence spoke to her of not only strength and power, but also tenderness.

Oh, why did he have to be a pirate? She had dreamed of finding someone like him ever since dreams of a future with a man began to materialize inside her brain. . . .

Brandon felt the need to tell her that it had not been his or Cyril's intent to fire upon an innocent American ship. But he did not confess to mistakes so easily! And would she even believe him? The reputation of the *Erebus* had been formed even way before he had boarded her those many years ago. Even now that the *Erebus* and its crew mainly sought out Mexican ships, it made the *Erebus* no less the threat it had always been in the past, to American ships.

"If you don't wish to tell me how many, or who is in the other cabins, then I shall find out on my own," he growled. "But do as I've told you. Go on up, to topdeck. From there you shall be transferred to the *Erebus.*"

"*Erebus?*" Leana murmured, her eyes wide.

"The devil ship, so you called the ship I travel," Brandon said, his eyes twinkling. "You are soon to travel on that devil ship."

"And . . . what . . . is the fate of this ship?" Leana dared to ask.

"It will be left to drift," Brandon said.

Leana looked over her shoulder, toward the cabin where she had left Father Bailey only moments before the first shot had been fired from the pirate ship. She had witnessed his last breaths. She would never forget the sound of the choking rattles as he had struggled to breathe. Would he now be left to float on a ship, to never have a permanent resting place for his body? The thought tore shreds of her heart away.

"Father Bailey," she blurted, pleading with her eyes as she looked up at Brandon. "What shall become of him?"

Brandon's eyes wavered with the mention of Father Bailey. Yet he felt the need to not reveal that he also knew the Catholic priest of his childhood. It was always the same. Brandon could never utter his last name to strangers for fear that doing so would lead authorities to Cyril, and he would be hanged for his kidnapping and all other crimes committed since then.

Brandon couldn't even speak of his past life to those he met. And he had yet to find anyone whom he felt close enough to, to completely confide in them of his deepest, hidden feelings and emotions.

It was the same now. To show a knowing of Father Bailey would only raise questions that he was not yet prepared to answer.

"Father Bailey?" he asked, lifting an eyebrow, trying to pretend that he was ignorant of such a name, or man. "Who is this Father Bailey that you make mention of?"

"He was the Catholic priest who was also traveling on this ship," Leana said, remembering to be cautious, to not associate herself too closely with knowing Father Bailey or anything that might lead one to know that she was related to Parker Seton.

She again looked toward the cabin where Father Bailey lay, quite dead. "He is in that cabin," she pointed. "He died a short while ago."

Again she pleaded with her eyes as she looked up at Brandon, remembering having seen the gentleness in this pirate's eyes, surely thinking that he would understand the need of a burial for this priest, where perhaps no other pirate would ever understand anything so civil.

"He is in need of a burial," she murmured. "Please do not leave him to just drift at sea on this ship."

Brandon's eyes lowered. He swallowed hard, wondering if Cyril would understand this need of burial at sea for this beloved man of God. But understand or not, Brandon, as well as Leana, understood, and Brandon was, by damn, going to see that it was done, and properly so.

"He will have a burial," he said as his eyes implored Leana. "But it will have to be here, at sea. Land is too far. He . . . he would not last. I am sure you understand, Leana."

"At . . . sea . . . ?" Margaret gasped, paling. "Lord . . ."

Leana drew her mother more closely to her side. "It's the only way, Mother," she whispered. "At least it is to *be* a burial. He could have been left here, on this ship. Surely you see the necessity of this type of burial."

Margaret silently nodded.

Leana smiled weakly up at Brandon. "Thank you," she murmured, then guided her mother on toward the companionway, and to upperdeck.

When she reached the upperdeck and saw the lifeless bodies spread out on the deck, she felt a light-headedness sweep over her and a sick feeling rise from the pit of her stomach. How could she have thanked the pirate for anything? This viewing was enough to prove to her just how inhuman *all* pirates were, even if the pirate showed sensitivity in his eyes and smile.

Protecting her mother, Leana drew her back away from the center of the deck and waited until everyone below deck had been herded to topdeck. She even watched as all valuables were being carried from the hold of the ship *Jasmine,* and on over to the pirate ship.

And when all of this was done, Leana glared at the pirate with whom she had had a brief encounter. He now stood beside a commanding figure who appeared to be the leader of all the pirates. And Leana was surprised when the lead pirate gave those men who were still alive of the ship *Jasmine* a choice to join the pirate crew, or join those who would be set out in longboats, to drift at sea. She had thought that all men who had survived the attack would surely be shot! But to be given . . . a . . . choice . . . ? She had to wonder what sort of choice the ladies might be given.

But she scoffed at this. The women were a different matter. No choices at all would be given them. Though only twenty women had been traveling on this ship to Texas, Leana had to believe she knew what would soon be happening to them all. She shuddered at the thought and held even more tightly onto her mother.

"Now, ladies," Cyril shouted, his hands on his hips. "Get ye over to the *Erebus*. And when there, you will be shown to yer quarters."

He chuckled low and his eyes gleamed as he looked from one lady to the other. His gaze settled on a buxom thing whose hair reflected the color of the sun back at him, itself being the color of copper. He could tell by the boldness in her eyes that she was not an innocent lass. Her idea of fun had to be a pleasurable romp in a bunk!

Feeling as though her world had suddenly come to an end, Leana followed along beside the pirates as they ushered them from one ship to the other. And once there on the ship that was as black as night, Leana awaited further instructions. And when she was separated from her mother, she began fighting the one doing the separating.

"No!" she screamed, clawing at the sweat-laden pirate who wore no shirt and whose breeches clung to him like a leather glove. His eyes were cold, his smile set. "You can't separate me and my mother! I won't let you."

A shadow fell across Leana and the pirate she was

battling, causing Leana's heart to lurch. Firm hands gripped her by the wrists and held her in place. She looked heatedly up and down those familiar dark eyes staring down at her, stunning her into speechlessness, they were so filled with warmth yet determination to make her behave.

"Stop that," Brandon said flatly. "It will do you no good to fight what is happening here, Leana. Just go along with it. You will be better for it. So will your mother."

"Take the older wenches to the hold!" Cyril barked out his order. "You know what to do with the younger beauties."

Leana paled. "The . . . hold . . . ?" she said in a shocked whisper. "My mother . . . in . . . the hold? Along with rats and Lord knows what else?"

"Like I said, don't question anything that is happening here," Brandon said dryly. "For now, let it be, Leana."

Leana felt defeated. She grew limp and let her eyes lower, knowing that what he said was true. She had no choice but to give in to whatever was chosen for her and her mother. Would they even be alive this time tomorrow? She doubted if she would ever see Parker or Matt Seton again. Texas! Oh, if she had only never heard that such a place existed! Oh, if only life didn't have such ugly twists.

She couldn't watch as her mother was led away from her. And Leana didn't want to watch where she was even being taken. She only went where the handsome pirate urged her to go. And when she found herself in the privacy of his very own cabin, she looked up at him, anger again flashing in her eyes, and she couldn't help herself. . . . She spat at his feet.

73

Brandon chuckled and walked away from her, leaving her alone in the cabin. She tensed when she heard a bolt lock being slipped in place outside the door. She was this handsome pirate's personal prisoner. A part of her was glad . . . yet she felt guilty for this and decided to make every moment for him, while with her, miserable. . . .

Chapter Five

Leana paced the cabin, concerned about the welfare of her mother. She didn't even want to think about the conditions of the hold of the ship. It pained her sorely to believe that her mother had been taken there.

Stopping to look about this place in which she herself had been brought, Leana knew that she should feel lucky to be in such a fancy cabin. The walls were paneled in a dark oak. Two red leather chairs sat on opposite sides of an oak table, where upon it lay books and a scattering of papers and two cups as well as a half-emptied bottle of French champagne.

Her gaze went to the outside wall, measuring the bunk positioned there. It was large enough to hold two people. It looked enticing with its colorful blankets and pillows arranged neatly atop it.

Leana's gaze traveled from the bunk, then to the bottle of champagne and two empty cups.

"He must have a different bunk partner every night," she hissed. "What does he do? Pick them up at one port and drop them off at another?"

The thought of her being next on his list of seductions sent a tremor of involuntary desire to rush through her, and she couldn't understand why. She couldn't want a seduction with such a man. He was a pirate. Pirates seized ships for cargo and plundered coastal towns for riches. They organized powerful gangs to exact tribute and demand ransom for prisoners. They committed armed robbery on the high seas. Their ghastly deeds were against all the laws of nations. They couldn't even fly the flag of any nation, except to deceive others.

So vividly recalling this pirate who had claimed her surely as his own for a night's fun, or possibly even longer, Leana had to wonder how someone as handsome as *he* could be such a rogue. He was among those who made anything but an honest living. *He* was nothing but a swarthy sea robber!

Leana placed her hands to her cheeks and shook her head, trying to clear her thoughts. "What am I doing?" she whispered. "My worries should be of my mother. Nothing else. What am I to do?"

The porthole above the bunk showed that night had fallen in its total darkness. Her face flamed scarlet, wondering just when the pirate who had chosen her as his own private playmate would make his appearance again. This *was* his personal cabin. To comfortably retire, he would have to return for the night.

Leana swallowed hard, wondering if his seduction would be swift. Would . . . it . . . be painful? She had yet to be introduced into the ways of making love. Only innocent kisses had been stolen by her gentlemanly escorts. And even these sorts of opportunities had been drawn to an abrupt halt when she had been forced to live in Father Bailey's rectory for two long, lonesome years.

She had to believe that it was this lonesomeness, a restlessness *caused* by this absence of men in her life these past two years, that made this young, handsome pirate so appealing to her. She had wondered about how it would be to experience more than a mere kiss from a man. Her body had strangely hungered for knowledge of a man's touch . . . a man's full possession of her. . . .

"Oh, Lord," she groaned, whipping her skirt around, again pacing. "What am I thinking of? Father Bailey is dead . . . Mother is perhaps even shackled. . . ."

The sound of movement just outside the door drew Leana quickly around. She froze in her steps, watching, wide-eyed, as she heard the bolt lock on the door being slipped aside. She took a cautious step backward, wishing there were somewhere to hide, for she knew that there were more pirates on board this ship than that one who made residence in this personal cabin. Any one of the half-naked, swarthy men could come and take their pleasure with her, then leave her for even another! Would the handsome pirate interfere? Or would he even stand aside and watch, getting his pleasure in that perverse way, before taking her himself after a long line of men had had their way with her?

The thought made a sick sort of feeling course through Leana's veins, now suddenly realizing just what sort of danger she *and* her mother were in. Somehow she had to try to find a way of escape for them both. But how? She was doomed. Her mother was doomed. . . .

The door creaked open. Leana squinted her eyes, trying to make out the figure standing in the shadows. But the lone whale oil lamp positioned on the wall of this cabin was just not enough light by which to see anything except for a tray of fruit and cheese which was now being placed on the floor and slid on inside the room.

Leana didn't have a chance to say anything before the door was closed again. She stood in silent awe, staring down at the feast awaiting her, wondering who had been the generous one who had ordered this be sent to her.

"Only one person would offer me such sort of nourishment," she whispered. "First feed me, get me pleasantly relaxed, then seduce me? Yes, that is surely his plan."

Combing her fingers through her hair, Leana looked at the red shine of the apple, the thick wedges of cheese, and the purple grapes so plump and enticing. Her mouth began a slow watering; her stomach ached. But guilt would not let her feed so freely, thinking that her mother surely was being neglected of such a kindness as this.

"I can't eat . . ." Leana moaned, shaking her head. "Not while my mother . . ."

Her heart skipped a beat. She stared openly at the closed door, remembering. . . .

"The lock," she harshly whispered. "I didn't hear it being slipped back in place after the tray was left. . . ."

With weakened knees, knowing what this sort of negligence by her anonymous visitor might mean, she tiptoed to the door and placed her trembling fingers to the latch. Barely breathing, she moved the latch downward and slowly opened the door, surprised to find that the door *hadn't* been locked.

"I can't believe it," she whispered. "Is it even . . . too . . . easy? Is it a trap?"

But she knew that she wouldn't think about that. She had to think of her mother, first and foremost. She would take her mother some nourishment, then they would sneak to topdeck and try to find a way to lower a longboat into the water. She knew the dangers of being in the sea in such a small craft, but at least she would have paddles, whereas those men from the ship *Jasmine* had been left to drift without any such means by which to guide themselves to land.

"I really have no choice but to at least try," she decided.

Closing the door, she turned and grabbed the wedge of cheese and an apple and tied them securely in the fullness of the skirt of her dress. She then again opened the door, stopping to peer into the darkness, relieved to not see anyone so close that she might be caught, and possibly even reprimanded for having escaped.

Again she thought about this possibly having been a trap, but again brushed such a worry aside and began inching her way along the darkness of the narrow corridor, her eyes searching for steps that would lead her to topdeck. She had no idea where to look for the hold of the ship, but she had to risk everything to find it, for the sake of her mother.

On both sides of her, through the many closed doors, she heard an assortment of sounds. She heard men laughing greedily and soft squeals of women. She heard snores from other cabins and the popping of a cork from an unseen bottle from another.

The aromas were varied, from that which smelled of dried sweat and urine and others of mildew and rot. And then there would be the faint aroma of perfume drifting from beneath another door, from behind which came the sound of a lady receiving pleasure. It was evidenced by her sweet murmurings back to a man, and in her erotic groans. Leana had to wonder which lady of the twenty captured could be enjoying being with a lowly pirate! It wasn't decent!

Yet Leana knew that she had let her mind wander to how it might feel to be with the handsome pirate.

Again shame engulfed her and she moved more quickly onward, trying to leave the lustful sounds behind her.

But suddenly she heard more than those sounds that had disturbed her. She was hearing footsteps behind her, moving quickly toward her.

Daring to not look back, to see who it might be following her, Leana began to run, panting, now seeing the steps only a few footsteps away, but she was not to reach them this night. Strong hands were now on her waist, stopping her, and by doing so, caused the food meant for her mother to spill from the folds of her dress.

"No!" she softly cried. She was forced around, to look up and onto the sweaty, bearded face of the same pirate who had roughly held and fought with her earlier in the day before the handsome pirate had come and led her to his private cabin. She was aware of this ugly pirate's bare chest and its preponderance of matted hair circling his dark nipples.

Her gaze lowered to the tightness of his leather breeches, revealing the outline of his passion's need of a lady, *any* lady, but having chosen *her* to quench his manly thirsts.

"So ye took the bait, eh?" the pirate laughed. "Ye found that I left yer door unlocked?"

"You. You did that purposely," Leana hissed, trying to squirm free from him, but finding herself too pinioned against the steel frame of his body. She gagged, smelling his very distinct aroma of dried perspiration. And his beard showed the shine of grease beneath his mouth, evidence of having only recently eaten.

80

The press of his hands into her waist was paining her, but the thought of what might happen in the next moments pained her even more. To be initiated into the ways of that shared between a man and a woman by this man made her stomach roll and a bitterness rise to the inner depths of her throat.

"Aye, I planned it well, didn't I?" the pirate bragged, his voice deep and scratchy. "Now when Brandon asks how it was that you are found in my cabin, I will say that ye found a way to escape from his, to be with *me*."

"Brandon? You are speaking of the pirate whose cabin I just escaped from?"

"Aye. The one and the same," the pirate chuckled.

"And you think he will believe you?" she said, laughing sarcastically. "No woman would ever choose you over *him*."

Then the name *Brandon* formed in her consciousness. She had only known of one man with that name, Brandon. But it couldn't be possible that this Brandon was one and the same. It was too foolish to even consider. Though she had never had the opportunity to meet her stepbrother Brandon before his abduction, her mother not having married Brandon's father yet, she knew that no son of Parker Scton would choose a pirate's life over that of living with his family.

No. She would discard such a thought. There were many men in the world with the name Brandon. She wouldn't give such foolishness of wonder of this name another thought. Her mind was playing games with her, just as life seemed to be enjoying doing!

"Aye, you might say that now," the pirate scoffed, now grabbing her by the hair, yanking her lips close to his. "But, wench, just ye wait till ye get a taste of what I offer. Then you'll change yer tune."

Leana began shoving at his chest but his hold was too strong. And when his lips bore down upon her in a savage kiss and his tongue lashed out and ravaged her mouth, she gagged all the more and felt a light-headedness begin sweeping through her.

But then she was suddenly jerked back to full consciousness when she felt the pirate jerked away from her. She stepped back, awestruck, watching the handsome pirate flailing the other pirate with his fists, knocking him from one side of the corridor to the other, until the other pirate fell to his knees and began to beg for mercy.

"Get away with you," Brandon growled, placing a hand on his manchette, tempted to use it on this vile creature who dared to touch, even dirty Leana with not only his hands, but also his mouth. "And if you ever so much as draw near my woman again, I'll not only horsewhip you until blood draws into bitter welts on your back, I will also *kill* you."

"It won't happen again," the pirate mumbled, scampering to his feet. "She's yers, Brandon. She's yers."

"Just remember that," Brandon snarled, having always thought that Cyril had been wrong to let this particular sailor join their pirates' crew. He had caused more trouble than not. He was not one to be trusted. If it wasn't food he was stealing, it was something else. And this time a lady?

Brandon turned his gaze to Leana and how she was cowering against the wall, her eyes wild. Even in the soft glow of the wall sconces lighted by whale oil, he could see her pale cheeks and trembling fingers. Yet she was still so beautiful. Adrenaline flowed through him like an unwelcome antidote to magic, his need for her was so great.

Then his gaze lowered and saw the wedge of cheese and the apple at her feet, and he only had to guess as to how she happened to be free of his locked cabin.

He nodded in the direction of the fleeing pirate. "He's responsible for your escape, is he?" he said hoarsely, stooping to pick up the cheese and apple. "He baited you well, did he?"

"Yes," Leana murmured, biting her lower lip in frustration.

Brandon offered the food back to Leana, which she didn't accept. He noticed how still she stood, as though a statue. He hated the fact that she appeared to be so afraid of him. But he hadn't given her cause to like him, had he? He must change that.

"I was the one to give orders for the food being brought to you," he said. "But I did not leave orders that your door be left unlocked." His golden eyebrows came together to form a straight line as he frowned. "That's the way it was done, wasn't it, Leana?"

"Yes," she said, swallowing hard, feeling imprisoned now by dark, fathomless eyes, much more than when behind the locked door. The way he was looking at her was causing her heart to begin a crazy pounding, so much that she felt as though her insides were a hollow tunnel, echoing her desire of him.

"You were taking the food to your mother?"

"Yes."

"Is yes all you can say back to me?" Brandon asked, taking a step forward. "Are you so afraid of me, you are rendered almost speechless? I mean you no harm."

His free hand touched the gentle curve of her jaw and his lips lifted into a soft smile. "I'm sorry about what just happened. Come back with me to my cabin. I'll make all wrongs right for you."

"The only thing that you can do to make things right for me and my mother is to let us go," Leana said, slapping his hand away from her face, though the touch had sent sparks of fire throughout her. This had seemed to revive her power to speak *and* think. She knew that she couldn't let him use his charms on her, to make her do what she knew would be sinfully wrong.

"That's impossible," he said thickly. "But I can promise you that your mother will be fed and made to be comfortable."

"Oh, yes," Leana mocked, squaring her shoulders. "While the others are made to look on and not share in any of this? Mother would rather be dead."

Brandon chuckled low. "You were taking her food," he said. He held the cheese and apple out before him. "Did you plan to feed the lot of women with these offerings?"

"Well . . ." Leana stammered, her face reddening with humiliation.

"Or did you believe to act as Jesus, who had but five loaves of bread and two fish and fed a multitude with them?" he teased.

"Who are you to talk of Jesus or anything that He did?" Leana said, placing her hands on her hips. "How *can* you, a man like you, know *about* the words of the Bible?"

Yet she was now marveling at how well he spoke, as though one who might have been educated, nothing like the other pirates with whom she had become briefly acquainted. He *was* different. Yet he was . . . a . . . *pirate.*

Her initial wonder of his name and who he truly was came back to haunt her. . . .

Brandon's brow knitted into another frown, reminded again of Father Bailey and that he was now dead. It had been this kind man who had taught Brandon much about the words of God, and now Father Bailey was *dead.*

"Let's return to my cabin," he grumbled, taking Leana by an arm, leading her back down the corridor. He cast her a sour glance. "And I'll see to it that everyone is well fed. Now do you feel better?"

"I'd feel better if mother was with *me,*" Leana said softly, yet relieved to know that her mother at least wouldn't starve.

"That's impossible," Brandon growled. "And I don't want to hear any more about it."

Leana jerked at her arm that he held, then ouched as his fingers tightened. "You don't have to be so rough," she complained. "I know that I have no other choice but to go back to your cabin with you. But I don't have to like it."

"You'll be left there alone for a while longer," Brandon snapped back. "So relax, beautiful. I have more chores to look into before retiring, myself, for the full night."

"Like flogging that nasty sailor, I hope," Leana hissed, again ouching as he gave her a shove back into his cabin. "He deserves it, even more than that. I think he should be made to walk the *plank.*"

"God. Walk the plank?" Brandon chuckled, his eyebrows forking. "I believe you've been reading too many pirate books, Leana. Neither I *nor* Cyril have ever made a man walk the plank."

He was still laughing when he closed the door in Leana's face, laughing still as he bolt-locked the door. She could even hear his low chuckles as he began walking away, back down the corridor, and away from her.

"Oh!" she whispered, swirling around, to again take notice of her prison. Before long she would have to share it with him. And perhaps . . . even . . . more?

"No," she grumbled. "Not if *I* can help it."

Heavy footsteps stopping outside the door and the sound of the lock being removed again made her stiffen and stare openly at the door as it swung widely open. She watched, struck numb, when a huge tub was brought into the cabin and placed in the center of the room. And she became even more amazed as buckets of water were brought into the room by several pirates and poured into the waiting tub.

Finally she found the ability to speak. "What do you . . . think . . . you are doing?" she said, afraid to hear the answer. Was Brandon planning to take a bath in her presence? She would simply die of embarrassment if that was his plan!

A more pleasant-appearing of the lot turned and smiled at Leana. "You're to take a bath, ma'am," he said, handing her a bar of soap.

A flush of embarrassment rose to Leana's cheeks, now knowing the truth. "And who gave such a command?" she softly asked.

"Brandon, ma'am," the sailor said, flashing his white teeth back at her through the thickness of his beard.

A fragrance, similar to that of roses, floated up from the spa, yet it was offensive to Leana, causing anger to well inside her. How dare Brandon imply that she needed a bath!

Then another thought came to her in a flash. The bath was to precede lovemaking! Surely it was! That was why he wanted her to have a bath, so that she could smell more sweetly for him when seduced!

Leana grew furious. She stomped to the tub and knocked a bucket of water from one of the pirate's hands. "Get out of here!" she screamed. "All of you! Now! Do you hear?"

She was surprised when they rushed from the room and left her alone, as though they had heeded her command because she had the power *to* order them around.

But then such power faded into helplessness when she again heard the door being bolt-locked from the outside. Again she was a prisoner, awaiting her fate. . . .

She stood back, eyeing the water. She glanced down at the soap in her hand, then a slow smile lifted her lips and her eyes began to gleam. "I'll show him," she giggled.

She tossed the soap into the water, then turned slowly on a heel and looked toward the whale oil lamp and the whale oil floating in the base of it.

"It surely can't smell pleasant," she said, kneading her chin contemplatingly. "What if . . . ?"

Now knowing what she must do, she began a frantic search through the cabin until she found a candle beneath the pile of papers on the table. Smiling wickedly, she placed the wick of the candle down into the flames of the whale oil lamp, and when the candle's wick captured flame at its tip, she hurriedly uprighted it.

"So far so good," she whispered.

She walked determinedly back to the table and let some candle wax drip onto its surface, then positioned the candle in the wax until it dried solidly to the table.

"Now to remove some of the whale oil from the lamp," she said, taking the lamp from its perch on the wall.

She first snuffed the fire out, removed the glass funnel, then took the lamp apart until the whale oil splashed openly before her eyes.

"But first I must undress," she whispered, placing the lamp on the table beside the burning candle. "I must be sure to smell sweetly all over."

Before long she was standing in the nude. And fearing time was wasting, she splashed the whale oil into the palm of her hands and began rubbing it over her body. She was disappointed that the whale oil didn't smell as bad as planned, yet it wasn't something so pleasant a man would welcome it as he pressed a woman against his bare flesh.

"At least I don't smell like roses," Leana giggled. "What a surprise he will get."

When her body was a glossy sheen, she ran to the bunk and grabbed a blanket and wrapped it around her. She stood poised beside the tub of water, awaiting Brandon's arrival. At first glance she would look wet from the bath. Ah, but when he touched her . . .

Chapter Six

Leana smiled daringly at Brandon as he opened the door and stepped inside his cabin. Her pulse raced, waiting for him to discover her trickery. But she was surprised when he gave her only a half glance, then moved on away from her to sit down on his bunk.

Breathless with wonder, Leana turned and openly gaped at him as he so casually began tugging at his glossy black boots, tossing first one and then the other aside. And when he yawned and stretched his arms above his head and then fell back onto the bunk, still ignoring her, she didn't know what her next move must be. Surely he wasn't going to go to sleep with her standing there covered by only a blanket.

And a thin layer of whale oil, she worried. Neither she nor how she was attired seemed to matter to him. Perhaps a seduction wasn't at all what he had had in mind when he had ordered her to bathe. . . .

"Well? Are you going to stand there all night?" Brandon suddenly blurted. He raised himself up on an elbow and gave her a slow smile. "And did you enjoy your bath, Leana?"

"Bath?" Leana said in a near whisper, caught off guard by his sudden decision to pay attention to her after all.

Brandon chuckled. He reached and untied the leather string that held his reddish-golden hair back from his face. He then moved to sit on the edge of the bunk, toying with the string, twisting and untwisting it around a finger, as he continued to set Leana afire with the heat of his eyes.

"Yes. Bath," he said, amusement etched across his handsome face. He nodded toward the tub of water. "I believe that's what one does when water and soap are offered them."

Leana's lips became set and anger caused her eyes to flash arrows back at Brandon, again feeling humiliation soaring through her with the thought of him implying that she had been in need of a bath.

Forgetting that only the blanket hid her full nudity from Brandon, Leana jerked her arms to cross them over her chest and, while doing so, caused the blanket to flutter from around her, to settle in a gentle heap at her bare feet.

"Oh, Lord . . ." she gasped, her eyes and face hot from added embarrassment. She quickly bent her back to rescue the blanket but was stopped when she felt strong hands on her wrists, urging her back into a standing position.

Her insides floundered in strange, tremulous feelings when discovering herself being scrutinized by Brandon's hypnotic gaze. She had never been so aware of her status of "woman" as now, Brandon's eyes teaching her that which until now had only been speculation on her part as to how it would feel to be desired by a man, and to desire

90

him . . . in . . . return. . . .

And then Leana became aware of Brandon's puzzled expression as his hands slipped on her wrists, unable to hold firmly onto her. The whale oil clung to his hands as he placed one before his eyes and gaped openly at it.

"What the hell . . . ?" he further puzzled. "This feels like some sort of *oil*. How . . . ?"

Leana's eyes gleamed. She held her chin high, laughing mockingly beneath her breath, awaiting his further reaction. She could hardly hold back a burst of laughter when he released her other wrist and began smelling first one of his hands and then the other, his nose crinkling with discovery.

"Whale oil?" he said, an eyebrow raising quizzically as he looked down at Leana, his gaze slowly raking over her, seeing the full shine of her body. Though he was now seeing what her game might be, he couldn't help but get caught up in her loveliness. The oil shine enhanced her exquisite, flawless features, making her more vibrant, even glowing.

Her night-black hair spilled over her shoulders and tumbled down her back, her liquid curves tantalizing his eyes into points of fire, seeing how her waist was so narrow and supple and her hips so invitingly rounded.

Her overripe breasts were taut, tipped with rose-colored nipples, and the triangle of dark hair at the junction of her long, tapering legs caused a crazed madness to almost engulf him!

But it was the game that she seemed to be playing with him that quickly numbed the desire that flooded his senses. He glanced over at the table, seeing the whale oil lamp void of flame, the cabin instead being lighted by a lone candle.

Brandon's eyes crinkled into an amused smile. "So whale oil is preferred over perfumed soap, is it?" he chuckled. "Well, we'll see about that."

Leana gasped as he lifted her fully up into his arms and then dropped her into the tub of water. She spat and flailed her arms as the coldness of the water seeped into her pores, sending shivers up and down her spine.

"You cad!" she screamed, now wiping water from her eyes, and then her hair back from her face.

Her voice caught in her throat when she watched him shed his shirt, then drop to a knee beside the tub. "What are you going to do . . . ?" she blurted, eyes wild.

"I gave orders that you were to have a bath," he said flatly. "Now you need a bath even more badly than before. I don't think whale oil is a good substitute for soap, do you?"

"You're despicable," Leana screamed, pummeling her fists against his chest. "Leave me alone. I've never been so insulted. How dare you continue to insist that I need a bath? Do you always treat women this way before you . . . you . . . seduce them? Do you think women are filth, or what?"

Brandon again chuckled amusedly. He held one of her arms firmly with one hand while his other hand began sudsing soap over her back. "Truth?" he said. "You want the truth?"

"You surely don't know the meaning of the word," Leana hissed, squirming. When he dropped the bar of soap into the water and began using only his hand to smooth the suds over her back, a sensual thrill coursed through her, feeling fires being ignited everywhere he touched anew.

She fought the feeling, yet her mind, as well as her

body, was again betraying her. Oh, Lord, did she have no shame? Why wasn't she able to control such feelings of ecstasy? Of want?

But it was all new to her, this being with a man in so intimate of terms. Would it soon be more intimate? She couldn't let it happen. She hated this man who had taken her as his personal prisoner! She felt a loathing for him that she did her stepbrother Matt!

Matt, she thought suddenly. *Brandon. That name Brandon . . . ? Matt's brother . . . ?*

She stopped her struggling and let her gaze move over Brandon, seeing so much of the Setons in his features. . . .

"The truth *is,*" Brandon said, splashing water over her back, clearing it of the suds, "I offered the bath at first for your *pleasure*. It was not something that I felt that you needed. I thought you might enjoy it . . . be able to relax in these surroundings that have been forced upon you."

"Oh, yes, I am sure," Leana said mockingly, giving Brandon a sour frown, yet still studious of his features. . . .

"But . . ." he continued in his deep, resonant tone of voice, "now that you've chosen to anoint yourself with whale oil, I've changed my mind. Lovely lady, you can't share my bunk with me while reeking of whales."

Leana gasped softly, yet hadn't she known all along what would be required of her? But hearing him speaking it and knowing that moment of seduction might be so near made her thoughts stray from her wonder of his name as she again tried in earnest to battle him.

Her free hand splashed the sudsy water up into his face. He jumped with a start and emitted a loud yelp as the burn of the soap soaked into his eyes. He jumped to

93

his feet and began wiping at his eyes, oblivious of what Leana was now about.

Scrambling to her feet, she became unsteady, feeling the slick whale oil that had settled to the bottom of the copper tub. With a scream she felt herself tumbling back down into the water. Landing with a loud splat, she softly cursed to herself, then looked up at midnight-dark eyes looking down at her, accusing and angry.

But when she discovered the red streaks in the whites of Brandon's eyes, resembling veins on the back of a leaf, she laughed victoriously. The soapy water was leaving its mark and she knew that his eyes had to be painfully stinging. He was not winning her easily! And if she had anything to do about it, he would have to fight her even more for the moments ahead in his bunk!

"You're a hellcat," Brandon snarled, placing his hands on his hips. "But I've tamed worse."

Leana again tried to get her footing on the bottom of the tub as she held tightly to its sides to pull herself up. She had to forget that she was nude and that this pirate's eyes were touching her all over, for it was not of her doing that she had been forced to be here under these circumstances.

But she had to win this battle raging inside her that was being caused by his nearness, or the fault of what might happen as a result of these feelings could quickly revert to her. The excitement felt by being with him alone was not only alarming to her, but she knew it to be also dangerous.

She could hardly keep her senses about her when she gazed up at him, oh, so teakly tanned and finely chiseled was he! And now that he was without a shirt, she was keenly aware of his muscled chest lightly furred with golden hair and how the chest hair tapered down his flat belly, disappearing into the waist of his black leather breeches.

Color rose into her face, from letting herself imagine where that hair traveled to. Being leather, his breeches could not conceal the bulge at the front, nor the muscles abounding at his powerful thighs. Even now they flexed as he stepped closer to the tub. . . .

"So you think you will climb from the tub before your bath is completed?" Brandon growled, again positioning himself on a knee beside the tub. His long tapers of fingers grabbed her by the waist and forced her back down into the water. "Now I am determined that we will finish what was started here. It will do you no good to fight back."

A dark frown creased his brow. "And I wouldn't splash any more of that damn water in my face," he growled. "Or I will quickly repay you in kind."

Resigned to the fact that she *would* have to have this bath, now even wanting it herself to remove the dreadful whale oil, Leana settled down into the water, at least glad that the suds were covering her breasts. She had felt his eyes on them more than once. She even could still feel the sensuous thrill that this had caused and felt awash with shame for this.

"I understand my need of a bath," she blurted, feeling his fingers now on her shoulders, smoothing the suds into her skin there. Surely he wouldn't be so bold as to try to touch her lower!

A desperate pleading crept into the blue of her eyes. "I can give myself my bath," she said in another rush of words.

But his hands were much quicker than her words.

They were now cupping each of her breasts, causing Leana's breath to catch and her face to flame.

She blinked her lashes nervously up at him as her breasts pulsed warmly in his hands. The euphoria that filled her entire being was uncontrollable. It was causing a strange ache between her thighs. It was a mixture of pain *and* sweet pleasure. And when Brandon's mouth lowered and possessed Leana's lips with the gentle warmth of his, she found herself lost to the ecstasy, no longer caring who he was, or how it was that she happened to be with him. She was now only aware of being filled with a flaming passion, compelling her to twine her arms about his neck to return the kiss, lost to him in a helpless surrender.

Brandon's heartbeats were almost swallowing him whole, having never wanted anyone as badly as he wanted Leana. Though it was not his usual plan to seduce a woman when she did not wish for such a seduction, there was no turning back the hands of time that had led him into the seducing of this beguiling wench. Nothing could be sweeter than her kiss. Nothing could ever be as soft as her breasts! He had to have her or his loins might burst from denial!

Yet he couldn't force her. It was not his way with women! He had been taught the ways of a gentleman. He had always remembered Parker Seton's private talks when Brandon had begun to mature into a young man at even his youthful age of ten.

Though no longer under the guidance of his father, Brandon still obeyed what *had* been taught him those many years ago.

With a quiver in his lips, Brandon drew away from Leana. His eyes were passion-heavy, dark to the core with need. "Take your bath," he said hoarsely, moving to his feet.

He kneaded his brow, seeing how her face was so flushed and her eyes so hazed. Was it from surprise of what had happened? He had felt her return his kiss. She had even openly invited it to continue, for she had actually placed her arms about his neck!

Or were the flamed cheeks from shame that she had so willingly accepted the kiss?

Or was it because she sorely desired him, as he did her?

Turning his back to her, he stooped and grabbed the blanket up from the floor. "I shall get you a towel," he said huskily. "And I must see to it that we discard this blanket. It reeks of whale oil."

Leana was sitting quietly, still numb from his kiss and the passion that the kiss and his hands on her breasts had aroused inside her. She had been willing to let him touch her . . . kiss her! Even now she desired him, wanting to fully explore these building emotions that were setting her afire.

Then she lowered her eyes, shame engulfing her. Should her mother ever find out what a shameful hussy she had raised, her mother would surely disown her!

The thoughts of her mother made her head jerk upward. "Did you see to my mother as you said you would?" she blurted. "Did you see that she was properly fed?"

Brandon turned on a heel and looked down at her, amazed that she could turn her thoughts from one subject to another so quickly. Only moments ago she was most surely filled with the pleasures of a kiss. And now? To think of other things? He was so damned troubled by *her*, nothing else could possibly take her place in his mind. How was it that she could be so flexible? Or had she not desired him as he had thought? Had she planned to use her body to get what she wished for her mother? He hadn't thought of those possibilities before.

But, yes, surely she was a scheming bitch. She *had* spread whale oil all over her body, hadn't she, in an effort to keep him from her? What else might she try? He must be sure to sleep with his manchette beneath his pillow!

"Yes," he growled. "I saw to your mother. Now you see to yourself and get that bath completed. I have to get some sleep. That won't be so easy having to share my bunk with you."

"I didn't ask to share your bunk," Leana said icily, splashing water onto her face, rubbing suds hard against her flesh, finally feeling that the whale oil was leaving her.

She didn't want to wash her lips, though. They were still warm from his kiss. The way he was acting, he probably wouldn't do the same again. And she knew that she should be happy about this, yet deep down, where her desires were formed, she knew that she was not. She had even wanted his kiss to continue when he had cut it so abruptly short.

But the fact that he *had,* proved to her that he was surely not the rogue she had at first thought him to be. He seemed to be sensitive to the fact that she had never been with a man before as she was now. . . .

"That can be remedied, you know," Brandon snapped back. "You can join the other wenches. Would you prefer to be taken to the cabin where the younger ones are being held? Or would you prefer to be sent to the hold with the older ladies? If you choose the first of my choices, you will be among those picked over each night by the rest of this pirate's crew for filling their hungers of the flesh. I think you would find that none would be as thoughtful as I. Some even use whips to get what they want."

He began to unbutton his breeches. "But if that's what you prefer, I can arrange it, Leana," he said dryly, now revealing his full nudity to her as he slipped out of his breeches.

Leana paled and cast her eyes quickly away from him. "Please cover yourself," she gasped. "I've never . . . seen . . . a man naked before. It is quite embarrassing."

Brandon went to the bunk and spread out atop it, then pulled a blanket up to his armpits. "I don't know why I feel a need to please you," he growled. "But I hope this makes you feel more at ease."

Leana still didn't dare look his way.

"I am quite decent," Brandon half shouted. "Now, will you just get that damn bath over with?"

Slowly turning her head, Leana looked across the room, relieved to see him hidden beneath the blankets. Her gaze then saw the lack of space left beside him and she had to know that she had more than seeing him nude to cope with. She was going to be forced to lie next to him. Oh, did she dare? He had already caused her insides to dangerously flame. Would she be able to even stand it if he touched her again, even if only accidentally in his sleep?

She began rubbing soap briskly on her legs, poising one on the edge of the tub, feeling free to do so now because he had scooted to his side, with his eyes facing the outside wall of the cabin. She scrubbed herself until her skin felt raw, all the while watching Brandon, still battling feelings that were new to her.

Then she eyed the floor, then the extra blankets rolled at the foot of the bunk. She now knew what she must do. She had to make a pallet on the floor. Surely he wouldn't argue over her doing that. He would have the full use of his bunk, would he not?

Then she frowned. No matter where she chose to sleep, surely he wasn't going to leave her alone sexually. Why else had he brought her to his cabin? He surely was now only playing a game with her. He was probably pretending to leave her alone only long enough for her to be finished with her bath. Wasn't that why he was urging her to hurry?

Shaking her head, Leana felt pulled in two directions. She was filled with this strange hungry need, a need surely felt by a woman who felt desire for a man. Yet she wanted to not feel these things . . . wanting to remain an innocent virgin until she was speaking words of marriage with the man whom she loved. Only this was the right way to approach these crazed feelings that were paining her even now, as she continued to cast troubled glances Brandon's way.

Brandon turned over on his other side and glared toward Leana. "Christ, I've never seen a woman like water so much," he groaned. "What's taking you so long?"

Leana tilted her chin haughtily. "Oh? You've witnessed many a lady's baths?" she dared.

"Enough to know that it doesn't take that long to get through," he argued.

"Well, sir, I am different," Leana said smugly.

"You certainly are," he scoffed. "You're the first to take a bath in *whale oil*."

Leana glowered over at him. She tossed the soap aside.

100

"If it makes you feel any better, I am now finished and ready to leave the tub," she said icily. "I would appreciate it if you would again turn your eyes away from me."

Brandon's eyes rolled. "Why do I continue to put up with you?" he groaned, then again flopped over on his other side. "I should've known when I found you fighting Jack that you'd give me a hard time. I should've left you for Jack and the others to tame."

Leana stepped gingerly from the tub and quickly grabbed the towel around her. "Jack?" she queried, a feathery brow lifting inquisitively.

"The pirate who has twice tried to accost you," he grumbled. "He wouldn't have offered you a bath. He doesn't even ever take one *himself*."

"I can certainly believe that," Leana said, shuddering at the remembrance of the nasty pirate's smell. "And I *do* thank you for saving me from . . . from his clutches. I do appreciate it. Truly I do."

"Prove it to me by coming on to bed," Brandon said, giving her a half glance. "Daybreak comes early while on the high seas."

Leana toweled herself dry, then reached for her petticoat and slipped it over her head. She left her dress spread out on a chair, hoping the wrinkles might loosen from it, and chose to sleep in only her petticoat. She felt safe to do so. She had definitely decided to sleep on the floor.

"All right," she finally said. "I'm ready." She went to the bunk and quietly took the roll of blankets from it, then jumped with a start when Brandon jerked around to face her.

"Now what are you doing?" he snapped, raising himself up on an elbow.

"I've inconvenienced you enough," Leana said, swallowing hard as she saw anger darken his eyes. "I'm going to sleep on the floor."

"You're *what?*" Brandon said, his golden eyebrows forking.

"You heard me," Leana said stubbornly, already spreading the blankets on the floor.

A quiet amusement softened Brandon's eyes. "Oh, I see," he chuckled. He lifted a shoulder into a shrug. "Fine. If that's the way you want it." Again he settled down on the bunk, drawing the blanket snugly beneath his chin.

Leana was awestruck that he was so agreeable. She would have expected a fight, not indifference. Suspicious, she cautiously climbed onto her pallet, grimacing when the floor seemed to reach through the blankets like hard fingers to dig into her flesh.

A pillow suddenly fell upon her face.

"Take that," Brandon said softly. "You'll be more comfortable."

Leana was even more confused. She couldn't believe that he was *this* agreeable. But she was not one to argue a good thing when she was staring it in the face!

"Thank you," she murmured. "You're so . . . so . . . suddenly *kind*."

"Think nothing of it," Brandon grumbled. He rolled over on his other side and looked down at her. "Oh, by the way," he added. "Watch out for the rats down there on the floor."

He chuckled low beneath his breath, so low she didn't hear him. He then turned his back to her again, listening to her gasp of horror.

Leana shot up from the blankets, her knees weak. "Rats?" she cried. "Lord, Brandon. Do you have rats in your . . . cabin . . . ?"

Brandon shrugged. "Only on the floor," he chuckled.

Leana quickly understood what he was trying to do. He was trying to use any means he could, besides that of actually forcing her, to get her in the bunk with him. She reached for the pillow he had given her and struck it across his head in two powerful blows, causing him to emit a yelp, then she very politely stretched back out on her pallet.

But she couldn't forget what he had said. She looked toward the door, cringing when seeing the large gap beneath it. She knew that perhaps he had been only jesting, but she knew that rats *could* get into this room should they decide to. She now knew that it would be hard to close her eyes in a restful sleep. She would even probably see rats *in* her sleep. . . .

Chapter Seven

The candle had burned low, then out, to now be only a circle of hardening wax on the table. Leana lay on her pallet, tense, her eyes wide, her throat dry from fear. The cabin was almost pitch-black. Leana could only see a trace of light spilling in beneath the door from the corridor. Something compelled her to watch this light, watching for any sudden scampering movement, still worrying about Brandon's mention of rats. If one should enter this cabin, it would quickly find her. She shuddered at the thought!

Brandon was smiling to himself in the dark, hearing Leana's troubled, shallow breathing. He had to guess that this was due to a mixture of fears on her part, but one in particular if he had correctly read the gasp of fear when he had teased her about the possibility of rats coming into the cabin through the night.

Inching his way to the edge of the bunk, he slowly lowered his hand over the side. Only barely brushing the tips of his fingers over one of her arms, hoping that she would mistake this for a rat, he chuckled to himself when he heard her loud shriek and the rush of feet as she moved quickly from her pallet.

Brandon pretended to not have heard her, hoping what her next move might be after having teased her into thinking that she had just been accosted by a rat. He inched his way back to the farthest edge of the bunk next to the wall, waiting. . . .

Leana stood trembling, her hands to her throat, almost wild with fright. The night sounds were now as though thundering inside her consciousness . . . the water slapping against the sides of the ship, the creaking, the groaning of the timber, the sound of the wind as it howled around the outside wall of this cabin where she was now imprisoned.

Her feet cold against the floor, afraid that what she had just felt was surely not her imagination, she looked anxiously about her, fearing the touch of a rat again.

She then peered through the darkness, trying to make out the still figure of Brandon on the bunk. Surely he was asleep, for he had not made notice of her alarming scream. If she should slip into the bunk with him, perhaps he wouldn't even notice. She just couldn't return to her pallet. She had to take a chance at Brandon's side. It was much safer than trying to sleep on the floor!

Barely breathing, Leana tiptoed to the bunk. Lifting the long skirt of her petticoat, she placed one knee on the bunk, and then the other, then slowly lowered herself; relieved to find that Brandon was asleep on the other side.

Snuggling her knees up to her chest, Leana lay on her side facing away from him, but still she was tense. What if Brandon would scoot over in his sleep and find her there? Would her presence awaken him? Or might he just continue sleeping, undisturbed?

Oh, please let him stay asleep, Leana silently prayed.

Her eyelids grew heavy with the need of sleep. But the continuous howling of the wind outside the ship kept her awake, as well as Brandon's presence so close behind her. She could smell an enticing aroma of expensive men's cologne emanating from him, and she could hear his steady breathing.

Both made Leana's heartbeats become erratic, so remembering how he could send her senses to reeling with the seduction of his eyes and how passion burned so within them.

Forcing her eyes closed, she clenched her arms about her knees, also trying to will herself to not think on these sinful thoughts of this rogue pirate.

I must go to sleep, she kept forcing herself to think. *I must go to sleep.*

And then her eyes jerked open widely when the ship pitched with the thundering of a massive wave, causing Brandon to flop over on his other side, facing the back side of her. Leana swallowed hard, drowning in tremulous passion when Brandon's arm draped over her and his hand rested upon one of her breasts. A sensual tremor engulfed her when she became aware of his breath hot on her neck.

And when she felt the hard frame of his body fit into hers, even recognizing the risen strength of his manhood pressed against her back, she closed her eyes and bit her lower lip in frustration. She couldn't move or it would awaken him. She couldn't let him find her there in such a seductive embrace or he would most surely believe that she was there purposely *to* invite even more from him.

Hadn't she brazenly returned his kiss only a short while ago? Oh, she had become a person even she didn't recognize!

Every nerve in Leana's body was taut, her pulse raced, waiting for any sort of movement from Brandon that might suggest he was awakening. She closed her eyes and fought back the urge to moan in ecstasy when his fingers tightened about her breast. He was surely dreaming of being with a lady, for even his breathing was becoming more rapid, his breath even hotter on her neck. And when his lips grazed the flesh of her shoulder, Leana bit her lip to stifle a soft cry of desire. Oh, Lord, what was happening inside her that she could let this man so wickedly disturb her? Even now, as in his sleep he was cuddling closer behind her, she couldn't deny this rush of pleasure that splashed through her.

"Leana . . ." Brandon whispered. "My . . . Leana . . ."

Leana's eyes flew open widely. Brandon had whispered her name in his sleep! Had he been so taken by her that his dreams were now filled . . . with . . . her . . . ?

Warm fingers began kneading Leana's breast. Leana was becoming dizzied from emotions spiraling throughout her. And when Brandon's other arm circled beneath her and drew her around to face him, Leana even still could not tell if he was awake or still dreaming. The cabin was too dark to see anything. The only thing that she could think to do was to let him have his way with her, or he might awaken. She didn't want him to know that she had been too afraid to sleep on the floor.

She most certainly didn't want him to be aware of how his touches were affecting her. If she let him know, then it seemed that all would be lost to her. Her respect . . . her logic . . . her desire to escape from this man who had

107

stolen her heart from even that first look into his dark, fathomless eyes. . . .

Long, lean fingers began to weave through Leana's hair. She felt herself being drawn around, and when she felt the burn of his lips against hers, she realized that no man could kiss with such demand if he were asleep! She had been tricked!

Anger replaced desire. Leana began shoving at Brandon's powerful chest, pulling her lips free from his. "You rogue!" she hissed. "You almost had me fooled. Unhand me. I made a mistake. . . ."

Brandon was suddenly atop her, his hands holding her wrists to the bunk. "I felt you responding to my touches, Leana," he said hoarsely. "*Now,* by damn, you try and tell me that you want to leave my bunk."

"Release my hands and I'll show what I wish to do," Leana snapped angrily. "Though I can't see your face, my fingernails can find it in the dark."

"Oh? So you wish to brand me, eh?" Brandon chuckled. He released one of her hands. "Go ahead. I will proudly wear any mark made by you."

Leana gasped, in awe of this man who surprised her, it seemed, every time he opened his mouth. "Just release my other hand," she sighed. "I only wish to return to my pallet on the floor. That's all."

"Oh? And why did you even *leave* it?" he asked, his free hand finding the gentle curve of her jaw, tracing it.

"I guess I . . . walked . . . in my *sleep*," she stammered, lying. "But now I am fully awake. I now know what I'm doing."

"Ah, yes, I believe you even know what you were doing moments ago when my touches were making you quite atremble, Leana," Brandon said huskily.

108

His fingers traced an invisible line down from her jaw to a strap of her petticoat. "And I believe I even feel you trembling now," he said, lowering the strap.

His fingers crept lower and fully cupped the breast, feeling it tightening against his palm.

"Please . . . don't . . ." Leana whispered, her heart soaring from rising passion.

But Brandon was no longer speaking. His lips and tongue were now skillfully teasing Leana's taut breast while his hand was removing the other strap of her petticoat, now baring both breasts to feast upon.

A guttural moan surfaced from inside Leana. She closed her eyes and tossed her head, having never felt anything so delicious. It was as though she were floating above herself, being enveloped in sensuous splendor.

"Leana, I want you. . . ." Brandon whispered, his hands wandering eagerly down the supple lines of her body. "You also want me. I feel it in the heat of your body. I hear it in the nervous beating of your heart. Don't deny yourself what your body is begging for."

Leana' breath caught in her throat when she felt his hands now wandering up the inside of her petticoat, traveling slowly over the curve of her thighs, and then daringly on upward, where she felt a strange throbbing at the core of her womanhood.

Never before had she felt these longings . . . this sweet pain between the thighs . . . until Brandon! Surely this was what her mother had spoken of when telling her that one day a man would make her aware of all those feelings that were meant to lie dormant until the right man came along. And when this happened, she had found the man of her dreams, the man she would want to conquer, *and* marry. . . .

But surely her mother was wrong. Leana didn't want to think that she had let herself fall in love with a pirate! There was no future in such a love. . . .

Leana again began shoving at his chest. She had to fight all feelings. She would have to be insane to let this go any further. "I don't want anything from you except for the right to leave this ship with my mother," she said shakily. "Please, Brandon. Please . . . let . . . me go. Let me go to my mother and assure her that you are going to release us at the next port."

Brandon's lips were his only response. His kiss was that of intensity, searing her mouth with his, evoking her hungry response.

Slipping his hands beneath her, he pressed her body upward, against his, letting her feel the hardness of his manhood, dizzying her.

Slowly gyrating himself into her pliable limbs, Brandon could feel her weakening in her defenses. He moved deliberately, teasingly, then smiled to himself when he felt her joining him in these movements, even flowering her legs open to him. Yet she still had the shield of petticoat between them. . . .

Drawing his lips only a fraction from hers, he whispered into her ear, "Now tell me that you don't wish to be with me in this way," he said. His lips nibbled on the lobe of her ear, his hands now slowly pushing her petticoat down . . . down . . . down. . . .

"You're confusing me so," Leana whispered back, feverish with desire. "I've never . . . felt . . . this way before."

"Nor have I, and I have been with many women," Brandon whispered.

He slipped the petticoat on past her ankles, then tossed

110

it aside. He only wished that he could see her. Yet feeling her, memorizing her in this way was, indeed, enough. His hands sought out the feel of her from her toes upward, on past her thighs, to the perfect firmness of her breasts.

And when his hands found her lips parted, he let her tongue draw one of his fingers inside her mouth to seductively suck on it, causing his loins to ache and his senses to spin. Though she spoke of having never been with a man in this way, she seemed experienced. He welcomed anything that she might even teach *him*, for she was behaving in ways only that were coming natural to her, innocence making what she was doing even more beautiful.

As though she were willing him, her body provocatively soft against his, her breasts warm and pulsing against his chest, Brandon lowered his man's strength downward, placing it against her tendrils of hair which lay triangled at her thighs.

He withdrew his finger from her mouth and let his lips find hers, ripe and quivering. He kissed her with fire, his hands now beneath her hips, lifting her against him as he began to slowly enter her from below. When he found the thin membrane of skin still intact, he moved slowly yet deliberately, then made the one thrust that claimed her finally as his . . . totally his. . . .

Leana emitted a soft cry of pain against Brandon's lips, but the pain was forgotten when he kissed her more passionately. Her body began responding to his strokes as sweet currents of warmth began sweeping through her. She lifted her hips and melted against him, her hands seeking out the sleekness of his back and the tautness of his buttocks.

She had not been prepared for the intense passion that

111

accompanied being wholly with a man. The pleasure made tears burn at the corners of her eyes, totally lost to the ecstasy introduced to her by him. . . .

Brandon's fingers wove through her hair; his lips rained kisses across her face. And when he felt the coil of desire becoming unwound inside him, reaching for completion, he slowed his strokes, wanting to delay this moment of delight, that which may never be duplicated again. Surely when she left his bunk, she would hate him even more. He had robbed her of her virginity, that which was usually saved for the man whom a woman married. . . .

He let his thoughts wander to what seemed to be forbidden him because of Cyril's warnings about women. He knew that if he would have ever wanted to choose a wife, he would have more than likely chosen such a lady as Leana to be his wife had he not been introduced to the pirate's way of life at his tender age of ten. It was then that the sea became more important than a future with only one woman. The sea had become his bride. . . .

Leana felt Brandon's hesitation. She opened her eyes, drugged, it seemed, oh, so wishing she could see him, to be able to trace his handsome profile with a finger. She so wanted to feel free to tell him of these exquisite feelings he had aroused inside her, yet she knew that she must never be so open to such a man. When he did eventually set her free, they would never meet again.

Strange that this should trouble her, Brandon being who he was. Yet it did, for he had stolen her heart. She was even troubled by what she might say to the man she would eventually meet to take Brandon's place in her heart. Would he even know that she had been sensually with a man? Oh, how she wished that she didn't have that

112

to think about. Oh, how she wished to always be with . . . Brandon. . . .

Searching out his lips in the dark with her forefinger, she delicately touched them, then with her other hand placed at the nape of his neck, encouraged his lips again against hers. Twining her arms about his neck, she gave him a sweet kiss, again lifting her hips to invite him to continue his manly strokes inside her.

Brandon groaned. His hands sought out her breasts and hungrily kneaded them, his thrusts inside her having become even, determined, demanding. He swept his tongue between her lips and tasted the sweetness of her mouth. He trembled as the release was building inside him. . . .

Leana felt his steel arms enfold her. She felt his thrusts becoming harder. And when she heard his soft moans and felt the quiverings of his body, she was sent into a moment of rapture as it seemed flames reached out inside her, blossoming, then scorching her, leaving her breathless, even strangely spent. . . .

Brandon drew easily away from her. His fingers swept around her breasts, guiding his lips to them. He softly kissed one to tautness, and then the other. And then he reached for Leana and held her tightly in his arms. "Did I hurt you?" he asked thickly, hearing her uneven breaths.

Leana felt hot tears again burning her eyes, shame now fully taking hold of her. Yet she buried her face in the curve of his arm, not yet wanting to relinquish these sweet moments with him. He had awakened more in her than she would have ever thought possible.

Love? Was it possible that she could be in love with him? Could it happen so quickly? Could she *let* herself love such a man? A . . . pirate . . . ?

But, yes, she knew that she would always love him. She had no power over such feelings. They had wholly claimed her, body and soul. She even knew that no one could *ever* replace him inside her heart. She was now more than just a prisoner on a pirate's ship. She was a prisoner of this pirate's love, and she hated herself for such a weakness. . . .

"No," she murmured. "You didn't hurt me. How could you even think that you did? Didn't you feel my response to your lovemaking? I still feel quiverings from it."

She paused and swallowed hard. "Yet I know that I shouldn't and I know that what we just did was sinfully wrong. I . . . shall . . . rot in hell. I know that I will."

Brandon held her more tightly. "What you are thinking is foolish," he softly scolded. "You are a woman with healthy woman desires. There is nothing wrong with that. We shared in something more beautiful here than most do in a *lifetime.* Even most married men and women don't know how to love in such a way."

"But I don't wish to love a pirate," Leana softly groaned. "Oh, why did you have to steal me and my mother from the ship *Jasmine?* Now my life will never be the same."

"Nor will mine," Brandon said thickly. He eased away from Leana and left the bunk, searching in the darkness for a match. And when he found one, he lighted a fresh candle, filling the cabin with a low glow of light.

Turning, Brandon let his gaze settle on Leana and how lovely she lay, so beautifully satiny pink in her nudity. Her hair lay about her head in soft, dark waves, her eyes were luminous blue, fringed by thick lashes. Her lips were ripe and red, yet pouting in her unhappiness with

114

herself over what she had allowed to happen.

Brandon was drawn back to her. He knelt to a knee beside the bunk and drew her closer to the edge. Leana's breath was stolen away from her and her neck arched backward as Brandon's lips closed over a breast, sucking the nipple between his teeth; all the while his hands were again setting her afire as they teased and taunted her into a renewed mindlessness.

And when his tongue began leaving a wet trail of warmth downward, across her taut belly, and then even lower, Leana's heart began a crazy beating. She closed her eyes and enjoyed this way in which he had chosen to worship her body.

His lips kissed, suckled; his tongue urged Leana to new heights of wonder. And when her body pitched and rolled in another awesome passion's flame, she couldn't help but cry out.

But Brandon was soon there, silencing her outburst of passion, kissing her hungrily. He buried himself deeply inside her and again they shared the sweet explosion of splendid joy until they lay panting, embraced, clinging.

"This is a night I shall never forget," Brandon whispered against Leana's heaving breast.

"Nor I . . ." Leana whispered back, her fingers twining through his reddish-golden hair. She didn't want to leave his arms, feeling strangely safe while there, though he was the one who had forced imprisonment upon her.

But not the seduction. She had willingly joined him on this bunk, and this was something that she would have to learn to live with . . . that knowledge of being so wantonly brazen with a pirate, a man she should despise, even kill if given the chance. . . .

"Do you have a man waiting your arrival at some

port?'' Brandon suddenly blurted, moving to lie beside her. He left a hand resting on her thigh, not wanting to give her up so easily, not now that he had found her, a woman whom he could truly love, forever. . . .

Leana laughed softly. ''You ask me that now?'' she said, trembling beneath the warmth of his hand, so possessive in its touch.

''I saw no ring on your finger,'' Brandon said, lifting a shoulder in a casual shrug. ''You spoke of no commitment. Only now did the wonder enter my mind.''

A shadow of a frown creased Leana's brow, thinking of once more having to do battle with Matt once she did arrive in Texas. It tired her even now, thinking about it. ''No,'' she murmured. ''No man.''

Brandon's fingers went to her furrowed brow. ''And what has caused the frown?'' he asked, lifting an eyebrow inquisitively. ''Something crossed your mind that wasn't pleasant. It was after my mention of another man. Why is that, Leana?''

Leana stiffened. She was remembering her stepfather's warnings, those of not speaking of family, not even the family *name*. She couldn't confide in Brandon of her hate of her stepbrother. She didn't even understand why she felt she should even want to open her heart so fully to this man.

But there was a way about him that surely could cause her to do anything, even when knowing that she mustn't. She must learn the art of restraint, especially while in his presence, though it was already too late where it was most important. He had already led her into that which she still couldn't believe had happened. . . .

''It is nothing,'' she said, lowering her lashes. Then the thought of *family* had again made the wonder of

116

Brandon's name enter her mind.

Fluttering her lashes more widely open again, she studied Brandon momentarily, then blurted, "Tell me of your family. Where are your parents? Before you were a pirate, where did you make your residence? Or is the older pirate . . . your . . . father . . . ?"

Brandon drew his hand away from her in a jerk. His face drew within it a guarded, strained expression. His eyes grew as though dark pools as he glowered over at Leana, then looked away from her. He reached for his breeches and rose to his feet to pull them on, still silent.

"Brandon . . . ?" Leana said, rustling her petticoat over her head, feeling more secure with herself now that she was at least partially dressed, glad even more that he had chosen to hide his most private parts from her eyes.

"I do not discuss my family with anyone," Brandon growled. He spun around and totally faced her. "Not even you, Leana, though I seem to have already revealed even my soul to you this night."

His hesitation made Leana tense, wanting so badly to tell him of knowing the name Brandon before having met him. Though she had never met her stepbrother Brandon, he was on her mind more than not. It had been his disappearance that had caused so many changes in the Seton family. It had caused Parker's first wife to die from the shock. It had prompted his remarriage to Leana's mother. Leana knew that it was even a big reason for Parker to want to leave New York. He had wanted to leave all bitter memories behind him.

But she again couldn't tell Brandon this that bothered her heart. And how foolish of her to even think that this Brandon could possibly be *that* Brandon. Brandon Seton was most surely dead.

"If speaking of family causes pain, then I will not pursue the subject," Leana faintly uttered. "But I would hope that you would respect me as well, and not speak of my private life."

Brandon nodded. "That's fair enough," he said. He went to the table and poured a glass of champagne into one of the cups. He looked toward her. "Would you care for a drink of champagne? It's refreshing. It might even help make you relax and go to sleep. It *is* still the middle of the night, you know."

Leana raked her fingers through her hair, then stretched and yawned. "Yes, I'm quite aware of the time of night," she said. "But I doubt if I can go to sleep. I seem to be so wound up. Perhaps making love causes this?"

Brandon strolled to the bunk and sat down beside her. "Making love, being *in* love, causes many sorts of complications," he said thickly. He placed the cup to her lips. "Here. Take a sip. It's the finest of champagnes. Made just for such a beautiful thing as you. It *will* relax you."

Leana looked guardedly toward him. "Do you wish for me to relax so that I will go to sleep, or do you wish to entice me into another seduction?" she asked, not so sure that she could live with herself if she let him touch her again in all the sensual ways to which he had only moments ago introduced her. Already she had much to learn to live with. . . .

"Now, would that be so terrible?" Brandon teased. He placed the cup back down on the table and leaned to brush his lips across the hollow of her throat. "Perhaps that would be a better substitute than sleep."

Leana's breath caught in her throat as he slipped the

petticoat from one of her breasts and his tongue flicked around its taut nipple. "Brandon, no," she whispered, already feeling the flames being ignited inside her.

She shoved his lips away. But that was not enough to dissuade him. He instead drew her fiercely into his arms and kissed her savagely, his one hand squeezing her breast, the other already slipping up inside her petticoat, touching her where she so unmercifully throbbed between the thighs.

Leana drifted toward him, no longer resisting this that was like a madness, tormenting her into never feeling to have gotten enough of Brandon. Ecstatic waves splashed through her, flooding her with rapture as his lips continued to scorch her and his hands coaxed tremors to rise upon her flesh.

But this was suddenly drawn to a halt when a series of taps on the door drew Brandon quickly to his feet. His fingers went to his hair, straightening it back from his eyes; his eyes shifted from Leana to the door, then he hurried to it and opened it a crack. His face suffused into an angry frown when finding the one pirate that he despised most standing there.

"Well, Jack, what is the cause for this interruption?" Brandon growled, making sure he blocked the way for Jack to see past him, not wanting Jack to see Leana stretched seductively across the bunk.

"It's a lady in the hold," Jack said, wiping a bead of perspiration from his brow. "I think she's gone sick on us, Brandon."

"Do as you usually do," Brandon grumbled. "Doctor her the best you can, give her laudanum for pain if she needs it, then leave her be. She's probably ailing from the motion of the ship. It's hard on the ladies to be in the hold, so much closer to the thrashing sounds of the sea."

Brandon felt pangs of guilt enter his gut, never having agreed to placing *any*one in the hold of the ship, especially ladies. But this was a part of pirating, one that he had had to adjust to. . . .

Jack leaned up into Brandon's face. "This ain't just any lady," he said in a loud whisper. He nodded toward Leana. "The one who's ailin' is the mother of yer wench Leana."

Brandon paled. He turned with a start and peered toward Leana, then looked back down at Jack. "How ill *is* she?" he mumbled.

"She's burnin' up with fever," Jack said, squinting an eye up at Brandon. "It was her groans that woke me. She's a mighty sick lady, she is."

Brandon kneaded his chin, again looking toward Leana, then placed a hand to Jack's bony shoulder. "Bring her here, to my cabin," he said thickly. "I'll see to her myself."

"Aye, aye, sir," Jack said, then turned on a heel and hurried away.

Brandon closed the door and went to Leana. He knelt to a knee beside the bunk and took her hand into his. "Leana, there's something I must tell you," he said hoarsely.

Leana's heart skipped a beat, seeing so much in the depths of his eyes, and hearing a strained quality to his voice. She hurried to a sitting position. "What is it?" she asked anxiously, wishing her heart would quit pounding so.

But there could only be one reason for Brandon's cautious alarm. Only one other person besides herself, and now Brandon, was on this ship who meant anything

120

to her. Her mother. Oh, God, was . . . it . . . her mother . . . ?

"Your mother is being brought to my cabin," Brandon said, understanding when she jerked her hand free of his. She had to know there would be only one reason for her mother to be taken from the hold and brought to a more comfortable place.

Leana's hands went to her throat. "Mother?" she whispered harshly. "Is . . . she . . . ill? Or what? Why else would she be brought here?"

"Yes, she's ill," Brandon said. "She has a fever. I mean to see to it that she be made comfortable. She can stay here. You can be with her, Leana. I'll leave you two alone."

Tears sprang forth in Leana's eyes. Guilt caused her heart to ache. While she had been making wanton love with Brandon, her mother had been in the cold, dark hold of the ship, ailing. She glowered toward Brandon as she jumped from the bunk to fully dress.

"I think your generosity perhaps has come too late," she hissed. "My mother should've never been taken to such . . . such a place as the hold. I should have never been separated *from* her."

She went to Brandon and spoke hotly into his face. "Oh, how I . . . hate . . . you . . ." she spat. "Oh, how could I have ever . . . ever let you touch me?"

Brandon clasped onto her shoulders. "Because you know that you do not hate me," he said thickly. "Now I will leave you. You can ready the bedding for your mother."

He swung around and left Leana wordless, torn by her feelings. She went to the bunk and a sensual thrill coursed through her with remembrances of embraces

121

only moments ago shared there. Then a spot of blood on a blanket made her grow ashen in color, knowing what those embraces had led her to agreeing to do. She was no longer innocent. Oh, and what if her mother could tell that she had been with a man in such an intimate way just by looking onto the face of her daughter?

Jerking the soiled blanket from the bunk, she threw it across the room, having never been so angry or disappointed in herself as now.

Yet she knew that the smoldering memories of this night would forever be with her. . . .

Chapter Eight

In the dim lighting of the cabin, Cyril stood back admiring his latest prize. The wench's hair was long and free, red as the blaze of the sun, hanging down to the small of her back. Her hazel eyes were tempting him; her smile was seductively wicked. Placing her hands on her hips, she dared him, thrusting her bosom out, bold and proud.

"So what are you waitin' on?" Wanda Rhodes purred, running her tongue across the ruby red of her full and pouting lips. "I'm not puttin' up a fight. Or does that take away the excitement for a pirate?"

Cyril chuckled low. Though this fiery creature did not resemble his fair Amelia in the least, he felt that she might be the one he had been patiently waiting for all these years. She could put the fire back into his blood. She was the sort who could make a man never lack for excitement in the bed. Daring him as she was at this moment, she appeared quite skilled in the art of tempting a man. Traveling alone, she had to have had her goals set for, perhaps, working in a house of women.

Well, Cyril would keep her as his own, making it well worth her while, for he would shower her with gold trinkets, so much that the shine would never leave her eyes.

Taking a wide step forward, Cyril grabbed Wanda roughly around the waist and jerked her into his arms. "Wench, you talk too much," he growled. He kissed her savagely, his teeth cutting hard into her lips, drawing a wince of pain from between them.

He forced her downward, onto his bunk, ravaging her with the largeness of his hands. The sound of silk ripping whispered through the cabin, the smell of her perfume intoxicating Cyril even more as his lips now trailed downward to the magnificent swell of one of her breasts.

"Ah, so sweet," he mumbled, flicking his tongue around the nipple, tasting her flesh. He then raised up on an elbow and smiled down at her. "Undress me, wench. Then this pirate will teach you ways of making love that even you are innocent of knowing."

Wanda laughed softly, her long fingernails digging into the corded muscles at his shoulders. Her gaze traveled over Cyril, seeing that though he was much older than she, he still held within him that commanding look of power in both his gray, smoldering eyes and his set jaw.

She could tell that at one time his hair must have been jet-black, but now was threaded with gray. He wore it tied back with a strip of leather, and he displayed gold loops of earrings at his ears, and a bright gold religious medal hung around his neck.

"Are you truly a religious man?" Wanda purred, enjoying flirting with him. She had always wondered about how it would be to make love with a pirate. In her years as a confessed prostitute, she had yet to bed up with such a man. The thought excited her. It was the best way to have been taken prisoner. . . .

Cyril laughed low; his lips formed a half smile. "Just because I wear a gold piece around my neck doesn't make me religious," he said. His smile faded. "Now, wench, do I have my way with you without a fight, or not?"

"You wanted me to first undress you?"

"Aye, that is what I have ordered you to do."

"Ordered?"

"Aye. And do you not take to orders all that well?"

"I am the one usually handing out orders," Wanda said dryly. "When I am with a man, he is usually even glad *to* be ordered about by me. You see, I am one of a kind. It will be *I* who will teach *you* a few tricks about the ways to fornicate."

Cyril's eyebrows raised. "Oh?" he chuckled. "Is that right? Well, wench, again talkin' is gettin' in the way of doin'."

Wanda rose to her knees before him. She smiled seductively at him while her fingers began deftly lifting his satin shirt up and over his head. After the shirt was tossed aside, she splayed her fingers across his chest and lowered her lips to suck on first one of his nipples, and then the other. She could feel the thundering of his heart against her lips; she could hear the intake of his breath as her tongue began to trace a path downward, through the curled hairs of his chest.

And when she came to the bright red sash that he wore about his waist, she moved behind him and with her teeth unfastened it and began unwrapping it from around him; all the while her fingers were tantalizing him as she boldly touched and squeezed his hardness through the

125

sleekness of his breeches.

"Enough," Cyril growled, taking her by a wrist, throwing her back onto the bed. He frowned down at her as he continued to undress himself, and when finished, he leaned over her and ripped the rest of her clothes away. "Now we shall see who is the wiliest here. My lady, you are about to be made to see just how much a man this pirate *is*."

Wanda laughed sarcastically low, slithering across the bunk away from him, then smiled to herself as he bent and grabbed her hair, forcing her lips into his. For the first time ever in her life of being with men, she felt a tingling of actual desire! Always before she had only pretended. The ravagings by her father when a small child had made it impossible for her to feel anything about men. She had always thrilled in humiliating them. It had made her feel powerful to have them beg for what she so skillfully gave.

But now? Her heart was erratic with excitement, her skin felt aglow as his hands now skillfully searched out pleasure points that she hadn't ever been aware of having. A sweet melting, a current of warmth, enveloped her senses as she locked her arms about his neck and returned his kiss. She moaned as he stroked her between the thighs, awakening in her a euphoria that brought a rush of thankful tears to her eyes.

Cyril felt the trembling in Wanda's body and wondered about it, thinking to find her cold and even *hard*. But he could feel her responding. His tongue brushed her lips lightly. "Do I sense response in my lady?" he said huskily, arching an eyebrow as he looked down into her feverish eyes.

Wanda was in a daze, not even knowing what to say.

She didn't want to admit to feeling anything for this pirate. It was something that she had never thought to even experience. And so quickly? He had only touched her, kissed her, and such a delicious languor had crept over her.

Cyril smiled softly down at her. His large hand went to her hair and brushed it back from her face. "Ah, so you do not want to tell me that I've won with ye, do ye, wench?" he chuckled. "Well, that's quite all right. You see, in a way you've also won with *me*."

His mouth again closed hard upon hers; his hands were like fire upon her flesh as he captured a breast and kneaded it. His thumb rolled around a taut nipple, then he lowered his teeth to it and softly nipped it. Wanda moaned and lifted her hips from the bunk, placing a hand to his head, guiding it downward.

"Take me," she whispered huskily. "Fully take me."

Cyril's insides were like molten lava; his face was flushed. He did as she requested. She writhed and moaned when he entered her with his hardness, and as their bodies tangled, she emitted a soft scream and began pounding his back with doubled fists.

Laughing softly, having never bedded such a wild thing before, Cyril greedily worked with her, his hands cupping her breasts, his muscles cording with each eager thrust inside her. He placed a kiss to the slender curve of her throat; he scorched her skin with his mouth.

Passion swelled inside Wanda, pleasure spreading through her body like wildfire. Her hands wandered eagerly over his wide shoulders and his tight back. Her teeth bore down into his upper right arm, laughing softly when he winced with pain, then fading into a thick, husky groan as she soothed the pain away with fiery kisses.

Cyril drew momentarily away from her. His eyes swept silently over her, his hands playing homage to her perfect, supple body. He was left strangely shaken with desire for her, then his breath quickened with a yearning when she began moving her body against his, urging his strokes to begin again.

"You're a mixture of many types of women," Cyril whispered; then his mouth seized hers again in an explosion of searing flames. They blended into a torrid embrace and together they reached the peak of exquisite sensations, sighing and whispering against the other's cheek. . . .

"Stay with me," Cyril said huskily. "Be me queen. Wench, you'll never want for another thing for the rest of yer life."

Wanda was still tremulous from the sheer joy of having finally felt something when with a man. This troubled her. If a man had such power over her, wouldn't she again be playing the role of submitting to a man as when with her father? She had vowed to never let a man rule her again.

Rolling away from Cyril, Wanda rose quickly from the bunk. Barefoot, she strolled to the liquor cabinet and withdrew a bottle of wine and a gold goblet, looking about her at the richness of this private cabin. She knew that what he offered was real. He did possess riches. Even though they were riches taken from innocent travelers, they *were* riches, and they were now *his*. If his offer was true, she would never have to work another day. She could have everything that she had ever wanted out of life. Security. Even . . . love . . . ? She would have sensual moments that now meant something to her, and

128

she would have gold, diamonds, rubies. . . .

Her gaze moved farther about her, seeing the rich paneling of the cabin, the leather chairs, and desk with its top rolled closed.

She turned and eyed Cyril daringly. "Do you even have something with which to entice me right now?" she asked, wondering just what might be hidden behind the closed door of the desk.

"You need proof, eh?" Cyril laughed. His muscled legs flexed as he climbed from the bunk and walked smoothly to the desk. He had seen her eyes surveying it. Well, he was ready to show her what he kept hidden there. If she needed convincing, then she would have her way!

His eyes aglint, Cyril rolled the desktop up and withdrew a gold chest displaying rubies and sapphires encrusted into its sides. Wanda's breath caught in her throat as she viewed the shine of the jewels. Her fingers were trembling as she replaced the wine and goblet back inside the liquor cabinet. Her knees were weak as she walked toward Cyril, humbled by what she was now seeing as she now looked down into the opened chest.

Cyril ran his fingers through glittering pieces of jewelry, smiling a half smile toward Wanda. "These are yers, wench, if you will agree to be me lady," he offered. "But when I say me lady, I mean forever."

Wanda paled. Her eyes grew wide. "You don't mean marriage . . . ?" she stammered, feeling ice form around her heart. Marriage hadn't meant anything to her father. Her mother had suffered endlessly by his abuses and had died a weak and embittered woman at the age of forty. Wanda now being only thirty, she wanted to never believe that she would have that same fate.

Cyril threw his head back and laughed boisterously.

"Marriage?" he said, almost choking on the word. Then he sobered. His eyes squinted into two narrow slits. "Never. Once was all I needed to turn me heart against such an act as that."

Relief washed through Wanda. She smiled wickedly up at Cyril. "Then let me see those jewels," she said in a thick hiss. "I think we may be able to strike some sort of bargain here, handsome pirate."

His insides warming with her words, Cyril went to her and placed an arm about her waist. He handed the chest to her. "These are yers in exchange for yer promise to be faithful to me wishes," he said thickly.

A warning shot through Wanda. Men were born to inflict pain. She must remember that! Men were born to *betray*. Yet she would humble herself to this man for his jewels. What woman wouldn't?

"I think I may be happier now than ever before in my life," she said, a wicked glint still in her eyes, yet mostly hidden in the guise of a smile.

"Is it because of the jewels that I offer you?"

"It's much more than that. It's first because of *you*."

Wanda then let her eyes feast upon the treasure spread out before her eyes. She let her fingers sink down into the coldness of the gold chains and bracelets, the crispness of the sparkling diamonds, all of which were taking her breath clean away.

"So you feel the exchange is fair?" Cyril asked, stepping away from her. He went to the liquor cabinet and opened the bottle of wine and poured two goblets full of the red liquid.

Wanda wished she could relax to fully enjoy her victory. She should even be feeling as though having been given the *world*. "Fair? What can I say? I've never

130

met a man as generous," she said, almost choking on the words, hating having to say this to a man . . . any man. . . .

Cyril lifted his shoulder in a shrug. "That is only the beginning," he said, going to her. He held out the goblet of wine. "If you wish, some wine?"

Wanda once more let her eyes absorb the jewels, then she placed the chest back down on the desk and accepted the goblet. "Wine would be nice," she murmured warmly up at Cyril.

She sipped it slowly, watching him, seeing further than the pirate, seeing the man. She could see strength, yet a touch of sadness in his eyes, and had to wonder what woman had done this to him. He had mentioned a first marriage. She had to wonder where his wife was. Was she dead? Or had she fled from the dangerous life that surely pirating offered a lady . . . ?

Having never thought of the dangers of being this pirate's woman until this moment, Wanda's insides bubbled with the thought of such excitement.

Yes, she had it all, and perhaps, just perhaps, she would never let it go. . . .

"To us . . ." she said, tapping her goblet against Cyril's.

"Aye," Cyril chuckled.

Together they drank, then Cyril took the goblet from Wanda's hands and placed it beside his on the desk and led her back to the bunk. Gently he urged her downward, seeing the haziness enter her expression as his hands once again discovered every hidden curve, every pleasure point.

"I want you to feel special," Cyril said softly, feeling the pressure building inside him, that which could ex-

131

plode if she so much as touched him.

"I already do," Wanda whispered, wriggling seductively on the bunk as his mouth now closed over a breast. She bit her lower lip, she closed her eyes, again filling with ecstasy. She clenched her fists to her sides, so caught up in the rapture that when someone knocked on the door, it sounded as though only an echo of her nervous heartbeats.

"Cap'n?" a voice rang out much more loudly. "We've some trouble on board."

Cyril's face became engulfed in a pinched look. He wanted to ignore Jack's interference. But he knew that though Jack was disliked by all who met him, he *was* a dependable sailor.

Giving Wanda a brush of a kiss across her lips, Cyril rose from the bunk. He reached for a blanket and gently covered Wanda with it. "I must see to business," he grumbled. "But I won't be gone long."

In a flash he was dressed and slipped out into the corridor. "Let's have it. What's the trouble, Jack?" he stated flatly. He spread his legs and placed his hands on his hips, finding it hard to concentrate on anything but what lay waiting for him in his cabin. She was a rare find, a jewel *herself*.

"It's sickness aboard the *Erebus*," Jack scowled. "Just thought you'd best know. I've already informed Brandon."

"Eh? And what does Brandon have to say about it?"

"A plenty," Jack said, laughing low.

"What do you mean?" Cyril said, forking an eyebrow when having heard the mocking laugh.

Jack leaned into Cyril's face. "The one ailin' is the mother of the wench Brandon's claimed as his own," he

132

uttered. "I think we should put both wenches afloat, don't you, Cap'n?"

"I'm sure that wasn't Brandon's suggestion," Cyril grumbled, squaring his shoulders, stepping back away from Jack and his terrible stench. "I'll go and see for myself."

"The one ailin's been taken to Brandon's cabin," Jack interjected. "But I think she ought to be put overboard. We don' need sickness spreadin' on the *Erebus*. No matter *whose* mother she is. It's trouble, Cap'n. Trouble."

With a shadowed frown creasing his brow, Cyril hurried to Brandon's cabin. He didn't stop to knock. He jerked the door open and went on inside. He found a dimly lighted room and a tender scene, where daughter was looking after mother with affection.

Leana turned her head around when she heard the door opening, thinking it might be Brandon. She was still angry with him and hoped to not have to face him again so soon. Yet she had to wonder about herself when feeling the plummeting of her heart when seeing the older pirate standing there instead of Brandon.

Walking quietly across the room, Cyril towered over Leana. He gave her a weak smile, then kneaded his chin when he gazed over at the lady whose face was colored with fever.

"How's she farin', lassie?" Cyril softly asked, yet more concerned for his pirate crew than this mere stranger. This sort of sickness could change the luck of his ship. He felt as Jack did . . . that the sick one, at least, must be placed on shore as soon as possible.

"She's not at all well," Leana murmured, taking her mother's hand, dying a slow death inside when feeling the complete hotness of it. It seemed as though bathing her brow hadn't helped reduce the fever. And the way her mother now lay, so lifeless, Leana had to expect the worst. She didn't know if she could bear the loss. Her mother was everything to her. Without her . . . ?

Brandon moved silently into the cabin. He clasped a hand onto Cyril's shoulder. "Someone passed the word on to you, I see," he said thickly.

"Aye. It was Jack."

Brandon sighed heavily. "Aye. I could have guessed as much," he said, nodding. He looked over at Cyril, his thick brows coming together into a frown. "So? What do we do?"

Cyril gave him a set stare, his face solemn, his eyes dark. "You know what must be done," he said dryly. "She must be put from the ship. You know the dangers of fever."

Brandon placed his back to Leana. He spoke quietly into Cyril's face. "But you know that if she is sent away in a longboat, Leana will go with her," he said. "I just can't do that, Cyril. You know the chances are that neither would reach shore alive."

Cyril locked his hands together behind him. "So what do you suggest, lad?" he grumbled.

Brandon urged Cyril back and away from Leana. "The port of Rufino is not that far away," he whispered. "We can keep Leana's mother isolated until we get close to the port, *then* let them find their way to shore."

"That's what you want, Brandon?"

Brandon looked Cyril square in the eye. "At Rufino, they will be close to our headquarters in the Big Thicket," he said, realizing even when he was saying this to expect Cyril to lash back at him for giving special thoughts to one certain lady. "This will give me the opportunity to look in on Leana and her mother from time to time."

Cyril chuckled beneath his breath. He patted Brandon on the shoulder. "Lad, I guess it's about time you be thinkin' seriously on ladies." He nodded. "Aye. We will do as you wish. I respect yer judgment. Always 'ave. Always will."

Brandon's mouth dropped open, not ever thinking that Cyril would be so agreeable, especially where a lady was concerned. What had happened to change him?

Then the heady aroma of perfume emanating from Cyril gave Brandon cause to know that Cyril had bedded himself quite a charming lady himself. Had she had some effect on him? If so, this was the first that Brandon had ever witnessed. . . .

"Then it is agreed?" Brandon said, smiling knowingly at Cyril.

"Anything you say, lad," Cyril said, again patting Brandon's shoulder. "Anything you say."

Brandon watched Cyril walk away. Was there a skipping sort of quality to his step? If Brandon didn't know better, he would think that that hardheaded pirate was in love!

Shaking his head, smiling to himself, he turned and looked down at Leana. He was remembering her anger and accusations, placing the blame of her mother's illness on him. Even now she would not look his way. He ached to draw her up into his arms, to comfort her. But he knew this wasn't the time.

But he would not give up so easily. He would not give *her* up all that easily. . . .

Chapter Nine

Exhausted from sitting vigil at her mother's bedside for many endless days and nights, Leana savored the touch of the sea breeze caressing her face and the feel of the sun as it warmed her through her thin cotton dress. At the ship's rail she felt she could see forever, yet quietly wishing to see at least a trace of land. Though her mother's fever had broken, it had already taken its toll and she now lay spent, colorless, and sometimes even mindless. When Margaret hadn't been able to even speak Leana's name, it had almost broken Leana's spirit as well as her heart.

"I'm glad you're taking advantage of this beautiful day," Brandon suddenly spoke from behind Leana. "The *Erebus* is moving through the water so smoothly, it's as though it's a sea animal, alive and breathing. Would you tend to agree?"

Hearing Brandon's voice made Leana's heart skip a beat. Though still feeling a deep resentment toward him, she knew that at this moment he was the only one with whom she could be at ease. All of the other pirates seemed to be undressing her as they looked at her. At least Brandon treated her with respect due a lady.

Turning her head only slightly, only enough to let Brandon know that she had heard him, she smiled faintly at him. Yet she didn't want to speak to him. She was afraid that her voice would reveal too much of how his nearness still affected her. Even now her knees were weak and her pulse was racing. In her mind's eye she could see him making love to her. She could even feel the same strange, sweet ache between her thighs when recalling how he had sent her into another world of exquisite sensations. Dare he touch her, surely she would be lost to him again. . . .

"Still angry with me, I see," Brandon said, stepping to her side. He clasped his hands tightly to the ship's rail and squinted his eyes against the brilliant reflection of the sun, which was casting its beams into the emerald-blue waters of the Atlantic. Soon they would be lowering two longboats into the sea. Leana and her mother would travel in the one alone, while the rest of the captured ladies would be placed in the other. Brandon would make sure they reached port alive, for he would watch through his telescope until he saw that they did.

Brandon gave Leana a questioning glance, seeing that she still offered him only a slight smile. He tried to ignore her silent coldness by offering more small talk, hoping by doing so, her reserve would thaw.

"Aye, the *Erebus* is a good ship," he said, again gazing out to sea. "And would you like to know how this masterful ship got its name?"

He kept his eyes locked straight ahead and his spine stiff when she still refused to talk to him. But *still* he would try to draw her into the conversation without having to outright demand to know just how long she would choose to behave in such an unfriendly manner.

"Cyril gave the *Erebus* her name, long before I ever knew him," he said thickly. "I remember the first time he told me about it. He explained that Erebus was a Greek god, also known to be called *Darkness*. . . ."

Hearing Leana emit a quivering sigh as though she was bored caused Brandon's words to be cut off.

"You *are* still angry with me, *aren't* you?" he blurted.

"My feelings for you are torn," Leana finally confessed, weaving her fingers through her wind-tossed hair, arranging it more neatly around her shoulders. "I appreciate having been given your cabin for my ailing mother. But I hate you for placing both me and my mother in this impossible position of being on the ship *Erebus*."

Brandon scowled. His dark eyes implored her, drawing her eyes to his like a magnet. "I will not apologize for anything that I have done," he growled. "This is my life. I was introduced *into* this way of life at a young age. I know nothing *but* pirating. The fact that you are among one of the prizes taken is another result of the ways of pirating."

He moved his hands to her waist. "I will not apologize for that either," he said thickly. "For had I not boarded the ship *Jasmine*, I would have never met *you*. And had I not, our destinies would have never become intertwined. That would have been more of a crime than having taken all the gold and silver pieces from your abandoned ship."

Leana's eyes wavered; her heart was mellowing and she did not want this to happen. "I do not want to believe anything that you say about destiny and that you and I were at all meant to meet," she said, hating it when her

138

voice cracked as she spoke. "Brandon, you and I are from different ways of life. How could you even for one minute believe that we could ever be wholly together? You will continue sailing the seas, plundering. I want nothing of . . . of . . . that sort of man who does these terrible deeds."

Brandon dropped his hands down and away from her, turning on a heel to place his back to her. He knew that what she said was true, yet it was hard for him to give in to this knowing.

Yet wasn't it true that he soon would be putting her out to sea? Wasn't it true that he soon would be again acting out his role of pirate as soon as he had the much-needed time away from such a life while spending it on his horse riding free on land close by the Big Thicket?

Somehow he couldn't envision Leana there with him, for he *was* still remembering the warnings that Cyril had beat into his head these past seventeen years. Women should not be trusted. Especially fiery-natured ones. And Leana was quite the high-spirited female!

Leana felt a numb ache circling her heart, realizing that her words had perhaps cut Brandon as though she had pierced him with a knife. The hurt transferred to her, having seen the gentle side to his nature, having even been a recipient *of* this gentleness when he had held her in his arms. For a moment she had to brush aside the fact of how he made his living. She felt the need to reach out to him, soothe the wounds caused by her harsh words.

Trembling, she stepped around him and looked up into his eyes, which were smoke-black with emotion. His reddish-golden hair was tousled, unencumbered with its usual leather string. It was fluttering free in the sea breeze. His bronzed face was somber, his lips set.

"I'm sorry," Leana murmured, so badly wanting to place a hand to his face, tell him just how much she did love him.

But there were many eyes on this ship, always watching her. She didn't dare show any signs of affection to this one man, for it might arouse desires in others to come and take the same from her in the cold black of the night.

And she knew that she didn't even dare confess her love to Brandon, for she was going to continue fighting these feelings that plagued her.

She must, for soon they would be separated, forever.

Brandon's insides quivered with warmth. His eyes lit up, as did his hopes. "Do my ears deceive me?" he asked, forking an eyebrow. "Or did I just hear you say that you were sorry?"

Leana placed her hands to the skirt of her dress, holding it down from the blow of the wind. "I am sorry," she repeated. "Though you do anger me, I feel I have been rude. I cannot ever thank you enough for letting me and my mother use your cabin. Nor do I forget how you have protected me twice from that swarthy pirate, Jack. Do you understand what I'm trying to say, Brandon?"

Brandon's eyes crinkled into a warm smile. "Yes. I believe I do," he said.

He looked from side to side, knowing that privacy could never be found on the topdeck of the *Erebus*. And at this moment, he wanted full privacy with Leana. Their goodbyes were only a few heartbeats away.

Yet it was he who knew that they *would* meet again. Little did Leana know that he would also be docking near the port of Rufino.

But Brandon couldn't wait until then to be with her

again. He wanted to say goodbye to her *now* in the only way lovers knew.

He turned his full attention back to her, seeing how her sleek black hair spilled over her shoulders, and her eyes the color of the sky seemed to be reaching clean into his soul. Where her cotton dress opened at the throat with gathers of lace, he could see a trace of her deep cleavage, causing a knot to coil inside his gut with the need of her.

In a rush, he had his arm locked about her waist and was guiding her toward the companionway.

Leana's breath was stolen from her in this surprise move of his. She looked up at him, awestruck. "What are you doing?" she harshly whispered, brushing past sailors at work. "I believe you misinterpreted my apologies, Brandon. Let . . . me . . . *go.*"

He held her as though in a vise and led her on down a flight of stairs, and then another, and then walked her into a small, dimly lighted cabin and closed the door behind them.

Turning to face her, he gave her a heavy-lashed look, then drew her into his arms and suddenly kissed her with an urgency. Leana couldn't help but shudder with desire as his lips taunted her into responding. He held her with one hand while the other skillfully reached inside her dress to cup a breast.

Leana felt as though a puppet, as though some unhidden strings were drawing her arms about his neck to cling to him, every nerve in her body crying out, being again awakened to pleasure that Brandon, only Brandon, had borne inside her. His was a kiss that melted all anger, a kiss that left her weak . . . left her mindless.

Brandon leaned away from her, framing her face

141

between the largeness of his hands. "I must have you," he said huskily. "Leana, don't fight it. You want me as much."

Leana was too weak with desire to protest. She welcomed his hands removing her dress; she even moved toward a small bunk in a dark corner along with him. She let him urge her downward onto this bunk and she watched as though in a trance as he shed himself of his own clothing until he stood perfectly nude before her. The lamplight caught the look of desire in his midnight-black eyes, the expanse of his tanned, sleekly muscled body, and how he filled this tiny, drab cabin with his masculine presence.

And as her gaze lowered and saw his risen need of her, her face flamed and the heat of desire coiled inside her, threatening to break.

He went to her in a rush, drawing her into his arms, their bodies tangling as they wrestled in a lover's embrace, passionately kissing and touching.

"Oh, how I need you," Brandon whispered, his lips demanding, his knee spreading her legs apart. He pressed his hardness against the throbbing core of her womanhood; his hands kneaded the softness of her buttocks as he positioned her beneath him. "I've never wanted a woman as much, Leana. Only you."

Leana let her fingers again discover his wide shoulders, his muscled thighs, and then the largeness of his manhood pressed hard against her. Brazenly, she let her hands touch him there, and when he moaned she went as far as to encircle his shaft with the trembling of her fingers.

"Move your fingers on me," Brandon said, burying his face into the sweet curve of her neck. "Pleasure me,

142

Leana. Pleasure me."

Filled with rapture's abandon, Leana did as he asked, her fingers reveling in the velvet touch of his manhood. It seemed separate from the rest of him, alive even, as it pulsed and throbbed against her fingers.

Hearing his heavy breathing, Leana leaned away from him, and when her eyes locked with his and held, she saw that she had aroused in him a passion so keen, only their fused bodies could complete what had begun here.

"Brandon . . ." she murmured, her insides melting beneath his dark, stormy gaze. She reached her arms out to him.

His powerful hands reached for her waist and drew her to him. He lifted her up and urged her legs to lock around him. With her clinging around his neck, he positioned himself inside her, then began his sure and easy movements, then began thrusting hard, then again gently, his whole body atremble from the intenseness of their coupling.

Leana threw her head back, sighing with pleasure. Brandon placed an easy kiss at the hollow of her throat. And then he again pressed harder into her, moaning with joy as she began gyrating her hips, spinning some sort of silver magic around his thrusting shaft.

"Leana, your lips," Brandon whispered. "I . . . must . . . kiss you."

Intoxicated by passion, Leana's mouth closed hard upon his. Her tongue surged between his teeth; their kiss became that of flame as Brandon placed Leana gently on the bunk. Still locked together in a torrid embrace, Brandon recklessly drove on inside her.

Leana then unlocked her legs from around him. She urged him from her. "I must . . . get . . . my breath . . ."

she murmured, wiping beaded perspiration from her brow. "I did not know how weak and tired . . . I . . . was from having tended to my mother so much."

"My poor baby," Brandon whispered, cradling her close. His lips paid homage to one of her breasts, kissing it tenderly. His tongue left a trail of fire around the nipple, then lower, to tease her tiny navel.

And again he entered her. "I will make you relax," he said huskily. "There will be no work required on your part. Just close your eyes and feel the tension leave your body. There will be only one wild moment . . . that which will send your mind spiraling through the universe."

Her face inflamed with desire, Leana smiled up at him, then closed her eyes and forgot everything but the delicious warmth of his mouth gently kissing her and how his easy strokes inside her were making her feel as though she were soaring . . . floating . . . above herself, even him. . . .

And after the joy had spread over her like the flames of a candle touching her everywhere, Leana framed his face between her hands. "I know you are purposely holding off your own moment of total pleasure, wanting to be sure I have been satisfied," she said softly. "Do not torture yourself any longer. I have already been to heaven and back, darling."

Brandon gave her a warm smile, then drew her into his arms and held her close, and in three strokes he felt the release splash through him like lightning scorching a towering tree. He closed his eyes, his muscles tightened, he shuddered as he felt his warm liquid fill her insides.

Breathless, they moved apart, yet still held hands as they lay side by side on the bunk. "How can I ever say goodbye to you?" Brandon said huskily, scowling.

Leana didn't say anything. She was still in a state of rapture. She didn't want to think of any tomorrows. She knew that she had many battles to fight, and all without Brandon.

"When will we reach land?" she finally blurted, turning on her side, facing him.

"Possibly tomorrow," Brandon said, looking away from her.

"And how is it that you can feel safe enough to take the *Erebus* to any port, to set everyone free?" Leana continued to question. "Surely this pirate ship would be spotted and all the pirate crew . . . even you . . . will be arrested."

"You have to know that isn't the way it will be done," Brandon said, moving from the bunk, fearing telling her the truth. Up to now, it had been easy to avoid talking about the day they would separate. He hadn't told her that she and her mother would be placed from the ship and would have to find their way to shore, alone.

But now it was time to confess everything to her. He knew that she would not understand. He was again giving her cause to hate him! But there was no other way. Brandon wasn't only thinking of his own safety, but he had always placed Cyril's welfare before his own. Cyril had become a substitute father, and having betrayed his own father, Brandon could never do the same to Cyril.

Leana gathered her clothes and began dressing. "What do you mean?" she asked, fluffing the skirt of her dress as its gathered waist fell into place on her.

Brandon slipped into his leather breeches, then went to Leana and clasped his fingers onto her shoulders. "I mean to say that I will not be accompanying you nor your mother to shore," he said thickly. "The ship *Erebus*

145

would never dare dock at any port. You see, you are right. The ship *and* its crew would be quickly seized."

Leana swallowed hard; her face paled. "What are you trying to tell me?" she asked.

"That you and your mother will be placed at sea in one longboat and the rest of the prisoners will be released in another," he said in a rush of words. "Each longboat will be required to find its own way to shore."

"No . . ." Leana gasped.

She jerked away from him, her eyes filled with fire. "Now I see," she hissed. "You make sure you have this one last romp in the bed with me before telling me that you are not even worried about my welfare after releasing me and my mother to the sea. You will leave . . . us . . . to drift . . . as though we were nothing more than animals."

Brandon took a hasty step toward her, making his muscles to stir down the length of his lean, tanned body. Again he possessed her by the grasp of his fingers. "I would never do that," he growled. "And you should know that I wouldn't."

"Then what?" she said, trying to stifle a sob of frustration.

"You will have oars and I will keep watch from the ship until I see that you have safely reached shore."

"And then what? I will have my sick mother to look after."

"You will be able to find all the help you need in Rufino," he said thickly.

Again Leana paled. Rufino? She had never told him that Rufino was her original destination. Yet, no, he didn't know even now. It was just a coincidence that he had chosen that seaport. If he knew she had been heading

146

for Rufino, he would know that she would have family to go to, not strangers, and he hadn't made any mention of that.

Caution breathed through her like a pale breeze of evening. She still mustn't let him know about her family. She knew the dangers of any pirates knowing the family name. Brandon Seton . . . one Seton family member . . . was enough to have been taken for ransom by pirates. . . .

The thought that *this* Seton, the man she loved, was a pirate again grated on her nerves. She took a bold step up to him and spoke into his face. "If you were anything but a pirate, you could—" she began, then was silenced by the crush of his lips.

"Be silent, my love," Brandon whispered between kisses. "I *am* a pirate. And you love me . . . even . . . still. You have proved it to me more than once."

Leana felt the same power in his fierce, possessive kiss and knew that, yes, she knew that he was a pirate and, yes, she *did* love him still. Oh, a future without him was . . . no . . . future at all. . . .

Chapter Ten

Rufino sat at the mouth of the Sabine River, nine miles from the Gulf of Mexico, closer to Houston than San Antonio. The docks were alive with men, howling and sweating, loading and unloading ships. Leana moved easily through the crowd, having successfully brought her mother to shore on the longboat. She now clung around her mother's waist, helping her along, tired from both the rowing and struggling to keep her mother to her feet. Leana couldn't hate Brandon more than at this moment, now fully realizing her helplessness, and now fully blaming him.

Casting a look over her shoulder, she looked for traces of the *Erebus* on the horizon, but as it was the last time she had looked, it seemed to have vanished into thin air, having even seemed to have done so as soon as Leana and her mother had been sent away from the devil ship. Though Brandon had said that he would keep watch until Leana had safely landed at Rufino, she now doubted that he had. If so, he would have to have done so only in spirit!

"I'm so tired," Margaret whined, leaning more heavily

against Leana's side. "I . . . must . . . rest, Leana. My head. It keeps spinning so."

"I know, Mother," Leana said, at least glad that her mother was aware of what was happening. It was a relief to hear her say something. "I'm doing the best I can."

Frowning, Leana looked about her, seeing the indifference in all the men's eyes as they hurried on, attending to their morning duties. None had even questioned her as to why she had landed in a longboat. They seemed to have one purpose in life . . . that of looking out for themselves.

Leana had to wonder what had been the fate of the other longboat that had left the *Erebus*. An involuntary shiver raced across her flesh, Leana at least thankful that she had been given oars with which to propel the longboat in which she and her mother had been sent out to sea. The other women could drift for days, perhaps never to reach shore.

A hurtful stab at her heart caused Leana to even wince when thinking of the one lady who had been left on board the pirate ship. She had stood brazenly smiling beside the captain of the ship, gold shining at her ears, throat, and fingers, all signs of having been bought. . . .

Leana couldn't help but feel a wave of jealousy splash through her, wondering why Brandon hadn't tried to bargain with *her* to stay on board with him.

But then she suddenly realized why. . . . It was because of her ailing mother. All aboard the *Erebus* had been equally glad to see the sick lady removed from the ship. Brandon had to know that this could only be done with Leana accompanying her mother.

Shaking her head, clearing her thoughts of any further wonder of Brandon, Leana became seriously involved in wondering what her next move must be *now*. She had to find out where the Seton *ranchero* was located. She must get her mother there, *soon*.

But Leana was afraid to stop and question any of these sweating, filthy men. If she drew undue attention to herself in this way, might they take full advantage of her and her mother's aloneness?

No. She had to find a small, private house, where a proper lady might be found from whom to ask assistance.

"We must get away from the waterfront, Mother," Leana murmured. "I've got to find help. Please do your best to follow along beside me."

"It's . . . so . . . hard . . ." Margaret said in a harsh whisper, panting. "Oh, where is Parker? Lord, where . . . is . . . Parker . . . ?"

Leana suddenly realized that her mother had thought that Parker was going to meet them. Her mother had forgotten just how they happened to be in Rufino. It seemed that the past weeks had been erased from her mother's mind and that she seemed to believe they had just been set free from the ship *Jasmine* instead of the *Erebus*.

"I'm going to take you to Father," Leana encouraged, tears scalding the corners of her eyes. "Just trust me, Mother. You will be with Father soon."

"But where is he now?" Margaret whined. "Why didn't he meet the ship?"

Leana cast her mother a troubled glance, seeing how her mother's eyes were hazed over, as though in a drugged stupor. Her face was ashen; her hair had lost its sheen and now hung in wiry wisps across her thin shoulders. She was dressed in a silk dress that displayed a row of gathered lace at her throat and at the edge of its long sleeves. A few months, even weeks ago, Margaret Seton would have been a vision of loveliness in the dress. But today it hung from her like a droopy sack, Margaret's body having been wasted away by fever.

This tore at Leana's heart. She looked quickly away from her mother, not even aware of her own appearance and that her face was a glowing, vibrant pink, an aftermath of her many hours of lovemaking with Brandon. Her hair was free, a cloak of black as it hung about her shoulders. Her dress was a soft cotton, billowing in the wind, revealing her lace petticoat lifting up and from around her tapering ankles as the breeze blew steadily in from the sea.

But it was her eyes that showed her true self. In their deep blues, there was a determination. And her jaw was set as well as her chin lifted. She would make things right for her mother if she had to die *trying*.

Now glad to be away from the docks, Leana led her mother along a board sidewalk, one of which was found on each side of the dirt streets that were packed with jostling men, horses, mules, wagons, and very noticeably Mexican soldiers. The town of Rufino was a mass of warehouses and wooden and adobe structures scattered along the few dusty streets that led to the bay.

Leana's gaze moved from building to building. There was a general store, a hotel, post office, jail, and a thin line of saloons, even a bordello. She could hear the faint calliope of voices from the saloons, the tinkling of a piano. She jumped when she heard the breaking of glass and distant gunfire.

When she saw many men gathered in groups before the stores, now staring openly back at her, she swallowed hard and urged her mother hurriedly onward until she left the main thoroughfare behind and began walking before gray and brown adobe houses.

"Leana . . ." Margaret rasped, trembling. "Where's Parker? You said . . . that . . . you were taking me to him. Lord, where's . . . Parker . . . ?"

Feeling desperation rising inside her, Leana studied the houses now available to her, then chose the closest. It was a crumbling adobe house, yet had a yard that was neat and clean of debris, which meant that surely the owner had the same sort of disposition. . . .

"I think we can find help here," Leana reassured her mother. "Just a few more steps, Mother."

She clung to her mother, her own body aching from her labors. If she would come face-to-face with Brandon at this moment, she would surely plunge a knife into his heart! Her misfortunes were all because of him! Should she ever see him again, oh, what she *would* do to him!

There was no porch at this adobe house, nor steps for which to propel her mother up. Leana instead only had to step to the door and knock, breathlessly awaiting a reply. Perhaps she should have gone to the hotel instead of a private dwelling. What if a sweating, vile man opened the door she was now standing before?

But from what she had seen of the town's hotel, she knew to have found perhaps more rats than people inhabiting the rooms. There seemed to be a lack of pride on the part of the owner of the hotel. If she should have the chance, she would make such a place a grand showcase, not a place that women were afraid to enter because of its broken windows and dark, foreboding entranceway.

And I don't have money for even renting a room for a night, which I must do if I don't find out the directions to the

Seton rancho, she stewed to herself. *I don't have anything to offer* anyone *for payment of any kindness rendered me and Mother.*

Leana was drawn quickly from her reverie when the heavy wooden door opened with a jerk before her weary eyes. Relief flooded her senses, seeing a young woman instead of a man. Leana took a quick second glance at the woman, seeing something familiar about her. Was it the gray of her eyes? Or the slight crook of her nose? Her hair was jet-black, naturally curly in appearance as it blossomed into tight ringlets of curls about her square face and across her shoulders. She was of a medium height, attired in a dress that was bold not only in color with its great splashes of red roses in its design, but also in the way its drawstring bodice lay low, revealing too much of the swell of her breasts.

Leana gathered that the young woman might be seventeen, yet in her face there appeared to be a trace of what one found in one who had lived beyond those youthful years, having possibly experienced hardships, tragedies, more than one that age should have been burdened with. The lines were there at the corners of her eyes, lines put there by worry. . . .

But, still . . . besides these things . . . Leana still felt as though she had met the young lady before, but scoffed at the thought, knowing that she surely had to be wrong. How *could* she know her? Until this very moment they had been worlds apart, Leana being from New York City and this young woman seemingly to have had her roots planted in this drab settlement in Texas.

"Yes? What can I do for you?" the young woman said in a cautious tone of voice, looking first at Leana, then at Leana's mother.

"We've just arrived in town," Leana said, groaning beneath her breath when her mother seemed to have become heavier as she leaned more into Leana's side. "Perhaps you may be kind enough to help us? My mother. She is ailing. She needs a place to rest momentarily. We have kin near here, but I'm not sure just where. I need to find someone who will help me locate my stepfather's rancho."

"Did you arrive by ship?" the young woman asked, again closely scrutinizing Leana and her mother.

A frown darkened Leana's features. "You might say that we did, in a way," she said sourly.

The young woman's brows knitted together, also in a frown. "You did or you didn't," she said, gazing back over her shoulder as the sound of a cough surfaced from inside the house. "Now, which is it?" she asked, again gazing with suspicion at Leana.

"Parker?" Margaret said in a bare whisper, squinting her eyes as she looked over at the young woman. "Is that . . . you . . . , Parker?"

Leana shook her head sadly. Her lips formed a narrow, straight line as she glared at the young woman still blocking the door. "I see that we are wasting our time here," she snapped. "My mother is gravely ill and you can stand there so cold, not willing to help us? You are most certainly not a kind young lady."

Supporting her mother, Leana leaned and spoke into her face. "Come on, Mother," she murmured. "I seem to have chosen the wrong house. We'll go to the next one." She eased her mother around and began walking away, then stopped when she heard the soft voice from behind her asking her to stay.

"Please. Forgive me," the young woman said, gesturing with a hand as Leana cast a glance across her shoulder to look at her. "I've learned to not trust. It is something that you learn when living without men in your house to protect you. Please do come in. Your mother does appear to be quite weak. I know how it is to have a sick mother. My mother is not well either."

"We don't want to be a burden," Leana said, helping her mother back around. "But we *do* need someplace for my mother to rest. It shouldn't be for long. It surely shouldn't take too long to locate my stepfather. He said that he had built a ranch not too far from Rufino."

"My name's Darla. Darla Yates," the young woman said, stepping on Margaret's other side, taking on some of the weight as Margaret now half leaned into *her*.

"I'm Leana Rutherford," Leana said, being directed into a room dimly lighted by the faint glow from a kerosene lamp sitting in the middle of a kitchen table. "Margaret is my mother's name. Margaret Seton."

Darla's eyes widened. "Oh? You and your mother have different last names?" she said.

Leana felt safe enough to explain the difference in the two last names now that she and her mother had finally arrived in Texas. She even was compelled to tell Darla about everything that had happened at sea, except for the fact that Leana had fallen in love with her captor.

"After my mother is made comfortable, I've much to talk about and glad to have somebody that I can confide in," Leana sighed, hoping that she wasn't trusting too quickly. But she didn't see any choice *but* to trust. It was this young woman who was going to have to help her find Parker Seton's ranch. And to do this, the woman would *have* to know the name. . . .

"My mother is asleep in her bedroom, so we can take

155

your mother to mine," Darla said, seeing now how Leana was taking in everything of this drab house with the wandering of her eyes.

Darla's gaze swept over Leana and her mother, seeing the expensive taste of the two women in the way they were dressed. It was evident that these two women were used to the best, probably of *everything*.

The usual shame engulfed Darla, never anxious to let anyone see how she or her mother lived. But that had been the way of life since Darla could remember. When her mother had been well, they had constantly kept on the run, with Darla never understanding from *what*.

But since her mother's illness, the strange melancholia that had robbed her of her senses and will to live, they had stayed in one place, in this drab town of Rufino, and it had been hard, oh, so damn, damn hard to make ends meet.

Darla had lost respect for herself many years ago, and almost even her mother, because of the way they had been forced to live. Had there been a man to support them, things would have been different. But her mother had never spoken of a man . . . Darla's father. Darla hadn't even ever been told her father's name. . . .

"Offering your room would be more than kind of you," Leana said, seeing the cracked cement walls, the mismatched furniture, and the floors bare of carpet. A fireplace glowed orange; the smell of spices lay heavy in the air as a pot hung over the live coals, steam spiraling from it in gray swirls.

An Indian blanket hung over one doorway. Leana surmised that Darla's mother slept in that room. Colorful beads, the only colorful item in this house, hung over another doorway. Darla directed Leana and Margaret through them and into a room that was furnished with only a bed and a table beside it, where a candle had burned low, sputtering in a bed of melted wax.

"Let's help her down onto my bed," Darla encouraged. She held onto one of Margaret's arms while Leana held onto the other. And when they had Margaret comfortably in bed, covered by a blanket, and the candle was blown out, they went out to the living room and sat down in front of the fireplace on an upholstered divan.

Leana leaned her head back, stretching her neck and tired shoulder muscles. She combed her fingers through her hair. "It feels so good to sit down," she sighed. "It's been a long morning. Lord, I even feel lucky to be *alive*."

"Can I get you anything? Some wine? Some tea?" Darla asked, her cheeks rosy, now glad to have company. It had been a long time since she had been offered companionship and conversation with a decent woman from the States. Now that she knew that she could trust Leana, she was going to revel in the pleasure of her company, no matter how short the time spent with her might be.

"I really care for neither wine nor tea," Leana said, smiling back at Darla, still seeing something familiar in her features. "Just a moment to rest before I begin my search."

"How do you happen to be in Rufino?" Darla questioned, drawing her bare feet up onto the divan, clasping her arms about her drawn-up knees. "How is it that you and your mother are alone? Where did you travel from?"

Leana settled into the back of the divan, her eyes taking on a faraway cast as she peered into the dancing flames of the fireplace. "Nothing is as it should be," she murmured. "If not for the pirates—"

"Pirates?" Darla said, straightening her back. "What about pirates?"

Leana again sighed, then proceeded with her tale of how the ship *Jasmine* had been accosted by the pirates and what had happened from there on, except for the sensual moments shared with Brandon. . . .

"And now I must find my stepfather," Leana continued. "Do you happen to know a rancher by the name Seton? He said something about settling close to the Big Thicket. Do you know where that might be?"

Darla smiled awkwardly. "Everyone knows where the Big Thicket is," she said softly. "But not too many dare to go near it. There is much mystery about the area. Some speak of mysterious golden lights. Some say that bandits, perhaps even *pirates,* live there."

Leana's breath caught in her throat. She moved to the edge of the divan and gave Darla a steady stare. "Pirates?" she said in a strain. "Truly? There are rumors of pirates making their residence there?"

With a swish of skirt Darla moved from the divan, laughing softly. "Ah, I doubt it," she said. "Most of these tales are a product of superstition. Do not let such things frighten you. If your stepfather has chosen to make his residence near the Big Thicket, he has done so because he feels it is safe enough."

Moving to her feet, straightening the lines of her dress, Leana shook her head slowly back and forth. "He would not know of such things," she murmured. "He is a man of large city ways. What would he know of myths and superstitions? Lord, if pirates *are* harboring themselves close by, my father hasn't bettered himself at all."

Then Leana's cheeks colored with wonder. Pirates?

Could they be the same pirates among whom could be found the man who had set her insides aglow? Was that why it had been so handy for Brandon and Cyril to set the two longboats free from their ship? Because they, too, were close to their hideaway . . . ?

"Leana . . . ?"

Leana turned with a start. When seeing the questioning in Darla's eyes, she knew that Darla had seen her silent questionings. She laughed awkwardly. "Oh, I guess my mind wandered just a bit," she said. Her fingers again combed through her hair. "I really must find a way to locate Parker Seton. Could you help me? I feel so . . . so lost so far away from New York. From what I've seen of Texas, I don't find it to my liking."

"It's a rugged territory," Darla said, frowning. "First the Mexicans want the Americans to settle here, and now that the Americans have, the Mexicans want them to leave. There is even rumor that the Mexicans are paying the Indians to cause trouble for the white settlers, to scare them off. If you are wise, once you find your stepfather, you might try talking him into returning to New York."

Leana shook her head. "No," she said softly. "Once Parker Seton starts something, he finishes it. He loves a challenge."

"But this time he may have more than he bargained for," Darla said, nodding. "If I had a chance, I'd leave this horrid place. But as it is, with my mother so sick, I don't have any choice but to stay on."

"I'm sorry about your mother," Leana said, looking toward the Indian blanket that hung at the one bedroom door.

"There's nothing much that can be done," Darla said,

bending to place another log on the fire. She moaned as she placed her hands to the small of her back, again facing Leana. "But let's see if we can do something at least about *your* mother. I think I know of someone who can help you find your stepfather."

Leana's heart began to race. "You do?" she blurted. "Who?"

"He's Mexican," Darla said, caution edging her words.

Leana's insides tingled in an unknown fear, remembering Darla's very recent words about Mexicans and of their hate now for the Americans. "Would a Mexican truly help an American?" she asked, forking an eyebrow.

"For payment, this Mexican would."

This time Leana's insides grew cold, knowing what payment was usually expected of a woman. "Oh? And what might that be?" she said icily.

Darla's gaze again traveled over Leana, her mind having absorbed all that had been implied about Parker Seton. Only a rich man could change his lifestyle in midstream. "Your stepfather would be willing to pay the price?" she murmured, drawing a cheroot from a leather pouch. She lighted it, seeing the surprise in Leana's eyes. She smiled and gestured with the cheroot toward Leana. "This is something only recently introduced to me," she laughed. "It is my one pleasure of life. There aren't too many, you know."

Awestruck, now realizing that this woman was quite educated in the ways of life though she was so young, Leana was momentarily left wordless. Then she grew angry inside, thinking that Darla surely would get a share of what was given this Mexican for information handed her.

She moved to the fireplace and drummed her fingers

160

against the solid oak mantelpiece, peering into the flames. "And what would you get from this Mexican?" she said coldly. "An even split of the money given him for services rendered?"

"How I wish I could," Darla laughed. "But, no. I'm afraid I must make my money in different ways. I only suggest this Mexican to you out of the kindness of my heart. I'm afraid I know of no one else that you could scarcely trust."

Feeling guilt for having suspected her newly found friend, though a questionable type of person she was, Leana went to Darla and placed a hand on her arm. "I'm sorry for having doubted you," she apologized. "But much has happened only recently that makes me mistrust everyone. I'm sure you understand."

"Yes. I understand," Darla said, flicking ashes into the fireplace.

A soft whine of a voice filtered through the Indian blanket at the bedroom door, calling for Darla.

Darla tossed her cheroot into the fireplace, her eyes wavering as she looked over at Leana. "It's Mother," she murmured. "She's awakened. I must go to her first. Then I'll go and find Diego Rufino."

"Diego Rufino?"

"He's the Mexican that will help you. He's a Mexican general. This town bears his name. It *is* his town. He *will* help you, Leana. Trust me?"

"I must, mustn't I? I have no other choice."

"I hope to earn your trust soon," Darla said softly. She took one of Leana's hands. "Come on. Meet my mother. Rarely does she have the opportunity to have visitors."

Leana walked alongside Darla into the bedroom, then recoiled somewhat when she saw the shriveled-up woman

161

on the bed . . . a woman who couldn't be even forty yet, lovely in a haunting way, but whose face was drawn tautly across bone. Her hair was golden, her eyes a lovely violet color, searching Leana's face as Leana was guided to her bedside.

"Mother, this is Leana," Darla said softly. Darla turned to Leana. "Leana, this is my mother. Mother, Leana and her mother are here visiting for a while. They had some troubles at sea. A ship of pirates kidnapped them from their ship. Isn't that terrible?"

Darla's mother placed a hand to her mouth, yet that couldn't stifle a sob. She was remembering another pirate . . . another time. . . .

Darla paled, seeing the response in her mother's eyes. This was the first in many weeks. She leaned down and over her mother, placing a hand to her cheek. "Mother? What did I say to . . . to . . . make you aware . . . ?" she whispered.

Darla's mother turned her eyes away, letting the tears warm her cheeks. But nothing could ever again warm her heart. . . .

Chapter Eleven

The buggy rode along pleasantly rolling country, the trail occasionally knifing through tall, cool trees. Sycamores brightened the darker bottomland with their mottled trunks and branches. Magnolia trees were gargantuan, growing fifteen feet high with a twenty-two-foot top spread. Cottonwoods spread shade, scattering on the wind their winged, cottony seeds, their silver-lined leaves making a continued noise of rain. The fugitive scent of pine perfumed the air; the sun glared out of a platinum sky.

Leana held possessively onto her mother's hand in this fringe-topped buggy, casting troubled glances up at General Diego Rufino, the Mexican in the driver's seat guiding a brown mare. Though he had assured Leana and her mother safe arrival to Parker Seton's ranch, Leana still didn't trust the Mexican general. Beneath his black hat his face was ruddy; his lips seemed to always hold a hint of mockery in them, twisted into a smug smile beneath his razor-thin mustache.

His dark eyes held a dangerous glint within them. He

was squared-off and stocky and walked with a limp. The saber worn at the side of his black suit trimmed with silver caught the shine of the sun in it; a pistol belted at his other side behaved as a threat to Leana.

Yet Leana had no other choice but to take Darla's word that this Mexican general was an honorable man and that he had been telling the truth when he had given his word that he would see to her and her mother's safety while taking them to Parker Seton. Leana only hoped that the price asked of Parker Seton for Leana and her mother's safe arrival wouldn't be too steep. . . .

"How much farther?" Margaret said in a muted whisper as her head bobbed from the movement of the buggy. Her eyes were scarcely open, her face ghostly pale.

"I have no idea," Leana whispered back, smoothing some of her mother's wisps of hair back from her eyes. "Just relax against me, Mother. At least we know that we are finally *on* our way to Father's ranch, which, of course, is also yours."

Margaret managed a quivering smile as she looked up into Leana's eyes. "And also yours, darling," she uttered. "And also yours. You know that Parker looks to you as a daughter. I only wish that adoption papers could have been drawn up. I would feel . . . feel much more comfortable about things. Out here in the wilderness, who knows what might happen to me? Even Parker? What . . . might . . . happen to you *then?*"

"Nothing is going to happen to you *or* Father," Leana scoffed, smiling reassuringly back at her mother. Yet in her heart, she knew all too well the dangers of living in Texas. As if Indians weren't threat enough, it was now a known fact that the corrupt Mexican government was

164

now even more a threat!

Leana cast General Rufino another glance, thinking he must be the most corrupt of all. He was surely going against his command by helping two American ladies in distress.

Yes, the price *would* be high when delivering these two ladies to Parker Seton, and Leana had had no other choice but to let it happen in this way. Her mother was too ill for her to not have accepted help from the Mexican general. Alone she could have found other means. But her mother's well-being had to be placed before everything else. Even money. . . .

A thundering of hooves drew Leana's thoughts from all but that which her eyes were now filled with. She placed a hand to her throat, seeing a herd of buffalo rushing across the land, appearing to be brown streaks with their massive, shaggy bodies silhouetted against the blue of the sky.

And then the buggy came alongside a different sort of animal grazing contentedly on land where wildflowers exploded and retreated in masses of gold and scarlet, pink and purple.

"Señoras, what do you think of the 'mossy horns'?" General Rufino shouted from across his shoulder. "They are impressive, *si?*"

"Mossy horns?" Leana shouted back, leaning forward.

"*Si,*" General Rufino said, giving Leana a quick glance. He nodded toward the grazing longhorns. "The older longhorns have moss on their horns. They are called 'mossy horns.'"

"Oh, I see," Leana said, flicking a stray curl that had whipped around into her eyes.

"These wild cattle of longhorns that roam the

165

unfenced Texas plains have descended from stock introduced by early Spaniards," General Rufino further explained. "After they live in the swamps and wet thickets of this part of Texas for a year or two, they grow moss, like most everything else around here."

"Are you familiar with the Big Thicket?" Leana asked, glad to at least have someone to question about this new land that she was being introduced into. Also, she liked talking with this Mexican, hoping that if she was friendly enough, he just might not demand so much payment from Parker Seton.

"*Sí*," General Rufino said, his face shadowing into a frown. "It is a place of ghosts and bandits. Señora, it is a place not fit for a beautiful señorita like yourself. Do not go there. You would never return."

Pinpricks of fear laced Leana's heart. If this place was so off-limits, why did her stepfather buy land adjacent to it? Of course, she knew that he wanted to be kept isolated from the rest of the settlers, to remain anonymous, but he hadn't achieved these wishes, it seemed. For if so, how was it that this Mexican general had known so quickly just where the Seton ranch was located?

But the wonder of her stepfather was quickly replaced by thoughts of Brandon. Could it be possible that he and Cyril and his pirate crew did make residence in the Big Thicket? Was it the pirates whom this Mexican general feared?

Shaking her head somberly, Leana didn't want to think anymore on pirates *or* the Big Thicket. Right now she only wanted to get her mother safely to her husband. Then Leana could worry about her own future and who she could think of including *in* it.

A cool breeze touched Leana's bare arms. Her gaze was

drawn quickly to the dark and menacing wilderness that now spread out on the one side of her. From her very first notice, she knew that she had just seen her first glimpse of the Big Thicket.

A shiver raced across her flesh and it seemed that something cold edged about her heart when she saw how this region was that of enormous trees and scattered swamps and black-water sloughs, laced with dense tangles of yaupon and titi and interspersed with open savannas. It was *not* the familiar Texas of the big sky and far-off horizons that Leana had just recently become acquainted with. And she knew that she was not afraid, but, instead, intrigued. . . .

The buggy rattled onward, still skirting the edges of the Big Thicket. The afternoon was ebbing; the distant hills were shaded in purple and gray. Only an occasional ranch could be seen in the distance, and then finally one in particular was pointed out to Leana and her mother. Its full spread of simple buildings and corrals and ranch house was nestled beneath the shelter of shinnery oaks and cottonwoods beside a glittering stream, interspersed with mesquite, chaparral, and prickly bear bushes.

"Señoras, may I introduce you to the Seton rancho," General Rufino said in his gravelly tone of voice. "I have never had the pleasure of meeting Señor Seton, but it is my business to know of each of the land owners. Do you understand?"

Leana was too engrossed in what she was seeing to hear anything that the Mexican general was saying. Her heart was thumping wildly against her ribs, her eyes were wide, absorbing this that her stepfather had managed to build in his two-year absence from New York.

Her gaze moved from one end of the property to the

167

other, seeing the pasture dotted with horses and longhorn cattle. Several gray-silvered shacks, which she had to guess were used for bunkhouses, were set far back from the main house with bitter orange and chinaberry trees near them. Beyond this spread the corrals, the barn, the grain sheds, and even a blacksmith shop.

But then Leana's gaze was drawn back to the ranch house. It was low and gray, built of adobe and tufa, which was a porous limestone. It was one-storied except for an airdome roof which was railed and flat, which she surmised was used as a lookout.

The sunlight was quickly fading now, liquid gold pouring over the Seton ranch, and from each of the windows of the adobe house more golden light could be seen, fusing with that of the outdoors.

Excitement welled up inside Leana. She looked down at her mother, wondering if she had also seen what Parker Seton had built.

Then her heart seemed to plummet to her feet when seeing that her mother's eyes were peacefully closed and there wasn't a trace of a heartbeat at the base of her throat.

"Mother . . . ?" Leana said in a harsh whisper, now realizing that her mother's fingers were tightly closed over her hand, in a death's grip.

"No!" Leana then screamed, fully realizing what had happened. Her mother had died, perhaps even only seconds ago.

"Lord, no," Leana cried, cradling her mother close, oblivious of the fact that the buggy had just come to a halt before the ranch house and that Parker and Matthew had stepped from the house, their eyes wide with wonder and confusion.

"Margaret? Leana?" Parker gasped, raking his fingers confusedly through his thinning carrot-colored hair. "How . . . ?"

Leana sobbed. She wiped tears from her eyes, unable to release her mother's hold on her other hand. "Father, Mother . . . is . . . dead . . . ," she cried. "She died only moments ago. Please . . ."

Ashen, Parker rushed to the buggy. Pain showed in the lines of his face and he moaned with remorse as he unlocked Margaret's hand from Leana's. Matthew came to the other side of the buggy, his eyes dark with questioning.

"We didn't receive word of your arrival," Matthew said thickly. His gaze traveled to General Rufino, then over the buggy, seeing no luggage. "What's happened, Leana? How is it that you've arrived in such a way? How did Margaret die? I don't understand any of this."

"Matt, just help Father with Mother," Leana said, sniffling. She wiped her nose with the back of her hand, looking over at the lifeless form of her mother now being lifted into Parker Seton's powerful arms. It didn't seem real . . . that her mother was dead. Only moments ago her mother had even talked rationally to her!

"Father is doing just fine without my assistance," Matthew said dryly. A small smile lifted his lips as he reached for Leana. "It is you who needs assistance. You are quite distraught, Leana. Let me help you from the buggy."

"Yes, I'm distraught," she snapped, again sniffling. "Why shouldn't I be? My mother just died. We've traveled from hell and back to get to Texas. Shouldn't I be distraught, Matt?"

Matthew reached and placed his hands to her waist.

"Come, come," he said dryly. "This isn't the time for old antagonisms, is it?"

Leana slapped Matthew's hands away, having dreaded being placed in the position again of defending herself against him. Well, this time she would tell Parker. That would put a stop to this nonsense from Matthew, forever!

General Rufino intervened. He climbed from the buggy. He brushed Matthew aside. "Gringo, if the beautiful señora doesn't wish to be bothered by you, then I shall do her the honors of helping her from the buggy," he said in a snarl. His dark eyes gleamed as he looked up at Leana. "Señorita, may I?"

Leana sighed wearily. It seemed that she now had two vile men from whom to protect herself. She could see it in the Mexican's eyes. He liked what he saw and Leana was afraid that he might use his powers as a general of the Mexican army to get what he wanted.

But she would fight him. Every inch of the way. Neither he nor Matthew would ever touch her in the way they so openly desired!

Leana squirmed free of the Mexican's hands. "Sir, unhand me," she hissed. Her eyes wavered as she saw Parker carrying her mother into the house. "I must go and help Father. I must comfort him. He has . . . has . . . just lost his wife. I have just . . . just lost my mother."

"*Lo siento,*" General Rufino said, stepping back away from the buggy. He turned to Matthew and held out a large, very finely manicured hand. "*Dinero? Pago total,* Gringo," he said smoothly. He shrugged. "You pay, I leave. It's as simple as that. I do not deliver these two señoritas to you and your father for nothing."

Matthew straightened his back, his full six-foot height

170

dwarfing the Mexican. Yet in Matthew's eyes there was an evidence of silent fear. "Yes, I should have known to expect such a demand," he said hoarsely. "*Espere un momento.* I will have to see what my father is willing to pay."

General Rufino emitted a low snarl. His hand locked over his pistol. "*Pronto,* Gringo," he said. "And make the payment enough so that I do not have to ask for more." His gaze moved to Leana. "Do not force me to take the beautiful señorita back to Rufino with me to work out the payment."

Matthew blanched. "*No se preocupe,*" he gasped. "Do not worry. I am sure my father will pay you very well."

Leana climbed from the carriage, barely breathing. When her skirt got caught onto a nail and the pale evening's air was disturbed by the shrill ripping of cotton, she gasped, seeing that the pink of her thigh was now exposed to the naked eye. She looked from Matthew to General Rufino, seeing both their gazes fused to her flesh.

"Matthew!" she hissed, jerking her dress free of its ensnarement. "Go and tell Father what General Rufino is needing so the general can go on his *way.*"

Matthew's lips lifted into a nervous grin. He nodded and hurried toward the house.

Leana straightened her back and smoothed the skirt of her dress. "Now, sir, if you will excuse me," she said dryly.

General Rufino grabbed her by a wrist as she swung around and attempted to go on her way. "*Espere un momento,*" he growled. "I have more to say to you."

"Oh, I do believe I forgot to thank you for your courtesies of bringing me and my mother to the Seton ranch," she said icily. She searched her brain for the proper Spanish words to say, having only been taught a few words while in school.

"*Muchas gracias,*" she blurted.

She jerked herself free from his hold and began stomping away from him. "And *buenas noches,* Señor."

Leana's heart was paining her, so dreading having to look upon the dead face of her mother. She only barely glanced at Matthew as he brushed past her with a chest. She didn't even wonder how much she and her mother had been worth. She only vaguely chose to wonder if the Mexican might even be back for more payment, possibly even demanding Leana *be* that payment. Leana could only think about how her world seemed to be continuously torn apart.

Looking toward the dark shroud of the land that led into the Big Thicket, her thoughts strangely were suddenly filled with Brandon. She knew that it was his arms she craved at this moment, to comfort her, and she knew that want . . . that need . . . was wrong. . . .

A guitar sobbed its music in a far corner of the mission. Banks of flowers decorated the sanctuary; a cloth of red, white, and green—the colors of Mexico—veiled the tabernacle. A brilliantly striped serape served as an altar cloth; the casket lay closed, shrouded by red roses, velveteen in their sheen.

The voice of the priest mumbled low blessings over the casket and then the ceremony was moved outside, to a fenced-in plot of ground where tombstones rose ghostly from the ground.

After the burial was completed, Leana walked beside

Parker, reveling in the touch of his strong arm about her waist. Out of the corner of her eye she saw the drab edifice of yellow brick of the Spanish mission, built by Spanish friars in 1718. The sun crowned it this evening; the sky was orange-streaked as night ebbed darkness along the horizon.

"It's over," Parker mumbled. "I can't believe that I have truly lost her. Leana, what am I to do without her?"

"What am *I* to do without her?" Leana murmured, tears sparkling in her eyes. "I even feel responsible for her being *gone*."

Parker helped Leana up into the stately family carriage, nodding to Matthew as he walked around the carriage and boarded it at the other side. "If anyone is to blame, it is I," he grumbled. "Had I not left New York. Had I not . . ."

Leana's eyes sought Parker out as he settled down onto the seat across from her, the sun having now set for another day, the moon exchanging places in the sky with the sun. She had noticed how his words had dropped off into a nothingness. And again she was filled with wonder as to why he had felt such a need to leave his way of life in New York. Would she ever know . . . ?

She settled back against the plushness of the seat, letting her gaze absorb Parker's handsomeness as the moonlight silvered him through the window. His carrot-colored hair had thinned, yet in his expensive woolen suit he still showed quite an expanse of muscles at his shoulders.

Though suffused with painful sadness, his face was still that of a handsome man, strangely stirring something inside Leana. She was seeing something in Parker that she hadn't thought to wonder about before. But now

173

that she thought about it, there was quite a resemblance in him . . . and . . . Brandon, not his son Brandon, but the Brandon who had stolen Leana's heart away.

Leana felt the need to mention this to Parker, yet there was no need in causing him to start thinking about his son again . . . a son whom he would never see again. The pirate Brandon surely wasn't Brandon Seton. Yet Leana had never been told her lover's last name. It *was* possible.

But she would not trouble Parker with this. Surely she was wrong. . . .

The coach lurched as it began moving away from the mission, the driver of mixed Mexican and American descent. Parker leaned toward the window, frowning. "There's a 'Comanche moon' tonight," he grumbled. "That's what the Comanches call a full moon. I pray to God the moon doesn't lead them to our ranch."

"Father, don't begin worrying about that again," Matthew scolded. "Just because we've seen some Comanches scouting close to the ranch, that doesn't mean they are going to bother us."

Parker slouched his shoulders and drummed his fingers nervously on a knee. "It's going to happen," he grumbled. "One day it's going to happen. Damn the Mexicans. First wary of America's blatant expansionism, they sought, through an influx of settlers, to check the Indians who dominate the province. Now it is rumored that the Mexicans have been sending agents to meet with the Indians, antagonizing them against the Americans. The Mexicans know that with the Indian attacks from the north and the Mexican Army from the south, Texas would be hard-pressed to survive. . . . Texas could never win its total independence."

Leana leaned a hand to Parker's knee. "This isn't the

174

time to worry yourself about such things," she murmured. "You are troubled enough with the death of Mother. Try to not crowd your mind with other worries."

Parker slammed a fist into the seat beside him. "Damn the *pirates*," he growled. "First pirates take my son Brandon and now they take my wife. It *is* their fault that she is dead."

He gave Leana a lingering look. "But I am lucky that you were strong enough to make it through the ordeal unharmed," he said in a strain.

Leana cast her eyes downward, afraid that Parker might see the truth that lay in their depths. She didn't want him to see that though she was unharmed in the sense that he implied, she had not come through the abduction untouched. Brandon, oh, Brandon . . .

"We want to hear all about your experience one of these days," Matthew said. "But of course it must be something you don't wish to labor over. Pirates are a swarthy lot. I am sure there is not one among them who has a decent bone in their body."

Matthew leaned over, closer to Leana. "Perhaps one even tried to force himself upon you?" he whispered, low enough for his father to not hear.

Leana glared over at Matthew, seeing his perfect profile in the moonlight. It would seem that any woman would melt beneath the gaze of his smoldering eyes, yet Leana still felt nothing but coldness for him.

"Of course your mind would conjure up all sorts of ugliness," she quietly hissed. "Just leave me alone, Matt. Don't include me in your twisted, devious thoughts."

A low chuckle was Matthew's only reply. He straightened his back and looked away from her, knowing too well what must have happened to her on the pirate's ship.

She was too beautiful to ignore. Surely one, possibly even more than one, pirate had had his way with her. Well, whoever it was had just prepared her for what *he* soon would introduce her to. She could not deny him forever. In this wilderness where men were scarce, she would even beg for it now that she knew the pleasures of the flesh.

Ah, yes, Matthew gloated to himself. *I would enjoy seeing her beg . . .*

The ranch house was finally reached. Everyone unloaded from the carriage and sauntered into the house, silence a burden, that which always accompanied death in a household.

Parker walked to the liquor cabinet and poured himself a shot of whiskey. He gulped it down in one swallow, then slammed the glass back down inside the cabinet. He turned on a heel and looked from Leana to Matthew. "We've much to talk over," he said thickly. "But tonight isn't the time. I've got to retire to my bed. I just can't seem to think about anything now, other than missing my Margaret."

"I understand," Leana murmured. "I shall be retiring, also."

Matthew gave Leana a quick glance, then nodded. "Yes, I guess it's time that we all say our goodnights," he said thickly. "I'll be going on to my room, also."

Leana nodded toward him. She watched him leave the room, then she felt the warmth of Parker's arms enfold her, then leave her much too soon as he also left the room.

Feeling the aloneness, Leana looked about the room, knowing that her mother would have enjoyed living here in the house especially built for her. The walls had been covered with Mexican mahogany on white oak, girdled with hard pine. The room was well furnished with a figured carpet, sheer curtains hung immaculately white at the windows, and cherry wood tables with marble tops sat beside chairs and a sofa upholstered in horsehair.

A fire had burned low in a magnificent stone fireplace at the far end of the room, casting pale orange light about the room.

Leana walked into the tallest room of the house. It was a room of mostly windows. An airdome. She had seen the railed roof and its lookout upon arrival to the ranch. And she wondered if there was a true threat of Indians. And was this the reason *for* such a room having been built onto the house?

Weary, Leana lifted a shoulder into a casual shrug and went to her bedroom, closing the door behind her. Again she observed what lay before her, feeling the touch of Parker's choosings in everything that she saw. She loved the four-poster bed with its luscious embroidered bedspread and skirt. A lit brass lamp hung suspended from the ceiling, the wick only barely turned up.

But the lamp emitted enough light from it for Leana to see a movement in the mirror over the chest of drawers and see that Matthew had just opened the door behind her and had silently entered the room.

Spinning around on a heel, Leana glared up at Matthew as he closed the door. "What do you think you're doing?" she hissed.

"It's been too long, Leana," Matthew whispered, taking a wide stride, grabbing her in his arms. His mouth crushed down upon hers, stealing her breath from the quickness of his actions. She tried to wriggle free but his arms were imprisoning her, his tongue now surging

177

through her lips, invading her mouth.

And then the door slammed suddenly open and the wrath of God seemed to come down upon Matthew as Parker was suddenly there, jerking Matthew away from Leana. "I saw it coming," Parker growled. He slapped Matthew across the face, first one direction and then the other. "Have you no respect for the dead? Have you no respect for your stepsister? Matthew, God! If you weren't my son, I'd horsewhip you!"

Matthew was ashen in color. Blood curled from his nose and lip. He glared from his father to Leana, smearing the blood as he wiped it with the back of the hand.

"Apologize to your sister!" Parker demanded, clasping Matthew by the shoulders, giving him a rough shake. "Apologize to *me*, Matthew. I just did bury my *wife*."

"I apologize," Matthew gulped, yet the hate in his eyes told Leana that the apology was a lie. She now knew to be wary of his each and every move. . . .

Parker eyed Matthew with a longing, then drew him roughly into his arms and sobbed against his shoulder. "God, Matthew, you're the only son that I have left," he whispered. "And I hit you? Oh, God, I'm sorry. God, I'm sorry. You . . . you and Leana? You're now all that I have."

Leana's eyes widened, her hands went to her throat, seeing Parker humbling himself before both her and Matthew. And when she saw a look of triumph enter Matthew's eyes, she knew who was the true victor here. Matthew. Only Matthew. . . .

"That's okay, Father," Matthew said, patting his father on the back. "Damn if I didn't deserve what you gave me. But I had only come to Leana's room to embrace her, to tell her how sorry I was about her mother's death.

She just suddenly got under my skin, being so beautiful and all. I just forgot myself. Honest. It won't happen again."

Leana's insides grew cold, seeing how he looked at her from across his father's shoulder. She knew to expect more . . . much more . . . and perhaps soon. She now wondered if she could even ever expect help from Parker. With his breaking down in such a way, humbling himself to his son, he surely would think twice before facing Matthew again in Leana's defense.

Leana turned her back to Matthew, having never felt so helpless as she did now. . . .

Chapter Twelve

A sumptuous fare of ham, eggs, grits, orange blossom muffins, and mayhew jelly had been served for breakfast. Leana sat at the dining table with Parker and Matthew, sipping on her coffee. She sat in silence, peering over the coffee cup's rim at Parker and how he was faring this morning, the first day after his wife's burial.

There was a strange determination in Parker's dark eyes this morning. His jaw was set and he was dressed much differently than Leana had ever seen him before. This day he wore a cotton plaid shirt with a thin western tie at its collar, and before he had sat down she had seen his tight jeans and western boots. His carrot-colored hair had been brushed to lay impeccably back from his brow, and at his waist he sported a belted pair of pistols.

Placing the coffee cup back in its saucer, Leana nervously cleared her throat, drawing Parker's attention from his deep thoughts. She welcomed his slow smile and his look of admiration at how she was dressed this morning. She had gladly accepted the jeans and cotton shirt given her to wear, even the boots that Parker had suggested she wear while out in this wilderness of mainly men. He had encouraged her to look less the seductive woman that she had become, feeling that she would be less apt to draw undue attention to herself from the hands at his ranch.

She had never worn a man's breeches before and had laughed at the thought. But now she felt comfortable in them, even enjoyed the sense of freedom they evoked, not having to be on guard at all times, as she would if she wore a delicate dress.

"Well? What do you think of Texas?" Parker asked, shoving his plate away from him, though it still displayed uneaten eggs and biscuits.

Leana scooted her own plate away from her, and then also her empty coffee cup. "I at first detested it. But now? I can say that I haven't seen enough of Texas yet to state an honest opinion," she said, lifting a shoulder into a casual shrug. "Perhaps you might show me around this morning, Father?"

Parker's brow furrowed into a frown. "Maybe tomorrow," he mumbled, lowering his eyes. He toyed with a knife, turning it from side to side. "I need to be alone, Leana. I thought I might get on my horse and take a ride. Think things through. That sort of thing."

Matthew poured himself another cup of coffee. He frowned toward his father. "Do you think that's wise?" he asked. "Don't you remember the Comanches? Surely you don't intend to ride alone."

A bruise showed at the corner of Matthew's mouth and a contusion was browning beneath his right eye. He was still remembering the blows from his father, and his insides seethed with contempt *for* his father. Even though his brother, Brandon, had been gone those many years, Matthew still felt as though second in his father's heart, the largest portion being still reserved for a son who would never return.

Jealousy festered inside Matthew like a sore and he knew that he would never be free of it. Not as long as the memory of Brandon was still alive. And how did one kill . . . a . . . memory . . . ?

"Oh, hogwash," Parker scolded. "You worry too much, Matthew. What you need is to work out your fears." He gestured with a hand. "Get out there with the rest of the men. Damn it, son, mingle. Go and help rustle some cattle. There are many longhorns runnin' free. One day they'll be worth a lot of money to those who have claimed them as their own."

"I'll stick to bookwork," Matthew grumbled. "Somebody's got to do it."

"I can hire that done," Parker argued. He slammed a fist down onto the tabletop, causing dishes and silverware to bounce. "Damn it, son. Since our arrival to Texas you seem scared of your shadow. That's not like a Seton."

Matthew rose angrily to his feet, knocking the chair over in the process. He placed the palms of his hands flat on the table and glowered down into his father's face. "I'm not the only one afraid in this family," he grumbled. "Father, you uprooted the entire family and came to Texas because of your *own* fears. Fears that you won't even talk about. So don't go calling me the black sheep of the Seton family."

Matthew's face turned crimson as he leaned even closer to his father's face. "Want to tell me about what you were runnin' from, Father?" he glowered. "Huh?"

Parker rose from his chair in a fury. His face was beet-red, his heart was pounding. But remembering how he had lost control only the night before, he only now doubled his fists to his sides and stared in silent rage at his son.

"Matthew, just go and do what you do these mornings," he said blandly. "I'll forget your disobedience." He flailed an arm into the air. "Get on away with you. Do you hear?"

Straightening his back, his callus-free hands now smoothing the silk of his shirt back down into his fawn breeches, Matthew gave Leana a lingering look, then spun around on a heel and stomped from the room.

Shaking his head, Parker went to Leana and helped her up from her chair. "Sometimes I don't even believe he's my son," he said thickly. "Now, if that was Brandon, there would be respect. Brandon would never talk to me in that tone of voice. He was a son . . . of . . . sons."

The name *Brandon* stung Leana's heart as though a bee were there, torturing her with its stinger. The Brandon whom she had become acquainted with would have been a devoted son. He was kind. He was gentle. He treated the aging pirate, Cyril, with respect due a father. Leana had to wonder where Brandon's true father was. Could he be the Brandon of Parker's dreams and Matthew's nightmares?

But still she couldn't take it upon herself to tell Parker about the likenesses. It would only add pain to the misery if she was wrong. Why give the man hope, when hope surely was only a figment of *her* imagination?

"I'm sure Matthew is under much strain from the move from New York," Leana tried to encourage. She felt the usual warmth touch her insides when Parker swung an arm about her waist. She leaned into him as they began walking from the dining room. "Matthew loved New York. He was quite socially active, you know. Think of the beautiful women he had to leave behind."

She bit her lower lip with those last words. She knew that she had been his choice of women. Leana knew that his reasoning was surely because she had become a challenge. He wanted what he could never have. This had made life more exciting for him. Leana knew that he had begun to sorely enjoy the cat-and-mouse game that he played with her.

"Father . . ." she blurted, thinking this was the time to tell her stepfather of her fears of Matthew. Hadn't Parker gotten a taste of what his son was capable of the previous night?

Yet her words stuck in her throat, not wanting to worry Parker any more than he already was this morning. She had seen the awkwardness that was growing between son and father. Leana was puzzled at this change. But she gathered it was because with Parker leaving New York, he had lost all hopes of ever seeing his other son again. It was as though Parker had purposely closed that chapter in his life, yet he didn't appear as though he was living with his decision so well.

Parker guided Leana down a narrow hallway, into his study. "You were about to say?" he asked, studying her out of the corner of his eye. "Is something bothering you, Leana? Is it the death of your mother? Can I do anything to help ease the pain?"

Leana shook her head. "It's nothing, Father," she sighed. "It's nothing I can't handle myself."

Nodding, Parker laughed softly. "My dear daughter, I think you are capable of handling any problem that might come your way," he said. "You managed to survive the pirates, didn't you?"

He swung her around and faced her, his face troubled. "You never did say," he mumbled. "But . . . did . . . you truly come out of that ordeal, uh, unscathed?"

A blush rose to Leana's cheeks, rosying them. She cast her eyes downward, so vividly remembering that first time with Brandon. It was a mutual seduction, one that was repeated more than once before she left the *Erebus* with her mother.

But it was not a thing that she would share with anyone else. She most certainly couldn't confess such a thing to her stepfather. Only *she* fully understood why, and how it had been allowed to happen.

Unashamed, she tilted her chin upward and met Parker's questioning stare. "As I told you before, I was unharmed," she said dryly. "The pirates weren't all that bad a lot of men, Father. In fact, there was one—"

She clasped a hand over her mouth and gasped, having come so close to telling him about Brandon.

"Yes?" Parker said, his eyes widening. "You were about to say . . . ?"

Leana looked up into his trusting eyes and felt a tearing of her heart. She combed her fingers through her midnight-black hair and strolled on away from him, yet feeling his eyes on her, burning her, it seemed.

"There *was* this *one* man," she murmured, now knowing that she was compelled to tell him about Brandon. She had worried and stewed over it long enough. If it was Brandon, Parker's son Brandon, couldn't it change Parker's life? He would no longer be remorseful. He would even welcome each new day with a smile! It had been a long time since Leana had seen Parker truly, truly happy. . . .

"Yes? What about this man?" Parker asked, going to Leana. He placed his hands to her shoulders and gently turned her around to face him.

"Parker, his name was Brandon," she blurted, wide-eyed. "But surely this pirate couldn't be your son. Could he?"

Parker's hands dropped away from her in a jerk. His face paled and his eyes drew to sharp points of black. "What are . . . you . . . saying . . . ?" he gasped.

"One of the pirates, a very gentle, a very handsome man, called himself by the name Brandon," Leana said, already knowing that she had been wrong to tell Parker. She saw the hurt and confusion etched across his face, lining it.

"And you think . . . this pirate . . . could be my son?" Parker said. He then threw his head back and laughed fitfully. "My son? A pirate?"

He grew somber, his jaw squared angrily. "Never," he hissed. "If my son was alive, he would be with *me.*"

Leana was barely breathing, watching Parker as he began to pace. His shoulders were slouched, yet his muscles were corded. "No. That couldn't have been my son," he said, his voice trembling. "Never."

"Yes, I know," Leana murmured. "And I'm so sorry for even suspecting that it might be. I know that Brandon, *your* Brandon, would have returned home if he were alive. There are many men with the name Brandon. How foolish I was—"

"You're never foolish," Parker said, his mood softening. "You're special, Leana. I've been lucky to have you as a daughter."

He went to his massive oak desk and sat down behind it. He unlocked a drawer and motioned for Leana to come to him. "I've something to give you," he said hoarsely. "Just in case something might happen to me, I want to be sure that you have what is due you. I'm not sure Matthew can be . . . uh . . . trusted, Leana. He's not as devoted to you as I am. And sometimes I even think that he's . . . uh . . . a bit too greedy for his own good."

Parker's words about greed caused a sick feeling to eat away at his gut. Greed? He was the *king* of greed. If Leana ever found out the full truth about him, her devotion to him would falter, even possibly blow away with the wind.

But there was no reason for her to ever find out what he had done in New York. She would never know to what extent he had gone to enable him to leave his memories behind him in New York . . . memories that had not been left behind so easily, as he had found out upon arrival to this new land. Brandon was always with him . . . always. . . .

Full of wonder, Leana stepped up to the desk, then beside Parker as he motioned for her to even get closer. "Father, what is it?" she murmured. "I can't imagine what you're talking about."

"Money and jewels," he said, looking up at her, his eyes dark with feeling. "Leana, you must have something with which to bargain should anything happen to me. And, Leana, you must never tell Matthew that I have given you these things. There's already too much strain between us. If he knew the complete distrust I had in him, my only surviving son, he would never forgive me."

Leana was rendered speechless by his confession and a gold chest that he had withdrawn from a drawer and had opened. The shine of diamonds and the glitter of coins and even the dull green of dollar bills met her eyes. She jumped as though startled when Parker offered the chest to her.

"This is yours," he said softly. "There should be enough of value in here to take care of you quite properly for a while should the need arise." He moved it closer to her. "Take it, Leana. It is the only insurance I can offer you."

"But, Father, so . . . so much . . . ?" she said in a whisper. "I don't know what . . . to . . . say. . . ."

"You need say nothing," he said, easing the chest into her hands. "Having you as a daughter all these years has been thank you enough."

"But I am not truly . . . your . . . daughter," Leana dared to say, fearing hurting him. But she felt that he was being too generous. Did he care for her that much?

But, yes, she had always suspected that he did. Theirs had been a special relationship from the very beginning. He had become a substitute father, as she had become a substitute daughter.

"Yes, you are," Parker said, smiling warmly down at her. "In every sense of the word, you are."

He picked up a sombrero from a chair and plopped it on his head. "Take the chest to your bedroom," he said, walking toward the door. "Put it in a safe place. I'm now going for that ride I promised myself."

"Father?" Leana said, her voice sounding thick and strained, full of emotion.

Parker turned on a heel and faced her. "Yes?" he said, eyeing her warmly.

"Thank you. And be careful," Leana murmured. "I'm sure Matthew isn't worrying over nothing when he makes mention of the Comanches."

Parker laughed softly. He went to a chair where he had left his guns and holsters draped. "Yes, I must remember to wear these," he said, buckling them in place about his waist. "In New York I never had need for such protection."

"Please be careful?" Leana repeated, walking toward him, the chest heavy in her arms.

"Always," Parker chuckled. He leaned a kiss to her cheek and then hurried from the room.

Leana was still in a semi state of shock over his generous gift. She studied the jewels and the money, having never before seen so much at one time. "I must get this to my room," she whispered. "Should Matthew see this, Lord, what would he *do?*"

She walked in a half run down the hallway and breathed much more easily when she closed the bedroom door behind her. Placing the chest on her bed, she closed its lid, then looked cautiously about her, wondering where she might put it, away from searching eyes.

Her gaze settled on a larger chest at the foot of her bed. She could hide this smaller chest beneath the most delicate of her underthings, only herself the one to ever touch them. At least there, they were safely hidden from Matthew.

And after getting it well hidden, she strolled to the window and drew back the sheer curtain and watched as Parker rode away on a proud steed. A chill coursed through her, fearing for him.

Yet surely he traveled alone often. She was being foolish for worrying about him. He wouldn't take any undue risks.

Yet she knew that he felt as though he didn't have much to live for. And wasn't it strange that he would give her this chest now? It was as though he *expected* to die. . . .

189

Leana blanched. "Lord, no . . ." she whispered. She watched Parker become only a blur in the distance, then turned from the window and stared blankly into space, filled with fear and wonder. . . .

Parker enjoyed the touch of the wind against his face, thinking that the best time in Texas had to be dawn. The sun was flaring above the prairie and sere hills; hawks were planing overhead. There was an almost mystical attachment that seemed to be here this morning linking Parker and his horse and the explosion of nature all about him. Somehow he was feeling better about life than usual. It even felt good *to* be alive.

"Giddyap!" he shouted to his roan, hearing his voice echoing back at him. He laughed. He thrust the heels of his boots into the horse's flanks.

And then his face lost its excitement when he saw the most identifiable figure of an Indian approaching him.

"Damn . . ." he whispered, drawing his reins tightly, causing his roan to come to a shuddering halt.

He waited for the Indian's approach, knowing to turn his back could be disastrous. He didn't even reach for his gun, knowing even that could mean his quick death.

But he did look around him fleetingly for possible other Indians, relieved when seeing none. Perhaps a bargain could be made with only one Indian. . . .

The sun was hot. Parker pulled his sombrero lower over his eyes and sat straight in the saddle, still waiting. The Comanche then finally drew up next to him on his pony. He wore only a loincloth and a wide, multicolored beaded wampum belt. His long, lank black hair hung

190

around his shoulders; his dark eyes were fathomless. He carried a lance decorated by colorful feathers, and his copper skin shone as though waxed beneath the powerful rays of the sun.

Parker raised a hand in a gesture of a friendly salute, yet saying nothing, not knowing the language of the Comanche.

The Comanche's eyes didn't waver. He held his chin high, then suddenly his gaze moved to Parker's saddle and nodded. In a staccato sort of speaking, the Indian pointed his lance toward the saddle, that which had been hand-tooled with a silver horn and mounting.

Parker immediately knew that the Indian wanted the saddle. And when the Comanche removed his wampum belt and offered an even trade, Parker growled to himself. "You thieving bastard," he mumbled. "Who wants a wampum belt? The saddle cost me an arm and a *leg*."

But Parker knew that he had no choice but to comply. He dismounted and angrily jerked the saddle from his horse and handed it to the Indian, shaking his head discontentedly as he accepted the wampum belt in return.

Parker then mounted his roan but waited for the Indian to ride away with his prize before turning his own back on the Indian. And when he felt it was safe enough, he swung his roan around and began riding away in a trot. But when he heard the thundering of hoofbeats coming up quickly behind him, he understood that the Comanche had tricked him.

Before Parker had his head turned to see the Indian, he saw the lance pierce his chest, having first entered his back.

"Oh, God . . ." Parker cried, then saw nothing but black as he slumped over on his horse to lock his arms about the horse's neck.

The Comanche rode up next to Parker and jerked the wampum belt away from where Parker had tucked it loosely into the waist of his jeans, then started to knock Parker from the horse, to also take the horse, but was stopped when seeing many men on horseback suddenly appear on the horizon.

Emitting a loud shriek, the Comanche rode away, leaving a curtain of dust behind him. . . .

Another death. Another funeral. Leana felt drained from the losses. She entered the ranch house and went on into the parlor, letting her black veil flutter from around her face and to the floor, at this moment not caring about anything. Life was unfair. First her mother. And now her stepfather? What was she to do?

"Are you all right?" Matthew asked as he moved into the parlor with Leana. "You're as pale as a ghost." He went to her and framed her face between his hands. "You know, don't you, that it's just you and me now, Leana?"

Leana's insides froze, hearing so much in his words without him even having to voice his intentions aloud. Her thoughts went to the chest of valuables hidden in her bedroom. She must escape with the chest, and soon. But first she must play the role of an innocent, helpless ninny. This was the only way.

"Yes, Matt," she said, casting her eyes downward. "I guess you're right."

"You *will* marry me, won't you, Leana?"

"Please give me time . . . to . . . think, Matt. We've only just returned from Father's burial."

"Yes. I understand. Perhaps you should go on to your room and rest, Leana."

"Yes. I'm sure you're right, Matt. Thank you for being so kind."

Matthew placed a finger beneath her chin. "Do you want me to help you to your room?" he asked thickly.

"No. I'm fine, Matt. Just fine. I'm sure you've much to do yourself. You've just lost your father. Don't worry about me."

Matthew eased away from her. Leana looked at him closely. She felt as though she saw traces of remorse in his dark eyes. Was he truly missing his father? But, yes. He must. Who could not miss Parker Seton?

Yet wasn't it the same as when her mother had died? It didn't even seem real that Parker was *dead*.

"I'll be going on to my room, Matt."

"Fine. I'll look in on you later, Leana."

Leana turned and smiled smugly to herself, knowing that when he looked in on her, she would be gone. As soon as she got her things together, she would sneak away from this place. Without Parker, it could never be home. And to stay could mean a possible ravaging by the man she detested. She could never let Matthew touch her in . . . that . . . way. Only Brandon. Only Brandon. . . .

Hurrying to her bedroom, she removed the chest from its hiding place and opened it to once again peer down upon the riches it held. "Father must have known this would happen, that Matt would presume that he was all I had, and that I would marry him," she whispered. "Father even must have truly known that he would soon

193

be dead."

Tears blinded her eyes. She stood there long enough to cry out her complete sorrow, then she began moving determinedly around the room, knowing that she had to be swift. And could she move away from the ranch in the buggy without Matthew hearing? Oh, Lord, she had to be able to. Her future had to be found elsewhere. . . .

Chapter Thirteen

Rufino was dark as Leana entered its empty streets, the time of night not that which was popular for being up and about. It was three in the morning and all seemed to be asleep, even the ships moored at the docks, their bows creaking in the lapping of the waves.

Keeping her eyes moving cautiously all about her, as she had done since having left the Seton Ranch, Leana slapped the reins against the horse pulling her buggy. She had at first thought to go to Darla Yates's house, to again ask for her help, but the time of night had changed her mind. She must go to the hotel. But she would just have to be sure to keep her stepfather's pistol close at hand, having taken it from his desk, where Matthew had placed it after having taken it from Parker's body after his murder.

She shuddered when remembering how she had felt when she had looked at the hotel that first time. She could envision it being filled with rats. *I've got to keep my eyes watching for more than rats,* she argued to herself. *I know the dangers of being alone. I'm going to have to make it known quite quickly that I can take care of myself. No man is going to take advantage of me if I can help it.*

But she worried to herself as to whether or not she could stand up against all odds now facing her. She had never been alone. And women alone anywhere were targets for all sex-starved men.

"But Darla seems to have done all right for herself," Leana whispered. "So can *I*."

The dreary hotel came into view, only a dim light emanating from the open front door. Goose bumps rose on Leana's flesh, feeling a keen dread for what lay ahead of her. Perhaps she should even go and sneak aboard a ship instead of staying in the town of Rufino.

But she knew that she must stay where Brandon could find her, should he *try*. Though a pirate, he was the only man she would ever love. . . .

Drawing the horse next to a hitching rail, Leana unboarded the buggy and stood momentarily looking about her, hearing the silence, smelling the identifiable aromas of horse dung and dead fish. Occasionally the fresh scent of the seawater washed the air clean, but then again the foul odors would become more prominent.

Shaking her head disgustedly, Leana took her large valise from the buggy, the gold chest hidden well within it beneath her fineries. In a black cape with its hood drawn about her face hiding most of her delicate features, Leana hurried inside the hotel, to the front desk.

A boy, appearing to be no more than in his late teens, sat sleeping, his head bent, snoring. He was of Mexican descent, his coarse, black hair worn straight to his collar. His clothes were mussed, emitting a strong aroma of dried perspiration. His lips quivered as another snore rose from between them.

Pausing momentarily before awakening him, Leana looked about her at the hotel's decor. She winced when seeing bare floors covered with tracked-in mud and upholstered chairs with stuffing hanging from them, as though bubbles from an overfilled bath.

The tall windows were curtainless; the walls were of crumbling plaster. Spiders had weaved intricate designs across the ceiling, resembling lace, and mosquitoes buzzed noisily around the room.

A lone lamp hung from the center of the room, its glass chimney smoked black, its wick only slightly turned up with fire eating the kerosene at its tip.

"Señorita. *Como se llama usted?*"

Leana's heart lurched when hearing the Mexican speaking from behind the desk. She turned with a start and found him now widely awake, his gaze traveling over her. She was glad that she had chosen to wear a cape, for she knew that his dark eyes would surely mentally undress her should he be given a chance.

"I need a room," Leana finally blurted.

Then her gaze fell upon a sign. Part of it was written in Spanish, and part of it was written in English. She could read enough of it to know that it was a sign advertising the sale of this hotel.

Her mind began to work overtime, knowing that she had enough money for such a purchase. The thought was not only intriguing, but exciting as well! She would most surely gain respect quickly from the male populace of Rufino if she was a property owner.

She looked about her. In her mind's eye she could already see the changes in this lobby. She would make it a showcase. . . .

Then her mind was drawn back to the present and the

drabness of the hotel as it was now. It was not a place in which she desired to spend even *one* night. But with the thought of it one day possibly being hers . . . ? That made being there more tolerable. . . .

The Mexican thrust a hand toward Leana, turning it palm side up. *"Dinero?"* he said in a twangy tone of voice. *"Por favor?"*

"Money?" Leana said, knowing what he was requesting of her. She had known to have a few coins ready for payment of a room, and not wanting to have to open her chest for all eyes to see, she had slipped just enough money in the pocket of her cape to pay for a room for at least the one night.

She placed her valise on the floor and reached inside a pocket and pulled out a hand full of coins. Hoping this would be enough, she placed these into the palm of the Mexican's hand.

When he smiled up at her, pleased enough for the amount, Leana sighed with relief.

Then again her gaze moved to the sign. She hoped the Mexican could speak English, for she now knew that no more thought would have to be paid to a decision about the hotel. She wanted it. It would be the future she had only recently been forced to make for herself, alone.

Resting her hands on the desk, splaying her fingers across its top, Leana looked the Mexican square in the eye. *"Habla usted inglés?"* she said slowly, rounding off each word, carefully enunciating, hoping that she was using the proper Spanish words to ask him if he could speak English.

A broad smile lifted the Mexican's wide lips. *"Sí, sí,"* he said proudly. "José speaks *good* English as you also speak good *Spanish."*

"Gracias," Leana said, laughing softly, knowing that she had only mastered a very few words in Spanish. Thank the Lord they had been enough to get her this far. It was apparent, though, that she must study some more, for it seemed that this town of Rufino was made up of more Mexicans than Americans.

Slipping the hood of her cape from her head, letting it drop to lay around her shoulders, Leana pointed to the sign. "Who must I speak to about the purchase of this hotel?" she said dryly.

José's eyes grew wide. He laughed beneath his breath. "Is the señorita interested in buying the hotel?" he said mockingly, dropping the coins Leana had given him to the countertop. He began counting them, giving her an occasional amused look.

"Yes. I wish to purchase the hotel," Leana said, squaring her shoulders. "I don't see anything so amusing about that. I see nothing amusing about this *hotel*. It has been terribly neglected. I would like to change that."

The Mexican scraped the coins from the countertop and dropped them into one of his front pockets. He kept one hand inside the pocket, noisily jangling the coins. *"Que le vaya bien,"* he laughed. "Just you tell General Rufino what you theenk about his hotel. We will see how amusing *he* finds your comments."

Leana paled. She moved her hands from the countertop, so remembering the Mexican general and the glint in his eyes when he had first met her. She had hoped to never have to face him again. But she had known all along how impossible that would be. Rufino was his town, and perhaps he owned everything and everyone in it as well.

But she would not be dissuaded. She had decided to purchase the hotel, and by damn, she would!

"Where can one find General Rufino?" she asked icily. "When I needed his services before, he was informed and came to me."

"*Esta noche?*" José asked, leaning forward, speaking in an almost whisper.

"No. Not tonight," Leana said, sighing heavily. "Tomorrow."

José nodded toward the door. "He lives in a villa on the edge of town," he said, shrugging. "But you will be lucky if you find him sober early in the morning. It is no secret that General Rufino is addicted to opium, which he chews mixed with chicle. Perhaps you will find him more sober in the early afternoon. *Sí?*"

"Opium?" Leana gasped, placing a hand to her throat. "Lord. How . . . terrible. . . ."

Leana's mind went back to the day she had met General Rufino. He had appeared sober enough when he had taken her to the Seton Ranch. But, yes, of course, he would surely have his good and bad days. He had to be levelheaded to bark orders to his soldiers. And he surely was a man of intelligence to have managed to develop a whole town, even giving it his name.

José lifted a bony shoulder into a casual shrug. "Most important men choose to play around not with only beautiful women, but also opium," he chuckled. He pointed a finger to himself. "But myself? I barely can afford to buy *whiskey.*"

He laughed hoarsely, then handed Leana a key. "Upstairs and to the right," he said, nodding toward the staircase. "I believe room number eight is vacant."

"*Gracias,*" Leana said, lifting her valise. She walked toward the staircase, casting José occasional suspicious glances, hoping he didn't have a duplicate key. When in the room she would have to move some furniture in front of the door to ensure herself full privacy. When she owned the hotel she would get special locks for her doors. She would never take a chance of being awakened in the middle of the night by an intruder in the dark. . . .

"What is your name, Señorita?" José yelled from behind her. "It is for my records. Do you understand?"

Leana hesitated, then replied. "Leana. Only Leana. I think my first name is all you will need, Señor."

"*Sí,*" José said, chuckling low.

Leana ignored his low laugh, still seeing no humor in this that she was about, but instead fumbled along the darkness of the staircase, moving steadily upward. She was relieved to see at least a dim light glowing softly from a candle placed on the upstairs hallway wall when she finally stepped up on the second-floor landing.

Squinting her eyes, she tried to peer down the semidarkness of the long and narrow corridor. Her heart pounded, feeling the aloneness, then she hurried onward when she found the room that had been assigned her.

Fumbling with the key, Leana placed it to the keyhole, then jumped, startled when the door squeaked noisily open without her even turning the key. Something cold seemed to touch her heart when she found that the key fit loosely in place and that it didn't even serve a purpose, for the lock was broken on the door.

"Oh, no," Leana whispered, her hopes waning of being able to feel safe enough for the rest of the night. But still . . . she had the furniture to place in front of the door . . .

Stepping on into the room, Leana found only darkness greeting her. She placed her valise on the floor and began searching through the dark for a table and lamp. And when she found neither, only the touch of a bed, she shook her head in despair.

"This is worse than I had even thought," she groaned.

She glanced back over her shoulder at the door that still stood open. Her knees grew weak, knowing the dangers.

Rushing to the door, she hurriedly closed it and leaned against it until she received the return of her breath. And when she did, she again felt around the room for more furniture, but found none. The bed was the only thing that she could use to bar the door for the night.

Determined, she went to the bed and tried to move it, but her heart plummeted to her feet, it seemed, for the bed was made of heavy iron and was not to be budged. She was going to be forced to go to bed and pray for her safety. She had no other choice. She felt as though in a trap, waiting for it to be sprung by some evil creature seeking pleasure of the flesh.

"Well, if anyone should try, they will find the cold steel of Parker's pistol in their ribs," she hissed, plopping down on the bed, clothes and all.

Leana lay on her back, staring into darkness in the direction from where she knew the door to be. She removed Parker's pistol from the valise and placed it to her side, her finger on the trigger, her heart still at her feet. Never had she been so afraid. Oh, Lord, never had . . . she . . . been . . . so . . . *sleepy*. . . .

Her eyelids heavy, her eyes feeling as though filled with sand, scratching them, Leana fought the urge to fall to sleep. But she was too bone-tired to last for long. It was so sweet . . . this floating, this drifting into oblivion. She let her eyes relax and close. She drew in a deep breath and sighed as she felt sleep enveloping her all over. . . .

Leana knew not how long she had slept when a noise in the room startled her to a full awakening. Her fingers tightened about the gun, yet she couldn't find the trigger fast enough. A hand was on her mouth; a body of steel was trapping her beneath it. . . .

"Leana, don't scream," Brandon whispered. "It's only me."

A sensual thrill coursed through Leana, hearing his voice, feeling the warmth of his hand, loving it, even though it was closed over her mouth, keeping her from speaking. She blotted her anger of him from her mind. He had come to her! That was all that mattered. She had truly begun to doubt that she would ever see him again. And, oh, she sorely needed him now. She was so alone. . . .

Leana dropped the pistol to the bed and reached a hand to Brandon's hair and wove her fingers through it, feeling that it was loose about his shoulders, free of its leather bindings. She reveled in the heat of his body pressed against her, even more so his lips that now were replacing his hand at her mouth. The taste of him was as familiar to her as her own spoken name. The feel of him as she now roamed her fingers over the corded muscles of his shoulders taunted her, making her mind begin a slow, drunken spinning.

Shuddering with desire, Leana welcomed his hands loosening the buttons of her dress, Brandon having already pushed the encumbrance of her cape aside. And when his fingers crept inside her dress and touched her bare flesh, she emitted a soft moan and also began working with the buttons of his shirt, oh, so needing the feel of him against the palms of her hands.

"Leana, God, Leana, I can't believe that I found you so

easily," Brandon murmured, easing his lips away from her mouth. "I only had to ask the young Mexican at the downstairs desk and I was directed up here, to your room. I was so afraid that I would never see you . . . hold you again."

"*Do* hold me," Leana softly cried. "I need you, Brandon, as never before. I can even forget that . . . that you sent me away from the ship unescorted. The only thing that matters is that you have cared enough to come to me. Love me, darling. Make all wrongs right. I need you. I . . . need—"

Brandon seared her mouth with a torrid kiss, brushing her dress on down and away from her in one sweep of the hands. He molded her breasts with his hands, enflaming her senses even more. And wanting him fully against her, Leana's fingers feverishly worked with Brandon's clothes. She drew his shirt from his muscled arms. She unbuttoned his breeches and took it upon herself to push them down. And when he drew away from her only long enough to shed them equally of the rest of their clothes, she tried to see him, ah, so happy that dawn was lighting the sky outside the window, enabling her to see the night-black of his eyes and the strength of his manhood as he now leaned fully into her.

Opening herself to him, she trembled with ecstasy as he began to entice her with his masterful strokes. It was as though he were a painter, she the canvas, as he worked so skillfully with her. She felt as though she could feel every color of the rainbow inside her consciousness. She could feel the warm of yellows . . . the heat of reds . . . the euphoria of blues and purples . . . and the touch of white, as though she were floating on a cloud of rapture.

His eyes were points of fire as he gave her a lingering

look, then sank his mouth down and over a breast. His teeth nipped, his tongue flicked. Her hands clung to his sinewed shoulders; her fingernails sank into his flesh, drawing a wince of pain, then a chuckle from inside him.

"My little she-devil," Brandon said huskily, then gave her another kiss of fire.

Leana could feel the storm building inside her, yet weakened by the passion as her body melted, fusing with his as together they reached that plane of pain and pleasure, sweet in its completion. . . .

Brandon gave Leana another kiss, his breath raspy, his body still trembling from his spent passion. And then he leaned up, yet only enough to give him space so that his lips could taste her all over. He kissed the soft petals of her nipples, her cleavage, and then he circled his tongue about her tiny navel. When he heard her intake of breath when his fingers spread her where she was still feeling a keen tenderness from his lovemaking, he kneaded her gently with a thumb.

"Kiss me, Brandon," Leana moaned, arching her hips as his caressing was beginning to make her even more lethargic than she already was. "Darling, kiss me."

Brandon lowered his lips to hers, then felt her explosion of ecstasy against his thumb as he continued pleasuring her in this way. He kissed her fiercely, then again lowered himself inside her. His hands were urgent on her body. And then he cupped both her breasts and squeezed them.

Brandon's and Leana's low moans revealed to each other that again their crest of passion had been reached.

Still clinging, Leana withdrew her lips from his and kissed the curve of his neck, and then closed his eyes with a soft kiss. "I feel so wicked," she whispered. "You must think me a whore, Brandon, for accepting you in my bed so willingly in the middle of the night."

"You know what my thoughts are of you," Brandon said thickly, leaning up and away from her. He straddled her, resting on his knees, his hands framing her face. One of his thumbs brushed some loose locks of hair back from her eyes; he saw how her cheeks were so pink and feverish. "I cannot deny myself my feelings. I love you, Leana. You love *me*. What we do between us is only right. Never think for one minute that I think less of you for being so free with me."

Brandon's words warmed Leana's heart. Yet the word *love* had been spoken so easily by him. Had it been spoken *too* easily? Was it a word practiced on many women before her . . . ?

Leana splayed her hands across his chest. "Brandon, how is it that you are in Rufino?" she dared to ask, knowing that up to now he never revealed any of his private life to her. She knew that he was a pirate. That was all. And she knew his fears of letting anyone onshore discover who he was. Was he risking everything to just be with her? Surely this was proof enough that he spoke truth to her when saying he loved her. It thrilled her thinking that he could care so much for her.

"I've never been all that far away *from* Rufino," he said thickly. "But I cannot say where."

Leana glanced down at the foot of the bed, now able to make out everything with the soft rays of the morning sun now coloring everything within its reach a pale pinkish hue. She wasn't seeing his leather pirate's breeches nor his shirt with its flowing sleeves. She was seeing western clothes instead.

She gave him a quizzical stare. "Brandon, have you

206

been on land instead of the sea?" she cautiously asked. "Or did you dress this way before you left the ship to draw attention away from the fact that you are a pirate?"

"Like I said, darling, I cannot tell you," he said, lowering a kiss to her cheek. "It would not be best for the crew of the *Erebus*."

Leana jerked her cheek away from the touch of his lips. "So you are saying that you cannot trust me?" she pouted. "You make love to me . . . I return that love . . . yet you feel that you cannot trust me? That doesn't say much for our relationship, Brandon. I may as well be . . . be a whore you frequent. Nothing more."

Brandon again stretched his body fully down against hers. Leana's face flamed when feeling the fullness between his thighs touching her so sensuously where the softness of her hair formed a triangle at the base of her abdomen. She was throbbing with need of him again and she felt so wicked, as though she just might be a whore and didn't even realize it!

"You are an angel," Brandon whispered. He parted her lips with his tongue and let it smooth over the fullness of her moist lower lip. And then he buried a kiss into the tiny nape of her neck. "Only an angel. *My* angel."

Feeling a mindlessness closing in on her again, Leana wriggled free. Her pulse was racing, her heart was troubling her as she pulled her petticoat up to hide herself behind it, feeling this was the only way to stop this loveplay started between them. She was ready for some answers. She knew that he had much to be told about what had happened to *her*.

"Brandon, much has changed since we last said our goodbyes," she murmured, hating to have to say the words that her mother and her stepfather were dead.

207

Speaking it aloud only made it all too true. It was so easy to just pretend they were away on an extended journey and that she would see them again, sometime way into the future.

"Like what?" he said, sitting on the bed, drawing his knees up to encircle them with his arms, oblivious of his nudity.

"My mother . . ." Leana murmured, lowering her eyes.

"Oh, yes, your mother," Brandon said, looking toward the door. "Is she in the adjoining room?"

Leana's eyes shot up, red with the burn of tears invading them. "No. She's not in the next room," she choked out.

"Oh? Then where *is* she?" Brandon asked, eyes wide.

Leana slunk over close to Brandon. She let her petticoat drop down and away from her. She eased his knees from his chest and instead placed herself close to him, fitting her cheek against his chest, needing his comfort as never before.

"She's dead," she blurted. "Mother is dead, Brandon."

Brandon tensed. Guilt washed through him. He had to believe that if not for him and the crew of the *Erebus*, Leana's mother would surely not be dead. But he would not voice this aloud. He only hoped that Leana didn't.

"She died even before I was able to get her to the Seton ranch, even though it was only a short ways from Rufino, to the west," she blurted, herself forgetting for the moment that she had at one time even blamed Brandon for this terrible mishap of her mother's death.

"Seton . . . ?" Brandon said thickly, knowing of Setons. His family. . . .

Leana's head jerked away from Brandon's chest. She covered her mouth with her hands, now remembering Parker's warning to never mention the family name to strangers, especially pirates.

Yet there was something in Brandon's eyes with the mention of the name Seton. If she spoke *Parker* Seton's name, what would Brandon's reaction *then* be . . . ?

"Parker Seton, my stepfather . . ." she murmured, growing ashen when seeing the look register on Brandon's face.

Brandon's insides rolled; his heart began to race. His father! He was only a few miles out of Rufino! Brandon had thought that he would never get the opportunity to see his father again, and now it had been handed him, it seemed, on a silver platter!

No matter the outcome, he had to go to him. He would not let the opportunity slip away from him again. Brandon would never forget the guilt that he had felt when he had heard that his mother was dead and that his father had left New York City.

Jumping from the bed, Brandon hurried into his clothes. He was remembering so many things. He was recalling the reason his father had left New York. Brandon was also remembering that in no way could he draw danger to Cyril by what he was about to do.

"Brandon, what are . . . you . . . doing?" Leana gasped, climbing slowly from the bed, in a semi state of shock at his reaction, yet hadn't she somewhat expected it?

Brandon fastened his breeches, all the while gazing intensely at Leana. The world was full of ironies. He had just discovered that he was her *stepbrother!* She was his *stepsister!*

But of course that didn't make what they had shared wrong; it only seemed to *complicate* things.

"Leana, I can't say anything right now," he said hoarsely. "I've much to find out for myself. I'm sorry, darling."

He spun around on a heel and rushed from the room. Leana emitted a low sob and went to the window and watched him ride away on a cottony-white horse. She knew who he was. Oh, Lord, she now knew who he was! And he was just about to find out that he no longer had a father. . . .

Chapter Fourteen

Fog lay like a large, shimmering ghost along the land as Brandon finally reached the Seton Ranch. He was regretting having had to frighten two families by having to stop and ask directions in the middle of the night. He had been lucky they hadn't met him with a bullet instead of only a cautious aim of a pistol. He had even been luckier that the name Seton had stood out in their remembrances. For had it not, he would still be floundering, searching.

Brandon urged his stallion, Cotton, along a narrow lane. Glancing toward the Big Thicket, he shivered at the thought of knowing that fate had led his father to him. Yet his father hadn't yet discovered that Brandon also sometimes made residence in Texas, in the Big Thicket, the land that lay adjacent to the Seton Ranch.

He couldn't help but wonder how his father would react to the knowing. Would his father even recognize him? Was it even as dangerous now to expose himself to his father as it had been in the past? He hated to think of placing Cyril in danger.

But Brandon's heart would not let him think of Cyril at this moment. He was too close to seeing his true father. He now knew that he shouldn't have waited so long. He would not let any more years pass without telling his father that he loved him. He even had many apologies to make to him. Brandon prayed that his father would, somehow, understand. . . .

Guiding Cotton through a tall, fortlike fence in the process of being built, Brandon had his first touch of apprehension. He was a stranger to all who lived at the Seton Ranch. There was a possibility that he would not be met as cordially as he had at the last two ranches. He knew that his father was not used to this way of life and that he might shoot first and ask questions later.

Brandon's brow creased into a frown. He was now thinking of Matthew and how cowardly he had behaved as a small child. He had to wonder if Matthew was the same, or possibly even worse, as an adult. Matthew would probably even be the type to shoot a man in the back!

"But hopefully Father will be the first to come to see who is calling at this early hour of day," Brandon whispered. "God, has he aged so terribly much? Did my mother's death affect him terribly?"

Then his jaw set angrily. He was remembering that his father had taken a second wife. This had to prove that his love hadn't been so deeply imbedded for his first wife to have taken on a second wife so quickly.

And a daughter, he thought, seeing Leana in his mind's eye, so adoring her, yet in awe as to who she truly was. She was his stepsister. God, she was his stepsister.

But he knew that this development did not matter. Leana was not of blood kin. If their futures could ever fuse into one, the fact that they had the same father would not matter. It *did* not matter. Brandon's love for her could never be tarnished just because they had the same father.

Stepfather, he corrected to himself. *He is only her* step*father.*

Drawing closer to the ranch house, Brandon let his gaze move cautiously about him. He was seeing that his father had put much time in carving out his own share of this land of Eden, that which had even managed at times to lure Brandon from the clutches of the sea. It had begun to be as rewarding to Brandon to ride on his stallion as to sail on a ship. The land and the ocean took on the same meaning to him, it seemed. Each stretched out for as far as the eye could see. The difference was that one was green . . . the other blue.

The click of a shotgun being prepared for firing took on the most meaning for Brandon at this moment in time. He ducked down and let his gaze search hurriedly around him, stopping when the shine of the barrel of a gun could be seen through the railing on the airdome roof of the house.

"Halt! Who goes there?" a voice rang out from the airdome.

Instinct drew Brandon's hand to the holstered pistol at his right side, yet he only grazed its handle with his fingers. He could never fire upon this house where his father now made his residence.

Yet what if his own life depended on it?

His heart pounded, perspiration laced his brow, even though the morning temperature was that which could surely slice an apple in its cold sharpness.

"I've come in peace," Brandon shouted back, hating it when his voice cracked with emotion. He squinted his eyes, wondering if the man holding him at bay with a shotgun might be his father. Or was it Matthew? Or might it even be a cowhand? Surely there were many under his father's employ.

Out of the corner of his eye he saw a rush of movement at his right side. And then he suddenly found himself surrounded by many men, pistols drawn and aimed squarely at him.

"Hey, wait a minute," Brandon said, forcing a laugh. He straightened his back and raised his hands in the air when seeing that none of these men seemed to be amused by his presence. "I'm not here to cause trouble. Do you think I'd be foolish enough to come alone if I had trouble on my mind?"

"Who are you? What do you want here?" one of the men shouted, taking a bold step forward. His spurs jangled as he stepped even closer. "We don't hanker havin' mornin' visitors around here. It ain't wise to trust critters you don't know. What's your name?"

Brandon felt as though he was becoming entangled in a web. He only wanted to disclose his name to one man. His father. "Names aren't important," Brandon said dryly. "I just want the opportunity to meet with Parker Seton. We're . . . uh . . . old friends. I knew him in . . . uh . . . New York City."

"That ain't good enough," another man shouted. "Tell us your name. Then we might listen to reason."

Brandon's cheeks flushed with anger. He set his lips in a straight line, then knew that he had no choice but to speak his name. But only his first name. That would be all that was required. Once his father heard the name *Brandon*, he would make himself known and readily welcome him into his house. His long-lost son. How *would* he react to the knowing?

Brandon slowly dismounted his horse and stood at its side. "If it's a name you need, then a name will be given you," he shouted. He looked up at the airdome roof, now able to make out a full figure of a man standing there.

But the fog was still too patchy between him and the house for Brandon to be able to fully make out the full facial features of this man.

"Brandon!" Brandon shouted. "My name is *Brandon.*"

"A first name ain't enough," another man shouted. "A full name is needed under these circumstances!"

Brandon's pulse raced, now seeing the airdome roof empty. Whether it was his father or brother, the name had registered and he was now working his way to him.

"I believe that is all that is needed to the Seton family's way of thinking," he said thickly.

"Maybe it would've been to my father," Matthew said, stepping from the house, a shotgun resting in the crook of his left arm. "But it isn't enough for me. There are many Brandons in the world. Which are *you?*"

Brandon's dark eyes grew midnight in color as he was taking his first look of his younger brother since those many years ago before Brandon's abduction. His brother had only been six at the time, Brandon ten. But Brandon was seeing the same raven's-wing color of black hair, Matthew's straight, aristocratic nose, the coldness of his eyes, and the stubbornness of his straight line of lips. A coward maybe back then, but stubborn as hell!

Brandon was battling a mixture of emotions tearing at his insides. He loved his brother and wanted to go to him and embrace him, yet there was still that feeling of rivalry exchanged between them, even though they hadn't even been together *to* be rivals.

Stepping closer, leaving the fog behind, Matthew's insides did a strange rippling. He couldn't believe his eyes. But damn it if he couldn't see his brother Brandon in this man. This man had the same dark, fathomless eyes as in Brandon's youth; his hair, if not burned golden by the sun, with red tints, would be the same color of Parker Seton's, and Brandon was as powerfully built as Parker Seton had been.

It was as though Matthew was seeing a much younger Parker Seton standing before him, yet knowing that this man was instead, indeed, his brother.

"Is there any true question in your heart as to who I am?" Brandon finally said. "I see recognition in your eyes, Matthew. Now take me to Father. If there *is* still any question about my identity, it is he who will clear this up at first glance *of* me."

Matthew nervously kneaded his chin, realizing that Brandon's sudden appearance in his life was that of bad timing. Wasn't Brandon the true heir of all the Setons' wealth? Brandon *was* the older son. Matthew felt that somehow he must keep the truth of their father's death from Brandon. What if Brandon thought that his father was still alive but didn't want to see him because of the hurt caused by a son who had been alive yet had chosen to keep this truth from his family?

Yes, that was the only answer. To Matthew, it made no difference that his brother was standing before him. Matthew had accepted the fact that he had lost a brother many years ago, even then not truly having too many emotions of loss over thinking that his brother was more than likely dead.

There had never been any true love shared between

them. Matthew had only felt the emotion of jealousy toward his older brother. This jealousy had increased through the years of Parker Seton's mournings for a lost son. This mourning had crowded out Matthew's time with his father. Matthew had even then begun to hate Brandon, even though Brandon was then only a memory. . . .

"No, I don't believe I need any proof as to who you are," Matthew said flatly. "But I would like to know why you have chosen to return to your family now, instead of earlier? Where have you been, Brandon? How did you even find out that the Seton family has made this move to Texas? I believe there are many questions to be answered, Brandon."

Brandon chuckled low. An eyebrow forked. "I see that you haven't changed," he said. He placed a hand on Matthew's shoulder and pressed his fingers into his brother's corded muscle. "You still don't like your older brother very much, do you? I guess I shouldn't have expected a brotherly hug when you saw that I was alive and well. Do you hate me so much, Matthew?"

Matthew's cheeks grew hot with a blush, seeing many eyes watching this reunion of brothers. It was not in Matthew's best interest to behave so coldly toward Brandon. It was important that the men under his employ respect him, for it was these men who could make the difference of failure or success of the Seton Ranch. It was these men who were industriously building the stockade fence around the Seton Ranch, to ensure safety *for* Matthew.

Without these men, he would never feel safe to remain in Texas, and he didn't desire being forced to take the long sea voyage back to New York. He wanted his feet securely on land, having never liked the sea or anything about it!

Forcing himself, Matthew placed a hand on Brandon's that gripped his shoulder. He squeezed it and smiled warmly over at Brandon. "I'm sorry if I've appeared cold," he said hoarsely.

Matthew again looked about him and at the gaping men. He thrust his rifle up into the air. "Go on about your business," he shouted. "Can't you see that two brothers want to be alone?"

Matthew waited until the cowhands had drifted away in all directions and he was finally alone with Brandon. He dropped his hand down and away from Brandon and nodded toward the house. "Father recognized you right away," he blurted. "He saw you from a front window. But he doesn't want to see you, Brandon. It hurts him like hell to know that you've been alive all these years and that you've ignored the fact that you have family wondering about you."

He glanced toward the house, then back to Brandon. "He asked me to come out here to tell you to ride on. It's as simple as that, Brandon. Father has thought you were dead for so many years, he can't think of you in any other way. To him, you're still the same as dead. So why not ride on and save the ol' man further pain."

Brandon's insides were growing numb; his face paled of color. He looked toward the house, then glowered at Matthew. "You always were a bastard," he growled. "You always will be. You know damn well that if Father knew I had come to see him, he would welcome me with open arms. Where *is* he, Matthew? Asleep? You know damn well that he didn't see me from any damn window."

With determination in his steps, Brandon began

218

walking toward the house, ignoring Matthew's loud gasp behind him. And when Matthew hurried to block his further approach, Brandon doubled his fists to his sides and glared at his brother.

"Step aside, Matthew," he flatly ordered. "If you don't, I'll be forced to knock some sense into your head."

"Now, you don't want to fight your brother, do you?" Matthew taunted. "If Father saw us fighting, think of how it would make him feel, Brandon. So just turn around and ride away on your horse. Let's say goodbye peacefully. There's no need for a fight."

"That's what *you* think," Brandon snarled. "Matthew, you'll always be a coward, won't you?"

Brandon swung a doubled fist and clipped Matthew's chin with a loud pop, causing Matthew's body to jerk and go crashing to the ground. Matthew lay there momentarily, fuzzy from the blow, then he watched, mortified, as Brandon made his way on to the house.

"Brandon!" he shouted. "You'd best not. Brandon!"

But his words were falling on deaf ears. Brandon would not be dissuaded. He had come to make peace with his father and he would not be denied this opportunity. But he had just found out that there could never be peace between brothers. Brandon's gut twisted, wondering about a brother who so openly despised him. Brandon had to wonder about this sort of hate and where the seed of it lay. . . .

A muted silence met Brandon's approach inside the house. There were no signs of life anywhere. Brandon rushed from room to room, searching for his father, yet not finding him anywhere. Going back to the parlor, he stopped to knead his brow, furrowed with questioning. And when Matthew entered the parlor, his face a mask of coldness, Brandon went to him and grabbed his shirt right below his chin and jerked Matthew to him.

"I think it's time you quit playing sick games with me," Brandon growled. "Where's Father? Tell me, Matthew. Tell me now or I might be tempted to knock your teeth down your throat this time."

"There's no need for further violence," Matthew said, eyes wide. He swallowed hard. "If you must know, then I'll willingly tell you. I only . . . only . . . wanted to spare you, Brandon. Honest. That's why I lied to you."

"Lied?" Brandon said, releasing his brother. He shook his head, trying to clear his thoughts. Suddenly his brains felt scrambled. He was beginning to feel that something was terribly wrong here. Where *was* his father . . . ?

"What is it that you wanted to spare me of, Matthew?" Brandon questioned, his jaw setting hard. "I can't imagine you wanting to spare me of anything. It's obvious how you feel about me, *and* my return from, shall I say, the dead."

Matthew took wide steps to the liquor cabinet. "I think I need a drink," he said shallowly. He grabbed a bottle of whiskey and poured himself a glass. "You may need a drink also, Brandon." He poured another glass and held it toward Brandon. "I advise you to take this. I think you're going to need it."

Brandon went to Matthew and knocked the one glass intended for Brandon from Matthew's hand. Glass splintered at his feet, and whiskey spread like tentacles of an octopus. "I said no more games," he snarled. "Tell me where Father is."

Matthew took a step backward, stumbling into a chair.

He steadied himself, then took a quick swallow of whiskey, all the while watching Brandon. Matthew now knew that he had no choice but to tell Brandon about their father.

But Matthew would do everything in his power to keep Brandon from claiming any of the Seton fortune. He didn't deserve it. It had been Matthew who had stood beside his father all these years, even taking mental abuse while being there. Brandon had conveniently chosen another way of life, and by damn, Brandon could *return* to that life!

"You've forced the truth out of me," Matthew said, slamming the glass down on a table. "But once I've told you, I hope you will have the courtesy to leave." His insides churned, realizing just how coldhearted he sounded. A part of him wanted to reach out and embrace his brother, yet the greed, the hunger for power in Matthew, wanted him to shun his brother. He didn't want to share. He had waited too long for what was now his.

"I make no deals with bastards," Brandon said, resting his hand on the pistol at his left hip. "Even bastards who just happen to be my *brother*."

Matthew's face flamed with anger. He clenched his fists to his sides yet he kept his anger intact, remembering the pain inflicted by Brandon's speedy blow. "Father is dead," he blurted, watching Brandon flinch as though shot when finally confronted by the truth. "He's been dead for a short while now. Seems you've missed two burials since your disappearance, big brother."

"Father . . . is . . . dead . . . ?" Brandon stammered, feeling a part of his heart breaking away with remorseful pain. "How? When?"

"Do you really care?" Matthew said with a flip of the head. "Where have you been all these years, Brandon? Why did you choose to come home now? Surely you were free to come and go as you please." His gaze swept quickly over Brandon. "It looks as though you're quite healthy, as though you haven't been imprisoned. Try and tell me that your hands were tied, making it impossible to let Father know you were alive."

"God . . ." Brandon said, sinking down into a chair. He held his face in his hands. "You haven't told me how . . . or when. The fact that I waited this long to return doesn't matter now. Father isn't here to even know that I *did*."

Matthew poured himself another drink and swallowed it in one gulp. "Comanches," he said matter-of-factly. "Or should I say *one* Comanche. A couple of days ago. The Comanche killed Father with a lance through his back. One must never turn one's back on a Comanche. Seems Father learned that lesson the hard way."

"An Indian?" Brandon said, his head jerking up, staring wide-eyed at Brandon. "A damn . . . Indian . . . ?"

"None other," Matthew said, himself now slouching down into a chair. "Father was distraught over the loss of his wife and wandered out alone on horseback. He knew better. Damn, he knew better."

"*Second* wife," Brandon said, combing his fingers through his hair. "I already know about mother's death. I even . . . visited . . . her grave."

"Bully for you," Matthew said sarcastically. "You're too late for everything, it seems."

"Not truly by choice," Brandon said shallowly, remembering Cyril, and his devotion to the aging pirate.

222

"Not truly by choice."

"What happened to you after you were abducted by the pirates?" Matthew asked, leaning forward. "Where the hell have you been, Brandon?"

Brandon rose quickly to his feet. He wiped a stray tear from his eyes. "None of my life is any of your business," he said dryly. "Only Father deserved to know. I owe you nothing."

Matthew rose to his feet and stepped closer to Brandon. "As I owe you nothing, big brother," he said, angry at himself when hearing his voice crack from fear of what he was about to tell his brother.

"I would never ask you for a thing," Brandon growled, leaning into Matthew's face.

"I'm glad to hear you say that," Matthew said, taking a step backward. "Since you *could* profess to being the rightful heir to the Seton riches. But you relinquished that claim long ago when you chose to not return home. Right?"

"What are you saying?" Brandon asked, forking an eyebrow.

"That you are due nothing of the family fortune," Matthew said, lifting a shoulder into a casual shrug. "But you know that. Don't you?"

Recalling what he had found out in New York about Parker Seton's illegal activities at the bank where he had been president, Brandon's lips lifted into a polite smile. "I wouldn't be sure of myself, Matthew," he laughed. "You just might have a surprise coming your way one of these days."

Brandon squared his shoulders and walked toward the door, ignoring Matthew, who was following along behind him. Brandon needed to get some fresh air. He needed even more than that. He had to go to Leana to get some answers. Yet he knew that what he needed most was the comfort of her arms . . . the joy of her kiss. He hurried and mounted his horse and didn't look back. He would deal more fully with his brother later. . . .

Chapter Fifteen

Though troubled by Brandon's findings once he arrived to the Seton Ranch, Leana had to think about her own future, that of which only she had control. Having purchased several dresses, she had chosen one in particular in which to make her appeal to the Mexican general. She did not wish to make an appearance of one who might make bargains in bed, so she was wearing a dress with a high, stiffly starched white collar and long sleeves, and highly gathered waist.

Having placed her hair atop her head in a tight bun, she appeared to be of a less frivolous nature, one who would be less apt to turn a man's head. She was hoping that General Rufino would not recall how he had last seen her, remembering herself how his eyes had mentally undressed her. She was hoping that the gossip of his partaking in the pleasures of opium was fact and that his head would be fuzzy in all matters this morning, except that which *she* wanted from *him*.

Sitting straight in her buggy, Leana snapped the reins, urging the horse onward. She felt out of place on these streets frequented mostly by soldiers and men who worked at the busy wharves. It appeared that women did not make it a habit to be seen. She wondered if they were ever even heard. It seemed that Texas was a place of all men. . . .

Well, I am about to change that, Leana thought smugly. Parker Seton hadn't left her a fortune in jewels for nothing. He had known what she would manage to do with them. He had always known that she was a woman of abilities and determinations. She had only now been given a chance to prove that he had been right in these assumptions. Her only regret was that he wasn't here to see. . . .

On the outer reach of Rufino Leana saw an adobe villa that looked to be hundreds of years old, its walls crumbling, yet made to look beautiful with its symmetry of dusty pink oleanders blooming in protrusion in the yard. Gallberry holly and red bay and sweet bay trees circled the house, as did cottonwoods.

But all of these things were blocked quickly from Leana's mind when she saw the soldiers guarding the entrance of the villa. She now knew that she had found General Diego Rufino's villa, and pinpricks of fear raised on the flesh of her arms. Suddenly she was no longer as brave or confident.

But she must give it her best. Her future depended on it. So far, a future with Brandon had only materialized in her midnight dreams. He was a pirate, though he *had* dressed much differently this last time she had seen him.

A ploy. She knew that it had been only a ploy to draw attention from himself, in truth a pirate. She could never share a life with a pirate. She could never share her life with any man except for Brandon. Knowing this, she had to carve out a life of her own, to be lived alone. . . .

Guiding her horse and buggy into a drive that circled in front of the villa, Leana watched, horrified, as the armed soldiers rushed from the door to grab the horse's reins from her.

A rush of Spanish being shouted at her made her recoil, not able to understand that which was being demanded of her. The soldiers were speaking much too quickly for her to translate! But she understood the meaning of rough hands on her wrist, jerking her from the seat of the buggy.

Falling in a heap on the gravel drive, Leana flinched. She glared up at the two men standing over her. "I see that Mexican soldiers are less than gentlemen," she hissed, rubbing a raw wound on the palm of one of her hands. Her breath was stolen from her when she saw the soldiers point their rifles threateningly down at her, drawing a complete silence from her.

"What is this?" a voice spoke in a drunken drawl from the doorway of the villa. "Who comes to visit me without an invitation?"

Even though the voice was changed, probably opium-induced, Leana recognized it to be that of General Diego Rufino. She rose shakily to her feet, straightening the lines of her dress as the Mexican general stumbled out into the open.

Color rose into Leana's cheeks, seeing that General Rufino wore only a satin robe, its front gaping open, showing his pot belly and what lay below it. She wanted to turn her eyes away but felt as though she had better be attentive, for he had the power to give the orders that would say that she lived or died.

Leana only hoped that he would recognize her and

remember that she was from a family that possessed much wealth. Wealth and possessions seemed to guide the Mexicans' decisions on many things. She only hoped that she had brought enough jewels and that she had chosen the ones that were worth enough to pay for what she had come to bargain for!

Tensing, Leana found herself looking down onto the face of the Mexican general, she being at least a foot taller than he. His eyes were red-streaked, his cheeks were rosy and bloated.

Ruffled and uncombed, his coal-black hair stuck out in all directions. He was barefoot and he reeked of an unpleasant aroma, causing Leana's nose to curl up with distaste.

"Ah, the beautiful señora, the daughter of Parker Seton," General Rufino said, raking his eyes over Leana, then stopping again at her eyes. "It *is* Parker Seton's daughter, *sí*? Why has he sent you to me?"

Leana nodded. "*Sí*, I am Parker's daughter," she said softly, aware now that this Mexican general didn't yet know of Parker's death. "But he didn't send me. I have come on my own."

General Rufino kneaded his chin contemplatingly. "Oh?" he said, chuckling low. "Have you come for business or *pleasure*, pretty señorita?"

Leana's face flamed with color, knowing what he was implying when saying the word *pleasure*. "Señor, I will have you know that I come for business," she said dryly. "Only business."

Her gaze went to the buggy and to her purse. The jewels were inside her purse. She had to make this general understand that she was serious when making mention of *business*.

She looked back down at the general. "Can we go inside your villa and talk?" she quickly added.

General Rufino shrugged. *"Sí,"* he said. He spoke some quick passages to the two soldiers, causing them to again take their positions on each side of the door. He placed a hand to Leana's elbow. *"Adelante. Pase usted."*

She had been able to translate what he had just said to her, relieved, yet apprehensive that he had asked her to go into his villa with him. Should he take advantage of her, his soldiers would only listen, perhaps even enjoy hearing an American señorita being ravaged by a Mexican general.

But that was the chance she had to take. He was the owner of the hotel that she wanted to purchase. He was the only one to talk business with *about* this purchase!

"Gracias," Leana said, but eased out of his grip. "But I need my purse. I must get it from the buggy."

"Pronto!" General Rufino growled, flailing a pudgy hand up in the air. "I have been taken from my pleasures much too long already. And to now have to speak business with a señorita? Ha! What sort of business can a lady transact? Only men have such abilities!"

His words grated against Leana's patience. Why was it always implied that women could not handle things as well as a man? Did all men think of women as half-wits? Yes. It seemed so!

Leaning up to grab her purse, Leana momentarily forgot its weight from the jewels inside it, and as she picked it up, it immediately fell from her fingers back onto the seat.

"Mas aprisa!" General Rufino shouted, glaring at Leana.

"All right, all right," Leana mumbled, now taking a

better grip on the purse as she again lifted it from the seat.

Supporting the purse in the palm of her right hand, holding its drawstring top with the other, she followed along beside the Mexican general until they were inside his villa.

Leana's eyes squinted from the brightness of the parlor, sun pouring in from not only several windows, but also a double door that led out onto a terrace that displayed a beautiful assortment of flowering trees and vines.

And when Leana's eyes became used to the bright light, she looked about her, seeing the richness of the decor. Lush, overstuffed furniture of bright flowered designs were positioned about a great stone fireplace. Many pillows of all designs and fabrics were before the fireplace, and Leana's heart skipped a beat when two beautiful women lumbered into the room to slink down and upon the pillows. Both were American, scantily attired, revealing their bodies through thin silk gowns.

One of the women, with brilliant red hair, looked drunkenly up at General Rufino and held out her arms to him, beckoning for him to come to her, her ruby-red lips curved into a pout.

The woman spoke to the general in a soft purr. *"Por favor?"* she said. "The morning is young. Come. Let us finish what we started. *Sí?"*

"Espere un momento," General Rufino said, going to the woman to softly kiss her. "I have business to attend to first. Then we shall finish with our pleasures. *No se preocupe."*

The woman continued to plead with the general, as though Leana weren't even there. Leana had to surmise that both women were in a drunken state. It showed in their eyes and in the way they were so lethargic. Leana knew that she must encourage the Mexican to get on with business or he might get the idea that she was enjoying being sidetracked by such sensuous behavior!

"Sir," Leana said, clearing her throat nervously. "Do you have an office in which to transact business?"

General Rufino gave Leana a sour look from across his shoulder, then softened in his mood and walked away from the lounging women. "*Sí,*" he grumbled. "We will talk business in my office. Come with me."

Swaggering, the Mexican general nodded toward a hallway and let Leana walk ahead of him. And when they were finally in his office and the door was closed behind them, Leana became impressed by what she was seeing. There were many awards framed on the walls and also many sorts of medals hanging from plaques. The room was that of plush leather furnishings and a grand oak desk, piled high with papers. Green plants grew from many pots, giving the room the sense of the outdoors. Crystal glasses sparkled from a wine cabinet; fat cigars lay in a gold chest.

Then Leana's attention was drawn back to the Mexican general. He was slipping his highly polished boots on, and when this was finished, he belted his gigantic saber at his side. Leana could hardly refrain from breaking into a fit of laughter. Squared-off and as stocky as he was, and having chosen his saber and boots, and yet not his clothes, for wearing, she had never seen such a comical sight.

And when he thrust a cigar between his thin line of lips and lit it, she couldn't help but let a soft titter of a laugh emerge from inside her.

"You find me amusing?" General Rufino asked, squaring his shoulders, frowning up at Leana.

Leana quickly sobered. She cleared her throat nervously. "No. I don't," she lied. "*Lo siento.* Truly I am sorry. It's just that . . . that you choose to wear boots and your saber with your . . . your robe. Why?"

"I never talk business unless I wear my boots and my saber," he growled, flicking ashes from his cigar onto a highly polished floor. He nodded toward a chair. "Please sit down."

Leana clasped her purse more snugly against her. "No," she murmured. "I prefer to stand. I would like to transact this business as quickly as possible. I didn't mean to interrupt your, uh, social activities."

General Rufino eased into a chair behind his desk. The chair was high-backed, resembling a throne. Rich bloodred tapestry worked with a faded golden coat of arms formed a backrest from which heavy carved arms flowed out, ending in intricately carved handrests like the paws of the lions of Castile.

General Rufino leaned back in his chair and placed his fingertips together before him. "Tell me why you are here," he said casually. "It is not every day a lady proposes business to me."

His cynical laugh made Leana's flesh crawl. She shifted uneasily from foot to foot, then placed her purse on his desk. "I have come to make an offer for your hotel," she blurted. "I do not know it by name since none was displayed on its front, but I can tell you it is the one that the young man José runs for you."

General Rufino's eyebrows forked. "You? You wish to purchase my hotel?" he said, surprise in his eyes. "*Caramba!* You? A lady? You come here to say you wish to buy my grand hotel?"

Leana smiled amusedly. "Grand? You say your hotel is grand?" she said. "I find it almost repulsive."

A low snicker rose from between General Rufino's lips. "Yet you wish to buy it?" he said. "Why do you?"

"Because I need means to support myself," Leana said dryly. "I chose your hotel because I see much promise in it. I can make it beautiful . . . a showplace for all those who visit the town of Rufino."

General Rufino crushed his cigar out in an ashtray. His brow furrowed into a deep frown. He gave Leana a lingering look, then again spoke. "You only just arrived in Rufino yourself," he said guardedly. "You were taken to Parker Seton's ranch. You were to make residence there. Parker Seton is a rich man. Why do you choose to not live with him? Is he not family?"

Leana's eyes lowered. "He *was* family," she murmured.

"Was?" General Rufino said, again forking his eyebrows. "Are you saying that he is no longer alive?"

Leana's eyes moved slowly up, to meet General Rufino's steady stare. "He was killed by a Comanche," she said softly, always hating to have to say the words. She still could not believe that Parker Seton was dead. He was such a strong, powerful man. But much of his strength had left him with the burial of his second wife. . . .

"Comanche?" General Rufino mumbled, drumming his fingers on the top of his desk. "Hmm. *Sí.* I've heard of many such incidents. The Indians have always been a problem. They always *will* be. The Mexican government had hoped that the coming of the americanos would drive the Indians away. But so far it hasn't worked."

Leana wanted to strike out at this ugly Mexican and tell him that she had heard the rumors of the Mexicans now bargaining with the Indians, paying the Indians to slaughter and terrorize the Americans, to scare them into returning to the states.

But she knew that if she accused him of these terrible deeds, she would never get what she had come for. It was best to be cautious with words while with this Mexican, surely her enemy.

"But I still do not understand your need to live away from the Seton ranch," General Rufino quickly interjected. "You still have family. Do you not have a brother?"

"A *stepbrother*," she quickly corrected. "I do not desire to live beneath the same roof as such as a man as he. I do not care for him. I would rather make my own way in the world as to have to take anything from him."

Pushing the purse toward the Mexican, Leana set her jaw firmly. "I will pay you well for your hotel," she said dryly. "Inside this purse you will find many jewels. My father gave them to me as a gift. They will now be yours if you will make an even exchange. The jewels for your hotel."

She thrust a hand out toward General Rufino. "Is it a deal?" she said softly. "Can we shake on it?"

General Rufino opened the purse and let his eyes feast on the shine of the jewels. One by one he took the pieces out and inspected them, all the while Leana holding her hand out before her, stubbornly waiting for him to shake it. She knew that she had to appear to be a determined, strong-willed lady. She almost felt as though she were making a deal with the devil!

"Is it a deal, Señor?" Leana persisted. "I could take

occupancy today."

General Rufino's eyes moved slowly upward. A crooked smile lifted his lips. He placed his hand in hers and gripped it firmly. "The hotel is yours," he chuckled. "But this isn't payment enough. You will pay me more later? Eh?"

Leana's face and eyes grew hot with anger. She clenched her teeth together, for fear of saying exactly what she thought of this man. And she wasn't sure what he would demand of her later. Would jewels or cold cash ever be enough . . . ?

"You know there are enough jewels there to pay for your fleabag hotel," she finally blurted, then when seeing his face pale, knew that she hadn't had enough control of her feelings as she should have. She had just possibly humiliated this man with whom she had just done business. Her eyes widened and a feeling of relief washed through her when she saw the color return to his face and heard his laughter.

"I think I like you, Señorita," General Rufino said, releasing his hand from hers. He rose from his chair and came from behind his desk, to stand before her. "Sí. I think I will like doing business with you."

"Then the hotel is mine? I can do with it what I please?" Leana said, accepting her empty purse as he handed it back to her.

General Rufino lifted a narrow shoulder into a casual shrug. "Do with it what you please, name it what you please," he laughed. Then his face became somber. "But you will pay me more later. Sí?"

"Sí," Leana said in a near whisper. "Whatever you say."

"Then get on along with you," General Rufino said,

taking her by an elbow, guiding her back through the parlor and on outside. "I will be seeing you. Soon. *Buenos días.*"

"*Buenos días,*" Leana said, walking on toward her horse and buggy. She gave the general a look from across her shoulder. "And *muchas gracias.*"

"*Sí, sí,*" General Rufino said, then turned and lumbered back into his villa.

Leana's heart was thumping wildly against her chest, envisioning so many things about the hotel that would make it truly hers in appearance. She climbed aboard the buggy and directed the horse around the circular drive, and then to the hotel. When she drove up before it, seeing its crumbling facade, she smiled and whispered.

"I now christen you to be called *Leana's.*"

With a flurry of skirt and a flushed face, she reined her horse at a hitching rail and rushed inside. When she saw José standing casually beside the door, she flung her arms about him and laughed with glee. "José, you are now working for *me!*" she shouted. "This hotel is now *mine. Mine.*"

José joined in the laughter. "General Rufino sold eet to you? *Sí?*" he said, dizzying from Leana's tight hold.

"*Sí!*" Leana again shouted.

"Leana?"

Brandon's voice broke through the merriment, sounding as though being spoken from a deep well, it was so filled with sadness and confusion. Leana lurched away from José and turned with a start, seeing Brandon's tall shadow in the doorway behind her.

"Brandon? You now . . . know . . . about your father?"

"Yes. And we must talk, Leana. Now."

Leana took Brandon's hand and together they walked up the stairs and to her room. When inside, they embraced, then Leana looked up into his eyes and knew that at this moment she was the last thing that he had on his mind.

"Tell me all about my father and how long you have known him," Brandon said, framing Leana's face between his powerful hands.

Leana swallowed hard, then began sharing her earlier years with Brandon, those which also included his father and brother Matthew. . . .

Chapter Sixteen

Brandon paced the room. Leana looked on, silent. She didn't know what to expect from Brandon now, seeing how torn he was from finding out the truth about his family. She knew that guilt had to be playing a major role in his frustrated behavior. It had been his decision to not return to New York those many years ago, to be with his family. He had chosen the sea *over* family. And now all of his family was dead but his brother, Matthew, and Matthew had behaved bastardly toward Brandon upon discovering him alive.

"Darling, please stop pacing," Leana softly said, taking a step toward Brandon. "That won't change anything. Please accept things as they are and look to the future. One rules his own destiny. But sometimes this is taken out of one's hands. That's the way it happened for Parker Seton. If not for the pirates who stole you away from him for ransom, things would have been different for your father. Quit blaming yourself for what *Cyril* did. It was not your fault that you were thrown into a world of what was sheer excitement for you. You were a young lad who did not know the true meaning of what your decision would do to your father and mother. Please quit blaming yourself, the *man*."

Though Brandon was a man, Leana could see so much of the boy in him that he surely was those many years ago. He seemed so vulnerable now with such a sullen look on his bronzed face. And in his eyes she could see such torture.

Yet so much of him spoke to her as the man . . . his powerful, lightly furred chest shown to her where his plaid shirt was half-unbuttoned down the front, and his tight jeans, revealing his muscled thighs. He *was* the epitome of a man framing a boy's heart that was saddened with loss of family.

Leana went to Brandon and grabbed a hand. She squeezed it affectionately, causing him to stop his pacing. He turned on a heel and looked down at her from his towering height. His eyes softened in mood and a soft smile touched his lips.

"So you're my stepsister, huh?" he said, laughing hoarsely.

"Yes. Does that change much between us, Brandon?"

"Only had you chosen to live with Matthew, Leana."

"Oh? Why do you say that? What does Matthew have to do with *us*?"

"Had you chosen to stay with Matthew, I would have known just what sort of woman you were."

Leana's eyebrows lifted with wonder. "Oh? And what sort of woman *am* I?"

"One who saw Matthew just for what he was. A conniving bastard who I don't even want to claim as my brother."

Leana eased into his arms and rested her cheek on his

chest. She hugged him to her, feeling the hard pounding of his heart against her flesh. "Does it truly matter that he treated you so poorly?" she murmured. "You've gotten along just fine without him all these years. You sure don't need him now, Brandon."

Brandon placed a forefinger beneath her chin. He forced her eyes upward, to meet his steady gaze. "And you? Can you do without him?" he implored. "You were a part of the Seton family for so long. You know that you rightfully belong on the Seton ranch, claiming a portion of the Seton riches. You know that my father would have wanted that for you."

"I don't *need* Matthew for *anything*. Parker saw to my future before he died," Leana said softly. "I guess he saw through Matt, the sort of son he was, and more than that, the man that Matt had become. For insurance purposes, caring for me so much, Parker took me privately aside and gave me many jewels and money." A wicked smile touched her lips. "And I have put his generous offerings to use. Even this very morning, Brandon."

"How? What have you done?" Brandon asked, now fully realizing how much Leana *had* meant to his father.

But, yes, she would. Who could not treat her as special? She was the first woman to cause Cyril's words of mistrust of women to grow hazy inside Brandon's head. Leana might even make him forget *all* of Cyril's teachings!

Leana pranced about the room, flipping the skirt of her dress about as she turned to face Brandon. "This is all mine," she laughed, gesturing with her hands. "I just bought this hotel from General Rufino. Isn't it just wonderful, Brandon? He didn't even argue about it. I paid him many jewels and he accepted the offer." She threw her head back, laughing. "Imagine! Mine!"

Brandon's brow furrowed into a scowl. He kneaded his chin contemplatingly. "Yours?" he said, watching her smile fade as she saw the doubt in his eyes. "And you trust that bastard Mexican, do you?"

"We made a bargain. Surely . . . surely he will not go back on his word," Leana said, now suspicious herself, remembering how quickly the Mexican had complied with her offer.

And hadn't he said that she would have to eventually pay him more? In her anxiousness, she had tossed the worry of what he had meant by that aside.

But now as she came back down to earth and with Brandon showing such doubt, she wondered just how much of this hotel she *did* own. . . . And when would General Rufino come to collect whatever else he would demand of her . . . ?

"Bargains are made to be broken," Brandon growled. But seeing her so downcast, he feared that he had worried her enough. What was done was done; and nothing could change that. It was her future that he would have to warn her about! Especially where that damn Mexican general was concerned.

Reaching for her, he drew her into his arms and held her against him. "But I'm sure you did what was right," he assured. "If that Mexican tries anything with you, he'll have me to answer to."

Leana looked up into his eyes, melting inside, seeing passion so warm in their dark depths. "Are you saying that you are leaving your pirate days behind? You're going to settle somewhere close by on land?" she dared to ask, already seeing that these words were causing his eyes to take on a different cast . . . that of a distant coldness.

"The sea has always been my first love," he said,

241

loosening the combs in her hair. "Until you. Now I am torn, Leana, as to the ways of life I do want. Yet, until I fight this thing out inside my head about my family, I surely will return to the sea. Even tonight. Please understand?"

Leana jerked away from him, recalling the ship on which she had been when she had first met him. The ship and its crew had been cruelly separated. The pirate ship *Erebus* had become the recipient of all that had been aboard the ship *Jasmine*.

"You are actually saying that you must return to the sea to plunder . . . to *kill*," she stormed, her eyes flashing angrily. "You *are* a pirate, aren't you? How could I ever let myself forget that?"

Brandon grabbed her by a wrist and yanked her to him. His eyes were afire with anger. "I never killed unless it was in self-defense," he snapped. "And if it would make you feel better, you are the reason I have decided that I no longer want any part in ravaging other ships."

"But you said that you were going to return to the sea even this night," Leana said, ouching when she tried to free her wrist.

"I need to clear my mind," he said, releasing his hold on her. "Does that sound like a person who would attack another's ship?"

"Well, no. . . ."

"If I would happen to attack a ship, it would be a ship delivering arms to the damn Mexicans," he growled. "Between them and the Indians, the Americans are sitting ducks in Texas. Until the land of Texas becomes independent of Mexicans, and the Indians are taught a thing or two, no one is safe here."

He framed Leana's face between his hands. "Even you.

God, Leana, how safe do you think you are here in this hotel, even if you *do* believe you are now its owner? You're a mere lady. You are asking for trouble by being here without a man."

"I will prove to you just how I can take care of myself," she snapped, again jerking away from him. "Mere lady, indeed." She placed her hands on her hips. "Just let any man try anything with me. I will quickly put him in his place."

Brandon laughed beneath his breath; his eyes gleamed. "My, but aren't you a sight to see all puffed up and huffy," he snickered. Then his smile faded. "But I must ask, how do you intend to protect yourself?"

Leana marched to the bed and bent to a knee. She withdrew a shotgun and pointed it toward Brandon. "I could blow you clean away should I choose to do so," she said icily.

Then, when seeing how his face had become suddenly pale, she lowered the shotgun to her side and went to him and smoothed her free hand over his bronze face. "So you see, darling, I have nothing to fear from anyone," she murmured. "I also have your father's pistol."

"So you believe you've thought of everything, huh?" Brandon asked, frowning.

"Well, I'm not sure *everything*," Leana shrugged, again slipping the shotgun beneath the bed. "But purchasing the shotgun gave me a sense of security."

"Things happen quickly," Brandon said. "You just might not have time to grab the shotgun. What then?"

Leana forked an eyebrow. "What would you suggest?" she asked, watching him begin to draw his left pants leg up, disclosing to her eyes a leather scabbard tied to his leg. Her eyes widened as he withdrew the leather

243

scabbard, which housed a manchette, and then handed it her way.

"I've carried this with me since I was a young lad," Brandon said thickly. "But I now give it to you. This is something that you can use quickly: By day wear it beneath your skirts. By night sleep with it beneath your pillow."

His insides did a strange rippling as she removed the manchette from its scabbard and lay it in her right hand. He had always treasured this weapon. It had been his first as a free spirit after having been taken aboard the *Erebus*. Ever since, he had treasured it. But for her? He could part with it. It could save her life, as it had his, many times.

"A manchette?" she said in a near whisper. She could tell by the wear of the leather scabbard and its darkened fabric, caused by sweat stains, that it was quite old. And by the way Brandon was looking at it, she could tell that it meant much to him. Somehow she knew that this gift was more proof than anything else before of how he felt about her. Perhaps it was even the beginning of his choosing between her . . . and . . . the sea . . . ?

"Will you take it? Will you keep it with you at all times?" Brandon asked, again working at removing combs from her hair, wanting it to be free for him to run his fingers through her lovely satin tresses.

"Are you sure you want . . . to . . . part with it?" Leana asked, feeling the passion inflaming between them at the mere touch of his fingers in her hair. "You do seem fond of it."

"I want it to now be yours," Brandon said huskily. "As I now want you to be *mine*." His lips lowered and grazed against hers. "Leana, I need you. My heart is so heavy over finding out the truth about my father. Help me forget. Love me, Leana. . . ."

"Oh, but I do . . ." Leana whispered, dropping the manchette and its scabbard on the bed behind her. "I don't think I shall ever love another. But, Brandon, our lives . . . they . . . are so different. Our love is futile."

"Let's cherish this moment we are now together," Brandon said thickly, kissing the pulse beat at her throat. "Let's worry about tomorrow *tomorrow*."

"Oh, Brandon," Leana said, becoming quickly breathless as his fingers busied at loosening her dress. "Why must you always cause my mind to become so scrambled? I need you, yet I so fear this need. I want *you* to be all my tomorrows. Yet, you . . . you . . ."

His lips swept down and silenced her words with a burning kiss. His hands lowered her dress down from her shoulders, baring them. And, as if by magic, he managed to free her of all her other things and eased her down onto the bed.

Still kissing her, setting her afire inside, he moved the manchette and scabbard to a table beside the bed, then lowered himself over her, placing the hardness of his manhood straining against his clothes against her soft patch of hair which was curled black between her thighs.

As Brandon was grinding into her, Leana emitted a soft moan. Her fingers worked with the buttons of his shirt; then she crept her hands inside and splayed her fingers across his chest. She could feel his heart against the palm of her right hand, feeling as though a thousand hooves of horses were thundering against it. She could feel the quivering of his lips as he moved them from hers to now kiss his way down to a breast swollen with desire.

So filled with lethargic heat, Leana removed Brandon's

245

shirt and then placed her fingers at the band of his jeans. Unsnapping them, she reached inside and reveled in the touch of his hardness. When he groaned, she knew what she must do next. She anxiously slipped his breeches down away from him. Her face flushed hot, she opened herself fully to him as he thrust inside her and began slow, gentle strokes, all the while consuming first one breast and then another with his lips.

Nude bodies fusing, satin skin touching skin tough as leather, Brandon's hand swept down Leana's back in a soft caress as she leaned up into him. Delicious shivers of rapture coursed through her, Leana feeling his animal heat transferring to her with each thrust inside her.

His lips were sweet as they sought her out; his eyes had grown smoke-black with desire. His fingers now wove through Leana's hair, which spilled over her shoulders, threatening to cover her breasts.

He lifted her hair back and crushed her breasts into his chest, trembling, working rhythmically, burying himself deep inside her.

He now kissed her more hungrily, feeling how her breath quickened with a yearning and how she clung so hard about his neck. Her mouth was hot and sweet, her body soft as cotton against his.

"Darling, this is what dreams are made of," Brandon whispered into Leana's ear. "I shall carry this moment with you inside my heart, forever."

His words pleasured her, as did his lips, hands, and the part of him that was now causing her heart and mind to soar with joy. She drew a ragged breath as he again kissed her, draining her of all emotions, except love. She sighed as his lips now paid homage to a breast, his tongue a point of fire, igniting flames as it flicked about its soft pink crest.

"I wish this moment would never *end*," she whispered, then closed her eyes in complete rapture as she felt his strokes become more intense, causing the familiar warmth blossoming, growing warmer, hotter, until she became momentarily blinded with the sheer bliss of release as he came to her, also, in a rush of uttered moans and spun golden magic. . . .

Bodies intertwined, Brandon rained kisses along Leana's neck and then gently spread her breasts and ran a tongue up and down her deep cleavage. Leana reciprocated by running her tongue along his chest, down and around one of his hardened nipples.

As he leaned away from her, her lips and tongue played even lower, now circling his navel. She laughed softly as she saw his stomach tremble with her touch. And when she saw that his man's strength was still solid, beautiful in the way it shone in its purplish hues, she dared a flick of her tongue on its tip, desire again inflaming her when hearing his short intake of breath.

His fingers wove through her hair and urged her mouth closer to where he again throbbed, and when she understood his bidding and let her tongue again touch him there, she closed her eyes and pleasured him in that way while he stroked her silken flesh with his tongue and fingers where her own pleasure points begged to be taken.

And then Brandon could stand no more. The ecstasy was too intense. He lifted her up above him. She straddled him, placing her knees on the bed on either side of him, and felt as though floating when he again entered her and began his easy strokes inside her. His hands worked on each of her breasts, teasing the nipples to hardness.

Leana arched her neck backward, letting her hair become dark streamers tumbling down her back to her waist.

And again they found the ultimate of what was shared between man and woman, and then lay in one another's arms, attempting to get their breaths.

"Can one find a bottle of liquor somewhere in your hotel?" Brandon laughed, perspiration sparkling as fine lace on his brow. "I feel I need something quite strong to awaken me from this perfect stupor that I have found myself in. If I don't, I may never leave you, Leana."

Leana leaned up on an elbow and traced his lips with a forefinger. "And would that be so bad?" she pouted. "I'm afraid that once you leave, it may be forever before I see you again. It may even be *never*. You know the dangers of you being on the sea *and* land. It seems your reputation as a pirate precedes you wherever you go, Brandon."

"But I've survived, have I not?" he chuckled, rising from the bed. He dressed, all the while devouring her nudity as she lay ripe on the bed.

"But you haven't even told me where you make your residence *while* on land," Leana further pouted, rising to slip into her petticoat. Once he left the room, she would feel too vulnerable. She *did* know to be wary, being a lady alone.

"Won't you tell me, Brandon?" She gave him a wistful glance, a forced look of humility. "What if I *would* need you? Where would I find you?"

Brandon placed his holstered pistols about his waist. He frowned toward her. "No one knows the hideout of

A FREE ZEBRA
HISTORICAL
ROMANCE
WORTH

$3.95

the pirates who travel on the *Erebus*," he said sharply. "Though I trust you, I don't trust those who might try to pry answers from you, Leana. I can't tell you. Not yet, anyway. . . ."

Leana fastened her dress and tossed her hair back from her shoulders with a sling of her head. "Then one day?" she asked hopefully.

"We'll see," Brandon grumbled. He went and placed his hands to her waist. "But for now let's just concentrate on something to drink. Do you think there might be some downstairs? I'd like to even have champagne if I can manage to round some up."

Leana laughed softly. "I don't think José would have champagne to offer you," she said. "But I'm sure he has something much deadlier to offer you. It would be something I would not dare share with you."

"Then I will have to go find champagne elsewhere," Brandon said, laughing across his shoulder as he marched toward the door. "Darling, I shan't be gone long."

"Brandon . . . ?" Leana asked, stopping him with the questioning in his voice.

Brandon stopped and turned to face her. "What is it?" he asked, forking an eyebrow.

"What are we celebrating?" she asked demurely. "You are leaving again to travel on the *Erebus*. I see no reason to celebrate *that*."

Brandon chuckled. "We then shall celebrate my *return*," he said, then walked in a gay trot from the room.

Leana went to the window and watched for him, and then saw him go into a saloon across the street. And when he came from it again so quickly, holding a bottle, she laughed to herself. He seemed to know how to get his way with *everyone*. . . .

She rushed to her dresser and grabbed her brush. Wanting to look her best for Brandon's return, she began taking quick, long strokes through her hair. And when she heard footsteps behind her, she turned, stars in her eyes, though knowing he would part from her again way too soon. She was going to take every moment she could with him and savor it. . . .

Gasping, Leana went pale. She dropped the brush to the floor and stared openly at General Rufino, who stood in the doorway smiling crookedly at her. The haziness had left his eyes, and his military black suit trimmed with silver was pressed to perfection, as was his coarse black hair combed, and his glossy black boots waxed. He rested his hand on his saber as he moved further into the room.

"*Se puede?* May I come in, beautiful señorita?" General Rufino said in a mocking tone. "You do seem to have settled in in my hotel quickly enough." He laughed throatily. "But, Señorita, where is the fanciness you promised? Ah, but it is too soon. We only talked business this morning, did we not?"

Leana's jaws tightened, as did her hands into fists. "You have no busines here, Señor," she hissed. "This hotel is *mine* now. I paid you fair and square for it. Or have you come to demand more? I thought you might at least wait a few weeks before demanding more of me. What is it that you want? Tell me and let's get this over with."

"You think that I was too drunk this morning to remember all details of the agreement, do you?" General Rufino laughed. "Señorita, it was you who made the mistake."

He took a step toward her, letting his gaze rove over

her, admiring the glow to her cheeks and the fire in her eyes. He was enjoying this lady even more than when bedding another. She was more a challenge than those who went so easily to bed with him!

"What do you mean?" Leana said, watching the door, expecting Brandon to return at any moment. Oh, Lord, she knew the dangers of this Mexican general discovering Brandon there. Even dressed as a cowhand, Brandon's face was that which no one would ever forget!

"As I see it, the hotel is not at *all* yours," General Rufino gloated, drumming his fingers against the handle of his saber. "So what is this that you speak of . . . that you owe *more?* Señorita, we did not make a set deal this morning. If you think so, you are a foolish americano. Your jewels you handed over to me this morning did not seal our deal. Surely you know that. Or is it that I could be accused of taking advantage of a fair lady?"

His throaty, mocking laugh caused Leana's throat to constrict. "What are you saying?" she said shallowly.

"There were no papers signed, were there?" General Rufino mocked. "Legal documents are needed when property is purchased, *sí?*"

Leana paled. Her fingers went to her throat, feeling suddenly had. "You aren't seriously saying that our deal wasn't for real, are you?" she said in a strain.

"No legal document was signed stating ownership," General Rufino said, shrugging. "So the hotel is still quite mine."

He cocked a brow. "But we can begin anew," he chuckled. "Give me more jewels and I will this time sign a document stating the hotel is yours." He coughed into a cupped hand. "But still expecting more from you time to time, for protection, eh, would you say?"

251

Leana's face now flamed with heated anger. "You are nothing but a swindler," she hissed. "But how could I expect anything but something like this from you? And it is because of my own stupidity. I should have known to have asked for you to sign the hotel over to me this morning before leaving your villa."

In her mind's eye she was remembering how he had been scantily dressed, and his drugged half stupor from the opium, feeling anything but safe with him, especially since he had already flaunted half-nude women in drugged stupors awaiting to service his every carnal need!

Her anxiousness to get away from him and her sheer joy to have purchased the hotel had made her only half think of what was needed at the time. . . .

General Rufino rubbed his thumb and forefinger together on his right hand, while withdrawing a legal document from his coat pocket with the other. "Pay me, and the legal papers will be turned over to you," he said dryly. "If not, I will have to ask you to leave. *Pronto.*"

"But you know I already paid you a fair amount," Leana argued back. "I shouldn't have to pay you the full amount again." She inched toward him. "Give me the papers, General. You know they are mine *now*. I won't pay double that I have already paid."

General Rufino stuck the document back into his pocket. "Well, then, your decision is made," he grumbled. "Get your things and get out. Now."

"I don't think so," Brandon said suddenly from behind General Rufino, coming into Leana's vision as he stepped into the room, his pistol drawn.

"Brandon!" Leana softly gasped, covering her mouth with her hand. She so feared for his safety. She cared not for her own, *or* the fact that she had been foolishly free with the jewels that Parker had given her. "Please go. Please . . ."

General Rufino turned on a heel and glowered toward Brandon, his hand reaching for his pistol. But Brandon was too quick. He jumped the Mexican and twisted General Rufino's pudgy arm behind him.

"I've been out in the hall listening for a while. I think you owe the lady something," Brandon growled. "I believe she bought this hotel fair and square this morning. She now needs the signed document stating ownership."

Brandon held his pistol in the Mexican's ribs. "Get the document and hand it over to Leana. Do it or die right here on the spot."

"You can't get away with this," General Rufino snarled. "You won't even get away from this hotel before being shot by my men."

"I doubt that," Brandon chuckled. "Now, do as you've been told. Let's make an honest Mexican out of you this morning. Give the lady what's due her."

General Rufino leaned up closer to Brandon's face as he reached inside his coat pocket for the document. "I know you," he said, his voice low and threatening. "You're wanted at all ports. And I don't forget a face. Yours is one I will be watching for."

"As is most of the country," Brandon shrugged. "But you don't see me pale from fear, do you?" He chuckled, disarming the Mexican as General Rufino handed the document over to Leana.

"Make sure it's signed, Leana," Brandon ordered, shoving General Rufino toward a chair.

"But, Brandon, even if it is, General Rufino will take it

253

away from me as soon as you leave," she said softly. "He might even . . . even . . . kill me once you are gone."

Brandon pushed General Rufino down onto the chair and tied him to it with the belt that he had jerked from the Mexican's breeches. "General Rufino won't do anything to you, Leana," he said. "This is *my* doing. Not yours."

He bent down into the Mexican's face. "And if I hear that you've hurt one lovely hair on her head, I will return and personally kill you. You know how well I elude those who seek me, to hang me. So shall it be when I search you out, to kill you if you harm Leana. You'd best remember that, General. And I would make sure your death would be slow and painful."

Brandon nudged the general in the groin with a knee. "I'd take delight in taking away from you the part of you that gives you such pleasure with the American women you drug and take to your villa," he growled. "One knife point at a time, and your screams would be heard from here to Cuba."

General Rufino gasped. "You . . . wouldn't . . ." he said, paling.

"If anything happens to Leana, you just try me," Brandon snapped. He leaned closer to the Mexican's face. "And don't forget who now truly owns this hotel. I'd suggest you don't taunt her anymore."

Leana unfolded the document and read it, seeing that it was written up quite legally and that the general had signed it. Her face became radiant, knowing that now, for sure, the hotel was hers.

Then her smile faded when watching Brandon gag General Rufino. "What am I to do once you're gone?" she said in a near whisper.

"Give me an hour to get away, then untie him,"

Brandon said, now finished with securing General Rufino to the chair. He placed his arms about Leana. "I'll be safely gone in an hour. Turn him loose. And, darling, you'll be safe, or I wouldn't leave you. This Mexican knows I am a man of my word. He won't harm you. In fact, he'll take special efforts to make sure no one else harms you. He knows what to expect from *me* if any harm comes to you by *anyone*."

"Oh, Brandon, if you only didn't have to go," Leana sniffed, clinging.

"The sea beckons . . . ," he murmured in her ear. "Maybe one day it can be different. But for now, *buenos días, vida mia*. My thoughts of you will keep me *with* you."

He gave her a lingering, quivering kiss, then fled from the room. Leana trembled as she turned and looked toward General Rufino. There was much hate in his eyes. She feared the future now, as never before. . . .

Chapter Seventeen

Cyril stared from his bedroom window, trying to see through the thick tangle of trees and climbing vines for Brandon's return. Of late Brandon had become too restless, leaving on his horse almost as quickly as the ship *Erebus* dropped its anchor. Cyril felt as though he was losing Brandon. If not to the ways of the land, perhaps to a lady? Cyril had seen how Brandon had so quickly been taken by that lovely wench on their last voyage.

Leana. Hadn't Brandon wanted to set Leana and her mother afloat in the longboat close to Rufino so he could have the chance to find Leana again? At the time, Brandon's genuine interest in the wench had amused Cyril . . . him*self* having just been mesmerized by such a beauty.

But Cyril had thought this infatuation of Brandon's would pass, as had Cyril's *own* feelings for the wench Wanda. . . .

"Cyril? Whatever is the matter with you this morning?" Wanda spoke in a purr from behind him. She slunk to the edge of the bed, pink velvet in her nudity.

"Are you tiring of me so soon? Are you sorry you brought me to your fancy house? Do I sense that I will soon be turned away? Is this how it is with a pirate? You tire of your women so easily? I had thought to be *special*."

Dressed only in black leather breeches, tight enough to define his every muscle, Cyril turned his eyes to Wanda. His gaze swept over her, seeing her loveliness, yet also the hardness in her eyes and the way she set her mouth when she talked. Her life had been one of struggle, and he could understand why she would grasp onto this opportunity to share his life.

At first the thought *had* intrigued him. He had even wanted her. But now he *was* tiring of her, as he always had other women in the past. Amelia had ruined life for him as far as women were concerned. None had ever compared with her. None had ever been as genuinely gentle and loving.

Though he knew that he should hate Amelia for having deserted him, also denying him his child, he knew that he would always love her. This was a love meant to be only once in a lifetime.

"Well?" Wanda purred, stepping gingerly from the bed onto white carpet that reached almost to her ankles, it was so plushly deep. It was the soft fur of many animals stitched together to spread across the full length of the room.

Cyril accepted her into his arms, yet again glancing toward the window, still worrying about Brandon. Brandon hadn't approved of Wanda. Brandon had disapproved even more the fact that Cyril had brought Wanda to their hideout! Was *this* why Brandon rode away so often now on his horse, Cotton?

"Well, what?" Cyril said, framing Wanda's face between his hands, wondering just how much longer she would be here with him. If Brandon so disapproved, she would be sent away!

Wanda's hair fell across her shoulders and down her back in auburn reds, silken in its texture, glistening beneath the rays of the evening sunset cascading through the window behind Cyril. She wrapped a lovely taper of leg about Cyril and drew him closer.

"You don't seem to want to answer any of my questions this morning, Cyril," she pouted. "Are you tiring of me? Please tell me you're not."

"And if I am?" he said thickly. "Would it matter? You seem quite capable of finding another man."

Feeling a knot forming in the pit of her stomach, suspecting that Cyril was trying to find a way to tell her that he *was* tiring of her, Wanda curled her fingers into his hair and drew his lips close to hers.

"But no man pleases me as you do, darling," she whispered, flicking her tongue across his lips. "Surely no other woman knows *my* skills. I have pleased you, have I not?"

With a low growl, Cyril moved his hands to her buttocks and cupped them. He jerked her into his hardness, risen from a need so ancient, it was not within his power to ever deny himself when the offering of such was at hand.

"If yer hair was black and yer skin olive, I would think you were born with gypsy blood running through your veins," he growled. "You have such a mystique about you. Where do ye come from? Where is yer family?"

Wanda laughed softly. "In a sense I *am* a gypsy," she said. "Until you I never stayed long in one place. And where I am originally from surely shouldn't matter to you, nor the fact that I do not have family. What should matter is that I am here, ready to pleasure you again, Cyril. Isn't that all you desire of me this morning? I can make it heaven on earth for you, my love."

She pressed her breasts against his chest and forced his lips down to hers. With skill learned from having been with so many men, paid *for* these skills, Wanda kissed Cyril with a kiss of fire while gyrating her body into his.

Becoming mindless, mesmerized by this woman whose slender, curving body had a strange sort of power that could drain him of all his senses, Cyril lifted her into his arms and carried her to the bed and its red satin sheets matching the red velveteen draperies lined in gold brocade. He placed her on the bed and quickly withdrew his breeches, all the while letting her body tempt him even the more while his gaze feasted upon it.

"Come to me," Wanda said, beckoning with her outstretched arms. "Let me make you want me, forever. Cyril, after this morning there will no longer be any doubt in your mind about me. You won't *want* to live without me."

A thick, husky groan accompanied Cyril's entrance inside her. He thrust hard, his hands squeezing her breasts, his tongue searching wildly inside her mouth. Wanda locked her legs about his waist and worked feverishly with him, oh, so enjoying having learned to find pleasure with a man. Only Cyril had brought out the sensuous feelings. Before him she had only lain cold, hating every minute of being with a man. The money had been all that mattered then.

Now it was this scorching passion that he aroused inside her that mattered. She was afraid that if he sent her away, she would never find such pleasure again with another man. There was something about Cyril, even though he was much older. She knew that she would do anything to assure a future with him. Anything. If she even had to kill, she would. . . .

Brandon wound his way around the trees, following the path that he had worn with his travels on his horse, Cotton. The world was entering the little death of night; the forest creatures were settling in. A distant, long, melancholy howl of a wolf reverberated through the trees.

But Brandon knew that it was not the wolf that was the threat . . . it was the Mexicans. He had to expect the Mexican general to call out all of his troops to try and find him.

Wincing as though shot, Brandon's thoughts went to Leana. Yet he had made *his* threat real enough to the Mexican general. Surely the Mexican wouldn't harm Leana. He was the same as any other man. He wouldn't do anything to place his virility in jeopardy. And the Mexican surely knew a pirate's word was as good as gold and that if Brandon himself wouldn't be around to do the honors, someone else would under Brandon's orders.

No. Brandon had to believe that Leana would be safe. And wasn't there the manchette that he had given her? One plunge and she would be rid of the Mexican!

But Brandon's thoughts weren't completely filled with Mexicans *nor* Leana. He was in awe of Cyril and the change that had come over him after becoming tangled up with that wench, that *whore*, Wanda! She was the first woman to ever be taken to the hideout. This wasn't like

Cyril. He was going against all his teachings to Brandon! How could Cyril endanger all their lives because of a guttersnipe like Wanda?

Yes, Brandon was disenchanted with his mentor and he didn't know quite what to do about it. . . .

The house came suddenly into view, awash with moonlight seeping through the ceiling of trees draped with Spanish moss, resembling fancy, fine lace. The mansion rose from the forest like a giant magnolia in its magnificence. It was a house as none other in this part of the territory of Texas. It was pillared, stark white against the blackness of the surrounding forest.

The golden glow of candlelight blossomed from only a few of the windows, the others having been close-shuttered for the night, to not only keep the dampness of the swamp from entering the mansion, but also the large, annoying mosquitoes that plagued this place that could be called paradise to many who had much, much less.

Swatting at a mosquito as it landed on his arm, its stinger even piercing through the fabric of his shirt, Brandon urged his horse onward, anxious to get into the house, away from the pesky things. Yet when there, what would he find? A Cyril who would not want to leave his wench to accompany Brandon out to sea? Or would Cyril welcome the thought to ride the waves again in his beautiful ship *Erebus?*

"But he must. He has no choice," Brandon grumbled to himself as he dismounted and reined his horse to a hitching post.

Brandon knew that the Mexicans must even be made to see the ship this time, to draw them away from searching the Big Thicket. There was too much hidden in this house for the Mexicans to ever get their hands on. All the riches

Brandon and Cyril possessed were there.

"Seems I got a mite careless this time in town," he whispered, scowling.

But he knew that he would again, for Leana was there. He had become like a moth being drawn into the flame of this woman whose eyes, whose laugh, whose hands sent his heart into a tailspin of loving her. Somehow their futures had to become fused, to live as one, to act as one. . . .

Knowing that thinking of Leana could crowd out all other things of importance to him, and knowing that this was a threat to even his life at this moment in time, Brandon shook his head, clearing his mind, then rushed into the mansion.

A fire burned low on the grate, casting shadowed images onto a room rich with pure gold accessories. The room was well furnished with a thick Brussels carpet spread magnificently across the floor.

Jewels sparkled and more gold teased his eyes from a glass-enclosed bookcase that reached to the ceiling. Rare vases of all shapes and sizes stood about the room. Brocade drapes were closed over the windows; a faint smell of magnolia rose from a bouquet on a cherry wood table with a marble top beside a velveteen sofa.

Low titters of laughter emerging from overhead drew Brandon's eyes slowly upward, knowing from whose bedroom the sounds were emerging. He clasped a hand on a pistol and stomped from the room and to the staircase that spiraled to the second floor. Seems Cyril's fun was going to be spoiled! And Brandon didn't even give a warning. He marched on into Cyril's bedroom, nonplussed by the tangled bodies on the bed.

"Are you with me, or not?" Brandon said, his voice

firm, his jaw set. He watched as Cyril's head jerked around and gaped surprisingly toward him. "I am leaving on the *Erebus* within the next hour, Cyril. I would think that you would accompany me. Or does this wench have too much of a hold on you?"

He again silently marveled over Cyril's attraction to this lady. It would be understandable if Cyril had become captivated with a gentle, sweet thing like Leana. But . . . this . . . wench who most surely had bedded men in every seaport. . . . ? She surely was not the type to change one's life for!

"Lad, you have a way of makin' surprise appearances," Cyril chuckled, easing away from Wanda, not angry at Brandon for his rude interruption. It amused Cyril to see such fire in Brandon's eyes and to know that he was bold enough *to* come to this bedroom where he knew to find two bodies quite nude, making love. He had taught Brandon well. He had taught him to not fear anything or anyone. Not even the man who had abducted him as a child and turned him into a pirate. . . .

"You . . . you . . . stupid man," Wanda hissed, drawing a blanket up over her to hide her nudity. "Who do you think you are coming in here like this, unannounced? Don't you have a thread of decency in you?"

Brandon placed his hands on his hips and spread his legs, throwing his head back in a hearty laugh. Then his eyes gleamed as he met the challenge of Wanda's glare. "Ma'am, who are you to speak of decency?" he said smoothly. He glanced over at Cyril. "Or do I speak out of turn, Cyril? What *is* she to you?"

Cyril drew his leather breeches on. His face was shadowed into a sudden frown, causing the furrows on his face to deepen. He went to a chair and withdrew a shirt from where he had earlier casually dropped it. Its flowing sleeves billowed out away from him as he slipped into the shirt, buttoning it only halfway down the front, making sure his gold cross showed as it lay boldly against his chest.

"We shall discuss Wanda *and* yer own wench while at sea," Cyril grumbled. He nodded toward Wanda. "Seems the lad has a need for a jaunt on the *Erebus*. I trust him even enough to not ask why. But we'll return soon. Just make yerself at home. There should be enough here to amuse you."

Wanda jumped from the bed, wrapping the blanket about her. She had paled of color. She went and spoke into Cyril's face. "You're leaving? Just like that? And you're leaving me here *alone?*" she said, trembling from fear and anger. "Cyril, please . . . don't . . ."

"I'll be downstairs," Brandon said with a flip of his head. "But don't take too long, Cyril. I've given the Mexicans cause to remove more than our heads."

Wanda gasped, paling even the more. "Mexicans . . . ?" she whispered, looking from Brandon to Cyril. Then she was glad when Brandon left the room. She let the blanket ripple from around her, to the floor. She clasped onto Cyril's hands. "Will I be safe here while you're gone?" she cried. "Cyril, let me *go* with you."

"You won't be entirely alone," Cyril said, easing his hands from hers. He went and belted pistols about his waist. "We never leave our hideout unguarded." His eyes darkened. "Mind you, stay in the house. If I hear of you and one of my men . . ."

Wanda smiled devilishly up at him. "Would you be jealous?" she teased.

"Jealousy isn't the word I'd use," he grumbled. "But I

can only warn you. You wouldn't like the consequences should you make a fool o' me."

Strolling to the bed, Wanda spread out across it. "Please don't stay away long," she begged. "I'm afraid Brandon will turn you against me. It is obvious he has little respect for me. Why is that, Cyril? I've done nothing to him."

"You're the first woman I've brought to our hideout," he said flatly. "This is the reason for Brandon's behavior. And you might say that *he* is jealous. Up to now it's only been the two of us. Like father and son. You're a threat. Just like the wench he's taken a liking to is a threat."

Wanda moved to her knees, her breasts bouncing. Her face was red with sudden anger. "So he is seeing a woman you do not approve of?" she snapped. "Is this the true reason you have paid so much attention to me? To upset Brandon into giving up *his* lady?"

Cyril's eyebrows arched. "Hmm," he said, kneading his chin. "Perhaps that *is* the reason." He left the room, chuckling. And then when he found Brandon pacing in the parlor, his lighthearted mood became heavy with wonder.

"Well?" he said, placing a hand on Brandon's shoulder. "Want to tell me about it, lad?"

"Are you even ready to listen?" Brandon said in a snarl, glowering down at Cyril. "Seems the lady has got you wrapped around her little finger. And, Cyril, if you *do* tire of her, how can you even let her go from here? She would tell everyone about our hideout. She might even lead the authorities *to* us. If she were the type to be trusted, I would understand. But surely you know she isn't."

"We'll worry about that later, Brandon," Cyril said

dryly. He lifted a brow and studied Brandon. "What sort of trouble did you get into while in Rufino?" he asked, already feeling the thrill of danger that Brandon may have brought along with him. Life was too easy with a woman. He needed danger to fuel his blood. . . .

"Seems I made an enemy with a Mexican general," Brandon said, then chuckled low, remembering how the Mexican had looked gagged and tied up. Then his smile faded. "Let's board the *Erebus* and I'll tell you all about it. . . ."

Chapter Eighteen

Several weeks had passed since Leana had released General Rufino from his bonds. To her surprise he hadn't bothered her then, nor any time since. Either Brandon's threats had stayed with the general, or was it solely because of *her*? The general seemed to always be looking at her with an air of amazement, seeming to be in awe of how she managed to get on by her own, a mere lady, without a man's assistance. Young José could not yet be labeled a man. And he was the only one whom Leana chose to confide in.

Darla Yates was never around, seemingly too busy with her own life to include Leana in it, though Leana could very well remember Darla's anxiousness to have Leana as company that first day of Leana's arrival to the town of Rufino.

Leana missed a female's companionship. She missed close friends. Oh, Lord, how she missed her *mother!*

Her thoughts returned to General Rufino. Having his own sort of harem at his villa at the edge of town, General Rufino only occasionally lightly teased Leana, making her face flush crimson with his implied remarks, though innocent they were. She had grown to trust him, yet guardedly. . . .

Proud of how she had renovated the hotel into a combination of general store, hotel, *and* saloon combined into one business, Leana stood back and admired what was now hers. The hotel lobby glittered from a crystal chandelier dripping with pendants from the ceiling. The chandelier had been shipped from New York purposely for her hotel, and she had never expected it to arrive all in one piece. But it had, and it was the object of many comments as customers came and went from Leana's establishment.

To her right side, a room was dimmed with smoke as men sat at the bar, smoking and drinking. The tinkling from a piano broke through the boisterous laughs of the men and giggling of women who moved from table to table, serving drinks and flirting.

From this vantage point Leana could see the handsomely carved back bar and countertop in her saloon and a billiard table lit overhead by kerosene lanterns hanging low over it.

To her left, she could see the room that served as a general store. It was the source of dry goods and candy, and foods families couldn't get from their gardens. Leana had begun to cater to the poor. It wouldn't be a normal day if she didn't take a jug of corn whiskey as payment in kind for household items to take home to a wife and family.

She smiled to herself, knowing that if she stepped outdoors, she would see the change even in the outside structure of the hotel. Iron-balustraded balconies now graced the handsome structure; flowers of red geraniums sat in large pots, flanking the brightly painted door, red having been chosen to purposely draw attention to her hotel.

But night had fallen in its total blackness, and Leana didn't venture to leave her establishment after dark. The Mexicans were taunting and tormenting Americans during the daylight hours, and there were reports that some Americans had been grabbed after dark and carried away and tortured.

One day soon Leana expected a rebellion against the Mexicans and their treatment of Americans now that the Mexicans had decided they wanted no more Americans to enter the territory of Texas. Leana knew the dangers. Yet she would not leave what she now called *home*.

Having given José the evening off, Leana settled down into a deep wing chair where with just a mere turn of the head she could keep her eyes open for any new customers who might arrive, yet mostly hidden herself by the high back of the chair.

She began going over a ledger, frowning when realizing that business had slacked off due to the annoyances of the Mexicans. Only the poor seemed desperate enough to come on into town, and *those* Leana made *nothing* from. She was too generous to make a profit herself.

But as long as the jewels held out, so could she. So far, Matt hadn't even bothered to come to town to goad her into returning with him to the Seton Ranch or to see if she was faring well enough. Either Matt was scared of General Rufino, or Matt hoped that by his ignoring her, giving her no helping hand, it would finally force her to return to him, to beg him to let her stay with him.

But she would never do that. She would die first!

A rustling of petticoats drew Leana's attention to the

door. She barely leaned her head out from behind her chair, then sucked in a surprised gulp of air when seeing Darla Yates. And she was entering the hotel, escorted by a rough-looking sailor.

And when the sailor began to lead Darla on up the stairs toward the hotel rooms, Leana tensed and pulled quickly back. She knew the man, but not personally. She only knew him because she had registered him as a patron to her hotel only a few hours earlier. And now it seemed that he had found him a lady who was willing to spend a few hours with him . . . a lady who appeared to not be happy with the situation, by the strained look on her face.

Yet it was obvious that Darla wasn't being forced. She was going willingly up the steps. Leana could only surmise as to why. Sleeping with men had to be the way Darla Yates kept herself and her mother fed and clothed. And the thought sickened Leana. . . .

Leana hurriedly closed her ledger and placed it on a table. Almost tripping on her skirts from leaving the chair so quickly, she rushed to the foot of the stairs. "Darla?" she said dryly. "Darla Yates?"

Darla stopped and turned, almost toppling down the stairs from surprise when finding Leana there, looking up at her. They had met only once, but once had been enough to know that Leana was a lady of breeding and would never approve of a woman selling her body.

Feeling a blush burning her face, Darla stiffened her back. "Why, Leana? I believe that *is* your name, is it not?" she said weakly. "But of course it is. And this establishment even now bears your name. My, but haven't you been fortunate. How *did* you do it?"

Leana straightened her shoulders. "Darla, *not* in the

way you are most surely implying," she said. She glanced over at the sailor, his rough features looking even colder, deadlier, as he glared down at her for having interfered.

Leana placed her hands on her hips. "Sir, my establishment is not used in the way you have chosen," she snapped.

Then she looked at Darla, knowing the embarrassment she must be feeling, but Leana couldn't handle this in any other way. Her hotel was *not* going to get the reputation of becoming a "house," nor was she going to contribute to Darla's chosen profession.

"May I have a word with you, Darla?" Leana then quickly blurted. Leana had a sudden idea. It could be a way to repay Darla for her kindness paid *her*. At least it could be a way for Darla to make an honest, *clean* living.

It might stretch the purse strings to pay an extra hand, but Leana felt compelled to do what she could for this young thing, who looked pitiful in her embarrassment.

And couldn't this solve the problem of her own loneliness for female companionship . . . ?

The sailor blocked Darla's way with an outstretched arm. He glared down at Leana. "Lady, just what do you think you're doin'?" he snarled. "I think you need to be taught a lesson or two on manners."

Leana's eyes flamed in anger. "Oh? And you're the one to teach me?" she hissed.

"If you don't butt out, it looks as though I'll have to," he spat.

"Sir, I believe you forget whose establishment you are in," Leana argued back, fear creeping its way inside her heart, causing it to thump wildly. This was her first true confrontation with anyone since she had opened her establishment. And this man did not seem the type to tangle with in *any* respect. His hands looked strong; his shoulders were bulky with muscles, as revealed through a soiled gray shirt. His stringy, greasy-dirty hair was tied back from his face with a leather string, and his face was dark with unshaved whiskers.

"And you think knowing you are the owner is going to change my mind on anything?" the man said, laughing mockingly.

Knowing that she had to finish what she had started or never have the courage to try again should this happen again, Leana was reminded of the manchette strapped to her leg. Strange how having it always made her seem close to Brandon, and stranger still that she should think of that crazy spinning in the head when thinking of Brandon *now*, when her life might be in danger.

Her gaze traveled downward, seeing the pistols belted at the man's waist and his knife in a sheath at his hip. What she would try was risky, yet if not now, never. . . .

Stepping determinedly up the stairs, keeping her eyes hardened to the man's, Leana finally reached Darla. "Darla, I don't think you want to be with this man, now do you?" she said softly, yet fearing the trembling in her knees, hoping her knees wouldn't buckle beneath her with lessening courage as the man again nudged his elbow in the way of Darla.

"Leana, please . . . just . . . leave me alone," Darla said, giving the man a frightened look.

"You don't have to go with that man," Leana said, taking a hand, easing Darla away from him. "I think I know why you feel you must. I can change that for you. Just trust me?"

Taking Darla by an elbow, Leana began guiding her down the stairs, feeling the heat of the man's eyes

272

following her. And knowing what to expect next, she stooped and slipped the manchette from beneath her skirt just as the man swept down and raised a hand to hit her.

When she turned, she plunged the manchette into the man's upper right arm, causing him to emit a loud yowl and then a steady round of curse words as he ran from the premises, grasping onto his bleeding arm.

Shaken by the experience, Leana blinked her eyes nervously, then looked down at the blood-streaked manchette, realizing what she had done. Brandon had given it to her to use as a weapon, and this was the first time it had become necessary. If not for Brandon and his generous gift, she would probably now be knocked out from the blow of the angry man. And later, while unconscious, perhaps even *worse*. . . .

Darla grabbed Leana by an arm as Leana sank down into a chair, breathing hard. "Are you all right, Leana?" she said in a rush of words. "Lord! You are so brave!"

Wiping a bead of perspiration from her brow, Leana laughed nervously. "Brave? Damn it, Darla, I was scared to *death*," she said. "But I won't tolerate his kind in my establishment. I just *won't*."

Darla settled down into a chair across from Leana. She hung her head. "I guess I just didn't think it possible for a lady to defend herself in such a way," she murmured. "And I haven't yet had the need. The men usually get what they want from me without much argument. I guess you now know . . . how . . . I make my money."

"It wouldn't take a genius to figure that out," Leana said, laughing softly. She shivered as she again looked at the blood on the manchette. She held it out away from her and focused her eyes on Darla, seeing her as she had that first time she had met her. Darla had to be around seventeen, yet in her face there appeared to be a trace of what one found in one who had lived beyond those youthful years, showing a hardness, that which came with selling one's body to men at such a young age.

And again Leana saw something about the gray of her eyes, the slight crook of her nose, and the jet-black of her hair that blossomed into tight ringlets of curls about her square face and across her shoulders.

But again Leana couldn't put her finger on whom Darla might resemble. It was now the bright colors of her dress and its low-swept bodice, and the bold, bright colors that had been placed on her lips and cheeks that Leana was seeing. Darla played the role of a whore well. It was perhaps even too late to change this way of life for her. What if she had grown to accept it to the point that it was blasé, even enjoyable . . . ?

"I have no other way to see to my mother's welfare," Darla said, her eyes wavering, realizing Leana was looking her over, seeing her as she did not want to be seen. She wished to be as Leana. Free. Wise. And able to make her own way in the world, honestly.

"I know of no other way to make money to buy food and pay rent to General Rufino," Darla added, her eyes now locked with Leana's.

Leana leaned forward, her eyes wide. "You rent the house you live in from General Rufino?" she said. "Darla, would you like to come and live here with me in my hotel? You could bring your mother. She could be close by while you work."

Darla shook her head, her eyes squinting. "I don't understand you," she murmured. "First you say that you don't want me being with men in your hotel, doing the

274

only thing I know to make money, and then you suggest I move my mother here while I do this work?"

A blank look crossed Leana's face, trying to understand what Darla had just said, and then when it registered, she bent over in a laugh. "Oh, Darla, you are such an innocent," she said.

She wiped a laughter tear from the corner of an eye and sobered as she looked over at Darla. "Darla, when I say *work*, I mean for *me*," she said softly. "You can help me here at my establishment. You can work in the general store. You won't have to put up with any men any longer. Those who come to the general store are usually those who come for household items. What do you say? How does my plan sound to you?"

Darla studied Leana, cocking her head sideways. "I still don't understand," she murmured. "Why would you do this? Why would you be so generous?"

Leana understood Darla's hesitation. It was apparent that Darla hadn't found too many in her life to trust. "Because I miss having a close friend," she said softly. "And because you seem to be the sort who could *be* that friend. I have no other motives. Yet I guess you could say selfishness *might* be one. My selfishness for needing someone to talk to occasionally."

Darla rose from the chair and went to Leana. She placed a hand gently to her shoulder. "Leana, I don't think you could ever have a selfish bone in your body," she said thickly. "I don't think I've ever met anyone quite like you before. You're kind. You are a woman of heart."

"Then you will accept my proposition?" Leana asked, rising from the chair.

"Are you sure you want to be bothered with me since I

also have my mother? I can't believe you'd be that generous."

"Let's say no more. Tomorrow we will, together, move your mother and your belongings into my hotel. I have two rooms that are adjoining. You can set up housekeeping there."

Darla rushed into Leana's arms, sobbing. "Thank you," she sobbed. "Oh, thank you. You just don't know how hard it's been these past years. Without a father, life's been hard, forever."

Leana felt awkward. She still held the bloody manchette out away from her, and on the other hand held a sobbing waif. "From this point on, your life will be different," she murmured. "I'll see to it personally."

But deep down inside where her worries were formed, Leana wasn't so sure about this statement. Could she continue to even see to her own welfare, much less anyone else's . . . ? Only time would tell. . . .

Chapter Nineteen

A stealthy movement in her room aroused Leana from a deep sleep. She slowly leaned up on an elbow, squinting her eyes to search through the dark. When she saw movement she eased her hand beneath her pillow and clasped her fingers about her manchette, hoping she would again have the courage to use it. It had been a full week now since she had. Perhaps this intruder in the night was even the same man she had wounded, come back to get his revenge. Would such a wound she had inflicted have healed so quickly?

Barely breathing, she slipped the manchette from beneath the pillow and readied herself for the plunge. But when a familiar voice spoke to her from the darkness, she dropped the manchette, gasping.

"Brandon?" she whispered, now noticing a limp as he moved through the darkness toward her.

"I hope I didn't give you a fright coming in your room like this," Brandon said, now standing over her. "Leana, I need your help. *Cyril* needs your help."

Leana didn't need to hear anything else. She jumped

from the bed and searched through the dark until she found the kerosene lamp on her nightstand, and then a match. Out of the corner of her eyes she saw Brandon limp to the window and draw a curtain aside to look down from this second story onto the shadows of the street. Again she noticed his limp and her heart sank, realizing he had been wounded. When the lamp was lit, would she see him wounded even more severely? Would she . . . see . . . blood . . . ? The thought made an ache pierce her heart.

"What happened, Brandon?" she whispered back, realizing the danger he was in if caught in the town of Rufino. The general would probably even hang Brandon!

When the wick caught the flame of the match and began to softly glow, Leana's breath caught in her throat when she was fully able to see Brandon. She covered her mouth with her hand and emitted a soft, painful cry. "Lord! You've been wounded!" she said, seeing the blood on his chest and on the flowing sleeves of his shirt. "How . . . how . . . did you even manage to get here?"

Brandon looked down at the blood, then understood her horror. She thought the blood was *his.* In truth, it was a combination of many. He had done all that was humanly possible to save his wounded crew. But a few just hadn't made it. The rest had remained aboard the *Erebus,* patching its own sort of wounds!

Going to Leana, he took her hands, kissing the palm of one, then his dark eyes searched her face, then the soft swells of her breasts through the thin fabric of silken gown as it clung to her, having so desired to be with her again. And didn't the fear having caused such a flush make her even more ravishing? And her eyes! The tears made them resemble the sea for sure! Luminous in their mixtures of blues . . .

"Darling, only my leg has been wounded, but only barely," he said, yet seeing her eyes again moving to look at the blood splashes on him. "The blood is someone else's. Not mine."

Leana so wanted to fall into his arms, hug him to her, savor his nearness, so relieved to know that he had only a minor wound, yet the blood was a deterrent to her need, as though a wall being held between them.

Then she felt ashamed for thinking of her needs when she should be thinking of others. If not Brandon's blood, then whose . . . ? Perhaps Cyril's? Brandon had said that Cyril also needed her assistance!

"Who is wounded? Where are they? I'll do what I can. But we must be careful. What if General Rufino should discover you *or* any of your crew here? Where is Cyril?" she asked in a rush of words.

"We moved soundlessly through the night," Brandon said, again going to the window to peer from it. "And I have several men posted at vantage points." He nodded toward the lamp. "But it's best if you turn the wick lower, Leana. It might draw suspicion when most all other lamps in town are snuffed of flame."

Leana did as asked. She then jerked her sheet from her bed and handed it to Brandon. "Place this up to the window. Secure it over the curtain rod," she said softly. "It should block out light. I shall see to it, tomorrow, that drapes are placed to the window. Lacy curtains are not enough to keep prying eyes from seeing inside. I should've changed them even sooner. But being on the second floor, I felt safe enough from being seen. But with you here, we mustn't take a chance."

Again her gaze roamed over him, her hands going to

her throat. This reminded her of her duty. "What can I do? Just tell me, Brandon," she blurted. "I'll do anything to help."

"I knew I could depend on you," Brandon said, taking wide strides to the door. Swinging it open, he nodded to two men supporting Cyril between them. "Bring him in here. And be quick about it." Brandon stepped out into the hallway and looked about, then rushed back into Leana's room and closed the door noiselessly behind him.

Leana grabbed a robe and slipped into it, then stood, stunned, as Cyril was placed on her bed. His color was gray, his eyes were closed, and blood seeped from a wound on the right side of his chest. She looked at the two pirates watching Brandon now ministering to Cyril, in truth, Brandon's father figure, as Brandon stripped the blood-soaked shirt from Cyril.

Then Brandon stood back, pale himself, as he gazed down at Cyril. He began slowly shaking his head. "Damn," he muttered beneath his breath.

Then his eyes met and held with Leana's. "We need someone who knows something about doctoring," he said thickly. "And this someone must be trusted. Cyril has himself a nasty knife wound. If not treated quickly and accurately, he just might . . . not . . . make it."

"I know . . . of . . . no doctors," Leana said, her eyes slowly rising to see the deep concern in Brandon's. "And if there *was* a doctor in town, he couldn't be summoned. General Rufino would surely find out."

Then her eyes brightened in remembrance. She placed her hands to her cheeks. "Darla!" she softly exclaimed. "She cares for her mother. She seems to know much about medicines! Perhaps *she* can do something for Cyril!"

Without even waiting for Brandon to comment, she rushed from the room and to Darla's door. Knocking softly, she was glad when Darla came swiftly and let her in. After lighting a lamp, Leana took Darla's hands and clasped tightly to them.

"Brandon is here," Leana whispered. "And he's brought a wounded friend. Darla, do you think you might possibly know something about . . . knife . . . wounds . . . ?"

Darla's gray eyes fluttered nervously. "The only person I have ever treated for anything is my mother," she softly whispered. "I know nothing of open wounds that would be made by a knife."

"But surely you can think of something," Leana pleaded, squeezing Darla's hands harder. "This wounded man is more than a friend of Brandon's. There is a special bond between them. At least try, Darla. Please? If this man dies, I believe a part of Brandon will die with him."

"All right," Darla sighed. Leana stood by while Darla wrapped herself snugly in a robe, then gathered together things in a box and walked with Leana back to Leana's room.

Darla knelt over Cyril, something inside her strangely quivering when seeing so much about him that puzzled her. It was as though looking into a mirror, seeing herself as she would look if she were a man, his facial features were so much like her own. Her gaze took it all in . . . the slight crook of the nose, the color of his hair, able to see that it once had been as coal-black as hers, and then was drawn into the wonder of his eyes as he opened them and almost swallowed her in their grays. . . .

"Who is this man . . . ?" she asked, looking from Brandon to Leana.

"Cyril. Cyril Dalton," Brandon said, seeing the troubled expression on this young lady's face. "He . . . he is the captain of the ship *Erebus.*" He would not say that Cyril was a pirate. This might frighten the young thing off. And what was Leana doing bringing a mere lady to minister to Cyril?

Yet he would not question her reasonings. His trust of her decisions was complete. Surely the young miss knew *something* of doctoring, or why else would Leana have brought her here?

His gaze went to the box and all of the strange objects placed inside it. Besides the sterile bandages and iodine, nothing else looked familiar to him that might be used for ministering to wounds. He kneaded his chin, not so sure now. . . .

Cyril saw the young lady leaning over him through a shimmering haze, seeing so much about her that was familiar. He reached a shaky hand to her and tried to speak, yet he couldn't stop the drifting lethargy from again robbing him of consciousness.

"Why do you ask about the man, Darla?" Leana said, glad to see that Darla had brushed her wonder aside and was checking the wound.

"Oh, I don't know," Darla said, then gave Leana a quick glance. "Get me a clean basin of water. Make it lukewarm. I will do what I can."

She gave Brandon a wavering glance. "But I can promise nothing. I . . . I have only had my mother to care for," she murmured. "Hers is only a strange sort of illness. She has never had . . . had such a wound as this for me to look after."

Brandon stepped to Darla's side and gently placed a hand to her shoulder. "I understand," he said hoarsely.

"Just do what you can. I appreciate any efforts lended."

Brandon nodded toward the two men who had helped bring Cyril to the hotel. "Go back to the ship," he softly commanded. "Make sure it's well hidden. The damn Mexicans would burn it and everyone with it if they found it." He looked toward the window. "And move swiftly. The night is dark, but has many eyes."

"Aye, aye, sir," the men said in unison, then left the room.

Leana moved to Brandon's side. "How did all of this happen?" she asked softly as Darla cleaned Cyril's wound. "And surely your ship *is* in danger if it is close by."

"I know all hiding places for ships," Brandon said, slipping his blood-soaked shirt off, wadding it up in his hands, cringing when seeing Cyril flinch in his unconscious state as Darla continued to cleanse the wound. "And what happened? It was the damn Mexicans. We came across a ship carrying supplies to the port of Rufino. Of course we couldn't resist the fight."

"And? What ensued . . . ?" Leana asked breathlessly, envisioning two powerful ships in a battle at sea. She could even almost smell the gunfire, her imagination was so vivid!

"Though the *Erebus* was the recipient of many of the Mexicans' cannonballs, we blew the hell out of their ship and, thank God, all the ammunition and firearms carried aboard it," Brandon said gruffly. "This was one time I wished for no prize from the ship we approached. It was a devil ship for sure. I'm sure the Mexicans have plans for quite an attack against the Americans since the Indians have failed in their efforts to frighten the Americans back to the States."

His eyelids grew heavy over his eyes. He tossed his soiled shirt aside, then framed Leana's face between his hands. "You surely can't feel safe here in Rufino," he growled.

"I couldn't be any safer," Leana said firmly. "You see, the town is General Rufino's. If the Mexicans begin burning cities, this is the one town that won't be touched. General Rufino will be sending orders *from* this town."

"A much better argument for worrying about your safety," Brandon growled. "Leana, perhaps you should return to the States until it is safer."

"Never!" Leana hissed, moving his hands from her face. "And I *don't* fear the Mexican general. He seems to respect me for who I am and what I *do*. I think he likes strength and determination in a woman. I have proved that I have both."

"And you actually feel as though you can trust such intuitions?" Brandon said, raising an eyebrow quizzically. "You trust that bastard Mexican?"

"I never know who I can fully trust," Leana said, her face shadowing into a frown. "But I can assure you that nothing is going to happen to me."

"Leana?" Darla said from Cyril's bedside.

Leana hurried to Darla's side. "Yes? What do you need? What can I do?" she murmured.

"I need two things," Darla said, holding a cloth against Cyril's wound.

"What do you need? I'll get them if I have them. Surely what you need can be found in my general store," Leana said anxiously.

"Perhaps one ingredient, but maybe not the other," Darla said, smiling sheepishly up at Leana. "You do keep a spotless establishment."

Leana was taken aback by this last comment. What could her housekeeping have to do with anything? "Just tell me what you want and I shall get them if at all possible," she blurted.

"Get me a cup of soot from the insides of a fireplace chimney, and also several spiderwebs, if you can find any," Darla said, her eyes wide as she glanced from Leana to Brandon, who stood staring at her with their mouths gaping in disbelief.

"What . . . ?" Leana gasped.

"Leana, please . . ." Darla said. "Don't question this method. It is something taught me long ago by a swamp lady after I had been bitten by a deadly snake."

"All right. Whatever you say," Leana said, smiling crookedly over at Brandon. "I shall get the soot. Brandon, take a lamp and go to the attic and find some cobwebs. I'm sure they are there. I rarely go into the attic except to kill a rat when I hear one scampering about in the middle of the night."

Brandon laughed beneath his breath. He took Darla's lamp and Leana lit another for Darla, then they left with each other. When Leana and Brandon met again in the hallway before taking their findings in to Darla, they softly laughed and shook their heads.

"Strange as hell, don't you think?" Brandon said.

"Darla's been around," Leana said, smiling softly. "So I'm sure she's been taught many things, by many people."

They took the asked-for ingredients to Darla and then stood by, watching, awestruck, as Darla began stuffing Cyril's wound with first a portion of the soot and then the spider webs until the bleeding stopped and the wound seemed to almost magically lose the rawness at its edges.

Darla sighed deeply, placed a hand to her back, and stood up away from the bed. She gave Leana and then Brandon another sheepish smile. "Well, that ought to do it," she said, stretching her arms over her head. "And since I won't be needed any longer, I think I'll go back to bed." She glanced down at Cyril. "We'll know by morning if he'll pull through." She gave Leana a soft look. "What he needs is much quiet and rest. I would suggest you and Brandon go to another room and get your own rest. Check on him first thing in the morning, and if you need me again, come for me."

"What if he becomes feverish in the middle of the night?" Brandon worried, kneading his brow.

"I truly don't think there is any worry of fever," Darla reassured. "From what I've observed, he's going to be all right."

"Then you do truly suggest we leave him alone?" Leana asked, giving Cyril a half glance from across her shoulder.

"Yes. Quite," Darla said, glancing down at Brandon's leg, having noticed his limp. Then she gave Leana another soft smile. "You might have your own doctoring to do. Seems Brandon has also been wounded."

Leana's face grew pale. Through all their worries of Cyril, she had failed to think even once of Brandon and his newly acquired limp. "Oh, Brandon, how could I have neglected worrying over you?" she softly cried.

"It's only a bruise," Brandon shrugged. "A topsail fell. I didn't move quickly enough to get out of its way. No more than a slight blow to my thigh, Leana."

Leana locked her arm through his, her chin held high. "But enough for me to do my own sort of nursing," she said, giving Darla a wink from across her shoulder.

"Come with me. I think I can find a vacant room in my establishment."

Darla handed Brandon a lighted lamp, smiling warmly up at him as he gave her a wondering glance. "I don't think I'll be needed this time," she said, now covering Cyril with a blanket.

Before blowing the lamp out beside his bed, Darla again studied him. Why, oh, why did so much about him cause pain to circle her heart? She didn't even know him! Why should she care what happened to him? Though Brandon hadn't said the words, she knew that this man was a pirate. How was it that so much about him made her think that he was much more than that . . . to . . . her . . . ?

Confused, she blew out the light and left him to return to her own room. Restless, unable to even think about going to bed, she lit a cheroot and paced the room. And when the cheroot was only a stub and crushed into an ashtray, she decided to check in on her mother.

Going to her mother's room, Darla heard her mother whispering in her sleep, yet Darla couldn't make out the words. But she knew by the expression on her mother's face that she was again dreaming about a man of her past . . . a man she loved; yet, while awake, she had always refused to share the identity of the man of her dreams with Darla.

Feeling so alone, Darla went back to her room and fell into a troubled sleep. . . .

Chapter Twenty

The room was small, only enough space for a bed. Brandon placed the kerosene lamp to the floor, lowering its wick to the point where only a shimmer of fire glowed orange on its inch-wide tip. Leana felt as though her whole body was a massive heartbeat, so close to Brandon, his breath was hot on her cheek.

"I so want you to kiss me," she whispered, looking up into his eyes, mesmerized by the heated passion in their dark depths. "Oh, how I've missed you, my love."

Brandon's loins ached, yet he knew that he must hold himself as well as Leana at bay until he had the stench of death washed from his flesh. He didn't want the sweetness of her spoiled by his own unsavory aromas.

"I want to do more than kiss you, Leana," he said huskily. "But first I must ask you for a basin of water. I don't want to transfer my smell to you."

Leana's eyes wavered, seeing the dried blood on his chest and lower on his leather breeches. "Yes, I can see why you would feel that way," she murmured. "Let me fix you a warm basin of water." Her eyes twinkled devilishly as she then looked up at him. "But only if you will let me bathe you, darling."

"What . . . ?" Brandon said, chuckling. His hair lay tousled boyishly about his face, loosened from its leather string; there were dark smudges on his nose and cheeks. "No woman has ever bathed me before. As I recollect, my mother never even entered my room when I bathed as a child. As far back as I can recall, I demanded to be left to my bath alone."

Leana cast him a wicked look from the corners of her eyes as she tilted her head. "Darling, the bath I speak of giving you is not the sort one's mother gives a child," she softly laughed. "Especially not one's *son*. I would hope that my way of giving you a bath would be much more, would you say, seductive?"

Her gaze darted down to his leg, she again having become careless as to forget his bruise. "But, of course, your leg will receive the first of my attentions," she quickly blurted.

Smiling coyly up at him, she caught the glimmer in his eyes and knew that he fully understood what she was about.

"Well? What are you waiting for?" he teased, giving her a light smack on her behind.

"I won't be gone long."

"Any time away from you is too long."

Leana turned and rushed away with the lamp, leaving him to stand in the darkness until her return. Brandon went to the window and drew the curtain aside and let his gaze scan the streets, the moonlight being only a sliver in the sky, not affording him a good enough look where he had posted his men. It was late. It was quiet. Not even the saloons were open.

289

But in a few short hours, the sun would be rising and nothing would be hidden from the Mexicans' watchful eyes. It was imperative that Cyril be moved into the Big Thicket before this dangerous time of morning.

Brandon swung away from the window and began pacing. Would Cyril be in any shape to be moved? Yet Brandon knew that it was not only placing Cyril's life in jeopardy by staying in Rufino, but most of all, Leana's.

Yes, the move must be made. And as soon as he had shared a few hours with Leana in the way in which he had dreamed since their last time together, Cyril would be taken home. It seemed that nothing else could be done for his wound. Strange as it seemed, Darla had seemed to patch him up quite well. Cobwebs? Soot?

Brandon chuckled. "Damn. Damn," he whispered. "Some swamp folk nonsense used on Cyril?"

Light footsteps and a faint sweep of light entering the room behind Brandon drew him around. He hurried to Leana and helped her with the basin of water, laughing softly, wondering how she had managed to balance the basin of water in one hand while carrying the lamp with the other. A smell as sweet as roses floated up into his nose and he then saw the round bar of soap, designed in the shape of a red rose, floating in the water, as well as a washcloth edged in white lace.

Leana placed the lamp on the floor, then closed and locked the door. But remembering the window and its thin curtain, she did the same as she had in the room where Cyril now lay. She handed Brandon a blanket to tuck over the rod, to ensure them of full privacy.

"Kind sir, after assuring our privacy with this blanket over the window, you can remove your *clothes*," Leana said, smiling seductively up at Brandon.

"I will remove mine if you will remove yours," Brandon teased as he spun around and faced Leana, taking the blanket, placing it to the window. "Fair is fair, don't you think?"

"It is not I who needs the bath," Leana teased back, flipping her hair back from her shoulders. "So why should I undress?"

Brandon's long, lean fingers went to her robe and swept it back from her shoulders, letting it flutter to lay in a heap about her ankles. And then his fingers went to the thin straps of her silk gown; he tucked his thumbs beneath each and slowly, teasingly eased them across the smoothness of her shoulders, stopping when they were at the very edges.

Leana's insides were mushy from passion, yet she was disappointed when he didn't continue with his playful ways of disrobing her. "Why did you stop?" she asked, her lips curling into a pout.

"I thought you said you didn't need a bath," he said mockingly. He sat down on the bed and began tugging on one of his black leather knee-high boots. "So why must I bother with removing your gown? You *do* look so lovely in silk."

"Oh? Is that how you truly perfer me?" Leana continued to pout.

"Darling, your face would flush crimson if I put into words how I prefer you," Brandon chuckled, dropping one boot, struggling with the other.

"Tell me," she said in a husky whisper. "Brandon, make me feel shameful. I love to feel wicked while with you. I've never felt that way while with another man. I've never *been* with another man. But you . . . know . . . that. . . ."

Brandon tossed his other boot aside and rose to stand before Leana. She stood on tiptoe and ran her tongue across his lips. "Lord, will you hurry and get those damn clothes off?" she then blurted, strolling away from him, standing with her arms folded impatiently across her chest, watching him.

"I see my absence has heightened the playful side of you," Brandon said, smiling devilishly down at her as he began unfastening his leather breeches. "I like that, Leana. But remember to reserve that side of you for me . . . only me."

Leana's pulse raced as the part of him was exposed to her eyes that she had been so pleasured by. She then felt as though she had been behaving as a brazen hussy, no better than a street whore in her craziness, and made her eyes dart upward, yet her admiring, hungry glances having been caught by Brandon.

"Well?" Brandon said, gesturing with his hands as his breeches were kicked away from him. "I thought you were so eager to give me a bath."

He glanced toward the small basin of water. "Yet I would argue my skills at being able to sit in such a small tub of water," he chuckled.

His eyes grew hazy with desire as he let them wander back to her. "Ah, but what I could do with a large tub of water right now. I would teach you something about giving a bath."

Leana laughed softly. "Brandon, do you forget that you already have?" she said.

"Oh? And when?"

"The time I had to have the whale oil bathed from my skin."

He threw his head back into a soft laugh. "Damn. How

could I have forgotten?" he said. He went to her and ran a forefinger over the soft curve of her jaw. "But I did one hell of a job, didn't I? You've smelled of jasmine ever since." He placed his nose to the hollow of her throat and inhaled. "As you do even now." His lips were hot as he pressed them against her flesh, and his tongue tasted. "And you still taste like something between expensive French cologne and a bouquet of lilacs plucked from the forest, your aroma is so sweet and intoxicating."

Hardly able to stand it any longer, her insides wild with want of him, Leana shoved him away from her. "Brandon, it's pure torture having to put off what we both so want," she said thickly. She nodded toward the bed. "Please stretch out on the bed. Let me wash you free of all memories of your sea battle with the Mexicans. And then let my body . . . my lips . . . my hands clear your memories of everything but me."

"I couldn't ask for more than that," Brandon said, going to jump on the bed. He stretched out on his back and spread his arms and legs out, watching her as she walked gracefully to the bed, one strap of her gown having lowered completely down and away from her shoulder, revealing the satiny gloss of her right breast. He hungered to set his teeth and tongue to that breast, but he knew patience was required and then he would *consume* her . . . *fully* consume every inch of her. . . .

Leana's fingers trembled as she knelt down over him and began soaping him with the wet cloth and bar of soap. She could see the rippling of his abdomen muscles when she touched him lightly there. She could hear the intake of his breath when she barely brushed his risen manhood with the back of a hand. Slowly she teased him with the cloth, hating the teasing, yet finding it quite effective in the way his eyes were closed and his teeth clenched.

And then the temptation became too great. She felt that he smelled as sweet as a garden of roses. His skin even glowed from her washing. And while his eyes were still closed, awaiting further strokes of the cloth, she hiked her gown up enough so that she could straddle him and lowered her mouth to his glistening, stiffened manhood and gave its tip a light kiss. She smiled as the spot she kissed quivered, and when she felt hands on her arms, urging her upward, she welcomed his lips as he urged her to lie down upon him.

With a spinning head and sweetness entering her heart, Leana spun her fingers through his hair and drew his mouth even closer to hers. She shimmered with ecstasy as his hands slid her gown down and away from her and he fully cupped her breasts and kneaded them. And then when he wrapped his arms about her and caused her breasts to press against the hardness of his bare chest, a soft cry of joy escaped from between her lips, against his.

"Take me," she murmured, drawing her lips from his to look down into the haunting darkness of his eyes. "Brandon, love me. Fully love me now. I need you so."

Brandon managed to turn her so that she was now beneath him. His fingers went beneath her and pressed into her hips and lifted her to meet his swift entrance inside her. She moaned as he so magnificently filled her with his hardness. His strokes were even, were luscious. His lips paid homage to first one breast and then another.

Leana's hands never lay still. She wanted to touch him all over, memorize every inch of him, to cherish and savor in her dreams while he was again away from her.

She knew that he was again here with her for only a moment in time. Hating to, yet knowing that was the way it must be for now, she accepted this truth and closed her mind to all tomorrows. There was only now, only Brandon, only the sheer pleasure he was again sharing with her.

Brandon lifted his powerful man's strength in and out of Leana, absorbing the wet warmth that greeted each of his strokes inside her. He buried his face into the delicate taper of her neck and nibbled her flesh. He was almost wild with the way her hands worked along his body, now at his buttocks squeezing, probing. She was skilled and he was proud, for he knew that he had been her teacher. . . .

And then their bodies arched against each other, both feeling release near. Flesh shimmered against flesh, lips sought lips, and then soft moans of complete pleasure were shared. . . .

Leana's hair was damp against her face. She could feel perspiration on Brandon's chest as she kissed him about his nipples. "Oh, why can't it last forever?" she whispered. "Why must you even leave?" She gave him a heavy lashed look. "For you see, I know that you must. And soon. I know that you plan to leave before daylight."

Brandon leaned up on an elbow, cocking an eyebrow. "Oh? And how did you know that?" he asked.

"While I was getting the basin of water, I saw a wagon being positioned at my back door," she said, moving to her knees over him. "How would your men know to do that if they didn't know even know if Cyril would be able to be moved?"

"Whether he had lived or died, or if he was even hanging on to life, I had planned to take him away from

295

here," Brandon said, touching her face with the palm of his hand. "I have endangered you enough by coming here in the first place. But I had to. I had to find someone to help with Cyril's wound. Seems I came to the right place."

Leana leaned her cheek into his palm, trembling with ecstasy at his mere touch. "Where will you go?" she asked softly. "If your ship is so damaged, will it carry you to safety?"

"By now the ship should already be moved to its usual resting place," Brandon said matter-of-factly.

Leana's eyes widened. She looked Brandon directly in the eyes. "That has to mean that when you leave here, you will be taking him to your hideaway on land," she said in a gasp. She leaned down closer to his face. "Brandon, *where?*"

Brandon's insides tightened. It wasn't fair that he couldn't share this truth with Leana when Cyril had gone against all they had ever said about taking women to their mansion in the Big Thicket.

Yet Brandon knew that now wasn't the time for him to *also* break this promise shared by Brandon and Cyril. Times were too dangerous. One day he would be free to take her there, but not now. . . .

"I can't say right now," Brandon said, drawing her into his arms, relishing the feel of her body pressed against his. "But I promise to take you there one day. You will be in for quite a surprise," he chuckled.

"Oh, all right," Leana sighed. "I have learned to wait for everything that has to do with you, it seems. If I didn't love you so much . . ."

Brandon pressed his forefinger to her lips, sealing

them of further words. "But you *do*," he said thickly. "As I also love you, darling. And thank you for not prodding me with further questions. That makes me know that you *do* trust me. Trust is important between two people in love."

She eased his finger aside. "How can you expect to get through the town of Rufino without being caught?" she asked, worried.

Brandon laughed lightly. "My dear, we will pull the brims of sombreros low over our eyes and wrap Mexican blankets about our shoulders. Me and a couple of my men will sit slouched on the seat of the wagon as old men about their early-morning business. Cyril will be spread out beneath more blankets, surrounded by fresh vegetables. Now, who would think to stop and question?"

"I will worry so. . . ." Leana sighed, snuggling into his arms, hugging him to her.

"There's nothing to fear," Brandon said, kissing her cheek. "I've learned much about life since having become acquainted with Cyril, and one important teaching was how to protect my hide."

He laughed, then kissed her with a fiery urgency. "But, darling, Cyril never taught me how much I could love a lady," he said, drawing only slightly away from her. "Never had I thought it possible, until you."

"When I think that we may have never met, I grow so cold inside," Leana said, visibly shivering. "And if I ever *lost* you now that I *have* found you, I would also want to die."

"Then, my dear, don't fret," he chuckled. "You will live and love *forever*."

Leana sighed and again became enraptured by him,

knowing that time with him this night was drawing to a too brief close. She only had a short while now before morning would come with its revealing light. She loved Brandon all the harder, with an urgency, oh, so fearing this light and the awakening of all the Mexicans in the city of Rufino. . . .

Chapter Twenty-One

Now at his mansion in the Big Thicket, Brandon lay somewhere between being asleep and awake, his full night having been filled with dreams of Leana and her loveliness. A soft rustling sound from somewhere close by made him stir on his bed and force one eye sleepily open. In the soft light of morning he thought he might be seeing an apparition as something voluminous and silken seemed to be floating toward him.

Blinking his eyes and leaning up on an elbow, the drawn draperies at his windows giving only a slight slant of light from their very edges, Brandon watched the white billows of silk and lace move toward him.

His heart began to pound, his blood was growing hot, this apparition now taking the form of a lady, and in the dim light he couldn't make out the facial features nor the color of the hair.

What mattered most to his eyes was the way the silk gown clung and then flowed out away from the lady, only momentarily revealing the outline of the magnificence of the breasts that lay beneath the thin material.

Having been so filled with dreams of Leana, Brandon held his arms out and spoke her name, thinking that surely he was still dreaming. . . .

"Leana . . . ?" he said huskily. "How did you find the pirate mansion?"

He swallowed hard when seeing more of the satin figure which swayed and silently spoke back to him as only a woman's body could. His loins were aching, his throat was dry.

When the lady reached the bed and soft arms enfolded Brandon, he moaned throatily, feeling hands arousing him, lips almost smothering him in their eager hotness. Flames shot through him . . . that which only experienced when feeling the intense desire for a woman.

Weaving his fingers through her hair, he forced her mouth to his. He turned their bodies so that he was now on top and he crushed his lips down upon hers, fitting his body into the sensuous curves of hers. He lifted her gown and again groaned when letting his free hand explore the utter softness of her buttocks and then around, where her triangle of hair came into a soft vee between her legs.

Gyrating hips against him made him not dally any longer with only his hands. He fit himself inside this body of tempting desires and began his fiery strokes. He became even more inflamed when letting a hand find and squeeze one of her breasts, feeling the nipple grow hard between his thumb and forefinger.

"Leana . . ." Brandon whispered, perspiration lacing his brow. The edges of the drapes disclosed more light, and a slant of sunshine fell across the lady's face, illuminating the wickedness in her eyes and the witchlike smile as she looked up at Brandon.

Brandon drew away from her as though shot, recognizing Cyril's wench, Wanda. He stared down at Wanda in disbelief, wondering how this could have happened. Had she cast an evil spell over him? Did she have such a power . . . ? How could he have thought her to be his beloved Leana . . . ?

Oh, Lord, what lust for a woman's body could do to a man's mind!

Stumbling from the bed, wrapping a blanket about himself, Brandon glared down at Wanda, who lay splendidly beautiful in the silken folds of her nightgown, her hair as though a red halo about her flushed face.

"How dare you come to my room like this," he hissed, yet still frustrated from having come so close to making love to Cyril's woman, and betraying Leana at the same *time*. "I've been right about you all along. You belong in the gutter. You're a whore and will never be anything *but*."

Wanda brushed her gown down over her legs and slipped easily from the bed, having lost in her experiment. Cyril had made her know what true romance was. She had feared that now that he had been wounded, he might no longer want her. She had to see if he was worth fighting for . . . if he was the only man who could arouse her.

If she could feel something with Brandon, then she would fight for *him*. He was younger, he was much more handsome. And his riches were the same as Cyril's. And she *had* felt *much* with Brandon. He even had more skills in lovemaking than Cyril.

But, alas, he did seem to detest her so. She had to concentrate on keeping Cyril as her own. At any cost, she would be Cyril's woman!

She went to Brandon and ran a hand over his cheek.

301

"But of course you won't tell Cyril," she purred. "The stress could kill him, you know. He's still quite weak from his injury."

Brandon grabbed her by the wrist and drew her close and leaned down and spoke in a growl into her face. "Now you listen to me, slut," he said. "Cyril will find out in his own way just what you are. Somehow you will give yourself away. But, no, it won't be I who will reveal the truth to Cyril. He *is* too ill at this time. And later, ah, yes, you will give yourself away. All I need do is wait."

He shoved her away from him. "Now get out of here. You've wasted your time with me."

He gestured with a wild fling of the hand. "There are many of our pirate crew who would like to have their way with you," he said in a snarl. "Go seek them out. But a warning, my fair lady, once you give yourself to one, you will have to give yourself to all. They are all starved for a woman, as most men are, no matter the hour of the day or night."

"I don't wish for anyone but Cyril," Wanda hissed, placing her hands on her hips. "You? You were just an experiment."

Brandon threw his head back into a hearty laugh, then sobered and glared toward Wanda. "I would suggest you try no more *experiments* around here," he said dryly. "In fact, I would warn you to watch your every step. It would delight me to see you caught up in your little scheme with Cyril."

Wanda stepped closer to Brandon, her eyes wicked slants as she peered up into his face. "If you do anything to spoil what I have here with Cyril, I will kill you," she spat. "So I would suggest you watch behind you, every turn of the way, filthy pirate."

Brandon let the blanket drop from around him. He raised a hand and struck Wanda across her face. "That was a first for me," he growled. "I have never struck a woman before. You deserve even worse for threatening me and for what you are doing with Cyril." He placed a fist to her face. "And heed my warning, bitch; don't you ever try anything with me again. I shall feed you to the swamp alligators."

Wanda rubbed her face where it was hot from the blow. She could even feel Brandon's finger imprints in her flesh as she stumbled toward the door. She knew that Brandon was a man of his word and she feared him. But now, she feared even more Cyril. Surely Brandon would tell him everything once Cyril was well enough to be told. If Cyril ever found out about her, would he toss her to his pirates as though she were a piece of meat to be chewed up and spit out?

The thought made her ill. She turned and ran away from Brandon, to Cyril's bedroom. Slipping inside, tiptoeing silently across the carpeted floor, she saw how Cyril lay so still, so pale beneath the soft shimmer of a candle at his bedside.

Crying, Wanda crept into his bed and lay down beside him, cuddling close. "Cyril, please don't stop loving me," she whispered, now truly fearing more than loving him. She knew the power of this man. She sniffled and then smiled devilishly when Cyril stirred and eased an arm about her shoulder.

"Why are . . . you . . . crying . . . ?" Cyril asked, wiping a tear from her pink cheek.

Wanda rose to an elbow, her eyes wide, tear-streaked. She almost shouted with happiness when knowing that Cyril was so much improved this day. Until now he had yet to even notice her presence when she had been beside his bed, sitting vigil. Not until now. . . .

"Oh, Cyril, you're going to be all right," she cried, throwing herself into his arms. When he winced with pain, she drew away and again cuddled next to his side. "Why was I crying? Only because I have missed you so."

Cyril turned and gazed upon her face. Though his eyes were hazy from pain and the medication of laudanum, he could see what resembled a handprint on one of her cheeks. "Wanda, yer face . . ." he said, forking an eyebrow. "Why is the one . . . cheek . . . so . . . so . . . much redder than the other?"

Wanda's heart skipped a beat. "Why, that is only from crying, darling," she said, covering Brandon's handprint with a hand. She grew cold inside, knowing that Cyril might have even been strong enough to walk this morning, and he might have caught her . . . with . . . Brandon. . . .

"Well, you can quit cryin'," Cyril reassured, kissing her on the brow. "As you see, I'm quite all right. I'll be back on my *Erebus* before you can snap yer little finger."

"Oh, please don't leave again so soon," Wanda groaned. "I . . . get . . . so lonely."

Cyril sighed heavily, now knowing he had to send her away. She was becoming a nuisance. Well, he would wait until he was well. He would be able to handle her much better then. Ah, but she must be blindfolded and taken aboard a ship and exchanged for something else worth much more. She would be worth many gold trinkets!

He closed his eyes and let sleep soothe his thoughts. He dreamed of the sea, instead of a lady's arms. . . .

*　　　*　　　*

Disturbed and frustrated by the confrontation with Wanda, Brandon mounted his stallion, thinking that perhaps this was the perfect time to confront Matthew again. If Cyril was so determined to keep this wench with him, then Brandon would have his own separate life, away from them. It was time to tell Matthew that he was going to claim what was rightfully his after all.

Brandon *had* been the first son born to Parker Seton. Brandon had never before hesitated taking what he desired. With Matthew and the Seton wealth, he wouldn't either.

And didn't part of the Seton wealth belong to Leana? As she had spoken of Parker Seton, Brandon had been witness to such a devotion that had formed between stepfather and stepdaughter hardly ever heard of before.

But who wouldn't have been drawn into the sweetness of Leana, *and* she the love of Parker Seton, Brandon remembering him so vividly as good-hearted and generous. It seemed hard to accept . . . this knowing that Parker Seton had embezzled money from his bank in New York. It seemed that no one had known Parker Seton at all well. . . .

Making his way through the Big Thicket, Brandon again became enamored by it, this region of enormous trees and scattered swamps, laced with dense tangles of yaupon and titi, interspersed with open savannas. Earlier pioneers had bypassed this region, thinking it to be impenetrable, too foreboding to homestead. It was in truth the home of the panther, the bear, the wolf, and the ivory-bellied woodpecker, and now the pirate mansion.

The Big Thicket seemed a dark and menacing wilderness to most, but to Brandon, it had been a perfect place to hide away, until recently, when the need to be kept hidden was the furthest thing from his mind. He hungered to settle down, make a home . . . a home for his Leana, and their future children.

But deep down inside him, he wondered if his restless side would again eventually win over this desire for a life with just Leana. . . .

Not wanting to think of this possibility, Brandon spurred his horse faster along the path he had made through the forest, the horse's hooves occasionally making sucking sounds as they thudded into mud, traveling through the old sweet gums and loblollies, while parula warblers buzzed in the canopy of trees above, and Carolina wrens sang exuberantly.

And then the big sky and far-off horizon that Texas was best known for was finally reached. Brandon scooted his sombrero back from his brow, welcoming the heat of the sun on his face. His attire was that opposite of what he wore while riding the high seas. He wore a blue plaid cotton shirt with a neckerchief at his throat where his shirt was left half-unbuttoned. He wore coarse denim jeans and boots with high heels.

Wheeling his white stallion around, he headed it in the direction of the Seton ranch, finding it hard to not send his horse in another direction . . . toward town, where Leana most surely watched and waited for him daily.

But she knew that he had business to attend to, yet not having any idea that this business included her stepbrother, Matthew Seton. . . .

At a full gallop now, Brandon absorbed the scene about him. The land seemed to him now a treasure greater than gold . . . endlessly abundant, thickly carpeted in grass and trees, fertile beyond dreams. Brandon had heard many pioneers spinning tales of twelve-foot cotton plants in soil so rich that "if you put tenpenny nails in the ground, you would have a crop of iron bolts." ‧

Brandon's interest was mostly the horses and longhorns running wild on this land. He could envision a future of riches being made by possession of such animals. The thought of working with these wild beasts caused a thrill to surge through his blood. It was the same as that first time he had felt the love and adventure of being a part of the sea after his abduction.

"Damn if I'm not torn by wanting the sea *and* the land," he growled, tightening his gloved hands on the reins of his horse. "Which will win in the end? And didn't choosing the land over the sea also mean choosing Leana . . . ?"

He rode even faster, enjoying the wind against his face, feeling wildly free. And then, when he saw the tall fortress of a fence that had been built about the Seton ranch, leaving only the corral and the few outbuildings on the outside, he drew his reins taut and commanded his horse to stop.

"Matthew's scared as hell," Brandon whispered. "He's just as I thought he'd be. A coward."

Smiling, he rode onward. He circled the fence, seeing a lone figure of a man in the distance, chasing wild mustangs. Brandon squinted his eyes and cupped a hand over them to shield them from the sun, then recognized his brother, surprised that he would be alone, away from the house. Coward? No. Stupid!

In a trot, Brandon rode toward the herd of mustangs, keeping an eye on Matthew, surprised that his brother had learned the skill of a rope so quickly. When close enough to fully observe, Brandon drew his stallion to a shuddering halt and rested his weight on his saddle horn and watched Matthew, who was unaware of being observed. . . .

Matthew, with one end of a thirty-foot oxhide rope snubbed to his saddle horn, galloped into the mustang herd and dropped the noose end of his rope over the neck of a lively beast. Matthew wheeled his horse, tightening the noose, then dragged the struggling mustang until it fell, choking, to the ground.

Jumping from his horse, Matthew blindfolded the mustang's eyes and jammed a huge bit into its mouth as the mustang moved shakily back to its feet. Matthew then put on a pair of spurs six inches long with rowels like penknives and jumped on the mustang's back, urging the mustang to its very utmost speed. When the mustang resisted, Matthew pulled roughly at the bit, tearing the horse's mouth, causing blood to flow from it in streams.

Matthew drove the horse onward, punishing, teaching, until Brandon could stand no more. He yelled at his horse, Cotton, thrust the heels of his boots into his horse's flanks, and rode in the direction of the bleeding mustang and Matthew.

His guts were twisting at the sight of the torture his brother kept inflicting upon this beautiful animal. Surely there were gentler ways to tame a wild thing other than that being used by Matthew! If Matthew was allowed to continue on, the mustang would soon drop of sheer exhaustion and pain. The wildness of the horse would be completely punished out of him, but also his spirit, that which was so important in any living thing!

Gaining ground, Brandon ducked low to his horse's mane, shouting at him. And the closer he came to Matthew, the more he saw the blood on the wild mustang, now where Matthew's hideous spurs were gouging . . .

gouging . . . gouging. . . .

Brandon readied himself. He straightened his back and came alongside Matthew. And before Matthew could even guess what was about to happen, Brandon had jumped from his stallion and had grabbed Matthew from the mustang, and both landed in a thud on the ground.

"What . . . the . . . ?" Matthew yelled. And then he was aware of dark eyes burrowing down into his as Brandon managed to get atop, to straddle him.

"Brandon? What . . . are . . . you doing . . . ?" Matthew gasped, his back aching and his knees skinned from the fall.

"Now I see why Leana dislikes you so," Brandon snarled down into Matthew's face. "From a coward has emerged a thoughtless, cruel bastard!"

"Leana . . . ?" Matthew said, panting.

"Don't act as though you don't know of whom I'm speaking," Brandon warned. "Though you *have* chosen to act as though she never existed in the Seton family. Why *have* you forgotten about her? Hadn't you even thought to go into Rufino to check on her?"

Matthew's face shadowed in a frown. "Leana? I was giving her time to see that she could not do without me," he laughed sardonically. "But now she has you? How convenient."

"She needs no one," Brandon said, grabbing Matthew by the collar, jerking his head up from the ground, snarling more down into his face. "If you had thought to check on your stepsister, you would have found out that she has made herself quite a profitable establishment in Rufino. And it was our father who gave her the means to *do* this."

Brandon leaned into Matthew's face. "Surely this

309

wasn't done in secret because father felt he couldn't trust you?" he goaded sarcastically.

"How . . . do . . . you know Leana?" Matthew stammered, ouching when Brandon tightened his hold on his collar, almost choking him.

"That's none of your business," Brandon said, then dropped Matthew's head back down to the ground as he moved jerkily to his feet. He gave the wild mustang a hard look, seeing the horse standing almost lifeless, removed of all his spirit.

Matthew's gaze followed Brandon's. "Was it the mustang or Leana that caused you to storm me by surprise?" he said, inching up from the ground.

Brandon reached for his hat and hit it against the thigh of his leg, sending dust flying from its brim. "Neither was my purpose," Brandon said, glaring at Matthew. "I came to claim what's mine." He again glanced over at the horse. "But after seein' what I saw this morning, I'm not sure if I want a part in this thing called ranchin'. It may not be for me."

"Can't stomach it, huh?" Matthew laughed, plopping his own hat on his head.

Brandon's eyes narrowed in fury. "You just said the wrong thing, little brother," he growled. "Leana *and* I will take what's ours."

Matthew went pale. Then he squared his jaw. "You wouldn't dare try anything," he warned. "I'd turn you in to the authorities. Wouldn't the Americans *and* the Mexicans love to know that a pirate is available for them to come and hang?"

"Don't get so smug," Brandon laughed. He grabbed his reins and swung himself up into his saddle. "I think I know of a few people who'd give their eyeteeth to know *your* whereabouts."

Matthew gaped at Brandon and idly scratched his chin. "What the hell are you talking about?" he asked, forking an eyebrow. "I haven't had trouble with the law."

"Maybe not you, but our *father*," Brandon said, laughing lightly. "Seems a lot of his profits you are living on came from embezzling money from his bank."

"What . . . ?" Matthew gasped, taking a step backward.

"Now, I don't think the authorities would hesitate at coming and demanding the money returned to them, do you?" Brandon said smugly. "As for me? I've had enough of you for one day. I need the fresh air only found at sea to cleanse me of the smell of you."

He whirled his stallion around and began galloping away. "But I'll be back, Matthew," he shouted. "I'll be back. . . ."

Chapter Twenty-Two

Conditions in Rufino had deteriorated to the point that even the poor were afraid to come into the city to make their bargains with Leana. And fearing for their welfare, she had begun to deliver food to them. At first she had been afraid to wander alone, but General Rufino had given orders to his Mexican soldiers to leave her be to her whimsical ways, in silence still admiring her adventurous, daring personality.

But not fully trusting the Mexicans *nor* the Indians, Leana had chosen to dress as a man while traveling to the homes on the far, outlying reaches of Rufino. Leana knew that she made a comical sight in her loose breeches and shirt with a sombrero hiding her hair beneath it and its brim low over her face.

Even now, as she rode the buckboard wagon along the muddy road, she bent low, keeping her eyes moving in all directions, her pistol weighting her down at the hip, the sheathed manchette secured at the calf of her leg a constant reminder of Brandon.

Snapping the reins, she urged the horse onward, yet

her gaze was now steady, looking into the Big Thicket, slowly being drawn into its mystique. Parker Seton had spoken of buried treasure, mystic lights that wavered from tree to tree in the darkness of night, and of hidden bands of pirates.

She had often wondered if Brandon's hideaway could possibly be in the Big Thicket. Were the lights Parker spoke about lights carried by *pirates?* It made sense that the pirates might use this place as a hideaway except that the trees and ground tangle were so intensely thick, how could one even make his way through to the other side *of* the thicket?

Tightening the reins about her hands, Leana drew the horse to a halt. Her heart pounded out her anxiousness to explore. She had a gun and a knife should a snake or anything even less desirable try to attack her.

Glancing back at her wagon, seeing it empty of wares, having just made her last delivery of the day, she felt it safe enough to abandon, for a while, at least. What could it hurt? She would only go a little way into the thicket. If she could only find some sort of path . . .

Determined, Leana jumped from the wagon and secured her horse's reins on a low tree limb, then took a deep breath as she stood and decided the best way of entry into the thicket. Spanish moss hung beardlike from great oaks; resurrection ferns grew like pale green fur along the branches of huge cypress trees.

A stream reached out dark and snakelike beneath these trees, making the break in the dense growth that Leana was needing. Though the edges of the stream were muddy and overgrown with tall weeds, Leana began making her way along beside it. And the farther she walked, the darker it became, as though night had fallen around her, the forest ceiling was so thickly entangled.

And then there would be a spray of sunlight ahead, giving her direction. She gasped low when she suddenly made out a winding path through the trees and the prints of horses' hooves in the spongy mud of the path.

"So someone *does* frequent the thicket," she whispered, hope rising inside her like a flaming candle burning brighter. Could . . . it . . . be Brandon . . . ?

Securing her sombrero more tightly on her head, she moved onward, ignoring the slant of the sun in the sky when she could see it, not thinking that true night would soon be there in its total darkness. She was too lost in excitement and hope of discovery to remember to think of her safety. . . .

Perspiring from the dampness closing in on her, Leana followed the path that led around huge, scaly-barked pines, hundred-foot-tall magnolias, and gray-barked beeches.

Her gaze captured lady ferns, their fiddleheads just unfolding, and vines of sweet-smelling yellow jasmine. A carnivorous pitcher plant was dining on an insect caught in its translucent craw, and Leana gasped in awe when she found quite a display of orchids at her right side. The many orchids were like ladies' tresses, flourishing in cloistered serenity.

Stopping, Leana cupped an orchid in her hand, yet she couldn't fully enjoy its loveliness, for she sensed that she was no longer alone. Turning, she let her gaze slowly scan the trees about her and then the path from where she had just traveled. The sound had not been that of a horse, but of stealthy footsteps, and then a snapping of a twig.

Growing coldly numb with fear, Leana tensed, realizing she had come much too far. She couldn't even see the outer edges of the thicket, where she had left her horse and wagon awaiting her return. And as she peered upward where splashes of sunshine had only moments ago been seen, all that could be seen was a sky darkening in purplish blacks.

"Oh, Lord, it's getting dark," she gasped, placing a hand over her mouth. "I must return to my wagon."

Turning, taking rushed steps back along the path, she panted, her pulse pounding in the hollow of her throat. And as it grew darker and darker, she struggled with seeing the path, suddenly having disappeared ahead of her into tangled undergrowth.

A wolf howled, causing the hair at the nape of Leana's neck to rise. The screech of a panther made her grow pale with fear.

Trying to hurry onward, she began stumbling, catching the toe of her boots on gnarled roots of trees growing up through the ground. Her hands tried to spread the low hanging limbs of trees. She ran into Spanish moss, which felt as though cobwebs trying to ensnare her.

And then she stopped, exhausted, her eyes wild. She had managed to get lost. Her eyes darted around her; she again heard the same sound of stealthy footsteps she had previously heard. But this time they hadn't stopped when she had stopped. They were approaching, getting closer. And now it was too dark to see *who*. It was so dark Leana couldn't even make out her hand as she held it before her. Whoever was traveling this land by night did so often, for no one could walk as determinedly as this person unless familiar with the area by dark.

Trembling, hugging herself with her arms, Leana began inching away from the sound of the approaching footsteps. A tree limb knocked the hat from her head, spilling her hair down and across her shoulders. She tripped on the gnarled root of a tree and fell helplessly to the ground, stunned when she hit her head on a rock. She shook her head as she rubbed a wound rising on her scalp, then screamed when a hand grabbed her by the wrist and jerked her up from the ground.

"Screams won't get you nowhere," a man's voice said. "I've been watchin' you since you left the wagon back at the road. I at first thought you were a man, but when I got a closer look at yer face, I knew better. I even *know* you. Leana, ain't it?"

Leana pinched her eyes half closed, peering in the direction of the voice, trying to see the face. The voice had a touch of familiarity to it, yet she couldn't place it.

But she knew that she had to fight for her life. It was obvious this man *did* know her, and she could tell by the mockery in his tone of voice and the tight, hurtful grip on her wrist that he was anything but a friend.

Leana began kicking, yet not finding her target. She began slapping at the man with her free hand, but attempts to fight back only drew a scornful laugh from the assailant.

"Ain't no use tryin' to fight me back," he laughed. "Miss Prissy in breeches, you're mine for the night."

"Who are you? Why are you doing this? How do you know me? Are you from Rufino? Have I done something to displease you in my establishment? What? Tell me. I will try to make any wrong right," Leana said in a rush of words. She squirmed, trying to loosen his grip. "Let me go, damn it."

"Ah, such vile words from such beautiful lips," the man laughed. Then his tone changed. "Shut up, fool. I plan to take my pleasures with ye, and all the cursin' and fightin' only enhances the anticipation of what I'm soon to get from you," the man snarled. "I'll teach ye to treat me as dirt beneath yer feet."

"What . . . ?" Leana gasped. "When . . . did . . . I do that? Surely you have mistaken me for another."

The man laughed throatily. "Well, I must say, in those breeches and loose shirt it could've been easy enough to think ye were a man. But my eyes are much sharper than that," he said. One of his hands reached in the dark and cupped her breast through the cotton shirt, causing Leana to flinch and feel a crawling along her flesh with distaste. "And I was right, wasn't I? What else can I find beneath those clothes? But I don't have to ask, do I? I *know*. And I intend to touch it *all*."

The sound of a horse's hooves resounding across the land in the distance made the man of the dark clasp a hand quickly over Leana's mouth. He dragged her away with him farther into the thicket and then held her against the hard frame of his body as the horse and its rider went on past.

Leana fought the hand on her mouth, she grumbled, she tried to work herself free, knowing that the man on the horse was getting farther and farther away from her, and with him, the chance of escape. . . .

"It ain't safe here," the man growled. "And it's not the best place to take full advantage of your body. I'll take you where we can be more comfortable."

With his hand still clasped over her mouth, the man forced Leana to walk beside him, though not seeing one inch ahead of her. Each step she took was a challenge, not knowing where it might take her. When she tried to again see the face of the man, it was effortless. He just forced her onward until she felt as though she might collapse from exhaustion. Perspiration laced her brow; her hair clung about her face in damp ringlets. Her legs had never been as sore, her feet so tired.

And after what seemed to be many hours of walking, Leana was forced onto a solid plank of wood. Her ears picked up the sound of water lapping, and she then felt the solid flooring of what she gathered to be a ship.

"I've got to get you below," the man whispered harshly into Leana's ear. "You're my prize. Nobody else's."

His low laugh grated against Leana's nerves. Her wrists ached where he held her so tightly. She again tried to see around her, hearing the creaking of ropes and feeling the sway of the ship as it lay moored next to the land. But the ship seemed to be moored beneath the same canopy of trees that she had just been beneath in the thicket, and not even a star could be seen twinkling in the heavens. Everything was still pitch-black.

But there was one promising development. She could hear the voices and laughter of other men from somewhere close by. And then the flash of a lantern as a turn was made on topdeck and she was able to see the white, folded sails of the ship and many figures of sailors lolling about, talking, smoking, and drinking.

But all of this was taken too suddenly from her sight as she was jerked down the companionway ladder, again into total darkness. She scrambled alongside her assailant, fear mounting inside her, knowing that surely this ship would soon be out to sea. *She* would soon be out to sea. . . .

Leana became aware of a door squeaking open and then felt the shove of her body as the man forced her into a dark room. And before she could scream for help, he was tying a gag in her mouth and bending her back, to tie her hands to her ankles, rendering her completely helpless.

"I can't draw undue attention to my prolonged absence from the ship," the man growled in a whisper. "I'll come back for fun with ye later. The voyage will be long. I'll have ye all to meself for many days. No one will venture into my personal cabin. They call me rat because of the filth of my cabin. No one wants to become contaminated by entering it."

Leana's eyes were wide, her nostrils becoming filled with the stench of the cabin, unable to identify any particular smell, only that it curled her nose and burned her eyes.

"I'll be back soon, pretty lady," the man said, and then Leana became aware of the door closing, and she was sitting in silence.

Fighting mad, more angry than afraid, Leana began wrestling with the bonds at her ankles and wrists, having noticed while he was tying her that in the darkness he hadn't succeeded in securing her as tightly as she knew he had wanted.

But still, it could take many hours for her to break free. She didn't have hours. She probably only had minutes before the ship would set sail. She must work. . . . She must get herself untied. . . .

Leana tensed when she heard feet scurrying about overhead and the drone of voices. The *slap, slap* of the water against the sides of the ship prodded her fingers onward. But she stopped, breathless, when she heard the cranking sound of an anchor being raised.

Desperate, she again struggled, her gag getting wet from her perspiration, her wrists stinging from her pulling and tugging at the ropes.

Then she had to stop and rest. And as each minute passed, she felt as though it was all useless. Now no matter how quickly she released her bonds, she knew that she would be at the mercy of the entire crew of this ship, for she could feel the movement of the ship and knew that it was making its way from land. Soon it would be taking her into the high seas. There would be . . . no . . . means of escape, whatsoever. . . .

Her thoughts went to Brandon, remembering the last time she had been aboard a ship. It had been with him. Tears burned her eyes, wondering if she would ever even see him again. If she escaped from her bonds, could the captain of this ship have a thread of decency in his blood? Or would he look to her as a prize, just as the man who had abducted her?

More determined to be set free, to find someplace to hide for the duration of this voyage, Leana again struggled with her bonds. Her heart skipped a beat when one hand slipped free, and then the other.

Breathing hard, hardly able to believe her luck, she scooted the ropes down and away from her legs and then jerked the gag from her mouth, feeling strength returning in her moment of victory!

But the door opening and hands groping for her in the dark made her aware that she had been too late. The sailor had returned and was ready to take what he had brought her to the ship for.

Not wanting him to realize that she was loose or that the gag was removed from her mouth, she lay there, breathlessly, yet one hand was moving to the manchette strapped to her leg. Brandon had been wise to give it to her for protection. It had saved her once. It was, hopefully, going to again.

Securing her hand about the handle of the manchette, Leana withdrew it from its scabbard and inched it back down from beneath the leg of her breeches, hearing a low snarl of a growl from the man when he discovered that she had moved from the spot where he had left her.

"Playin' games, eh?" he laughed. "Scooted yerself away from me, did ye?"

Leana huddled against the wall of the cabin, her fingers trembling on the handle of the manchette, her breathing coming in quiet rasps, awaiting the man's touch again. And when a hand touched her thigh and began working its way upward, she envisioned where his full body might be positioned and raised the manchette into the air and brought it down in a quick thrust.

First she felt the manchette make contact, and then she heard the gurgle of the man as he tried to cry out from pain. And then she heard the thud of his body as he fell to the floor, no longer making any sounds at all.

Her knees weak, her heart thundering, knowing that she had just most surely killed a man, Leana felt ill to her stomach. She was frozen to the spot for a moment longer, then felt the desperate need to get away from this death scene and the man who had been only inches away from raping her. Had it not been for the manchette, she would even now probably be in the process of being raped. The pistol at her waist could have been used, but it would have been too noisy, creating a disturbance on this ship she was not willing to take a chance with. Everything had to be done in silence or her fate was questionable. . . .

Holding the manchette out before her, Leana crept to her feet and began inching her way around the cabin, thankfully finding the door. And when she had her hands securely on its latch, she slowly opened the door and stepped out into the darkness of the corridor.

She followed the faint glow of a lantern ahead of her and then inched her way up the companionway steps to take a look about. If she could just get her bearings. If she could just steal a hat and get the coil of her hair beneath it!

But one thing at a time. First she would see the makeup of the ship, find a place to hide, and then make further plans. She looked upward, now able to see the twinkling of the stars and the full moon on the velvet backdrop of sky. Sails fluttered ghostly-white above her, spread to the wind, and the ship creaked as it glided smoothly through darkened waters.

And then a familiar voice rang out from somewhere close by. Leana's heart sang with happiness. Yet surely she was imagining things. She had thought she had heard Brandon's voice. Had she been . . . brought . . . to Brandon's ship . . . ? Had it been his horse she had heard while the man had held her captive in the thicket? Was it the *Erebus* that had been hidden in the Big Thicket's very edges, where the water had to be deep enough to harbor a ship? Had she been right? Was the Big Thicket where she could have found Brandon and Cyril's hideout had she wandered farther . . . ?

Footsteps drawing near and a face now being illuminated by the brightness of the moonlight made Leana almost faint with joy of discovery. She began laughing and crying at the same time, stepping out, also in the moonlight, for Brandon to see.

"My God. Leana?" Brandon gasped, seeing the silken flow of her hair as it hung across her drab shirt, and the breeches torn and mud-stained. "How . . . ? Why . . . ?"

Leana fell into his arms, sobbing. "I was abducted and brought here by some . . . some vile man," she said. "He tied me and left me . . . me . . . in a cabin. While he was gone I got loose. And when he returned . . ."

Her eyes wide, she looked up into Brandon's face, whose eyes were filled with puzzlement. "Oh, Brandon, I just know I killed the man," she said in a rush of words. "I used your manchette. I left him . . . him in the cabin below."

"Leana . . ." Brandon said, holding her close. "I'm sorry, darling. Damn it, which of my crew is responsible for this?"

"I'm sure he is now dead, Brandon," Leana repeated. "I had . . . to . . . protect myself."

"And that you should have," Brandon said, holding her at arm's length. "And to think that you have been treated in such a way. If the man *isn't* dead, he will damn well wish he were."

Tossing his head, he commanded that his men go below and search out the body. He then led Leana to his personal cabin and eased her down into a chair. "Now tell me all about it, darling," he said, sitting down opposite her. "Why are you dressed in such a way? Where were you abducted from?"

Just as she began to speak her words froze on her lips when she watched a man carry the lifeless body of a man into Brandon's cabin. She recognized the face. No wonder his voice had sounded so familiar to her. It was Jack, the pirate who had caused her nothing but trouble on her first voyage on the *Erebus*. He had never forgotten her and surely had planned his vengeance from the very first time they had come to odds. . . .

"I'll be damned," Brandon said, standing. He raked his

fingers through his hair. "Jack. It's Jack."

"He's dead, Brandon," the man carrying the body said. "What do I do with him?"

Brandon slung a hand into the air. "Toss him overboard," he shouted. "What else? Let the sharks have their way with him. He deserves nothing better."

Leana placed a hand to her mouth and bit her lower lip, uneasy, yet knowing not to be. She was with the man she loved . . . a man she trusted, wholly. She just hated to see the pirate side to his nature, cruel and heartless. Yet this sailor, Jack, did deserve Brandon's wrath as well as her own. Yet she would never forget how it felt to plunge the manchette into the flesh of the man. . . .

Chapter Twenty-Three

The water warm, a caress on her tired flesh, Leana laughed as Brandon's toes touched hers, sharing this warm, bubbly bath in the privacy of his master cabin. "If anyone would have told me this morning that my day would end in such a way, I would have called them daft," she laughed silkily. "Only moments ago I was thinking that I would never see you again, and here I am, with you, even bathing with you." She sank lower into the water, the globes of her breasts glistening as bubbles clung to them. "Brandon, don't pinch me. I'm afraid I might wake up and find that I'm dreaming being with you."

"Perhaps I was too rash in my feelings toward Jack for what he did," Brandon said, clamping his teeth onto a cigar resting between his lips.

"Oh? And why?" Leana asked, her eyebrows forking. "He most surely would have raped me, Brandon. And he had planned to keep me in bondage through your whole voyage at sea." Her lashes lowered over her eyes. "In the end, I wouldn't have been worth anything, to anyone."

Brandon reached and placed a forefinger beneath her chin, lifting it, directing her eyes to his. "Darling, I only meant to say that if Jack hadn't abducted you and brought you here, you and I wouldn't be together now, with many days at sea ahead of us to enjoy, just meant for us to be alone. Ah, just think of the many times we can be transported to heaven while in one another's arms."

A slow smile and a blush warmed Leana's face. "Where are you taking me, Brandon?" she asked softly. "This *is* to be a peaceful voyage, is it not? Or else how would you find time . . . for . . . just . . . me . . . ?"

Then she looked toward the door and back to Brandon. "And Cyril? Surely he isn't well enough to travel yet," she quickly added. "Is this voyage commanded solely by you?"

"Aye. Solely by me," Brandon said, taking the cigar from his lips, crushing it out into an ashtray on the floor beside the large copper tub. "And, my darling, now also by *you*. Is there anyplace special you would like to go? Your wish is my command."

"That sounds wonderful," Leana said, yet frowning. "But I really must return to Rufino. Darla would become quite worried about me. I was only supposed to be gone a short while today. Even now that I haven't returned, she must think I have had a mishap. I don't want to worry her, Brandon."

"Ah, now, we can get a message to her," he teased, scooting closer to her, easing her legs about his waist as he wrapped his arms about her. "Let's get away, lovers for at least a while, where no one can disturb us, Leana."

Feeling the hardness of Brandon's manhood pressing against her right thigh, Leana was fast becoming engulfed in desire for him. "Darling, why have you chosen to ride the seas on the *Erebus* without Cyril? You act as though driven by some unseen force. Was it from me? Are you only pretending to be glad that I am here with you?"

His dark eyes branding her, scorching her flesh as he looked from her soft spray of hair tumbling over her shoulders to her breasts, Brandon drew her next to him. "How could you ever think that I would only play games with you?" he said huskily. "Leana, I love you. You are a thing of beauty . . . a joy forever to me."

His lips bore down upon hers; he drew her next to him, relishing the touch of her breasts against his bare chest. Her lips tasted of jasmine, her skin smelled of roses. Lifting her more fully on his lap, he moaned softly as his manhood slipped inside her. Beginning slow strokes inside her, he kissed her passionately, hot and long, his fingers weaving ecstasy through her heart as they slid over her body and then around to fully enfold her breasts.

"Oh, my love," Leana whispered, easing her lips from his to place her cheek on his shoulder.

He was magnificently filling her, causing her to begin a sweet drifting. She clung about his neck. She nipped at the wet flesh of his shoulder. And when she felt the wetness of his tongue at her ear, and then lower, to trace the outline of the tiny taper of her neck, a tremor of ecstasy shuddered through her.

"I believe we've had enough of this damn tub," Brandon chuckled, easing her away from him.

He stood and lifted her fully into his arms and stepped from the tub, then carried her to his large bunk and placed her there. He knelt down over her, letting his gaze absorb her closeness. Bubbles still clung to her body, glistening. Her cheeks were flushed, her lips ruby red.

Her breasts heaved in her excitement of the moment, her abdomen was flat, leading Brandon's eyes on downward where her perfect vee of soft hair lay, tightly curled from wetness.

"How can you always be so lovely?" Brandon chuckled. "You are as beautiful wet as dry."

Leana reached a hand to his face and ran a finger over its full outline, again marveling over his magnificent masculine, handsome features. His hair was loose and wet, almost curling against his shoulders; the nipples of his breasts were hard, tempting her lips to them.

"I think I prefer you wet," she said in a purr, sinking her teeth softly into his nipple. "My darling, you look deliciously inviting."

Brandon's mouth lowered and kissed first one of her breasts and then another, feeling the hardening of each nipple against his lips. "We're not on a ship," he teased. "We're on clouds, floating high in the sky." He looked at her, his eyes dark with desire. "Come with me, darling. Let's float away together."

Leana sighed. Her sigh was stolen when his mouth possessed her lips, his tongue softly probing, touching hers as her lips softly parted. Fitting himself down and upon her, he again found entrance inside her as her legs parted and lifted around his hips.

As he thrust, she met him with eagerness, feeling the marvelous sensations beginning inside her head. She felt as though separated from herself as the pleasure mounted, as though someone else were experiencing this joy, and she was watching, yet feeling the same as this person entangled with Brandon.

Together, she and the one being observed felt the rapture building, and then exploded into a total bliss.

And then Leana felt as though she was one again, riding the clouds with Brandon, as though a ship high in the sky, and again experienced the same overpowering pleasure as only moments before, as his body shuddered with intense passion into hers. . . .

They rested cheek against cheek, each breathing hard against the other. Brandon slipped to his side next to Leana and smiled over at her. "I'm famished," he said, chuckling low.

Leana's eyes widened with surprise. "You can think of food at such a time?" she said, laughing softly. She doubled a fist and hit his chest. "Is that all what we just shared means to you? A means to build up your appetite?"

"Well, yes, in a way," Brandon said, reaching and drawing her up to straddle him. "But my voracious appetite is always for you, darling."

"Oh, I thought you meant you were hungry," Leana softly laughed, lowering a kiss to his brow.

"I *am,*" Brandon said matter-of-factly, then eased her back down onto the bed. He climbed from the bunk and slipped into his breeches. "And I plan to get us a feast."

Leana leaned up on an elbow. "But, Brandon, I thought you said that your appetite was not for *food,*" she marveled.

"I sometimes talk in circles," he said, laughing heartily. He gave her a mock salute. "Get decent. I shall soon shower you with wine and delicacies you never dreamed possible on a pirate ship."

Leana watched him leave, then looked slowly around and at the expensiveness of his cabin, lighted almost hypnotically by whale oil lamps, recalling it as when there before, forcing her thoughts aside of how her mother had lain in this cabin, ill. . . .

The plushness of Brandon's furnishings and the dark paneling highly glossed from a fresh polishing showed what he would expect when choosing furnishings for a house, and how he would expect it to be kept.

He was a particular, immaculate person, one she dreamed of one day pleasing. She wanted to choose furnishings to his liking. She wanted to hire maids who would cater to his every whim.

Their life together could be so grand . . . if only he would give up this life lived as a pirate.

But would he? Ever . . . ? Did he truly care enough for her to put his love for the sea completely behind him?

It was most certainly a challenge for her, the greatest in her life that she had ever tackled. But she was never one to back down from a challenge, especially one that could only mean her complete future happiness, if won. . . .

Not wanting to wear the dreadful breeches and shirt, Leana searched through Brandon's wardrobe until she found a pleasing silk robe, one that clung to her every curve as she slipped into it. She let it hang seductively open, yet drew it quickly closed when there was a light tap on the door.

Hurrying barefoot to the door, Leana slowly eased it open and then held it open more widely when finding a young man dressed in white carrying a heaping tray of food, and Brandon beside him, carrying a bottle of French champagne and two long-stemmed wineglasses.

"Ah, and how is your appetite, my sweet?" Brandon asked, stepping around Leana into the cabin, as the cabin boy followed him. He nodded to the floor beside the bed. "Place the tray there, Daniel. And see to it that someone comes right away to remove the tub of water. Then see to it that my woman and I are left strictly alone. Do you hear?"

The young man with carrot-colored hair nodded his head vigorously. "Aye, aye, sir," he said, placing the tray on the floor. "I'll have the tub removed quickly."

"Go and take a bottle of my wine from the hold for your own evening of pleasure," Brandon said, laughing softly as the young man's expression became that of awe. "Enjoy yourself, lad. You've always been one to jump at my command. Tonight go to your cabin and relax. I don't think you will have trouble with that, do you?"

"No . . . sir . . ." Daniel stammered. "Thank you, sir."

Leana covered a soft laugh behind a hand as the young man scampered from the room, his eyes as wide as saucers. And after the tub was removed and the door bolt-locked from any intruders, Brandon guided Leana down onto the floor beside him, where they both leaned their backs against his bunk.

"First some champagne," Brandon said, pouring the sparkling effervescence into a glass, handing it to Leana. He poured himself a glass, then offered a toast. "To us. To love."

Their glasses clinked. Leana sipped the champagne, watching him over the rim of the glass, smiling seductively up at him. Her skin shimmered as one of his hands reached inside the gown and slid its way up to a breast and cupped it.

Leana felt as though melting when he placed his glass on the floor and then hers, then eased her back to the floor herself and wove his fingers through her hair. His lips spoke to her in the only way they knew how, in a savage kiss, heated with something similar to electric bolts exchanged from cloud to cloud during an intense thunderstorm.

Leana moaned sensuously as she felt his knee parting her legs and his fingers began to softly rub her pulsing core until she felt near to exploding. And then she closed her eyes and threw her head back in rapture as his tongue began to trace a path downward and then stopped where his fingers had just paid homage.

Leana writhed, her fingers dug into Brandon's shoulders as his tongue caressed her into a mindlessness never experienced before. And when she felt his hardness enter her, the explosion that she had been holding back could no longer be held at bay. Her whole body shook. She saw shooting stars inside her head. She emitted a soft cry of wondrous pleasure.

"Food, hell," Brandon said huskily, feverishly working inside her. "All I want is you, Leana. Always. Lift yourself closer to me. Let me feel you. All of you."

Placing her legs about his waist and her arms about his neck, she pressed her breasts into him and closed her eyes, again feeling the delicious swimming inside her head. He was so skilled, he would have taken her to paradise four times this night, and the night had only just begun! Oh, surely this was heaven!

She trembled along with him as their pleasure was again fulfilled. Closing her eyes, she sighed. "Darling, darling . . ." she whispered. Her fingers wove through his hair. "Oh, how I do love you."

Brandon eased away from her and refilled their glasses with champagne. He offered her one which she took, her throat dry from spent pleasures. He smoothed the robe back onto her shoulders.

"And now we shall have a different sort of feast," he said, eyeing the tray of food. "I truly *am* famished, Leana."

Leana sipped on the champagne as she watched him fill a separate platter for each of them. And when he handed one to her, she laughed. "My Lord, Brandon, I do believe I might lose my waistline this night," she teased. "I've never seen such an assortment of delicious things in my entire life."

They feasted on lobster caviar, oysters on half shell, tortillas, pineapple, mangoes and papayas, and all sorts of cheeses placed on thin slices of French bread.

Leana fed Brandon tiny slices of apple, then they both washed everything down with another glass of champagne.

Stretching her arms, Leana fought a laziness that was creeping over her; so wickedly content and full, she now wanted to sleep. "Brandon, have you drugged me?" she giggled, yet knowing her euphoria was truly caused by everything combined, Brandon being the prime reason, so deliriously happy to be with him.

"No more than you have *me,*" Brandon chuckled, drawing her to his side, resting his head on her shoulder. "Now, tell me. Where were you when Jack accosted you? Why were you dressed in such ungodly garb?"

"Now you ask," Leana softly laughed. "Seduce me, feed me, fill me with champagne, then show concern for my welfare. I believe everything came in reverse order of priority, did they not?"

Brandon shrugged. "Not as I see it," he said. "Admit that it is best to talk of unpleasant things now that our heads are filled with contentment. Nothing can spoil those moments we just shared. Before? Such talk would have gotten in the way."

Leana leaned away from him and moved to her knees to face him. "Brandon, I was exploring in the Big Thicket," she said, watching his expression for telltale signs of anything that might prove that she had touched on a tender subject as far as he was concerned. The ship had been moored in waters that stretched away from the Big Thicket. Surely there was a reason for having left it there. . . .

Brandon's expression became sour. "You surely know the dangers of that," he snapped. "Men have been known to completely disappear from the thicket. Some have sunk in the swamp mud to their chins, and their heads eaten by wolves."

Leana grimaced, gasping. "Lord!" she said, moving back to his side to cuddle.

"You say you were exploring," Brandon said, his voice tense. "For *what?*"

"Nothing in particular," Leana lied, so wanting to blurt out that she was searching for his hideout! But perhaps later. This did not seem the time to question him about something that he so detested talking about.

She looked up into his dark, expression-filled eyes. "Now tell me why you are on the *Erebus*, and without Cyril? What was your destination, Brandon? You even now don't seem your true self. Did you have words with someone?"

Brandon reached for the champagne bottle. He poured himself another glass and took a sip from it. "It's Matthew," he grumbled. "And Cyril and that damn wench Wanda he's taken to. With both things bothering me, I just had to get away."

"What about Matthew? What happened with him?"

"He's a bastard, someone I don't feel related to at all. And he's my *brother*."

"What has happened between you two?"

"Nothing to worry yourself about," he said flatly. "I'll take care of it in time. And who needs him anyway? To hell with him."

"I feel the same," Leana said, feeling an iciness circle her heart when thinking of Matthew. "But who is this Wanda you speak of?"

"She's a wench that traveled the same ship you did from New York," Brandon growled. "Seems Cyril couldn't do without her. He's taken the bitch to our hideout. Now if she ever leaves, all of our lives will be in danger."

"That doesn't sound like Cyril," Leana said softly.

"Well, he has much to consider when he fully recovers from his wound," Brandon stormed.

"Then he is better?"

"Yes. Darla's witchcraft sort of potion seems to have done the trick. But now he's got to regain his strength."

Leana yawned. "Seems I've lost all of mine," she said, jumping when a crack of thunder was heard outside the ship. The ship tumbled and rolled ominously, then settled back in to ride the waves peacefully.

"Nothing to worry about, my sweet," Brandon said, kissing Leana's brow. "This ship has ridden out many a storm."

He set his wineglass down and turned to her and picked her up into his arms. Placing her on the bunk, he spread the robe open and kissed her navel. Her soft laughter was tonic to Brandon's nerves, having been grated raw from this day's events. He lay down beside her and held her in his arms.

"Sleep, my darling," he whispered. "Then when we awaken, ah, what love we will again make."

Leana closed her eyes and clung to him, trying to blot out the steady rolls of thunder and the toss of the ship as it fought the beat of the waves. Brandon kissed her breasts and nuzzled his head there and drifted off into a pleasant sleep. Leana's breath became shallow as her eyes closed to join him. . . .

Chapter Twenty-Four

Leana awakened with a start, not knowing if what she had just experienced was a nightmare or real. But there it was again . . . wild shouts from the upper deck and the howling of the wind. The ship was pitching so, Leana was becoming quickly sick to her stomach. She grabbed at Brandon as he jumped up into a sitting position, his eyes wild as things in the cabin began to be tossed about.

"What the hell . . . ?" Brandon gasped, the ship now bucking and rolling. He stumbled from the bunk, then fell hard against the wall as the ship tossed right, then left. "Get something on. Quick, Leana. This doesn't look good!"

Leana scampered from the bunk. Brandon braced his feet against the wall and held onto Leana as she breathlessly struggled into her man's breeches and then the shirt. "What are . . . we . . . going to do . . . ?" she cried, as the schooner continued to plunge and roll. The sound of thunder was like many gun blasts, the lightning lurid through the small porthole above the bunk. She eyed the manchette and, remembering its importance to her *and* Brandon, again secured it to the calf of her leg.

"You stay here!" Brandon shouted. He tossed her a rope. "Secure yourself to the bunk! If I see there's no hope for the *Erebus,* I will return for you, to abandon ship!"

"But you said the ship has always won the battle against storms!" Leana said, ouching when stubbing her bare toe against a chair as it rolled against her.

"This might be the one time it doesn't!" Brandon said, leaning with the movements of the ship as he reached for the door to unlock it.

"I won't stay below alone," Leana argued. "I won't leave your side! What if you would be swept overboard? Brandon, I must stay with you! I must!"

"Do I have to tie you to the bunk myself?" Brandon said, the door swinging open with a bang, letting in gushes of seawater.

"No! Nor shall *I* tie myself," Leana said stubbornly. Her feet slipped and slid in the water as she inched her way toward him. And when she reached him she grabbed him by the arm and clung desperately to him. "I *shall* stay with you. I'll help you, Brandon. I'm not a weakling. I'm sure your ship needs every hand it can get, to empty the ship of water!"

"Leana, damn it . . ." Brandon said, giving her a dark frown. Then he nodded. "All right. Come ahead." He held her hand as they began working their way down the dark corridor, water swirling around their ankles.

When they reached the companionway ladder, they coughed and sputtered as water rushed down the steps in torrents. Inch by inch they made their way up the ladder, the ship now shuddering and groaning as the sea hurled its mighty waves against it.

Almost blinded by the rain and the seawater, Brandon and Leana moved to topdeck. It was as though they had entered the dark pit of hell when seeing the destruction. Lurid lightning flashes revealed that topsails had toppled. The crew were wild, trying to hang on to anything close by to keep from being swept out to sea.

The waves beat incessantly against the bulwarks; the timbers creaked. The great rush of rain was making the ocean white with spume. The fierce wind was making the water swell higher and higher around the ship.

"Oh, God . . ." Brandon said, feeling helpless.

Leana clung to him, fear grabbing her at the pit of her stomach like a knife stabbing her. "Oh, Brandon . . ." she cried. "What—"

Her words were stolen from her when an even greater wave splashed against the ship, heaving it sideways, causing Leana and Brandon to lose their footing. Screaming, Leana watched Brandon sliding toward the edge of the ship. Seawater momentarily blinded her. Her fingers clawed at the deck as she felt herself sliding . . . sliding . . . until she felt the plunge of her body into the crazed, swirling waters of the sea.

She felt the saltwater stinging her eyes and throat as she sank into the icy depths of the water. It seemed that her life briefly passed before her eyes, death imminent as she felt herself being tossed about beneath the water, first sucked one way, and then another. . . .

And then she felt strong hands on her waist, pulling her along, until the surface was reached and she could see through the haze of water that Brandon was fighting to keep not only himself alive, but also her.

She coughed and choked, then sobbed as she clung to his arm as he treaded water, the storm seeming to have passed, the water suddenly calm, the morning sun an orange ball peeking up over the horizon.

"Are you all right?" Brandon asked, studying her face. "Darling, I thought I . . . had . . . lost you. . . ."

Leana cried softly. "I'm all right," she said. "What . . . are . . . we to do . . . ?" Her eyes scanned the wide breadth of the ocean. "Brandon, where . . . where is your . . . ship . . . ?"

Brandon coughed and shook his hair from his eyes. "I don't know," he said sullenly. "I don't know if the ocean claimed it, or if the wind blew it beyond reach of our eyes."

"We're going to die!" Leana cried. "We cannot . . . last . . . forever. You can only tread water for so long." Her eyes looked frantically down into the water. "And what if . . . sharks . . . ?"

Brandon's eyes again searched the water around him. Hope sprang forth inside him when he saw a barrel bobbing along the gentle push of the waves. "There!" he shouted. "We must get to that barrel! It's our only hope."

He gave Leana a questioning glance. "Leana, can you swim?" he asked guardedly.

"Yes. Quite . . . well . . ." she stammered. "But, Brandon, I'm afraid if we separate . . . the waves . . . will separate us *forever*."

"But we must," he said sternly. "To reach the barrel, I must swim after it now . . . *alone*. Follow along beside me, darling. It is our only hope!"

Leana brushed her hair back from her eyes and nodded. "All right . . ." she said softly, tears again blinding her, having no hope at all of ever seeing land again. "Let go. I'll . . . do . . . my best. . . ."

"I love you," Brandon said, brushing a kiss against her

340

cheek. He then let her go and began swimming, looking back to see if she was following. He sighed with relief when he saw her expert swimmer's strokes as she was fast reaching him.

Leana's arms and legs ached; her lungs felt as though near to collapsing. But she forced herself to go on. And when she saw Brandon tackle the barrel and manage to clasp onto it, then offer her an outstretched hand, she put more muscle into her swimming and was finally touching him. She groaned as he drew her next to him. Fingers raw, she grabbed onto the barrel and clung beside him.

"I knew you could do it," Brandon said, his chest heaving, his voice raspy. "Now we must watch for a passing ship. That's . . . our . . . only hope, Leana."

"And . . . what . . . if there is no ship?"

"We'll float until something passes by," Brandon said determinedly. "There *will* be a ship. We must think positive, darling. It would be too easy to give up. You and I were both born fighters."

"Your ship, Brandon?" Leana said, squinting her eyes against the brilliant rays of the sun as it rose higher in the sky. There were no traces of the storm left in the sky, not even a single floating fluffy white cloud!

"I shall hope that it makes it to land," he said, his eyes heavy with sadness. "That ship and I go back a long way. I'd hate to think I would never seek adventure on it again."

"After this, you'd even want *to?*" Leana softly cried. "Brandon, if we ever reach land again, I don't think I could ever get on another ship!"

"Ships . . . the sea . . . have been my life for so long, it would be hard to completely leave them behind," he said,

341

then coughed as his lungs began a slow ache. "We must rest, Leana. Lean fully against me and the barrel. We may be here for some time. Let's save our full energies for struggles to survive."

"Yes . . . oh, yes . . ." Leana whispered, fitting her body into the wetness of his.

Her shirt was torn, exposing one full breast; the breeches she wore had shrunk in the wetness and were binding on her legs. Brandon was shirtless, his black leather breeches slick against Leana as she pressed into him.

Her eyelids grew heavy with tiredness, but she forced them to stay open. Rest . . . but not sleep. Sleep would perhaps be forever should she let it possess her. It would be so easy to slip down into the water and close her eyes and give in to the lethargy creeping over her. . . .

The sun rose higher and higher. Leana and Brandon floated and bobbed in the water, along with the barrel. And then the sun began to sink lower, getting near the other side of the ocean, a bright orange ball in the sky, spreading its colors across the ocean. Leana's stomach growled from hunger; her lips were parched from thirst. Her body felt as though one large prune, warped and creased.

"Brandon, what if nightfall . . . ?"

But she didn't complete the question. Her eyes widened and she let out a loud shout. She began waving her free hand in the air when seeing topsails shivering in the breeze not far away, on the horizon.

Brandon joined in with her, shouting until he grew hoarse. But he had no need to shout any longer. The ship was heading their way. A longboat had even been lowered into the ocean and two sailors were hurriedly rowing toward Brandon and Leana.

"I . . . can't believe . . . it. . . ." Leana stammered, shivering from the intense chill she was experiencing as the warmth of the sun left her flesh. "Brandon, we're going . . . to . . . be rescued. . . ."

"I knew we would," Brandon said in a near whisper, his throat one massive, raw ache. "Faith. One must always carry faith around with them. It can pull one through the damnedest of situations."

As she eyed the massive schooner drawing closer, Leana's insides did a fearful roll. Whose ship was it? Were those aboard Mexicans, Americans, or *pirates?*

Then she glanced over at Brandon, her eyes wide with worry. Brandon's reputation preceded him. No matter who was aboard this ship . . . it could mean disaster for the man she loved. She couldn't wish for Americans over Mexicans *or* pirates! Surely each would recognize whom they had pulled from the sea!

Brandon saw the look Leana was giving him. It was not a look of joy, which she should have been experiencing for having been discovered. She looked even more fearful now than moments ago, when their fate was still in question.

But he didn't have time to question her. The longboat was now close enough to be within reach. He had to help Leana aboard, and then himself.

"Let me help you!" a sailor said, leaning over in the longboat, giving Leana a hand as Brandon gave her a shove upward, into the boat.

Leana's face turned crimson when seeing the sailor's gaze settle on her exposed breast, then up into her face, himself blushing. She was glad when another sailor took his shirt off and offered it to her, having himself seen the predicament she was in.

"Thank you," she softly murmured, easing it over her shoulders, clutching onto it, shivering. She was glad when Brandon was sitting beside her in the longboat and she felt the strength of his arm slip about her waist to hold her possessively to his side.

"Where the hell did you two come from?" a sailor with a full beard asked as he and his companion began rowing back toward the large schooner.

Leana knew she and Brandon had been rescued by Americans, and part of her was glad, yet she was silently praying they wouldn't know Brandon. . . .

"We were thrown overboard in a storm," Brandon said, keeping his eyes shifted downward, seeing how the men were looking so questionably at him. He already knew that he had been recognized. Most who sailed the seas knew of the black ship *Erebus* and the two who shared in its command. What would it mean for Leana if the captain of this rescue ship decided to throw him in the brig? Surely they wouldn't hold her also to blame for the dark deeds of *his* past?

"On which ship were you traveling?" the other sailor, sporting golden shoulder-length hair, asked, his voice revealing a cool caution.

"On . . . on an American merchant ship," Leana quickly blurted, her eyes fluttering nervously, knowing that she had never been a skillful liar. But Brandon's life was at stake. She had to try her best to protect him.

"I do not . . . *we* do not know the name of the ship," she quickly added. "Nor does it matter. What matters is that you were kind enough to rescue us. Thank you, oh, so much for seeing and rescuing us."

"Rarely do we find beautiful women in the middle of

the ocean," the bearded sailor chuckled. "It's almost as good as findin' a damn *mermaid*."

"Though I also thank you for coming to our rescue," Brandon said in a low growl, "I *also* warn you to forget any notions you might have about my lady here other than offering her dry clothes, food, and water. Should either of you lay a hand on her—"

"Hey, there, fella," the blond sailor quipped. "My friend here was only jestin'. We can see this lady belongs solely to you. And who rescued her first? *You*, or why else would she *be* with you?"

"Or maybe she's an unwillin' victim, eh?" the bearded sailor said, arching a heavy eyebrow. "Perhaps she was with you on your ship unwillingly, eh? It could've been just by chance that you saved her when you fell overboard? Maybe she's not your woman at all?"

Brandon doubled his fists, ready to fight, but the ship was reached and a ladder had been unrolled and was hanging for him to help Leana onto. Leana rose, weak-kneed, and grabbed the rope ladder. Her feet slipped and slid as she moved upward; her fingers burned from the tight grip she had to maintain to keep herself on the weaving ladder.

Glancing across her shoulder, she saw Brandon still in the longboat, steadying the ladder for her. In his eyes she could see a fear she had never witnessed before, and she knew this fear was for *her*. On a ship of men, she could be passed around, from one to the other, until she could even die from the attacks. Brandon was only one man . . . and one man against a ship of men . . . would not be enough. Leana had to hope for a gentle captain aboard this ship . . . one with compassion, one who valued a woman's pride in herself. . . .

Eager hands reached for Leana and helped her on board the schooner. She immediately came face-to-face with a giant of a man in a black suit with shiny gold buttons gracing its front. His eyes were so gray they were silver, his hair worn to his shoulders so red, it could be the sun in its brilliance.

His face was ruddy, his nose broad, his teeth white against his purplish-red lips. From his better, cleaner appearance, Leana had to surmise that this man was this ship's captain.

"So what have we here?" the man said. "A half-drowned waif?" He smiled devilishly as his eyes traveled over her, then his smile faded when Brandon climbed aboard and moved to her side. "Ah, the sea has been good to us this day, it seems. Look what it's coughed out of its bowels. Brandon. Ain't you the pirate they call Brandon?"

Brandon didn't speak. He squared his shoulders and lifted his chin. He would never deny his identity, proud. Yet he would not openly admit it, either, now that he had Leana to protect.

"Captain Newman at your service," Captain Newman chuckled, offering Brandon a handshake. "I've marveled at your tricks at sea. But only because you've not come across *my* merchant ship. Now, that'd be a different matter had you shot your great cannons at *us*."

Brandon knew the captain was playing games. His offer of a handshake was only in mockery. Brandon knew to expect being dragged away at any moment and thrown in the brig. Oh, God, what then for Leana? The only chance she would have *was* to act as though she had been *his* prisoner, taken on his ship with him by force. Then, perhaps, they would treat her gently, be sympathetic, realizing she had already been taken advantage of too much for her to be able to tolerate more, from others.

Captain Newman dropped his hand to his side, almost mechanically. "Take him away," he growled, nodding toward Brandon.

Brandon flinched when two sailors took him roughly by the arms. He glanced over at Leana. "And what do you plan to do with her?" he growled.

"What one would expect to do with a pirate's woman," Captain Newman laughed.

"She was my prize. *My* prisoner," Brandon demanded. "I took her aboard my ship by force. So would you also, eh?"

Leana paled and covered her mouth with a hand, not understanding why Brandon was so boldly lying about their relationship. Was it because he truly didn't care about her? Or . . . what . . . ?

Captain Newman's gaze roamed over Leana, seeing her attire. He kneaded a chin. "Yes, it seems she must've been forced aboard your ship. Even had her clothes torn from her," he speculated.

Then his face reddened with anger as he turned on a heel and glared at Brandon. "So she ain't your personal wench, eh? You son of a bitch. Whose ship did you steal her from? Just how long had you kept her on your ship of hooligans? How many have already taken her?"

His eyes wavered as he again looked at Leana. "On my ship you'll be treated grandly," he said thickly. "And surely I can find something more decent for you to wear until we reach port."

He turned and gave Brandon a pinched look. "And your ship, the *Erebus,*" he grumbled. "What was its fate? Is it a threat to us?"

Brandon laughed throatily. "And you think I would tell you?" he said.

Captain Newman raised a hand and slapped Brandon, causing Brandon's head to turn in a jerk. Leana gasped, seeing blood running in a stream from Brandon's nose and lips, now understanding why Brandon had denied that she was his woman. It had been a ploy to protect her . . . as he was now trying to protect his ship, though even he didn't know the fate of his crew. She wanted to run to him, to throw her arms about his neck, even place herself between him and the threat of this ship's crew.

But later. She would find a way to release him of the chains he was surely going to be placed in. However she would have to, she would get the key. They would then escape, together. . . .

Chapter Twenty-Five

Well fed and now in a cabin all to herself, Leana fought sleep. All she could think about was Brandon and what he might be going through. Was he alone in the brig? Were they mistreating him?

In the shadow of a misty candle's light, Leana crept from the bunk, a silk dress soft and clinging as she began pacing. How *could* she get the key to the brig? And once there, how could she even release Brandon . . . ?

The sound of footsteps approaching outside the cabin drew Leana around, to watch the door. Her heart pounded, not knowing who to expect to walk through the door. So far she had been treated as the lady she was. But should a man decide to take advantage of her, who would even *stop* him . . . ?

The door burst suddenly open, Captain Newman appearing with a crooked grin on his face, and carrying a bottle of wine. He swaggered as he moved toward Leana. "I've brung somethin' to warm you from your forced swim in the ocean," he said, hiccuping. He swung the bottle in the air, motioning with it toward her. "Take a swig, missie. Cain't do you no harm, now can it?"

"I truly don't care for any," Leana murmured, inching away from him. "And I would appreciate it if you would leave, sir."

"Oh, she thinks she's too good to drink with a mere sea captain," Captain Newman mocked. He stumbled toward her, then spoke into her face. "Tell me. Where does your family make their residence? Whose ship did the pirate Brandon take you from?"

Leana was beginning to believe that the two sailors who had rescued Brandon and her from the water had been talking to Captain Newman, more than likely while sharing drinks. They had most surely told this captain that she had given them a much different story while in the longboat than Brandon had given Captain Newman after being brought to the ship, and that she *was* with Brandon willingly. Captain Newman seemed to be mocking her now, only toying with her. . . .

"The ship's name was the *Jasmine*," she said, not truly lying. She *had* been taken from the *Jasmine*, but this captain didn't have to know that it hadn't been in the last week or so. She *had* to convince him that she *had* been a prisoner on Brandon's ship. It was the only way to keep her*self* from being thrown into the brig. How then could she devise a way to free *Brandon* . . . ?

"And my father?" she blurted. "He was a banker before deciding to make his residence in Texas. I . . . I was on my way back to New York to visit relatives when that pirate attacked and sank the ship *Jasmine*."

She fluttered her eyelashes up at Captain Newman. "I must thank you again, sir, for rescuing me from that . . . that rogue," she added smoothly.

"A kiss would be a kind payment for the rescue,

ma'am," Captain Newman said, his eyes bloodshot, his speech slurred. He closed his eyes, puckered his lips, and leaned closer to Leana, teetering.

"Captain Newman, my *word*," Leana gasped, swinging away from him. "I am not a . . . a . . . loose woman. Please do not take advantage of me."

Then her mouth dropped open when she saw a chain of keys hanging from a loop of his belt. Her pulse raced, knowing that surely the one that would unshackle her love was among those keys. If Captain Newman left the room, how would she ever have the chance again of getting the keys from him?

Everything in her warned her of the dangers of what she knew must be done. She was not used to playing dangerous games with men. But this man was already drunk. Perhaps if he had a few more drinks . . . ? If he would drink so much that drowsiness might overcome him . . . ?

Captain Newman's eyes opened. He wiped his lips with the back of a hand and belched. "You must pardon me, ma'am," he said. "It just ain't every day that I have a beautiful lady to share a bottle of wine with. *Nor* kisses. We're at sea for months sometimes." He chuckled. "My wife'd appreciate the likes of you. She'd like knowin' you kept me hones', at least this time."

He gestured with the bottle, his face crinkled into a clumsy smile. "But surely one little ol' drink won't hurt none, will it, missie?" he added. "I carry the best o' wines on this ship o' mine."

Leana swallowed hard. She forced a smile. "Well, I guess a drink of wine might relax me," she murmured. "Since my ordeal with that rogue of a pirate, I'm finding it hard to even think of closing my eyes to sleep. The evil

351

man has surely ruined my life."

"Ah, you poor little thing," Captain Newman said, placing a coarse-textured hand to her cheek. He nodded toward a chair. "Go and sit yourself down." He reached for a mug on the table and poured some wine in it, then handed it toward Leana. "Now, just sip on it, ma'am. You don't seem the type to have partaked in much alcoholic beverages. It just might go to your head a mite too quick."

Leana couldn't believe that this man could be so kind, yet she had to believe it was, again, only a ploy. She must be cautious or *she* might fall into a trap, instead of *him*.

"Why, thank you for being so considerate, sir," she said, taking the mug.

"Lance," Captain Newman said, plopping down on the bunk, sitting straight-backed on its edge. "Call me Lance."

"Why, thank you for being so considerate, *Lance,*" Leana said, laughing softly.

She sipped the wine, watching as he tipped the full bottle again to his lips and swallowed deep gulps of it at a time. And when the bottle was empty, she watched as his eyelids became heavy. When he stretched out on the bunk, she wasn't at all surprised.

Yet when his eyes opened suddenly and he directed them at her, she became frightened, seeing a hazy look of lust in their depths that she had grown to recognize when a man hungered for a woman. Tricked? She wasn't sure if she could call it that. But he was now rising from the bunk and moving toward her, and she knew that she was trapped, unmercifully trapped. . . .

"My wife need never know nothin' 'bout you *or* what I plan to do with you," Captain Newman said thickly. His large hands drew Leana up before him. He knocked the mug from her hands, then crushed his lips down upon hers in a wet kiss, his breath reeking of alcohol and stale cigars.

Leana began to struggle, pushing at his chest with her fists. But he was too strong. He clasped his fingers to her shoulders and turned her and directed her, backward, toward the bunk, his gray eyes silver slats, his purplish lips lifted in a menacing smile.

"I thought you . . . were . . . a gentleman. . . ." Leana softly cried. "Please unhand me, sir."

"Lance," he said huskily. "I told you to call me *Lance*."

"I don't want to call you anything," Leana protested. "I want you to *leave*. What you are about to do is . . . dishonorable. Please . . . don't . . ."

He shoved her down on the bunk and crouched down over her. One hand kneaded a breast through the silk fabric of her dress and his other was traveling up one of her legs. "Don't you see? I have to have you," he grunted. "It's been too long. I cain't wait no longer. And you're so damn beautiful. How can you expect me to *not* want you?"

Again his lips claimed hers, his hands wild on her body. Leana was growing frantic, feeling the hardness of his manhood clean through his breeches *and* her dress. If she didn't do something fast, he would succeed in raping her.

The thought disgusted more than frightened her. And when she caught sight of the wine bottle out of the corner of her eye where he had left it on the floor beside the bunk, she knew what she must do. But if she failed to strike him hard enough, she might not only be raped, but also *shot*. . . .

His fingers now kneading her between the thighs, his breath coming in short gasps as he continued to kiss her, Leana let her right hand reach for and grab the wine bottle. Slowly she lifted it, hoping he would continue kissing her for just a while longer, for proper distraction. She positioned it above his head and then crashed it down with as much force as she could muster and broke it over his head.

Fragments of glass sprayed in all directions. Several fell onto her face, stinging her flesh.

But it was his yelp and the lurch of his body, and then his silence, that made her know that she had succeeded in rendering him unconscious; he now lay quite heavy atop her.

Groaning, she pushed and shoved until he fell with a thud onto the floor. Before moving from the bunk herself, Leana carefully picked the shreds of glass from her dress and from her arms, only a few having pierced her enough to draw blood.

And then she stealthily stepped from the bunk and stooped beside Captain Newman. Her fingers were trembling so fiercely, she wasn't sure if she could unlatch his circle of keys to remove the one she needed. She clasped her hands together to steady them, then barely breathing, she reached for the keys.

Her eyes darted from the keys to Captain Newman's eyes, not sure how long he would remain unconscious. Her only hope that with all the alcohol he had consumed this evening might make him stay completely helpless until Brandon was safely removed from the brig and they were in the water.

But she worried about even that. Once they were in the vast stretches of the ocean away from the ship, how long would it take them to reach land? Could . . . they . . . even . . . ?

But casting all doubts aside, she sorted through the keys, moaning disconsolately when not able to figure out which exact key to take from the circle of many. She had hoped that it would be marked somehow. But to her, they all looked the same. It was even possible that the key to the brig might be kept somewhere else! What then?

Shaking her head, her hopes waning, she had no choice but to remove all of the keys from Captain Newman's person. And what did it matter? Hopefully he wouldn't miss them until she and Brandon were safely from his wrath!

The keys jangling ominously, causing too much noise, Leana grimaced as she took them from the captain and now held them in her perspiring hand. She glanced toward the bunk. She had hidden her manchette beneath it. She needed it now as never before. . . .

Barefoot, she tiptoed toward the bunk and got the manchette. She secured its leather scabbard to her leg but kept the manchette in her free hand, for protection. Again tiptoeing, she moved toward the door, yet still casting occasional glances from across her shoulder, the captain's way. When the door was reached she inhaled deeply and closed her eyes, saying a silent prayer, then opened the door and stepped on out into the darkness.

Whale oil lamps swayed somewhere ahead of her, casting ghostly, dancing shadows everywhere she looked. She swallowed hard as she began inching along the wall, not even knowing where to find the brig. She had to believe that it must be somewhere below, so steps leading downward were her goal.

As she stepped past closed doors, she heard a mixture

of sounds. She could hear deep snores from those in deep sleep; she could hear the shuffling of cards and the boisterous laugh of sailors as they gambled the night away; and she could hear someone retching, perhaps also from having consumed too much alcoholic beverage, as had the captain.

But Leana knew there most surely had been some sober sailors left in charge of the ship, and those were the ones she had to watch out for.

Yet couldn't it look innocent enough for her to be taking a nightly stroll? The captain had ordered that she was free to do as she wished. She had even heard him warn his crew to not bother her. Now she knew it was because he had planned to keep her to himself. The thought sickened her. . . .

Worrying about being discovered with the keys and holding the manchette in the open for all to see, Leana stopped to fold a portion of her dress about the hand holding the keys, tucking the edges around her fingers to hold the silken fabric in place.

And after she had also replaced the manchette inside its scabbard, she wandered casually onward, trying to not look so suspicious should she be seen. Her feet drew the clamminess of the damp floor beneath them into their soles; her nose was curling from the smell of the unclean ship. And as her hair lifted from her shoulders, she knew that she was dangerously close to the companionway steps. The light from the lamps was even brighter.

But she traveled onward, down one passageway and then another, up steps, down steps, and then she went lower and lower until she found what she was after. Rows of barred spaces, cells looking as though pits of hell in their filth, were suddenly before her eyes. And in the dim lighting of another whale oil lamp she could see many men stretched out on both the floor and bunks inside the close confines.

And as she slowly scanned her eyes from man to man, searching for Brandon, something else began to form in her consciousness. She knew these men! Lord! They were . . . the . . . crew of . . . the *Erebus!*

"Leana . . . ?" Brandon suddenly spoke, rising, making himself known from the many crowded in the one cell. "God, Leana. How did you manage to get down here?"

He glanced to the stairway, then back to Leana. "You shouldn't have. What if someone comes and finds you here?" he said in a loud whisper. He nodded with his head. "Don't you see? The captain likes playing games. All along he knew exactly what he had planned for us. He had even been searching for us when he found us."

Leana moved quickly toward the bars. She placed her fingers to them, relishing the touch of Brandon's as he twined his fingers over hers. "Brandon, he had found the *Erebus?* He abducted its crew?" she whispered back.

"Exactly," Brandon nodded. "And he bragged of knowing you were my woman. Since the *Erebus* had no other prisoners on board when the captain seized it and its crew, he *knew* you must be there by choice."

Leana's cheeks grew hot with anger. "Yes, he is a man of games," she spat. "Nasty games. He just . . . tried . . . to rape me, Brandon."

Remembering the captain and that he might awaken at any moment now, Leana jerked the chain of keys from their hiding place and jangled them invitingly in front of Brandon's eyes. "Brandon, we must hurry," she said anxiously. "I'm sure the captain will be unconscious for only a while longer."

Brandon was taken aback. "Unconscious?" he said in amazement. "Keys? Leana, what have you done?"

"I hit him over the head with a wine bottle," she said matter-of-factly, shrugging. "He was quite unconscious when I left him to come in search of you. But hurry, Brandon. I was lucky to not have been seen coming here. Our luck just might run out any time now. Thank God most men were too occupied by their wine and cards to notice me wandering the corridors."

She thrust the keys through the bars. "I just couldn't figure out which one would unlock your cell," she whined. "What are we to do? They all look alike to me, Brandon."

She watched as Brandon's crew began to stir, moving to their feet when seeing her there. A murmur of excitement rustled in the cells, eyes wide as most now clung to the bars, anxiously watching Brandon sort through the keys.

"Yes, most do look alike," Brandon grumbled. "But I have a brig of my own on the *Erebus*. There is a certain notch on the key that locks and unlocks prisoners. I can find it even by just feeling each key."

With deft fingers he searched and then smiled triumphantly and removed the key in question. "Now we'll show this Captain Newman that the crew of the *Erebus* is not to be fooled with," he growled. "He will be sorry he even set eyes on my pirate ship."

"The *Erebus*?" Leana said, taking the key as he handed it to her through the bars. "What is its fate?"

She greedily placed the key in the lock and quickly turned it, smiling triumphantly when the door swung widely open.

"The *Erebus* is floating not so many miles away, awaiting our return," Brandon laughed. "Though limping from the storm, it will soon be as good as new. But first we have this ship and its crew to take care of."

He waved the key in the air, letting his crew see it. "Okay, men, let's do what we know to do best," he said.

He hurriedly unlocked each door, the men huddling next to the stairway. They all knew that they must find weapons. But Brandon knew even where to look for those. He knew everything about a ship, *all* ships. He had had the best of teachers. Ah, if only Cyril could be here to join in the fun! This was the sort of adventure that made Brandon's blood burn with excitement. He anticipated seeing the look on Captain Newman's face when he realized that he had let his ship become overrun by pirates!

Brandon turned to Leana. He framed her face between his hands. "Darling, once we are equipped with weapons, your life could be in danger," he said thickly. "Oh, what am I to do with you? If you stayed here and one of the captain's crew found you, they would run you through with a cutlass. Or they might enjoy raping . . . you . . . first. . . ."

"I'll fight alongside you," Leana said dryly, her insides cold at the thought. But she truly had no choice. At all cost she had to stay with Brandon.

"If I only had a pistol with me now, I could give it to you to shoot the first man to draw near you," Brandon said hoarsely. "But I don't have *any* weapon quite yet. And where they are located is too far from here. Once we are discovered, I wouldn't be able to get back to you, to give you a pistol for protection."

He drew her into his arms and hugged her. "Darling,

359

you *must* go with me," he murmured. "But I will protect you. Fully."

"As I will do everything in my power to keep danger from *you*," Leana said, then leaned away from him when hearing his rumble of laughter. She placed her hands on her hips, and her eyes danced with anger. "Do you find that so impossible?"

"No. Not really," Brandon said. "You continue to surprise me with your bravery, darling."

Smiling wickedly, Leana lifted the skirt of her dress and showed the manchette to Brandon. "As I told you," she said, "I can very well protect you as well as take care of myself."

Brandon's eyes lit up. He gave Leana an admiring look, then thrust a fist into the air and turned to his men. "Onward to another victory!" he half shouted. "You know what must be done. Do it!"

The time of night was their true reprieve. Even the ones having assigned duties were snoozing as the crew of the *Erebus* and Leana made their way along the corridors of the ship. It was even almost too easy when the weapons were reached and Brandon began handing them out to his men. He gave Leana a lingering look, his eyes dark with worry, as he thrust a pistol into her trembling hand.

"Stay by my side at all times," he softly ordered. "And shoot to kill, Leana. Just remember, if we don't kill them, our lives wouldn't be worth spit. Once land is reached, myself and all of my crew would be handed over to the authorities. I'm not even sure what they would do with you once they knew that you were associated with me. Women are dealt with in a most indelicate way, if you get my meaning."

Leana nodded her head, gulping hard. "I understand,"

she whispered. "Let's just hurry and get it over with, Brandon. I'm not sure how long . . . my . . . wobbly legs will hold me up."

"Violence just may be spared if we can take Captain Newman's men by surprise since they are asleep," Brandon tried to reassure. The shifting of his men's feet and their low, impatient grumblings told him that enough time had been spent in conversation with Leana. Brandon drew her roughly into his arms, kissing her hard, then released her and held her hand as he began leading her up a dark staircase. . . .

One by one the cabins were entered. Loud bursts of surprise rippled from room to room. Leana led Brandon to the cabin where she had left Captain Newman. Slowly opening the door, they found him just beginning to stir as he raised up on an elbow, rubbing his head wound, wincing as he picked a piece of glass from his scalp.

"Seems you've just lost your ship *and* crew," Brandon said, stepping boldly into the cabin, pointing his pistol in Captain Newman's direction.

Captain Newman's eyes squinted, he licked his lips, staring numbly toward the barrel of the pistol. Then he looked on past it, seeing Leana smiling wickedly down at him. "You witch," he growled. "I should've never trusted you. I should've tied your hands and then had my fun with you."

His hand was creeping toward his holstered pistol, the room only barely lighted by the whale oil lamp, whose fuel was almost gone. The flame flickered on the wick, then it suddenly burned completely out. Leana emitted a soft cry and jumped with alarm when two shots rang out. She screamed and felt her head beginning a slow spinning, but when strong arms reached for her in the darkness and Brandon's voice spoke to her, she stifled a sob and threw herself into his arms.

"I thought . . . he . . . had shot you," she said, clinging. "Oh, Brandon. What if . . . he . . . had . . . ?"

"The fact that you hear nothing else from him is proof enough to me that you no longer have that worry," Brandon said thickly. "But I must check him, Leana. To be sure."

Feeling his way through the dark, his boot searching for the body, Brandon went to a knee when discovering it. His fingers knew where to touch for a pulse beat, and when finding none, he rose back to his feet and went and guided Leana out to the corridor.

Leana flinched when hearing more gunfire and the clanking of cutlasses as fighting erupted in all directions. She watched as Brandon's crew led men from cabins, some bleeding, some only half-clothed and sleepy-eyed from having been awakened from a deep sleep.

And then, in what seemed a matter of minutes, it was all over, and one ship's crew had been exchanged for another in the brig, and Brandon was now in command of this powerful merchant ship.

As daybreak began to show along the horizon in velvety streaks of crimson, Leana leaned against Brandon on the upper deck, their eyes scanning the horizon for any signs of the *Erebus,* which had been left to float as a ghost ship, one that could be seen by all passing ships, showing everyone that its crew had been captured.

Cyril? Captain Newman hadn't even seemed to worry about the aging pirate. It had been the young, more vigorous pirate who had been the important one to capture, for if not, this pirate could have had many years of pirating left in him!

"And what are you going to do with Captain Newman and his crew once the *Erebus* is boarded?" Leana asked, shivering as a cold spray of seawater settled on her face.

"I shall leave them to drift," Brandon said, a frown creasing his brow, still scanning the horizon for his ship.

"But once they are found and let loose, Brandon? What then?"

"We will be safely at my hideout," he said, letting his gaze slowly move to her. "Darling, even you must go with me. Now that you are known to be my willing partner, the authorities will also be seeking you out."

"Lord . . ." Leana gasped. "Will I have . . . to . . . hide for the rest of my life, Brandon?"

He laughed gruffly, then swept her fully into his arms. "No," he said. "Nor will *I*. I plan to become a rancher in Texas with you at my side. We will have children. Now, how more innocent could we look, living such a life as that?"

Leana's insides warmed. "It sounds like heaven," she sighed. "But *when*, Brandon?"

"It can't be for a while," he said, hugging her tightly. "But it will happen, darling. I promise you that. I now know that you are the most important factor in my life. The sea . . . has . . . become secondary."

Leana suddenly remembered what he had said about taking her to his hideout. Her eyes widened and she drew away from him. She looked up into his face, so again captivated by his handsomeness. "You said you were going to take me to your hideout," she said with an air of caution. "Are you truly?"

"If the *Erebus* can get us there," Brandon chuckled.

"Where *is* the hideout?" she prodded, her pulse racing.

"Darling, surely you already know."

"Should . . . I . . . ?"

"You were almost there when you were exploring."

Leana's heart skipped a beat. "Brandon, are you telling me that your hideout is in the Big Thicket?" she said, a slow smile forming on her lips. "You've always been so close . . . ?"

"Very . . ." he laughed.

Then loud, happy shouts erupting from all around him drew his head quickly around. His insides trembled when seeing the *Erebus* on the horizon, rocking gently in the ocean. He couldn't help but feel that he was just about to be received into the arms of another lover, he was so jubilant at seeing the ship that had been a part of his life since he had been a youth. Oh, God, *could* he ever say a final goodbye to his first love . . . ?

Then his heart ached, seeing the condition of the *Erebus* the closer the merchant ship drew to it. But it would get them to land, though limping like a true person having been wounded. . . .

Chapter Twenty-Six

The large and airy room was welcomed after the many days at sea. Leana stretched out lazily on the bed, looking over at Brandon, so at peace with himself as he slept. The *Erebus* was now safely moored and being repaired, Cyril was finally up and about, and all seemed well with the world, except for the bother of Wanda! Leana knew her type and she was not the sort to take a liking to. But Leana could very well see that it was not her personality that had attracted him to Wanda. She was beautiful beyond words, if even in a hard way.

But Wanda's jealousy showed in the way she glared at Leana when they were together . . . a jealousy brought about by Wanda no longer being the only female around the mansion. Wanda had bragged to Leana that *she* had been the first woman *ever* to have been brought to the mansion. Wanda had taunted Leana, saying that Leana had surely not been important enough to Brandon, or why hadn't he brought her sooner . . . ?

Leana leaned over Brandon and softly traced his jawline with a forefinger, studying his finely chiseled features, never sure of his true feelings for her, though he had told her enough times that he loved her. But Wanda's words were always there to haunt Leana. Why *hadn't* Brandon trusted her enough to tell her about the mansion earlier, only doing so when *forced* to by events no longer under his control?

Brandon stirred; his eyes crept slowly open. And then he grabbed Leana and rose over, to straddle her. "You're awake bright and early," he chuckled, glancing up at the shimmers of morning sunlight at the bedroom window. He then looked down at her, perfect in her nudity spread out beneath him, his hands holding her wrists to the bed.

"Are you anxious for the hog hunt?" he then chuckled. "This *is* what we've planned for this morning, is it not?"

Leana cast worried eyes toward clothes laid out for wearing this morning. A pair of man's breeches, a coarse cotton shirt bearing long sleeves and a high collar, and a sombrero with a wide brim had been loaned to her, almost identically matching the clothes also spread out, awaiting Brandon.

Then she turned her gaze back to Brandon. "Are you sure you want to go hunting this morning?" she barely asked. "Are you sure you want me to *accompany you?*"

Brandon released her wrists and moved a hand to cup her left breast. "Why, darling, I mustn't ever let you think that life with me could be boring," he chuckled. "I do understand your hunger for adventure. You've proven that to me more than once, you know."

"But . . . hog . . . hunting . . . ?" she murmured, curling up her nose at the thought. "Lord, Brandon, I can't stand the sight *or* stench of hogs!"

"Ah, but the *challenge*, Leana," Brandon teased, dipping his head down to let his tongue flick across the taut nipple of her breast. "Surely you can't turn your back on the challenge of the hunt, no matter what the hunt is *for*. Now can you?"

"But are there actually wild hogs in the Big Thicket?" she asked, shuddering when envisioning the snouts and mud-flaked skin.

"Ah, yes, there are wild hogs, and most quite fat," Brandon said. "They fatten themselves on acorn mast that accumulates on the forest floor. Upon our first arrival here we discovered the beasts. Didn't you see the penned-up dogs? They are the true hunters, Leana. They can track down a wild hog with their sensitive noses, stamina, and courage. It's a sport much liked by both Cyril and I. But I think the dogs enjoy it even more than we men."

He laughed softly, nuzzling his nose in Leana's cleavage, tickling her. She giggled. "Don't expect *me* to like it just because you do," she said, then her insides grew mushy as Brandon's lips began heating her flesh, kissing her breasts, then the tender softness beneath her arms, and then making a path of sheer ecstasy down the curve of her hips, and then her thighs.

"Let's not talk anymore about it now," he said huskily. "Darling, let's savor the quiet of the mansion while Cyril and Wanda are still asleep."

The name *Wanda* being spoken caused Leana's thoughts to stray from Brandon. "Is he going to marry her, Brandon?" she blurted, causing him to sit suddenly upright and look at her with wide, dark eyes.

"What . . . ?" he said, half laughing. "Cyril marry that witch?"

"Well, she *is* here, is she not?" Leana said, her lips

curved into a seductive pout.

"For only the moment," Brandon said dryly.

"And what does that mean?" Leana said, leaning up on an elbow.

"As soon as the *Erebus* is repaired enough to return to sea, Wanda will be the first to take a sea voyage on the ship," Brandon said, his jaw set firm, his eyes showing a coldness unfamiliar to Leana. "Until then she can *think* she has Cyril eating out of the palm of her hand. But later? She will be angry enough to *kill* him."

"Do you mean he's going to take her away and . . . dump . . . her somewhere . . . ?" Leana gasped, paling, wondering if Brandon might choose to do that to *her* one day should he truly tire of her.

"Something like that," Brandon chuckled, again paying homage to Leana's body with his lips and tongue. "But that's none of your concern. I can tell you don't like *or* trust her."

"Well, yes, you are right. . . ."

"Cyril trusts her even less. She must be taken far away from Texas. She will even have to be blindfolded as she is guided from the hideout. Now can you ask if Cyril will marry her?"

Leana brushed him gently aside and rose to a sitting position, hugging her legs to her chest. "Brandon, would you do the same to me someday should you tire of me?" she asked, giving him a half glance.

Brandon chuckled, then took her gently by a hand and drew her to him. He smoothed her hair back from her eyes, devouring her with his. "How could you ask such a thing?" he asked thickly. "How can you compare how I feel for you with how Cyril feels about that wench? I've professed my love for you, over and over again. Must I continually be showing you?"

"Yes . . ." Leana said softly, in a purr, being swept away on a cloud of desire for him when seeing the heated passion in his eyes. "Tell me. Over and over again. Do you think I would ever tire of hearing?"

"I would hope not," he said huskily. Curling his fingers into the black silk of her hair, he eased his mouth down upon her lips. He drew her into the hard frame of his body, leaving no space between them.

Leana's arms twined about his neck, pleasure spreading through her body like wildfire. Wanting to have the touch of him against her fingers, she searched with them across his wide shoulders, the expanse of his sleekly muscled back, and down to where his back tapered to narrow hips. And still he kissed her hungrily, his hands now wandering over her body, claiming her fully with hot, possessive touches.

Leana drew a ragged breath as his lips then moved to the hollow of her throat and kissed her there, and then to the soft pink crests of her breasts. Rapture blossomed inside her, as sweet, as beautiful as plucked roses in their height of headiness.

"Oh, my darling . . ." Brandon murmured, again looking into her eyes. "My Leana," he said, reverently speaking her name. "How I do love you."

"Please never stop," she whispered, tingling as he eased her to the mattress and stretched out above her, fire in his eyes, magic in his touch.

And then the intoxication of his kiss as his lips came sweetly to hers, at the same time entering her, filling her, slowly beginning his strokes inside her. She writhed in response, meeting him with upthrust hips. She clung to his rock-hardness, giving herself up to the rapture.

His tongue gently parted her lips and entered her mouth; he enfolded her with his solid strength. Together they traveled into an abyss of total ecstasy, then whispered heated words of passion against the other's cheek, softly panting. . . .

Brandon was the first to break their sensual bondage. He leaned up away from her, smiling, his fingers softly smoothing her perspiration-dampened hair back from her eyes. "Now I'm really ready for the hunt," he chuckled. "Darling, you've invigorated me. I feel as though I could conquer the world."

"But what you want is to just slay a few hogs?" Leana softly pouted, easing from the bed. She glanced from the waiting clothes to him. "Do you truly want to do this?" she prodded.

"As I said," he said, stepping from the bed, "I don't want to offer you a boring existence." He pulled his breeches on. "And a hog hunt is *anything* but boring." He nodded toward her clothes. "Come on, darling. Don't spoil the fun. It can be an experience you'll never forget."

Leana sighed heavily, drawing the baggy breeches on. "That's what I'm afraid of," she said, giving him a half glance. "Nor will *you*. I'm sure to make a spectacle of myself this morning."

"I will be the only witness," Brandon said, buttoning his shirt. "Oh, yes, and then there are the dogs. But I'm sure they won't tell."

"Oh, Brandon," Leana said, giggling. Her stomach growled. "But surely we'll eat first?"

"It's the early bird that catches the worm," Brandon further teased. "We must wait, to eat later." He winked toward her. "Yet, on second thought, by the looks of those loose breeches, you might not make it until dinner. God, they're baggy. But those were the only ones I could find that I felt would even partway fit you."

"Thanks a lot," Leana grumbled. She fastened the coarse cotton shirt, then circled her hair up into a bun as she placed the hat on her head. She didn't dare look in the mirror. And she didn't have to. She could see the amused look in Brandon's eyes and the way his lips were quivering, as though he was struggling to keep from laughing.

"If you laugh at me, I'll—" Leana said, doubling her hands into tight fists.

Brandon took a wide step and just as quickly had her in his arms, sealing her lips from further words with a kiss, all-consuming. Leana was becoming mindless, forgetting their moments of bantering. She twined her arms about his neck and fit her body into his.

And then he released her much too soon and placed his holstered pistols about his waist, nodding toward her own. "Get your pistols and let's go," he said.

"Sometimes I think you are a tease, Brandon," Leana said, still feeling and tasting his lips on hers.

"Just because I get the sudden urges to kiss you?" he laughed, plopping a sombrero on his head.

"Yes," she said sullenly, fastening her holster around her waist.

"Would you rather I didn't?" he asked, his eyes gleaming with amusement.

"Well, no . . ." Leana said, then eyed him wonderingly as he placed a rope about his waist, then slipped a strange-looking yet graceful translucent horn into the waist of his breeches. "What on earth are you doing with that rope? And what is that horn for?"

"In case the dogs bay a hog, I'll lasso the hog with the rope, tie it, and drag it out live, for further fattening in a pen. The horn is to be used on the dogs should they wander too far," Brandon said matter-of-factly. "Now, you could carry the rope while I carry the horn. *You* could lasso the hog," he teased.

"Good Lord, no," Leana gasped, then laughed as he placed his arm about her waist and directed her from the room.

The house was quiet, the rooms dimly lighted by golden sprays of light from kerosene lamps. Leana again silently marveled over this elegant house with its large and airy rooms of high ceilings, Oriental rugs, many gilt chairs and settees. She had enjoyed lounging in a library of rare books and original art, yet wondering how many ships it had taken to steal from, to get such a collection of rarities!

But she tried to not think on the pirate side of Brandon's nature. She loved him, no matter what type of life he had chosen. And she always reminded herself how he had been introduced *to* that way of life. It had been forced upon him. It had then been the heart of a young boy who loved the adventure he had been introduced to that had led him to continue, willingly, with such a life. So she could never fully blame him for the wrongs he had done. Even now he sometimes seemed to be that innocent lad of ten when he would look at her with his dark eyes and smile of pure gold. . . .

Hurrying on outside, Leana and Brandon together witnessed the world awakening to another day. Leana breathed in the fresh, jasmine-scented air, looking about her as Brandon led her to the pens where the dogs were kept. The air was cool among the virgin longleaf pines and magnolia trees, the wildflowers dotting the ground in a myriad of colors.

A cottony fog was just now lifting; the forest was coming alive. An ivory-billed woodpecker swept by and clung to a tree and began its constant tap-tapping with its pointed beak; a long, melancholy howl of a wolf reverberated through the denseness of the woods.

Leana shuddered. "Will we be safe enough while hunting?" she asked, locking an arm through Brandon's. "Panthers are even known to be in the thicket. My one time here, I even heard its *cry*."

The dogs in the pens began yelping, excited to hear someone approaching. Brandon urged Leana away from him. "I'll go in the pens alone to ready the dogs," he said. Then he laughed softly. "And about that panther. All the years I've been a part of the Big Thicket, I've yet to see the panther. It's as elusive as the treasure I've heard tales of being hidden here in the thicket."

"Yes. I've heard such tales of treasure," Leana said, flinching as Brandon stepped into the pen and seemed suddenly attacked by the dogs.

But when he smiled and began patting them, she knew they were friendly enough. She stepped up to the pen and looked at the dogs. They were ratty. "Cur dogs," Brandon called them. He had told her that fine-bred dogs lacked the courage to tackle a bad boar, should they come across one.

Leana inched her way toward the pen and looked inside, seeing two black-mouthed curs, and then jumped, startled, as Brandon released them and they lunged out of the pen, darting, yelping toward the forest.

"Shall we follow?" Brandon laughed, offering Leana an arm.

"I hope we aren't expected to follow close behind them," Leana said, eyes wide. "I've never seen dogs so anxious to be set free."

"They're not so anxious to be free as they are to make a big catch," Brandon chuckled as he led Leana into the dense forest, the dogs now out of eye range.

Leana peered into the darkness of the forest, the limbs dripping from a light rainfall during the night. The woodland floor was mushy, the air was close and steamy. "The day is so oppressive," Leana said, wiping a bead of perspiration from her brow. Her gaze settled on orchids opened to the light. "But this sort of climate seems to agree with the flowers. The orchids are exquisite, Brandon."

Brandon plucked an orchid and positioned it in a buttonhole of her shirt. "At least you've found something you like about this morning's outing," he chuckled, brushing a soft kiss across her nose.

Leana looked up at him, her lips quivering in a soft smile. "The orchids aren't the only things that delight me, darling," she murmured. "Being with you is worth all the mud and sweat I'm experiencing. But . . . it . . . is the thought of wild *hogs* that sets my nerves ajar."

"We'll just let the dogs worry about them," Brandon said, taking her by an elbow, resuming their walk through the thick ground tangle and preponderance of trees. "Just be thankful I didn't suggest *night* hunting."

"I would have *never* agreed to that," Leana laughed. "I've heard the tales of the mysterious lights of the Big Thicket. I don't care to tempt ghosts to appear. I've even heard tales of phosphorescent balls of fire appearing from nowhere." She turned her eyes up to Brandon. "Have you ever seen anything like that, Brandon?"

"Myths," Brandon said thickly. "Every bit of it myths. If one believes in the supernatural, then they would believe in the legends of ghosts and visits from the dead here in the thicket. That's why Cyril chose this place for his hideout. Most are too afraid to enter it. Even with talk of buried treasure . . . most would not dare come in search for it."

"Have . . . you . . . searched . . . ?" Leana said quietly, wincing when a red-tailed hawk swept suddenly from the trees, only barely missing Leana with its wide spread of wings.

"You surely know that I have," Brandon chuckled. He cocked an eyebrow as he looked down at her. "Darling, I'm a pirate. Remember? I have battled many times for treasure. To think that some might be buried in my own backyard, to take without a fight? Yes, I've looked. But none is here. I personally have confirmed that this is also a myth, made larger than life as the tale spreads from one person to the other."

As they moved into darker woods, so dark it seemed to be night, Leana cringed as she felt her boots sucking into the mud as she continued to thread her way through loblollies and tall palmettos beside Brandon.

And then she was forced to stop when Brandon clasped tightly to her elbow. "Listen," he said, cupping a hand to his ear.

Leana's flesh crawled. At the very threshold of her hearing, she could feel, rather than hear, the deep *yow, yow* of a cur's baying.

"They're one to one. Let's go," Brandon urged, helping Leana through the murky swamp, holding low tree limbs aside for her.

"Oh, Brandon, I don't know . . ." Leana fussed as he

led her deeper into the swamp. The palmettos grew higher until they were way above her head. She then found herself in a brier patch, and the spines snagged in her clothes and raked her skin.

And then they reached a stream, swollen from heavy rains, impassable.

"The dogs must have swum across," Brandon said, kneading his brow. He listened for the dogs. "They must have gone beyond our hearing."

Brandon removed the cow horn from the waist of his breeches and blew a series of strident blasts, a primordial sound that made Leana's skin prickle.

Brandon lowered the horn from his lips. "They've got a boar bayed up," he grumbled. "If it was a pig, they'd have killed it and come in by now. We'll have to give it up. They might stay all night now."

"How will you get them back?"

"They'll backtrack themselves and they'll just go back to the mansion," Brandon shrugged, replacing the horn in the waist of his breeches. "I only hope they haven't cornered an old boar. My dogs are smart, but the older boars are smarter. They can slash you with their curved tusks, beveled sharp as knives, quicker than you can wink an eye."

"What . . . if . . . we'd run across one ourselves?" Leana said, her shoulders tightening in fear.

"Just don't try to outrun him, because you can't," Brandon said thickly. "Just shoot the bastard, Leana. That is, if it gives you the time. . . ."

Leana laughed nervously. "You sure are encouraging," she said, then gave him a pained look. "Brandon, can we now return to the mansion? Please? I've had enough of this sort of pastime for one day."

"Whatever my lady wants," Brandon chuckled, placing his arm about her waist. "Home it is."

Again they made their way back through swamp, palmettos, and nagging mosquitoes. On all sides of them trees pressed in, dark. The air was still damp, heavily scented with sweet smells.

Then Leana grabbed at Brandon, stopping him, her heart thundering, her throat suddenly dry. "Did you see that?" she whispered. "Just ahead, Brandon. "Did . . . you . . . see it?"

Brandon squinted his eyes and then his pulse raced when seeing a dim light in the distance, showing up clearly against the darkness of the forest.

"A light . . ." he said shallowly.

"Yes. And where . . . is . . . it coming from?" Leana whispered, knowing they were too far from the house for it to be lamplight in the windows.

She watched the light. It was only a tiny point. But suddenly it grew brighter, a hot point of light. It moved. It grew brighter. Then abruptly it dimmed and went out.

Then it reappeared, as a dull glow, the color of a pumpkin, and then again was lost to sight, completely, for good.

"Was that . . . the . . . light of the Big Thicket that everyone speaks of?" Leana asked, clinging to Brandon.

Brandon's skin crawled and then he feared what he and Cyril had worried about all the years they had lived there. That someone might come looking for them. He didn't fear myths or ghosts. He feared what breathed and walked. The light had surely been a lantern. But . . . who . . . would be carrying it? Who *was* searching the darkness of the Big Thicket?

"Come on, Leana," he said hoarsely. "We've got to get

out of here."

"Then you *do* think it's something to fear," she said, tripping on ground tangle as Brandon half dragged her along.

"Not something. *Someone*," he said. "Perhaps the cow horn attracted something besides my dogs."

"Who . . . ?"

"Mexicans, perhaps . . ."

"Or . . . Americans . . . ?"

"Whoever . . ." Brandon said, ducking low beneath the gnarled branches of a live oak. "I only hope they don't wander in the direction of our hideout. . . ."

Chapter Twenty-Seven

Cyril tossed fitfully in his sleep. He fought off dreams of misty mountains and blackface sheep on distant hillsides. He groaned as neat slated houses came into view and a village church steeple rose tall and serene, mirroring itself in the calm waters of the Sea of the Hebrides. His mouth trembled and he emitted a soft cry of remorse when searching through the village for his Amelia, unable to find her. Her violet eyes burned through his consciousness . . . and then gray eyes were suddenly there looking up at him, as though his own were being reflected back at him from a mirror.

His eyes flying open, his jaw slack, Cyril scooted to a sitting position on the bed, perspiration wetting his brow.

"What is it?" Wanda said sleepily at his side. She rubbed sleep from her eyes as she leaned up on an elbow to look toward the windows. Scant light was showing at the edges of the closed drapes. "Why are you awake so early, Cyril?"

Cyril scarcely heard Wanda's words. He was recalling someone else and the gray of her eyes as she had treated his knife wound. Though drifting in and out of consciousness at the time, Cyril had known enough to wonder about how she so resembled *him*. Had she been a young *lad,* it *could* have been Cyril's double those many years ago. How could a young wench take on his identical appearance, unless . . . ?

With his strength fully regained, Cyril jumped from the bed and poured fresh water into a basin. He lit a kerosene lamp and stood studying his face in a mirror for a moment, then began slapping his razor against the razor strop. If he was to ride into Rufino, no one must recognize him. And go to Rufino he *must*. He had to find the young lassie who had most surely saved his life with her skills at ministering wounds. He had many questions to ask her. Had she always lived in Rufino . . . ? Where was her family . . . ? Hadn't he heard her make a mention of a mother to Leana . . . ?

"Cyril? What are you *doing?* Why are you shaving so early? Are you going somewhere?" Wanda asked, climbing drowsily from the bed. Her silk gown clung to her as she moved toward Cyril; her hair lay like red spun silk across her shoulders, not even mussed by her full night of sleep.

Cyril's eyelids grew heavy as he glanced over his shoulder and saw the peaks of her breasts thrusting against the silk of the gown. She slunk up next to him, clinging to an arm, looking up at him with seduction on her mind.

Forcing himself to forget what she offered, having already determined what her fate would soon be, that which would make her hate him, Cyril looked away from her. And if what he was thinking was possible, he might have another lady wishing *she* were dead. If Darla was

380

who he thought she was, he would finally be able to make his wife, Amelia, pay for having deserted him those many years ago.

Setting his jaw firmly, his eyes now two narrow slits of gray, Cyril lathered his face with white clouds of soap, still ignoring Wanda as she now stood with her hands on her hips, glaring at him.

"Cyril, I don't like being treated this way," she hissed. "You make love to me at night, but by day you have become a *stranger*. What am I to think? What am I to *do?*"

"Love? You call what we do at night love?" he laughed mockingly. "For me it is only a way to feed my hunger."

Wanda flipped her hair back from her shoulders, her eyes flaming. "You didn't feel that way when we first met," she stormed. "You even treated me *special*."

"That was my first mistake," Cyril grumbled, taking long swipes with his razor. "But my biggest was bringing you here."

A coldness splashed through Wanda. Her arms fluttered to her sides. "You're . . . sorry . . . you brought me here?" she murmured. "What have I done wrong, Cyril? I've catered to your every whim."

He turned his head and cocked an eyebrow. "And anyone else who winked yer way," he growled. "It's in yer blood, ain't it? This need to be bedded by many men." He laughed throatily. "Though it doesn't even light fires inside ye except with me. What is it, Wanda? A sickness?"

Wanda turned and rushed to the bed. She fell down upon it, sobbing, pounding her fists on the mattress. "You'll be sorry," she softly cried. "Somehow . . . I'll . . make you sorry."

381

She turned her eyes back to him, then stopped crying, gaping openly at him as he wiped his face dry with a towel. "Your . . . mustache," she gasped, seeing his face shaved clean. "You . . . shaved your mustache off. Why?"

Her breath then caught in her throat as she watched him begin to cut his hair. "And your hair?" she said, slowly rising from the bed. "Cyril, why are you doing these things? Where are you going? Why do you have the need to change your appearance?"

"I must ride into Rufino," he said dryly. "And no one must recognize me. Or do you forget the Mexicans? Brandon even thought they were wanderin' in the Big Thicket yesterday. One day they'll find us. But I don't want to be the one to *lead* them to us."

"Why must you even *go* into Rufino?" Wanda asked, slipping a robe over her shoulders. "Might I even go with you?"

Cyril turned on a heel and glowered down at her. "You're to stay right 'ere until I say you're to leave," he flatly ordered.

Wanda paled. "Then I'm now to be considered a prisoner?" she said shallowly. She went to Cyril and traveled her fingers over his bare chest, looking seductively up into his eyes. "But surely only because you need me. Say that you need me, Cyril." She fit her body into his and kissed him softly on the lips. "Please don't treat me as a whore. I need you, Cyril. Need me as much?"

Though feeling her words were poison to his soul and forgetting his purpose of this morning, Cyril couldn't fight the desire that was swelling inside him. Wanda could bewitch him with a mere touch, and he knew the dangers.

Yet he was momentarily blinded of these dangers as her tongue teasingly flicked into his mouth, arousing inside him the tortured needs of a man.

Guiding her back toward the bed, his hands hurriedly shed her of her clothes. And as he leaned over her he removed his breeches, seeing the fire in her eyes, scorching his flesh as she let her gaze move over him.

"You *are* a witch," he growled, grabbing her into his arms as he spread out atop her. He took her mouth savagely with his. He plunged his hardness inside her and began feverishly working with her. Her fingernails dug into the flesh of his buttocks as she wrapped her legs about his waist.

Sensuous moans were breathed against Cyril's lips as Wanda began feeling rapture spinning around her heart. He had been wrong to say that only he could make her feel pleasure. She now knew that she should have never confessed such a truth to him. For though at first that had been true, it no longer was. And she hated that he had heard of her rendezvous with one of his sailors. She had only wanted the feel of young flesh against her body. But it was still Cyril who she would kill over. He had the riches . . . the power over many men . . . that most men could not brag of. She wanted to share all of this with him. Forever . . .

Cyril's hand stroked her silken flesh, now cupping a breast. He felt the heat spreading inside him and then the full pleasure was reached, leaving him feeling drained, angry for having again let her take him beyond coherent thought.

Jerking away from her, feeling the need to spit into her face, he instead turned his back to her and slipped into his breeches.

"So you are still determined to go to Rufino?" Wanda purred. She slunk along the bed until she was close enough to reach and curl her fingers through his chest hairs while he was sitting on the edge of the bed, working with pulling on a boot.

Cyril grabbed her wrist and forcefully held on to it. "Aye, I'm going," he growled. "And while I'm gone try to not create any problems for Leana. I've seen how you look at 'er. You'd be 'appier if she were dead, now wouldn't ye? All women are a threat to you, eh, lassie?"

Wanda smiled coyly, jerking her wrist away from him. She rubbed it where it unmercifully burned and ached. "If you will worry so much over Leana's welfare, perhaps you'd best stay home," she taunted. Then her eyes narrowed. "Or maybe there's more to your going into Rufino than you've said."

She watched him rise from the bed and walk confidently to his wardrobe. When she saw him choose a shirt other than that worn by a pirate, she stormed from the bed and spoke into his face. "You're going to see a *woman*, aren't you?" she shouted. "First you make love to me, and then someone *else?* Who is she, Cyril? How long have you known her? Why haven't you brought her here, to live with you? Only a woman *could* draw you into Rufino. You know the dangers of being recognized." She stomped a foot. "Who *is* she, Cyril? I demand to know."

A growl rumbled from between Cyril's clenched teeth. He gave Wanda a shove. "If I *am* going to see a woman, it's none of yer damn business," he spat. "And she *would* be a *lady*. Nothing like you."

Wanda stood stunned numb by his words. She walked away from him and sank down on the bed, watching as he combed his newly cut hair to perfection and splashed after-shave onto his freshly shaven face. Then her gaze captured the bright gold religious medal hanging around his neck where his shirt lay half-buttoned in front.

"Everything about your appearance this morning has been changed except for the necklace," she murmured. "Why not also that, Cyril?"

Cyril's cheeks colored with remembrance . . . remembrance of a day his Amelia had presented him with this necklace. He had told no one it had been a gift from the woman he had made his wife. And though he had carried hate for her around with him these past years, the fact that he couldn't part with the necklace, and that he made it a part of his everyday apparel, was proof enough to him that a part of his heart still belonged to Amelia. . . .

"I would feel naked without it," he grumbled.

Fitting holstered pistols about his waist, he gave Wanda a quiet stare, then left the room. He knew he had a duty to Brandon to tell him that he was going to Rufino. And though Brandon couldn't be told why, Cyril knew that Brandon respected him enough to not prod him for answers. And Brandon knew that at least one of them had to stay behind since the mansion had to be kept watch over. Cyril feared that one day soon all their lives would change. They had made many enemies during their pirating years. Of late, Cyril feared that things were closing in on him, as though he could foretell doom possibly for them all. . . .

On horseback, his sombrero tipped low over his face,

his shoulders purposely hunched, Cyril entered the town of Rufino and began moving down its main street. His eyes moved steadily about him, watching for any sudden movements, yet seeing none. In fact, the town seemed to have almost turned into a ghost town, the streets and walks almost deserted except for a few horsemen in the streets and men walking along the boarded walks.

The sound of raucous laughter arising from various saloons and gambling houses was welcomed to Cyril's leaning ears, not wanting to be *that* conspicuous as to be totally alone in a town where he could now see Mexican soldiers at the far end of the street, none seeming to have yet seen him.

Anxious to get out of sight, he let his eyes begin scanning the buildings on each side of the street, trying to recall which one he had been taken to after being wounded. In his haze of semiconsciousness he had only vaguely seen things around him. But he could remember a red door, knowing that was the one through which he had been carried.

"That should be easy enough to identify," he whispered to himself. And then his heart seemed to stand still when his eyes searched and found. And then his gaze captured the sign on the front of the building, reading Leana's name.

Ah, yes. It *had* been her hotel that he had been taken to! And if he remembered correctly, the sweet thing who had treated his wound was called by the name Darla, and she worked for Leana, *in* the hotel.

Directing his horse to a hitching rail, Cyril quickly dismounted, secured his reins, and hurried inside the hotel, out of the corner of his eyes having seen two

Mexican soldiers suddenly come into view at the door of the saloon across the street from the hotel. He wasn't sure if they had seen him. But if so . . . what would it matter? He was just a drifter. That's how they would see him.

Yet were drifters even welcomed in Rufino these days? If so, why wasn't there more activity on the streets? And now that Cyril was thinking about it, he didn't recall seeing any ships moored at the pier. Had the Mexicans cut off all of the outside world? Would he even be able to leave, himself, to get back to the Big Thicket?

Placing such a worry from his mind, Cyril removed his hat and looked about him, marveling at what Leana had managed to do with this establishment. On his left he saw a room that had been converted into a general store, and to his right, he saw a room that had been converted into a saloon. But both establishments lacked customers this day, making Cyril feel vulnerable to those who might look closer at him, wondering about this new stranger in town.

A swish of skirt and petticoat drew Cyril's attention to the staircase ahead. His insides trembled when seeing the face and eyes of the young woman of his dreams of only hours ago. His fingers tightened on the brim of his sombrero, again seeing so much familiar about her. Was it the slight crook of her nose? Was it her jet-black hair, naturally curly, blossoming into tight ringlets of curls about her square face and across her shoulders? Or was it her eyes . . . eyes so much like his own in their color of gray?

It was all these things that had brought him to Rufino, and even more. He would first thank her for seeing to his knife wound, then he would find out about her past life. . . .

Darla glided down the staircase, her silk dress low-swept at the bodice and fully gathered at her waist. She had seen the man's approach from an upstairs window, had even watched him leave his horse reined in front of the hotel.

By habit she watched everyone's entrance into the city these days, having a certain gentleman caller coming now to see her on a regular basis, though she did worry what Leana would say when she returned and found out.

And when *would* Leana emerge from hiding? And where *was* she? Only notes had been sent, reassuring Darla that Leana was all right, yet never telling her what had happened to delay her return home. But it had been enough to know that Leana was alive and well. Where she was and with whom shouldn't even matter to Darla. . . .

Darla swept on down the stairs and moved toward the gentleman, who seemed to be staring an open hole through her, he was so closely scrutinizing her. There seemed something familiar about *him,* yet she couldn't put her finger on just what, so went to him and offered a handshake of friendship.

"Good morning, sir," she said, feeling the coarseness of his fingers as he returned the proffered hand. "Have you come for a room, supplies from the general store, or entertainment one can find in Leana's saloon? I can assure you that none of these things will disappoint you."

She eyed his hand questioningly as he still held on to hers, feeling a trace of fear enter her heart with him still watching her so intensely, and still not saying that first word to her.

"Sir . . . ?" she said dryly, inching her hand from his. "Is there something I can help you with? If not, please . . . be . . . on your way."

Cyril's lips lifted into a slow smile, his hands nervously turning his sombrero around and around. "You don't recognize me, do ye?" he chuckled.

Darla pinched her face into a wondering gaze as she looked up at him and, yes, began seeing traces of resemblances. "Should I know you?" she asked.

"Me wound is quite healed, lassie," he chuckled, leaning down into her face. "Yer spider webs and chimney soot did the trick. I've come to thank ye, lassie."

Darla's eyes widened, now remembering him, though his mustache had been shaved, his hair trimmed, and his clothes quite different than before. "Why, you're Cyril Dalton," she said, laughing softly. "You're the pir—"

Cyril gently covered her mouth with a hand. "No need in announcin' it to the world," he chuckled, glancing across his shoulder. Then he looked toward the staircase. "Do you have private quarters where we can talk? I've managed to elude the Mexicans thus far, but I'm not sure for how much longer." He chuckled again. "Ye see, wee lassie, I don' talk the Mexican ways of speakin'. You might say, eh, I've a brogue?"

Darla laughed softly. She leaned up into his face. "Yes, you do have a brogue," she whispered. She nodded with her head toward the staircase. "Come with me. We can go to my room. It'd be nice to have someone to chat with." She smiled sweetly at José as he entered the room from the general store, then pinched her face into a frown as she spoke again to Cyril. "José is a nice young man but not the best to have a decent conversation with."

Cyril placed his hand to Darla's elbow and began guiding her up the stairs.

"And you say that you are now well?" Darla asked, looking in the direction where she remembered his wound having been.

"Hardly a pucker of a scar left," Cyril laughed. "And because you were so skilled at what ye were doin'."

"Thank you, sir," Darla said, laughing softly. Then she remembered Cyril's association with Brandon and again wondered if Leana might be with him. "Sir, have you just left Brandon? Might . . . might you know something of . . . of . . . Leana's whereabouts? I've been so concerned about her, though she *has* managed to send me notes from time to time, telling me to not worry."

Cyril's eyebrows forked. "Oh? She has done this?" he said, wondering which of his pirate crew came and went from Rufino without his permission. Yet if they had Brandon's permission, wasn't it the same . . . ?

"Yes. But seeing her is what would make me worry less," Darla pouted. She stepped up onto the second-floor landing and made a turn to her left, taking a lingering look toward her mother's closed door, thinking her to perhaps still be asleep. Of late, her mother slept more than she was awake.

"If that is so, then I can tell you that she's farin' fine," Cyril said, nodding a thank you as Darla directed him on into her room.

"Oh? So then you've seen her?" Darla asked, her eyes wide. She turned the wick up on a kerosene lamp and got an even better look at Cyril Dalton. Something about him stirred an uneasiness inside her, yet as before, she couldn't put her finger on what. It could mean nothing that their eyes and nose so resembled. . . .

"Brandon and I have seen that she's been comfortable enough," Cyril said, walking about the room, seeing how neatly she kept it.

"Then she's been with you *and* Brandon all of this time?" Darla asked cautiously, watching him out of the corner of her eyes as she lifted a tea pitcher and slowly began pouring tea into cups. She knew that the pirates most generally did not wish to discuss anything private of themselves. But where was Leana? Where did these pirates stay when not on a ship . . . ?

"Like I said, she's farin' fine," Cyril said, placing his hat on a table.

"Tea?" Darla asked, offering him a cup.

"Tea?" Cyril chuckled, shivering at the thought. "Well, aye, I guess so."

"Please sit down and relax," Darla asked, laughing softly. "You did come here to talk, didn't you? Please relax while doing so."

Cyril eased down into a chair and accepted the cup of tea. He watched her move about the room, then tensed when she opened a door to an adjoining room and peeked inside, then closed the door again and came to sit down across from him.

She reached for her own cup of tea and took a sip as she smiled over the rim at Cyril, yet her smile faded when she saw him staring toward the closed door that led into her mother's room.

"You don't live alone?" Cyril asked thickly, his heart racing.

"No. I don't," Darla said, her voice strained, wondering why he was suddenly interested in who lay in the bed in the next room.

He turned his gaze slowly back to Darla. His eyes were steel-gray, his lips set into a straight line. "But you said you had no one to talk with besides José since Leana was gone," he tested, placing his cup of tea on a table beside him. He leaned forward and clasped his hands nervously together on his lap. "Darla, tell me a little about yerself," he said in a rush of words. "Are you originally from here? Where are yer parents?"

An iciness seemed to grab at Darla's insides. She inched up out of the chair, pale. "Why would you ask?" she said quietly. She gave him a cold stare. "Why are you truly here? You didn't come to just share idle conversation after you offered me a thank you for helping you in your time of need. Why do you ask me so many personal questions at once? Who are *you?*"

From nervousness, Darla took a cheroot from a case of many and placed it to her lips and lit it.

Cyril's mouth went agape, amazed at this dainty lady who chose to smoke cigars! But then he saw further than the cigar, seeing alarm in her eyes, most surely caused by his questions. He cursed beneath his breath. He hadn't handled this at all well. Now he had frightened her!

A weak voice spoke from the adjoining room. "Darla? Daughter . . . please . . ."

Darla jumped when she heard the voice of her mother calling for her. But she grew coldly numb when seeing Cyril pale as he again looked toward the door.

"Is that yer mother in the other room?" he asked, his pulse racing. Surely he was right to be thinking what he was thinking. It was all beginning to fit into place, like a puzzle. . . .

"Why should that concern you?" Darla asked, flinching when her mother again called out to her.

"I don't believe you ever told me yer last name, Darla," Cyril said thickly.

"Yates. Darla Yates."

Cyril's heart plummeted. He lowered his eyes and shook his head wearily. It appeared that he was wrong after all. . . .

"I must see to my mother," Darla said, resting her cheroot in an ashtray. She gave Cyril a sideways glance, then turned and hurried to her mother's room. She knelt beside her mother's bed and reached for a cloth in a basin of water and began bathing her mother's brow with it. Though her mother had been ailing for many years now, there were still traces of her past loveliness. Yet her cheeks were so sunken and gaunt, and her hair was so thin.

Cyril crept into the room and to the bed. Darla felt his presence, and her nerves tightened when she looked slowly up into his face, seeing how ghostly he looked in his paleness. Why . . . ?

"God almighty . . ." Cyril gasped, teetering. His sight went momentarily fuzzy, a light-headedness almost overcoming him when looking down onto the face of his Amelia, still recognizing her though the years had taken her youth.

But he could never have forgotten one inch of her lovely face. It had been etched into his brain as a leaf can become fossilized into stone. And now that he had found her, he knew that he could never truly hate her. And, oh, wasn't she so frail and ill?

"What's the matter with you?" Darla snapped as she rose and spoke into his face. "Get out of here. My mother is quite ill. Why are you acting so strangely? You don't even *know* my mother."

Cyril blinked his eyes nervously. As though willed to, he framed Darla's face between his hands, now fully understanding why her face had so haunted him. "Darla? My . . . daughter . . . Darla . . . ?" he said aloud.

Darla's heart skipped a beat. Her throat went suddenly dry. "What . . . ?" she gasped. "What . . . did . . . you say . . . ?"

"You must be me daughter," Cyril said thickly, tears burning his eyes. "God almighty, Darla. You *are* me daughter."

Darla slapped his hands away, panic rising inside her. "You must be mad!" she cried. She pointed toward the door. "Get out!"

"Darla?" Amelia whispered, her eyes fluttering open. "Did I hear Cyril speaking? Has . . . he . . . returned from the sea? Has . . . he . . . come for me . . . ?"

Darla's insides splashed cold. She turned with a start. Her mother had only recently begun to remember things and talk again after many years of being in some sort of a trance. But now . . . to say something so . . . so crazy . . . ? No! This man . . . Cyril Dalton . . . could not mean anything to her mother! He could not mean anything to *her!*

Cyril knelt to his knees beside the bed. He took Amelia's limp hand in his; he saw the violet of her eyes. He choked back a tear when he saw also a faint smile on her lips. "Aye. I've returned from the sea, my sweet, wee lassie," he said hoarsely. "'Ave you been a missin' me?

'Ave ye been waitin' long, me love?"

Amelia's eyes found the reflection of his gold necklace. "It *is* you, Cyril," she whispered, her voice slight, weak. "My love, you have returned . . . to . . . me. You've *found* me, Cyril. You've . . . found . . . me."

Cyril leaned his cheek into the palm of her hand. Then he spoke to Darla, who was stunned numb by what she was witnessing. "How long has she been like this, Darla?" he asked. "How long have you been in Rufino with 'er?"

"Mother has been like this for years," Darla said, going on the opposite side of the bed to get a better look at this man whom she now knew to be her father. "She's had a hard life. But of course you truly don't care. You left her with a child long ago, didn't you? If you are my father, I will never confess to anyone that you are. You are nothing but a filthy pirate who deserted a wife and child."

Amelia began slowly shaking her head back and forth. She looked up at Darla, her voice still weak, yet determined. "I lied to you, darling," she said, tears running in silver rivulets down her face. "It was I who left. Not . . . not . . . Cyril. I am to blame for . . . all . . . our misfortune."

Darla's knees weakened. She stumbled down into a chair, her face blank. "This is all too . . . much . . . for me. . . ." she murmured. She hung her head in her hands.

Cyril was torn. He wanted to comfort both his wife and daughter. But Amelia wouldn't give up her hold on his hand. "I was wrong, Cyril," she whispered. "I shouldn't have ever left. But once I did, there was no turning back."

"Yer last name. It is not the same as mine," Cyril said, choking back the urge to cry.

"I changed it to Yates," Amelia sobbed. She turned her face from Cyril. "I at first didn't want you to find me. Then after Darla got used to the name Yates, I couldn't change it." She slowly looked up at him. "Now, could I?" she said, pleading with her eyes.

"No. I guess not," Cyril said. He wiped his eyes with the back of his sleeve. "It's not too late fer us, Amelia," he said, yet knowing that it was. He could tell that she didn't have long to live. She had wasted away to almost nothing. But he could make her comfortable in her remaining weeks . . . months, yet surely not years.

"Oh, but . . . it . . . is. . . ." Amelia said, smiling weakly up at him. "And I'm so sorry . . . for . . . that."

"I'm going to take ye with me," Cyril said, ignoring Darla's gasp. "We will be together now, forever, my darling."

He bent his lips to her brow and kissed her, remembering how they had once kissed so passionately, making love for hours until satiated. But now? Her body and her mind would never know such love again. Only the type that could make her feel needed. . . .

Cyril slipped her hand from his and rose to go to Darla. He urged her up from her chair and touched the softness of her cheek. "Now do you believe that I'm yer father?" he asked. "And can you help me get yer mother ready? I *am* takin' 'er with me. Her final days must be spent with me. We've already lost too many years."

"But . . . how . . . ?" Darla said, finding it easy to accept this man as her father now that her mother had confirmed it. Darla had taken an instant liking to him when she had cared for his wound. He had even then probably been reaching out for her. . . .

"You arrange to get a wagon. I'll take 'er by wagon to me mansion."

"But where?"

Cyril's insides tightened. "Must ye know?"

"I must know where my mother is at all times," Darla said dryly. "She's all I've had all these years."

"Then you come with us."

"No. I can't. I must stay here until Leana returns. I gave my word. I must make sure General Rufino doesn't get the chance to take possession of *Leana's* in Leana's absence."

"You would trust yer mother with me?"

"Do I . . . have . . . a choice . . . ?"

Cyril chuckled. "Not really."

"But you *must* tell me where you are taking her."

"I have a mansion in the Big Thicket," he said quietly. "Only a few know where. You must give *me* yer word that you will tell no one."

"You have my word. But what if I want to come, to see my mother? How would I find it?"

"When that time comes, there will be someone come for you."

Darla knelt beside the bed and clasped onto her mother's hands. She placed her face to her mother's chest. "Oh, Mother," she murmured. "Is this what *you* want?"

"I've waited forever for . . . this . . . moment, Darla," Amelia whispered. "I've only lived in my dreams . . . dreams of being with the man I loved. Yes. I . . . want . . . to go with him."

Darla looked up at Cyril. "You must wait until after

dark," she said softly. "The Mexicans usually are too drunk by then to notice much what goes on. You will be safe to leave Rufino only then."

Cyril knelt down beside Darla. He placed his arm about his daughter's waist, then touched Amelia's . . . his *wife's* . . . face wonderingly. . . .

Chapter Twenty-Eight

Breakfast sat cooling on the table, no one having any appetite to eat. Brandon paced, Leana watched on, sipping a cup of coffee at the table, while Wanda stood vigil beside a window.

"Where could he be?" Brandon grumbled. "Cyril hadn't said he would be gone this long. He told me he was just going to the edge of Rufino, to see how things were there. I had thought it an innocent enough reason for him to have this outing. I'm sure he was getting restless, being so cooped up and all."

Brandon slammed a fist into the palm of his other hand. "Damn it. I wish the *Erebus* were repaired enough to get Cyril out on it. Seems that's the only way to tame his restless moods. And now that he is well, his moods will only darken."

"I pray you are wrong," Wanda said, turning pensive eyes to Brandon. "He has become hard to live with both day *and* night. Why, yesterday morning, I thought—"

The sound of a wagon approaching was cause for Wanda to go quickly silent. Brandon tensed, drawing a pistol from its holster as he edged toward the window. "Move, Wanda," he flatly ordered. "I must see who is approaching. It can't be Cyril. He left on horseback."

"But if it was anybody else, surely whoever it was would have been stopped by those guarding the mansion," Leana said, quickly rising from the table. The skirt of her cotton dress tangled in her legs as she went hurriedly to the door as the wagon drew closer, coming to the back of the house.

Opening the door, Leana saw Cyril as he guided the wagon close to the back porch. Her eyes quickly switched directions, now seeing someone stretched out in the back of the wagon, wrapped in heavy blankets, eyes the only thing visible through the wrappings.

"Who . . . ?" Leana gasped, placing her hands to her throat.

Cyril hurried from the wagon. He nodded toward Leana. "Tell Brandon to get the hell out here," he shouted, flailing an arm. "Hurry, Leana."

Brandon had heard the order. He slipped his pistol back in its holster and rushed from the house. He stopped short when seeing Cyril climbing into the wagon, where someone lay quite secured in blankets.

"Brandon, give me a hand," Cyril said, gently lifting Amelia into his arms, seeing the trust in her eyes as she followed each of his movements. His gut twisted, only wishing that trust had been there those many years ago. Oh, the years that had been wasted without her . . . even without his *daughter*.

"Who *is* this?" Brandon said, racing down the steps, opening his arms for Cyril to place Amelia into them.

"You won't believe it when I tell you," Cyril said in a growl. "Just hurry up and get her upstairs and comfortably in a bed." He gestured with a hand toward Leana. "Help him, Leana. Get the bed ready in the room that looks out over the garden. I want Amelia to have a pleasant view from her bed." He shouted to Brandon. "We've got to make sure the bed is close *to* the window. She's been kept cooped up in a damn hotel room long enough, away from all things pleasant."

Brandon was halfway up the steps when he heard Cyril say the name *Amelia*. He almost lost his footing as he turned questioning eyes back to Cyril. "Amelia . . . ?" he said shallowly. "Cyril, not *the* Amelia."

"The one and only," Cyril said, jumping from the wagon, going to stand beside Brandon, to check on Amelia's coloring as he gently drew the blanket away from her face. "Darling, you'll be in a bed real soon now. I'm sorry for the long, tedious ride in the wagon."

Tears misted Amelia's eyes as she smiled up at Cyril. "I felt nothing except happiness because I . . . I . . . was finally with you again," she managed in a weak whisper.

"God . . ." Brandon said, then hurried inside the house and up the stairs with everyone trailing along behind him. Leana brushed on past him and went to the window of which Cyril had spoken. She was numb from knowing just who Cyril had brought to his mansion, yet full of wonder as to *why*. Leana knew that Amelia was Darla's mother. But what was she . . . to . . . Cyril . . . ?

Drawing drapes open, lifting a window, and then throwing the shutters aside, Leana felt the freshness of the air as it fluttered on past her and into the room. She turned and watched Cyril shoving the bed close to the window. When Brandon lay the tiny bundle on the bed, she hurried to the bedside and began gently unwrapping the blankets from about Amelia, glancing at Cyril, wishing she knew what this was all about.

But the pained look on his face caused her to keep her questions to herself. She could see that he was hurting. It was obvious that it was because of this woman . . . a woman he surely had known sometime in the past. . . .

Wanda stormed into the room. "Who is this woman?" she shouted. "I demand to know. Why won't somebody tell me? Why did you bring her here, Cyril?"

Cyril's face became as dark as a storm cloud ready to burst. He went to Wanda and took her by a wrist and led her out into the hallway. "Now isn't the time for any type of show from you," he said stiffly. "And if you must know . . . the lady in that room is . . . me . . . wife."

Wanda paled. She took a quick step backward, trembling. "You never told me that . . . your wife was still alive," she stammered. "Where has she been? Why do you bring her here now?"

"I never knew where she was before," he said, not wanting to waste time explaining this to everyone. He just wanted to be with Amelia. But he knew that Wanda wouldn't rest until she had answers. "I only found 'er today. Now, will you just go to yer room and leave me to me wife and making 'er as comfortable as possible?"

Wanda gave him a steady stare, then turned and fled away from him, sobbing.

"Amelia, are you all right?" Leana softly asked as she pulled the last of the bulky blankets from about Amelia's frail body. "Did the long ride weaken you too much?"

"I'm fine," Amelia said, breathing hard. She closed her eyes, feeling the weariness she would not confess to. But her heart was singing, warmed with happiness. She had prayed for this day but thought God had forgotten her long ago when she had had to sell her body to make her way in life.

If not for her daughter, Amelia wouldn't have resorted to such a way of life. But after leaving Cyril *and* Scotland, she had been forced to do what she must to keep Darla clothed and fed. When she had become ill she even knew that Darla had begun making the same sort of living, and the knowing had almost killed Amelia. But then Leana, the angel that she was, had come along and Darla had been able to live a decent, clean life. . . .

Cyril came back into the room. Brandon cornered him. "Why did you bring her here?" he growled. "Cyril, I thought you hated her. And how the hell did you find her?"

"You know she's me wife. But do you know what else she is to me?" Cyril said, looking on past Brandon to how Leana was now bathing Amelia's brow with a damp cloth.

"How should I?"

"She's Darla's mother. Darla . . . is . . . my daughter."

Brandon's mouth dropped open. "Do you mean all along—"

"Aye. Me own wife and daughter have been so close."

"But how did you know?"

"Didn't you look closely enough at Darla to see the resemblance in me?"

"I had no need to think about it."

"I did, Brandon. Even when I was semiconscious I noticed it. It's bothered me since."

Brandon clasped onto Cyril's shoulders. "But as I said before, Cyril," he grumbled, "you're supposed to hate her for having deserted you those many years ago, and for taking your child from you . . . a child you never did even get to see. Why show pity on her now? It goes against everything you ever said about her."

Cyril's brow creased as he frowned. "Brandon, don't ye see her condition?" he said quietly. "She's not goin' to las' long. How could I turn my back on 'er?"

"How? Just the way she did *you*."

"But, Brandon, seein' 'er makes me realize just how much I still love 'er," Cyril said, almost choking when seeing her thin shoulders when Leana pushed Amelia's dress down, readying her for a gown. "Aye, I love 'er. Always 'ave, me lad."

Brandon's patience was narrowing. "And now what about Wanda?" he growled. "All these years you've taught me to not mingle seriously with women, and now it seems you've got *two* on *your* hands."

Cyril squared his shoulders and glowered at Brandon. "Lad, that's my problem. Not yers," he said dryly.

"Oh? I see," Brandon said. He flew from the room, seeing Cyril as a weak, confused man. Well, he was not going to be a party to such a weakness. He was going to break ties with his pirate friend, now and possibly forever.

Leana ran after Brandon. She grabbed his arm, seeing his anger. "Brandon, what is it? Where are you going?" she said, breathless.

"I'm leaving this place," he growled. "I'm leaving Cyril."

"Why, for God's sake?"

"That woman he's brought home?" Brandon said, nodding toward the bedroom.

"Yes? What about her?"

"She's Cyril's wife," Brandon said flatly. "The wife he's been tryin' to forget all these years suddenly appears again in his life."

404

Leana paled. "But, Brandon, if that is true, then Darla is—"

"His daughter," Brandon said, walking hurriedly onward, Leana anxiously at his side. "Are you going with me or staying in this house suddenly gone crazy?"

"Where are you going, Brandon?"

"To the Seton ranch," he growled. He stopped and gazed down at her. "Come with me. Let's show Matthew a thing or two. If not all, at least a portion of that ranch belongs to me. I am to make claim on it. After today I'm damn ready for a fight."

"You plan to . . . live at the . . . ranch . . . ?"

"Until I make other arrangements."

"Then I cannot go with you, Brandon."

"Why the hell not?"

Her eyes were innocently wide. "Because Matthew will be there. Or are you going to suggest he leave?"

"He can stay if he wishes," Brandon shrugged. "I'm not a horse's ass who would deny *him* of what is *his*. Part of the Seton fortune *is* his." His eyelids grew heavy over his eyes. "As part of it is rightfully *yours*."

Leana lowered her eyes. "Yes, I believe that, also," she murmured. "But as long as Matthew lives at the ranch, I can't. He and I were never meant to live under the same roof."

Then she looked directly into his eyes. "And I must go to Darla," she said softly. "I'm sure she's torn by the discovery of who her true father is. And do you see? She was loyal to me by staying at the hotel instead of coming here with her mother and father. I must go to Rufino, to see if she wants to come and join her family."

Brandon drew her into his arms. "Always one who thinks of others," he said thickly. "I will see you safely to

Rufino. After you see to Darla and your businesses, come to the ranch. Surely we can arrange something."

Leana leaned away from him. "As long as Matthew is there, I will not even enter that house," she said firmly.

"Then I will have to see what can be done about that," Brandon said, again drawing Leana into his arms. He gave her a tender kiss, yet not feeling anything but torn emotions, feeling as though he had just lost a father. How could he have been so wrong about Cyril, for so long . . . ?

Leana hadn't realized just how much she had missed her places of business until now. As she entered her hotel her heart soared with pride, wondering if she would ever be able to leave it behind.

But if she ever were to get married, she knew that a true home . . . a real family . . . would have precedence over her establishments. Having lost her father at such a young age, she had not had a normal family while growing up, though Parker Seton had tried his damnedest to take the place of her father.

And Brandon, after age ten, had lacked a true family sort of relationship.

When she and Brandon married . . . *if* . . . they married, theirs would be totally *family*. Leana wanted children . . . and she wanted any child brought into this world to have a normal family relationship.

But she cringed when thinking of Brandon's love of the sea. She now knew that she could never marry him until he promised to leave his pirating days completely behind him!

Stepping farther into the hotel lobby, she was not

surprised to find it quiet and empty except for José, who was now running toward her to greet her. Weren't the streets mostly empty as well? Leana feared what the next few days or weeks might bring to this community. She dreaded coming face-to-face with General Rufino again. It wouldn't surprise her if he forced her from Rufino and gained full possession of *Leana's* without even paying one cent for it!

José's face was beaming, his dark eyes dancing as he stopped and looked anxiously up at Leana. "Señora Leana," he said, clasping his eager hands tightly behind him. "We were all so worried." His gaze moved over her, seeing the breeches and shirt, and then upward, where her hair was circled beneath a sombrero. He laughed hoarsely. "It took me a minute to even recognize you."

Leana laughed lightly. She took the sombrero off and let her hair tumble in gorgeous black streamers across her shoulders. "Lord. I hope one day this sort of disguise won't be necessary," she said. She tossed the hat onto a chair and looked toward the staircase. Her smile faded. "How's Darla? Have you spoken with her since her mother left with Cyril Dalton?"

José's shoulders tightened, his head leaned forward as he looked cautiously from side to side. "I was told to not say that man's name aloud," he whispered, now leaning up to speak into Leana's face. "Darla fears her mother's life might be endangered if the soldiers know who her mother's husband is. And it is a total secret *where* her mother has been taken."

His small frame of a body shook as he laughed. "Isn't it exciting?" he said. "The intrigue of the situation. *Sí*, Leana?"

Leana reached a hand to his stiff, dark hair and tousled

it teasingly. "That's just what you need," she laughed. "Intrigue." She then glanced over her shoulder. "Though one day you just might have more excitement than you can handle. The streets are almost deserted, José. I saw no ships at the quay. General Rufino wants the whole town of Rufino to himself, it seems."

She gazed down into José's eyes and placed a hand to his smooth, bronze cheek. "The Americans will retaliate one day, José. I'm afraid the streets of Rufino will become a battleground. But, of course, that sort of excitement isn't what you speak of, is it?"

"No," he said, his eyes wide. "Before meeting you, I would be fighting the americanos." He shook his head and hung it sadly. "But now? I wouldn't know what to do. The Mexican are my people." His face jerked up and his eyes looked intensely into hers. "But you are also my people. You have even become family, Señora Leana."

Leana bent and drew him into her arms and hugged him to her. "I so appreciate that," she murmured. "And, José, when the time comes to choose loyalties, I don't think you're going to have a problem choosing."

A man's voice suddenly rang out from the staircase. "Well, now, isn't that a tender scene?"

Leana moved away from José in a jerk, her gaze now transfixed as she watched Matthew move down the stairs with Darla beside him, clinging to his arm. Leana blanched, looking from Matthew to Darla, not understanding why they should be together—and why was Darla clinging to him as though she more than knew him as a mere acquaintance? And when *had* they met?

Darla broke free and ran down the stairs and flew into Leana's arms. "I'm so glad you're finally here," she sobbed. "Leana, why did you stay so long?"

Leana hugged Darla back, yet her eyes were still watching Matthew wonderingly. "I see now that I shouldn't have," she murmured. "Seems the vultures preceded me."

Matthew chuckled, moving on toward her, now away from the stairs. He was, as usual, dressed impeccably, in fawn-colored, tight-fitting breeches, a frock coat, and ruffles at his throat and cuffs of his shirt. A cigar lay in the corner of his perfectly shaped mouth; his dark eyes were gleaming.

"Now, is that the way to talk about your brother?" he mockingly teased.

"Correction, Matt," Leana said dryly. "*Step*brother, thank God."

Darla eased from Leana's arms and stood wringing her hands as she looked from Leana to Matthew. She had expected something like this. But she was glad that Leana was here and this could soon be over with. Matthew and Leana could argue only so long, and then, hopefully, Darla could force them to make peace with each other.

It was necessary, since Darla and Matthew had already gotten married in Leana's absence. It had been a secret, even kept from Darla's mother. Her gut twisted with the thought of her mother, which now included, also, thoughts of . . . a . . . father. . . .

"I take it you've been with your other *step*brother," Matthew said, frowning. "How *is* the filthy pirate?"

Leana circled her fingers into tight fists, having to hold herself back from attacking Matthew. "If you wish to speak of filth, just look in the mirror, Matt, and you will see a perfect example," she hissed. "Now tell me. What are you doing here? I own this place and you're not welcome."

Matthew nodded toward Darla. "I think Darla would tend to argue that point," he grumbled. He gestured with a hand, beckoning Darla to come to him. "And you wouldn't want to argue with my wife, now, would you?"

Darla flinched when seeing the pinched, pained expression suddenly in Leana's eyes. She crept into Matthew's arms, awaiting an explosion from Leana.

"No!" Leana gasped, covering her mouth with a hand. She looked at Darla and then to Darla's ring finger. "Oh, Lord, it's true, isn't it, Darla? You married . . . this . . . bastard."

"Leana, please try to understand," Darla pleaded, letting Matthew possessively hold her at his side.

Leana nodded her head slowly. "I understand, all right," she said sourly. "Matt, you knew you couldn't have me, so you chose to get back at me by marrying my best *friend*. You wanted to cause friction between me and Darla, didn't you?"

Darla's face paled. She glanced up at Matthew. "You love me, don't you, Matthew?" she gulped. "Leana is wrong, isn't she?"

"Damn wrong," Matthew roared, jerking his cigar from his mouth, angrily tossing it across the room.

"Well, I hope so," Leana said, lowering her eyes, feeling suddenly so worn-out, drained. Then she let her eyes move slowly up and looked over at Darla. "When did it happen? How long have you known Matthew?"

"I met him even before you asked me to come and work for you," Darla said, swallowing hard. "You see, he first paid me . . . for . . . my services. I was even taken to . . . to . . . the ranch. I know it quite well, Leana. And I've been waiting for your return, so I can join Matthew there."

410

Leana's eyebrows forked. Was she seeing a side to Darla that she hadn't known to be there? Oh, but, yes. Surely Darla would have seen the riches of the Seton family. And being so poor, wouldn't she, if possible, take advantage of these riches?

Ah, it seemed that perhaps Matthew had been the one taken advantage of. Before Darla had ever met any of the Seton family, she had fought and scratched for survival. Now it would no longer be necessary. . . .

Knowing that Matthew might possibly have been "had" drew a contented, smug smile to Leana's face. "Darla, how do you feel about your mother and your . . . uh . . . father getting back together?" she asked, glancing up at Matthew, wondering if he knew the full details of who Darla truly was, who her true father was. . . .

"My mother has pined her life away for many years," Darla murmured. "And now I know why." She nodded her head. "Yes. I'm glad for Mother. I only hope Cyril . . . my father . . . treats her as gently as I. Mother needs gentleness. She is so frail. . . ."

"She will get the best of care, I am sure," Leana said. She kneaded her brow, yearning for escape. "I'm going to my room, Darla. Go on with Matthew if you like. I . . . I . . . understand."

Then she smiled wickedly as she let her eyes meet and hold with Matthew's. "But when you arrive at the Seton ranch, you might find yourself a little surprise," she said, knowing that Brandon would be there, waiting for Matthew's return.

Ah, and what a surprise *Brandon* would also have. Life seemed to continually get complicated by one thing or another.

411

"What are you talking about?" Matthew grumbled. "What *sort* of surprise?"

"Why not go and find out for yourself?" Leana said, laughing as she walked toward the staircase. . . .

Wanda paced the floor, anger and jealousy fused into one gnawing at her insides. Her skirt rustled as she made another turn and continued pacing. She was bitter . . . she was humiliated! All those times Cyril had been making love to her, his thoughts had been on a wife . . . a wife he was longing for, wanting *her* in his arms, not *Wanda*.

"Oh, what shall I do?" she softly cried, looking woefully up at the ceiling. She had struggled with life all these years, and now that she had found a man . . . a man who not only offered her pleasure, but also *riches* . . . it was all going to be taken from her again, and all because of a wife suddenly surfacing, almost, it seemed, from the woodwork!

"She's a sickly wimp," she whispered, knowing that alone would pull more attention Amelia's way.

Wanda stopped with a start, her heart pounding, her face suddenly flushed with an idea. "Sickly?" she whispered. "Might . . . she . . . even die? It could be sudden, could it not?"

Fear crept into her heart at what she was thinking to do. She had done many things in her lifetime to get what she wanted. But never had she . . .

"But I *must*," she murmured. "No one can have Cyril but me." She looked about the room at the richness of the gold satin draperies hanging plushly at the windows, and at the intricately carved oak furnishings. Velveteen chairs and pictures framed in pure gold drew a quivering sigh from between her lips.

Going to the mirror large enough to reflect a crowd, she began drawing a hairbrush whose handle was also pure gold through her hair, her eyes dark with greed, her pulse racing.

"Yes, I . . . must . . ." she whispered to her reflection in the mirror.

Slamming the hairbrush down on the dressing table, she inched toward the door, wondering if Cyril had given up his vigil at his wife's bedside and had retired, himself, for the night. Though now once again healthy, he tired more easily than before his chest wound. He needed a full night's rest each night, and the previous night had been taken up fully with travels while bringing his wife to his mansion. . . .

Opening her bedroom door, flinching when it emitted a low creaking sound, Wanda peered out into the hallway. White tapered candles in sconces along the wall cast dancing shadows along the floor, ceiling, and the closed doors on either side of the hallway. There were no sounds. The silence was even almost deafening.

"He must be asleep," Wanda whispered, stepping on out into the hallway. Her gaze locked on the door behind which the frail Amelia lay. Wanda had to believe that Amelia would be too weak to cry out for help. And, hopefully, Amelia would be asleep and wouldn't even know what was happening to her. It could be over . . . in . . . a . . . matter of minutes. . . .

Creeping stealthily to Amelia's door, Wanda placed her trembling hands to the doorknob and slowly began turning it. She barely breathed, hoping Cyril would not be there.

Yet would he leave his wife for even his needed sleep? He had just found her. What if he fought sleep and stayed with her this first entire night . . . ?

The thought made the hair raise at the nape of Wanda's neck. How could she explain why she was coming to Amelia's room in the middle of the night should Cyril catch her there . . . ?

Yet she wouldn't think on that. She would just hope that Cyril *was* too tired to do anything but sleep. . . .

Stepping on into the room, not taking time to close the door behind her, Wanda breathed more easily when seeing the chair vacant at Amelia's bedside. Cyril was not there. And if Wanda moved swiftly, the deed could be done and *she* would be safely back in *her* assigned room.

Knowing the wickedness of her plan, she only felt a trace of guilt as she moved to the bed. She could feel her pulse pounding in the hollow of her throat, her knees had grown bizarrely weak, looking down upon the face of sickness, so gaunt, yet strangely enough, so hauntingly beautiful. Amelia's thick lashes were closed over her eyes, she breathed peacefully, her hair lay in pools of gold tainted with threads of silver about her face.

But Wanda felt only hate and jealousy for this lady who was robbing her of her future most surely as if she had done it by gunpoint! And this was why Wanda was driven to do what she must for her own survival. . . .

The pillow was so close, one not being used by Amelia. Wanda's fingers trembled as she picked the pillow up, her breathing coming in rasps, so near to taking another's life. She would not wait for Amelia to die naturally! People like her were known to hang on for years! And now that Cyril had brought her to his house, and with his pampering, Amelia could possibly even live *forever!*

Wanda did not have that long. She would . . . not . . . wait. . . .

Raising the pillow into the air, she held it above Amelia only momentarily, finding her courage waning. But then she began lowering the pillow, lower . . . lower . . . and when she finally placed it to Amelia's face and began holding it there, she began to feel ill to her stomach when Amelia began struggling and gasping for breath.

Suddenly a shot rang out and Wanda felt a sharp burning pierce her back, and she knew that she had . . . just . . . been shot.

Dropping the pillow, she turned around in jerks, the pain robbing her of her senses. Everything was becoming hazy, yet as she fell to the floor she was aware of Cyril now standing over her with a smoking pistol in his hand.

"You lived the life of a whore, you *die* a whore," he growled. . . .

Chapter Twenty-Nine

Leana lit a kerosene lamp, turning its wick up to fill the room fully with its soft glow. She felt strangely alone, still numb from knowing about Darla and Matthew. Yet she smiled to herself when remembering how Brandon now surely awaited Matthew's return to the ranch. If she could be small enough, a mouse perhaps, she would sorely love to sneak into the ranch house and watch the two brothers' verbal attacks.

Matthew would surely be the loser. Brandon was quite skilled in taking what he wanted. He had been trained by a master, it seemed. Though Brandon seemed to think less of Cyril now, she knew that he would change his mind once he had time to think about his hastiness to condemn the man . . . his *mentor*.

A hot bath awaited Leana. She went to the tub and leaned against it as she pulled a boot off and then began struggling with the other. But heavy footsteps approaching outside in the hall drew her numbly quiet, her eyes moving slowly to her door. After filling her tub with warmed water, she had forgotten to lock her door. She tensed and rose slowly to her feet, teetering because of wearing one boot and the other only half-off, watching the doorknob turn.

When the door burst open, Leana's jaw tightened and her chin lifted, anger welling inside her. "Sir, don't you have even the courtesy to knock?" she hissed, yet fearing this Mexican now that she was only one of the few remaining Americans in Rufino.

Her gaze swept over General Rufino, seeing how immaculate his black uniform was and that his eyes were not bloodshot, which had to mean that he was quite sober, free of the effects of his pastime of opium.

A hand on the saber at his side, General Rufino laughed throatily as he lumbered on into the room. "Ah, beautiful señorita, have I disturbed your bath?" he said, glancing at the tub of water, then at Leana. "But, no. My timing was wrong. Had I been one *momento* longer, might I not have found you *in* the water, quite nude, *sí?*"

Her face growing hot with a blush, Leana folded her arms angrily across her chest. She teetered, the boot half-off making her still quite awkward, then she composed her stature and glared at the Mexican. "Why are you here?" she asked. "You've left me quite alone till now. What do you want of me? Or do I need even ask?"

General Rufino outstretched a hand and rubbed his thumb and forefinger together. "*Dinero,*" he grumbled. "I have come for more payment, Señorita. If you plan to stay in Rufino, you must pay me well. Do you understand?"

"No. I don't understand," Leana said shallowly. "I paid you well. And you see how I've bettered this establishment. I've spent much money renovating. I've made my places of business something you can look at and be proud to *have* in your town of Rufino. Surely you ask no more of me than that."

General Rufino came farther into the room. He kneaded his chin as he looked over her choice of furnishings, seeing the gentle colors of her drapes and the canopy of her bed. Even her carpet was of an earth-tone color of beige.

A slow smile crept onto his face as he turned and challenged her with a set stare. "*Sí,* I like what you have done," he said. "And you did pay me well. But things have changed, Señorita."

"What has changed?" Leana said, limping with her hanging boot to a chair. She jerked the boot angrily off and tossed it across the floor.

"But, yet, need I ask?" she said, rising to stand tall and straight now that she was completely barefoot. "You've managed to chase almost all of the Americans from Rufino. What you are doing here with me is a ploy to rid the town of me also, is it not? You don't truly want payment. You want me out of town so it can be all Mexican again. Aren't I right?"

General Rufino's dark, heavy eyebrows lifted. He laughed throatily. "I've always liked your spirit," he said. "Even *now* you challenge me. Even now that the news has arrived that General Antonio López de Santa Anna has won at the Alamo? Or haven't you heard about how General Santa Anna's great army attacked San Antonio? And that those fighting him retreated to join those at the Alamo? And then that all those at the fort were killed? Santa Anna this very moment pursues the americano Sam Houston, who my Mexican comrades will *also* kill."

"How horrible," Leana gasped, now truly fearing this

man and all Mexicans.

"But of course you have been too busy away from Rufino to know *anything* of what's been happening," General Rufino taunted. He leaned up into her face. "When I discovered you were missing, I sent my soldiers looking for you. I even sent them into the Big Thicket. But no one could find you. Where have you been, beautiful señorita? With what *man?* Were you with that pirate again?"

Leana grew cold inside, recalling the flashing lights while she and Brandon had been hog hunting in the Big Thicket. It *had* been the Mexicans. They had come so close to finding the hideout, it made goose bumps crawl along Leana's flesh. "Why do you even care about who I am with or where I am?" she asked shallowly. "You even now threaten to force me from my establishment."

"I want to protect my interests. This is why I search for you," he shrugged. "No one else could please me as you do in caring for this beautiful hotel." He shrugged again. "I do not wish to see you leave. Just that you pay to *stay*."

He walked to the window and peered outward. "I have the powers to force you to leave or stay," he grumbled. "All gringos are even being denied entrance *into* Texas now. And now that General Santa Anna has shown the americanos who is the toughest, all Texas will become Mexico's *again*."

He swung around and smiled at her, cocking an eyebrow. "But you, my beautiful señorita, I would like to see you stay." He moved to her and ran his hand down her arm. "Perhaps one day you would even join me at my villa for . . . eh . . . entertainment?"

Then he chuckled, glancing at her attire of breeches

419

and shirt. "But, of course, I would buy you beautiful silk dresses," he said. "Your choice of apparel is shocking."

He went to her wardrobe and opened it and ran his fingers through the silk and satin of her dresses. "Yet you have many beautiful dresses already, no?" he said, giving her a glance from across his shoulder. "The man's clothes is for when you sneak about like a thief in the night?"

Leana was standing quite still, wordless, listening, watching. She knew that she must watch every word spoken now. This Mexican's threat was real. He could say even whether she lived or *died*. If she could only give him cause to trust her . . . give him cause to leave her alone again . . . then she *would* flee in the night, no thief, but someone who must get to Brandon and warn him of what had happened in San Antonio. No one's life was safe. The ranches were now vulnerable to Mexican attack. . . .

"You came for payment," she said, watching his eyes light up. "I will give you my remaining jewels. Will that be enough to satisfy you?"

"You know I could take them forcefully, do you not?" he chuckled.

"Yes. But you have chosen not to. *Sí?*"

He shrugged. "*Sí*," he said. "But do not think that I wouldn't were you another sort of lady." He tossed his head. "As I see it, I need you. You have proven to be quite a lady of business. Sometimes this is more important than being a lady to *bed*."

"I'm glad you appreciate my accomplishments," she said dryly. Inching her way to her wardrobe, she brushed past him. "And I'm sure you also appreciate that I like my full privacy. After I give you the jewels, please leave me to my bath?"

"*Sí,*" he chuckled, gesturing with a hand. "*Por entero.*"

Leana fell to her knees and scooted boxes aside at the bottom of her wardrobe, then withdrew her box of jewelry. Standing, she handed the box to him. "Take them," she said dryly. "You needn't ask for more. This is all I have."

As he lifted the box, the light caught and reflected the diamonds and rubies up onto the Mexican's face. He smiled widely, then closed the lid and sauntered toward the door. "Until later, beautiful señorita," he said, tapping a finger to his brow in a half salute.

Leana stood trembling as he closed the door. She then rushed and locked it, leaning fully against it, knowing how lucky she was to be again left alone. He could have forced himself on her. He could have even killed her and no one would have even known, except for José, and José would know to not intervene. Though Mexican, he now had the reputation of liking Americans much too much.

Her knees wobbly, Leana went to the window and watched the Mexican general ride away on his horse. She watched until he reached his villa. She had to guess that he would celebrate his added victory with her and would lose himself in his pleasures of opium.

"I must get to the ranch," she whispered. "I'll wait until I think General Rufino is well inebriated and then I must again sneak from the town. And the Mexican won't even miss me this time. He surely thinks he's put enough fright in me to last a lifetime. . . ."

Looking up at the sky, she noted the slant of the sun. Soon. She would leave as soon as dusk fell in its utter grays.

She turned and looked at the waiting tub of water. She

shook her head. No need. She must stay in her breeches and shirt. She had to elude the Mexican watchdogs again at the edge of town. . . .

Comanche moon. Leana welcomed the full moon this night. Without it, she would have had trouble finding her way to the ranch. Yet she knew that beneath such light her way was not only made more accessible to her eyes, but also herself to whoever might come along on the trail.

Nudging the flanks of her horse with the heels of her boots, she urged it into a faster gallop. The night air was damp on her face, stinging it in its coldness as she rode against it. She kept her eyes darting about her, flinching when shadows moved beneath the swaying limbs of trees, then laughed softly to herself, knowing these shadows were from the swaying leaves and branches, not from the presence of a human.

The Big Thicket lay only a few feet alongside the one side of her, filled with its own sorts of shadows and night noises. Somewhere in the distance a panther screamed. It echoed from afar, where shadows didn't even penetrate in the utter darkness of the thick, high grasses, and trees pressed so closely together, one couldn't even walk through them.

The lonesome sound, the *threat* it carried with it, made a shiver ride Leana's spine. She ducked low over her horse, flicked the reins, and again nudged its flanks with the heels of her boots. She squinted her eyes as the air became sharper in its coldness with her increased speed. The moonbeams rode with her, silhouetting her likeness along the ground beside her, ghostly in its quiverings as she bounced low in the saddle.

And then she finally saw signs of coming close to the ranch, where ground tangle had been cleared and tall grass had been cut to at least eye level. And just as Leana began making her way around stumps of trees and knew to see her first glimpse, soon, of the tall, protective fence about the ranch, she stopped short and felt her heart skip not only one beat, but many.

Drawing her horse to a shuddering halt, she gaped openly at the Indians who were poised along the horizon on a high knoll, not that far from the Seton ranch. Her insides grew cold when letting her gaze move along the long line of Indians, silently counting many. She could make out the shapes of their lances in the moonlight and also war shields, which she knew the Comanche to carry.

"Comanches," she gasped. "Brandon. Oh, Lord, Brandon."

She knew that the Seton ranch had several men under its employ, yet surely not enough to fight off Indians! And she knew that even her riding to warn them wouldn't help matters any. She had to go for help!

Her thoughts became scrambled, wondering, who could she go for? The Mexicans in Rufino couldn't care less for any American lives. They had even enticed the Indians to go on a warpath with the Americans! She gathered these Indians must be a band of southern Comanches, the *Pehnahterkul.* The *Antelope,* the northern Comanches, remained aloof, refusing to listen to Mexican agents.

She again looked toward the Indians, seeing them sitting so quietly on their horses, wondering just how long they would wait before their attack. She then glanced up at the moon. It hadn't yet reached its highest point. Was that what they were waiting for? To attack when the moon was the brightest in the sky?

She looked over her shoulder, knowing that time was wasting. She had to go for help! But . . . who . . . ?

Her eyes moved in jerks toward the Big Thicket. Cyril! Surely he could get enough of his pirate crew together to come and help fight off the Indians! Though used to only fighting at sea, they still knew how to fire guns!

She again looked toward the Indians, and then in the direction of the ranch, torn. Should she just ride ahead and warn Brandon and Matthew? Or should she go for Cyril?

She set her jaw firmly. Surely Matthew had men on guard at all times! Surely they had already seen the Indians and understood the threat the Indians posed. What they needed were reinforcements!

Wheeling her horse around, Leana led it into the Big Thicket, hoping and praying that she could find her way to the mansion in the dark. She shook her head in despair. She had been on her way to the ranch to warn Brandon of the Mexicans. She had forgotten about the dangers of *Indians!* It was as though the ranch was being closed in on. Mexicans on one side . . . Indians on the other! It and everyone who resided there were surely doomed!

Determination spurred her onward, though quickly losing the aid of the moon as the ceiling of the forest blotted it from her sight. She touched the holstered pistol at her waist, for comfort. She felt the pressure of the sheathed manchette secured at the calf of her leg.

She breathed hard, frightened more than ever before in her life. Yet she knew she must go on. Brandon's life could even depend on her.

But what if she didn't return soon enough . . . ?

Ducking her head low, worrying about limbs, she inched her horse onward, letting it use its own animal instincts to guide her through the dark thicket. But soon her head began to swim with worry. She looked about her, seeing only silent darkness. She looked across her shoulder, seeing only silent darkness. Was . . . she . . . lost . . . ?

Her gut twisted, tears stung her eyes. Yet she urged the horse onward. Her thoughts were filled with the tales of people becoming lost in the Big Thicket, never heard from again. She was recalling her initial fear of panthers and wolves. . . .

Still she traveled onward until her limbs ached and her head throbbed, her legs burning from being pierced by briers that had reached clean up to where her legs straddled her horse.

Panting hard, she tightened her hold on her reins and urged her horse to stop. She hung her head in a hand, shaking it. "Oh, Brandon, I think I am truly lost," she softly cried. "And . . . what . . . about you . . . ? Will you survive the Indians' attack . . . ?"

Her horse neighed softly and shook its head. Leana raised her eyes slowly upward when she heard its neigh returned by another horse from somewhere close by. Her back stiffened, her eyes became alert, knowing that where there was a horse in this thicket, there was also *man*. She wasn't lost after all! Someone else was close by!

Then her hopes faltered, wondering who. Mexican, American, or Indian . . . ?

She tensed and watched as a shimmer of a light came into view, swaying with the movement of a horse. Leana swallowed hard, transfixed by building fear. Then a slow smile surfaced on her lips when she thought to recognize the face being illuminated by the lantern being carried by someone riding alongside the man.

"Cyril!" she cried. Then she screamed his name, over and over again, urging her horse onward to meet him.

"God almighty," Cyril gasped, racing on toward her when seeing Leana's outline against the blackened trees behind her. "Leana. What are you doin' out here all alone? Where's Brandon?"

Tears rolling down her cheeks, Leana leaned and grabbed one of Cyril's hands as his horse came alongside hers. "Thank the Lord, Cyril," she said, breathing hard. "If you hadn't come, I most surely would have gotten lost. And Brandon—"

"What about Brandon?" Cyril grumbled. "Where *is* he?"

"Indians!" Leana said, pointing behind her. "Cyril, I saw them. They were lined up on a butte overlooking the Seton ranch. Brandon's there! I was going to warn him about the Mexicans. The Mexicans . . . General Santa Anna . . . have . . . overtaken San Antonio and the Alamo."

"Why were you not with Brandon? Why did you separate?" Cyril questioned.

"Cyril, please. Now is not the time to ask questions," Leana said, looking on past him, seeing many of his pirate crew on horses, following him. "Please. Let's go and help Brandon. Thank God you've brought some men with you."

Then she straightened her shoulders. "Cyril, why *are* you here, with your men?" she asked shallowly. "Why aren't you with *Amelia?*"

Cyril's face darkened into a frown. "She's dead," he said dryly. "I was on my way to Rufino, to tell Darla. My

426

men were accompanying me in case I ran into problems with the Mexicans."

Leana blanched. "Amelia . . . is . . . dead . . . ?" she gasped. "How . . . ?"

"Wanda. She . . . suffocated me wife. . . ." Cyril said, then rode on past Leana, motioning with a hand for his men to accompany him. "Come on, men. Seems we've a battle to fight, except it's not the Mexicans! Let's go kill us a few Comanches!"

Leana watched Cyril for a moment, then hurried her horse and rode beside him, numbly quiet, so stunned by the news. . . .

Chapter Thirty

Brandon spread his legs and placed his hands on his holstered pistols, glaring at Matthew. "Now that Darla is in bed and we're finally alone, I think it's time we had us that talk we've been putting off," he said. He watched as Matthew poured himself another glass of whiskey, his brother's eyes already bloodshot from consuming too much alcohol.

Brandon nodded toward the half-emptied whiskey bottle. "And don't you think you've had enough of that rotgut? You're a hard enough one to communicate with sober, let alone try to talk to you with you half-drunk."

"As I see it," Matthew said, gesturing with the bottle toward Brandon, "we've nothing further to say to one another. You're even lucky enough that I was civil to you this long. Do you know how hard it was to sit at the supper table with Darla watching on, seeing how I hate your guts? Why'd you come back, Brandon? It was best when I thought you were dead." He laughed. "My brother is a *pirate*. My father was a *thief*. That doesn't say much for the Seton clan, now, does it?"

Matthew slumped down into a chair, his shoulders heavy. He threw the whiskey bottle across the room, spraying glass and whiskey in all directions. "If I could only keep Darla from knowing about Father," he grumbled, turning the glass around between his fingers. "At least she could think *part* of my family was decent." He glowered up at Brandon. "She already knew about you. *Leana* filled her in on *that.*"

"And is she supposed to be some sort of queen?" Brandon mocked, standing over Matthew, smiling knowingly. "God, Matthew, before Leana took Darla in, she was a whore. Her damn *mother* was surely a whore before her! How else did she make her way clear from Scotland? She had no skills other than that of her body." He flailed a hand into the air. "Darla's mother deserves none of the treatment now being given her by her husband." He laughed sarcastically. "Husband. Cyril's a fool. A damn fool. Even if the wench is ill, he owes her *nothing.*"

Matthew rose to his feet and spoke into Brandon's face. "And what would you suggest he do? Make her walk a plank for her past wrongful deeds?" he laughed, then teetered and steadied himself against the back of a chair. He took another long swallow of whiskey, then threw the glass across the room, shattering it against the wall. "You're the one who ought to be made to pay for your past wrongful deeds, Brandon," he said thickly. "You deserted Mother and Father, and now you come and demand to share in what was theirs?"

"Must I remind you that I was abducted?" Brandon said dryly. "Did you know that we were sailing past India when Cyril gave me a choice of where I would rather be? On the sea or land? What was I supposed to do? Jump overboard and swim back to New York? Or what?"

"You've told me that you stayed with pirates by choice," Matthew growled. "Now you're trying to say it was only because you were so far from New York?" He hiccuped, then leaned into Brandon's face. "Are you trying to tell me that your ship never returned in the vicinity of New York again? You know better than that, Brandon."

Brandon turned away from Matthew and went to the fireplace and stared down into the fire. "I was a mere lad when it happened," he murmured. "The sea . . . the ship . . . the adventure? It completely seduced me, Matthew. And later, when I was close enough to New York to return home, it was too late. I had already become a *part* of that pirate's crew. Had I shown my face in any port, I wouldn't have survived a full day."

"A pirate. A thieving, damned *pirate*," Matthew said, rising quickly to his feet. "My . . . own . . . brother . . ."

Brandon turned quickly on a heel to face Matthew. "Matthew, I never—"

Cracks of gunfire blasts outside and an Indian lance suddenly crashing through a window, sticking ominously into the floor between Matthew and Brandon, drew Brandon's argument to a close. For a moment Brandon and Matthew stood exchanging surprised glances, too stunned to think *or* speak, then both spoke at once.

"Indians!" they shouted in unison. "Comanches!"

Brandon drew a pistol as he began running toward the door, then glanced over his shoulder as he heard Matthew stumbling along behind him. He turned around and glared at his brother. "You fool!" he shouted. "You're in no condition to fight Indians! You're hardly able to even stand up, much less shoot straight." He

430

motioned with a fling of a hand. "Stay inside. Go protect Darla, if you can even do *that*. But don't go outside, where you'd get your damn head blown off before you'd even get your pistol out of its holster."

"Your show of caring touches me deeply," Matthew said in a drunken, mocking drawl. He gave Brandon a shove. "I'll show you who can shoot a gun. I'll outshoot you."

Brandon knew that Matthew truly *wasn't* in any shape to fight Indians or anything else. He wasn't even capable of protecting Darla. And knowing at this moment just how much he *did* still love his brother, Brandon thought the only thing left to do to protect *Matthew* was to render him unconscious *himself*. At least it would only be temporary!

Doubling up a fist, Brandon clipped Matthew hard on the jaw. Surprise registered in Matthew's eyes before he tumbled to the floor in a heap. Shaking his head and rubbing his stinging fist, Brandon hurried on to the door. Slowly opening it, he looked around him, seeing clusters of Indians climbing over the fortress type of fence and being picked off one at a time by Matthew's skilled hired hands.

And then there was a different sort of commotion and Brandon's eyes widened when he saw the gates fly open and Cyril and some of his pirate crew thunder inside on horseback, fighting off Indians all the way.

And then Brandon's mouth went agape, seeing Leana among those on horseback, shooting just as skillfully as any man.

"Christ!" Brandon shouted, paling as he watched Leana moving toward the house, her back bent low over the horse. Out of the corner of his eye Brandon saw an

Indian raise a lance and aim it at Leana. His heart down in his shoes, Brandon raced on outside and aimed, and just as Leana reached him, he pulled the trigger and killed the Indian before the Indian had a chance to release the lance.

"Oh, Brandon. You're alive! You're safe!" Leana shouted as she quickly dismounted.

Glowering, Brandon grabbed her by a wrist and rushed her into the house. "Woman, what the hell are you doing?" he shouted. "Why are . . . you . . . here . . . ? You could've been *killed*."

"Don't you appreciate anything I do?" she shouted, stomping a foot. "Brandon, I risked my neck to go for Cyril and now you're angry with me? If not for me—"

"You're saying you knew the Indians were . . . ?"

"Yes, damn it! I saw them! I had come to warn you about the Mexicans. I went for Cyril! I got . . . lost . . . in the Big Thicket—"

A whizzing bullet flew past them, making them grab for each other. And then they laughed awkwardly and moved back to the door and stepped outside together. "You shouldn't be here!" Brandon couldn't help but scold.

"But I am!" she said, squinting, aiming. "And I'm *glad*."

Her body jerked with the firing of her pistol. Brandon scooped a hand about her waist and half dragged her around the corner of the house. "At least show some common sense," he growled. "You can't just stand out in the open like that. You'll get killed for sure."

Laughing lightly, Leana positioned herself beside him, and together they began shooting as Indians came into view. Brandon caught sight of Cyril from the corner of his eye, proud to see that his vigor—his vitality—had returned. Ah, how he would have missed the old pirate. He loved him. How could he have turned his back on him? Hadn't Cyril come at a moment's notice to defend *him?* A camaraderie had been formed long ago . . . more than that of father to son. It had been a bond that fighting side by side all those years had woven between them. Fight to the death! Defend each other to the death! They had laughed about their promises to each other, yet knowing just how serious the declarations were. Brandon knew there could never be such a bond again. Even that shared between him and Leana was not the same . . . yet it *was* becoming just as solid. . . .

The battle continued for a while longer and then died down to only a few scatterings of gunfire. And then there was an awkward silence, the smell of sulphur and death heavy in the air. Leana gave Brandon a questioning stare and then, together, they stepped out into the open, seeing crumpled bodies lying everywhere, mutely lighted by the waning moon's light as it dipped lower in the sky. . . .

Brandon drew Leana into his arms and hugged her tightly to him, eyeing Cyril as he moved up behind Leana. "You're one hell of a lady," he murmured, then leaned away from her as Cyril stepped to his side, his eyelids heavy.

Brandon offered Cyril a handshake. "Thanks," he mumbled, smiling sheepishly. "You could've left me to fight my own battle and I wouldn't blame you. Not after the way I stormed away from you. But you didn't. I appreciate it, Cyril. *I've* been an ass. I should've been more sympathetic about your feelings about your wife."

Leana's stomach churned, suddenly remembering Amelia's fate and knowing that Brandon didn't yet know. "Brandon . . ." she said, nudging him with her elbow.

"Brandon, you—"

"My Amelia's dead," Cyril quickly interjected. "But I appreciate yer feelings, lad. I understood why you found what I had done so hard to believe. I harbor no ill feelings toward you for leavin' the way ye did."

Brandon shook his head, his eyes wide, surely having misunderstood Cyril. "What . . . did . . . you say about Amelia?" he said shallowly.

"Amelia's dead," Leana said in a near whisper, leaning up into Brandon's face. "Cyril was on his way to Rufino, to tell Darla, when I came across him in the Big Thicket. And he doesn't know yet about Darla. . . ."

"What about Darla?" Cyril growled.

"She isn't in Rufino," Leana said, swallowing hard. She nodded toward the ranch house. "She's here. At the Seton ranch." She gave Brandon a nervous glance, then looked back at Cyril. "She *is* a Seton. She . . . married . . . Matthew Seton."

Cyril's face pinched into a pained expression. He gave Brandon a lingering look, then gazed past him, seeing the death that cluttered the ground, and then at the house. Turning, he hurried into the house, almost stumbling over Darla as she knelt down over Matthew, sobbing.

Darla's eyes moved quickly up and then she winced when seeing Cyril Dalton peering down at her with a strange expression in his eyes.

"Is that yer husband?" Cyril barked, pointing at Matthew, who was now moving to an elbow, groaning.

"Yes. Matthew. Why do . . . you . . . care?" she sobbed, yet so relieved to see that Matthew was finally awakening. Having found no wounds of any sort, she knew that he hadn't been shot or pierced with an arrow.

434

She had only found a slight swelling and a yellowing bruise on his jaw. Yet finding him unconscious had frightened her almost to her deathbed!

"Maybe it's best this way," Cyril said, kneading his brow.

"What's best? What are you talking about?" Darla said, slowly rising to her feet. Her heart skipped a beat. Why was Cyril Dalton here and not with her mother? Surely he hadn't tired of her presence so soon! And hadn't he promised to look after her? How *could* he and be here fighting off Indians at the same time? What if the Indians . . . or Mexicans . . . found the hideout, wherever on earth it *was!* Her mother could be killed, for all Cyril Dalton cared!

In her robe with her coal-black hair cascading loosely about her shoulders, Darla placed her hands on her hips and dared Cyril with an angry glare. "Why aren't you with my mother?" she stormed. "I should've never let her go with you!"

Cyril lowered his eyes, his heart aching. "Aye. Perhaps ye shouldn't 'ave," he mumbled.

Leana and Brandon moved into the house, arm in arm. They looked from Cyril to Darla, realizing what had not yet been told Darla. Would she be able to take the knowing . . . ?

Leana went to Darla. She placed an arm about her waist. "Darla, come with me," she said softly, giving Cyril a look of understanding as he looked up at her. "There's something you need to know. Maybe it's best that I tell you."

"What . . . is . . . going on here . . . ?" Darla asked, her heart becoming thunderous inside her. "My mother.

Is this about . . . my . . . mother . . . ?"

"Yes. It is," Leana said softly. She nodded toward a chair. "Honey, maybe it's best you sit down. . . ."

Safely at the mansion in the Big Thicket, Leana lay in Brandon's arms. Darla and Matthew were in the next room, Cyril alone in his. Amelia's funeral had been short; she had been buried on the most solid ground that could be found close to the house.

Cyril had allowed Matthew to accompany his wife to the hideout, though aware of the dangers of too many people knowing the location of his hideout. He felt that a husband's place was to be at his wife's side during tragedy, for support. And he had to believe that his daughter and his son-in-law would never do anything to cause him undue harm, like disclosing his secret hideaway. Darla's bitternesses seemed to have been put to rest along with her mother, and she now even welcomed having a father. For so long she hadn't known the feeling of that sort of love. . . .

"Do you think it's going to be safe for Darla and Matthew to return to the Seton ranch?" Leana whispered, cuddling closer to Brandon. "The Indian raid was so . . . so savage. What if those who survived the fight return? Do you think Matthew's hired hands will even have the ranch cleaned up and ready for living again when Matthew and Darla return there tomorrow?"

"It's their decision to make. Not ours," Brandon said, tracing the outline of Leana's nose with a forefinger while his eyes roamed appreciatively over her. The faint light from the lamp cast a golden glow across her ivory skin, making it take on a silken sheen. Her black hair lay about her oval face, contrasting against her pink cheeks, luminous blue eyes, and lips, lusciously ripe and full.

Her body was supple and slender, curving into his, her breasts teasing the bare flesh of his chest. Perfect; ah, wasn't . . . she . . . so . . . damn . . . perfect . . . ?

"But do you think they will be safe?" Leana persisted. "Darla has recently been through so much. I would hate to think she had anything else to fear."

"No one is truly safe nowadays," Brandon said, positioning himself over her, looking moodily down at her with his piercing dark eyes. "Though you think you might be an exception," he added in a growl. "You still stubbornly insist to go back to Rufino tomorrow? Even though you know the town is overrun by Mexicans?"

"I have my property to protect," Leana said, curving her lips into a pout. "But that doesn't truly matter to you, does it? *You* insist that you must go with Cyril aboard the *Erebus* tomorrow, do you not?"

"I've explained why. Over and over again," Brandon argued, yet now sending feathery kisses across one breast, and then the other. "It's for Cyril. He needs to go to sea to rid himself of this nagging ache inside him. He found and lost his wife all in two days. That's enough to cause a man to go insane. I must do what I can to help pull Cyril through this crisis."

He cupped a breast and smiled softly down at her. "But of course you understand?" he said thickly.

"No. I don't understand," Leana said, squirming, trying to fight off the sensuous warmth building inside her, yet wanting it . . . needing it. "You'll never give up the sea. Not even for *me*. Brandon, how can we ever have a future if . . . if . . . you always find an excuse to go back to sea?"

"Cyril is not merely an excuse," he said, tossing himself away from her. "He's even more than a *friend*. I owe him much, Leana."

He turned his back to her and folded his arms across his chest, yet breathless with desire of her. Yet she had to be made to understand. If not now . . . never.

"Oh, Brandon, I do want to understand," Leana said, moving over him, sitting on her knees as she spoke down into his face. "I see how torn Cyril is. He *does* need you. But . . . so . . . do I."

Brandon rose to his knees before her. He clasped onto her shoulders. "Then go *with* us this time," he said, his eyes gleaming. "If you do, I vow to you this will be my last time."

He lowered his eyes, then shot them back up again. "I have a confession to make," he added. "Cyril says this is to be his last time at sea. He plans to retire from pirating altogether and travel back to Scotland, to live there. So you see why I must go with him this time? It will be our last time together. It will be the last time I will probably ever even *see* him."

"He plans to leave . . . to travel to Scotland?"

"It may take him longer than he thinks to cut all ties with the Big Thicket," Brandon chuckled. "It's become a vital part of his existence. But I can't take that chance. Surely you see why I must take this voyage with him."

Leana placed her hands to his cheeks. "Yes, I guess so," she murmured. "But, darling, I still cannot go with you. I *do* fear for my property in Rufino. I must return, to protect my investments."

438

He moved her hands away from his face. "After we're married, what *then* about your so-called investment?" he said sourly. "Will you insist to be only a part-time wife?"

Leana's face beamed, her heart soared. "Brandon, are you saying . . . ?"

"Yes. I think we should be married real soon. We will build our own ranch. I don't even want the Seton ranch. Let Matthew have it. I want my *own*. I want us to build it together. I want every damn inch of it to be *us*."

Leana rushed into his arms, laughing and crying at the same time. "Oh, darling . . ." she whispered.

Brandon spread her out on the bed, his lips soft and sweet, kissing her as his steel arms enfolded her. Leana moaned longingly, his lips drugging her. She ran her hands up and down his flesh, hungry for all of him. When he filled her with his man's solid strength, his strokes were slow, then faster with quick, sure movements, causing ecstatic waves to splash through her.

And when his mouth lowered, to flick fire into her breasts, she closed her eyes and threw her head back and let a sweet current of warmth sweep through her, ready to soar to heights only shared with Brandon

Her breasts throbbed with his kisses, and then her face and neck. And when he buried his nose into the depths of her hair and momentarily rested, she kissed his cheek, softly, sweetly, inspiring passion to inflame him even more.

He again began his strokes, his hungry mouth sealing hers with another heated kiss, blending one kiss with another while his hands moved to the exquisitely sensitive inside of her thigh and urged her legs up, to lock about his waist.

"Open fully to me, darling," he said huskily. "I want all of you. Completely."

"As I do you," Leana whispered, her cheeks flushed, her eyelids heavy with passion.

She placed her hands about his neck and drew his lips again to hers. She ran her tongue seductively along his bottom lip, she smiled gently up at him.

He locked his arms tightly about her and consumed her with fiery kisses along her neck, and then her lips. He then lay his head at her cleavage, her breasts two cushioned pillows as he closed his eyes and enjoyed the pleasure swelling inside him, spun gold, swirling, swirling, rising, rising. . . .

And then he thrust harder and more deeply inside her until they shuddered against each other, full passion reached . . . joy splendidly shared . . . awesome, winsome in the beauty of it. . . .

"How can I let you go to Rufino tomorrow?" Brandon whispered as he smoothed her hair back from her eyes, still breathing hard from their rapturous coupling.

"How can I let you go to the sea tomorrow?" Leana whispered, touching him wonderingly on his lips, scarlet-red from his savage kisses.

"Go with me, darling," Brandon asked, smiling down at her.

"Darling, we must go our separate ways, it seems," Leana sighed, again becoming mindless as he began to spin his silver web of desire about her heart again with his demanding kisses. She knew that he was going to try everything to change her mind. But her mind was set. As his . . . was . . . also. He *would* go to sea. She *would* go to Rufino. Yet she *did* fear this separation. Was she being too stubborn? Should she go with him?

440

But no. He had to see the importance of being with her. This could only be accomplished if she remained firm in her decision. When he got to sea without her he had to find out that it *must* be his last time if he was to have a future with her. Without her along with him, ah, surely this could be accomplished. Wouldn't he miss her, oh, so much . . . ?

Chapter Thirty-One

Going to a room at the back of her hotel, a room that overlooked the harbor and the wide, outspread waters of the bay, Leana positioned herself by a window, feeling empty, already missing Brandon. Her eyes searched the water for signs of glistening white sails out at sea, yet knowing if she even did see sails, they wouldn't be those of the *Erebus*. The pirates wouldn't let themselves be seen so close to Rufino, yet she knew they weren't that far away. How *did* they manage to elude the Mexican warships? Ah, but yes, they must always move by night. . . .

Swirling her skirt around, she went back to her own room, never feeling so alone. Her hotel, saloon, and general store sounded like one huge morgue. The Mexicans had now virtually sealed off the town of Rufino. She even knew how lucky she had been to be able to sneak *back* into town this early morning with Mexican soldiers everywhere, watching. . . .

"But was I truly lucky?" she continued to fret, whispering aloud, yet only to herself. She let her gaze move slowly about her room, seeing only possessions. Possessions couldn't warm her at night. They couldn't fulfill her desires.

"I should have gone with him!" Leana then said, looking woefully toward the ceiling, clenching her teeth. The way things were . . . the turmoil . . . the stench of death everywhere one looked in this territory of Texas . . . who could even say there might be a tomorrow for *any*one?

She went to her window and drew aside the new drapes only recently hung, letting her eyes scan the full width of the street, and then farther, where General Rufino's villa lay sprawled, not all that fancy, yet a palace in General Rufino's eyes with a harem always at his command.

"Thank God he never forced me. . . ." Leana whispered, feeling a shiver riding her spine.

Then her gaze searched farther, where she could see the darkness of the Big Thicket as it lay in the distance, as though beckoning to her. Only a few hours had passed since she and Brandon had said their goodbyes. Had Brandon yet left with Cyril and his pirate crew?

Torn, Leana began pacing. Then her eyes brightened and her heart began to race, knowing what she must do. She had to go to Brandon. She would go with him on the *Erebus*. He was her only future! Not her hotel, saloon, or general store! Why hadn't she seen that? Why did she always have to be so stubborn?

She rushed to the window and leaned against its sill, again looking into the distance, wondering if her decision *had* been made too late. If Brandon was already on the *Erebus* . . .

Spinning around, her petticoat rustling against her dress, Leana knew that she must at least try to reach

Brandon before he left, if he hadn't already. She stopped short and looked down at the way she was dressed. If she took the time to change, it could be time wasted. But rarely had she traveled away from Rufino in anything but men's clothes, so having always feared being detected. But this time she would have to take that chance!

The window drew her once again to it. Her fingernails bit into the palms of her hands as she circled her fingers into fists, looking down at the street, from one soldier to the other. How . . . ? Oh, how could she escape? She *was* a virtual prisoner.

Then she spun around, all eyes. She lifted the skirt of her dress and ran from the room and down the steps, going anxiously to José. Clasping eagerly onto his shoulders, she spoke down into his face.

"José, I need your assistance," she said, panting, her cheeks rosy from building excitement and plaguing fear.

"*Sí*, what is it, Leana?" José asked, his dark eyes fully assessing her. "What is it you want me to do?"

"José, I've got to leave again," Leana said, still breathless.

She leaned closer to José and spoke in a whisper, glancing toward the open door, seeing a Mexican soldier lumber past outside on the boardwalk. "I need you to get a horse to the edge of town for me. Stay there until I get there. And then keep watch until I am safely out of town," she said in a rush of words.

Her eyes searched his troubled face. "Can you do that for me, José? Can you?"

"You only just returned, Señorita Leana," José said, frowning. "It is not safe for you to leave again. You know that the soldiers—"

"Yes. I know," Leana sighed, dropping her hands away

444

from him. She went to the door and leaned out, looking from side to side. "But I can't let the scare of soldiers stop me from what I must do."

She spun around on a heel, her dark hair whipping in dark streamers, settling on her shoulders. "I've made a terrible mistake, José," she murmured, going back to him, to lean and speak softly into his face. "One that perhaps, if I move in haste, I might be able to remedy."

José shook his head. "This has to do with that pirate Brandon, doesn't it?" he sighed. "But of course it does. He is the cause of everything you do."

"Well? Will you help me, José? There *is* a risk. For *both* of us. Until now you've been untouched by the soldiers. General Rufino has even left me to do as *I* please. But now . . . with everyone having been told to not leave *or* enter Rufino, what I want to do could place both our lives in jeopardy."

José tilted a dark eyebrow. "You are sure you want to do this?" he questioned.

"I *must*," Leana said, determinedly lifting her chin.

José shrugged indifferently. "Then I will help you," he said. "Have I ever refused you anything, Señorita Leana?"

Leana laughed with joy, then drew him into her arms and hugged him. "Oh, José," she said. "How could I have ever been so lucky to have found such a friend as you? I will repay you, somehow, for your kindness to me."

"What I do is payment to *you*," he said, flushing with embarrassment as she stepped away from him. "I only hope what I agree to do doesn't lead to disaster for you, Señorita Leana. I would forever hate myself if anything would happen to you."

"And so would I hate myself, if what I do leads you

into trouble with your Mexican people," Leana said dryly. Then she raced toward the stairs. "Go now, José. Take the horse to the very edge of town where the trees are the thickest, away from the soldiers' watchful eyes. Stay there. I will get there, somehow, without being spotted. But I first must . . . get . . . my pistol and manchette."

"You be careful," José said, walking toward the door. "The soldiers have eyes in the back of their heads."

"Yes. I do believe they do," Leana said, laughing nervously. "But so do *I.*"

She rushed to her room and belted her pistol about her waist, placed the manchette at the calf of her right leg, and changed her polite, delicate slippers for sturdy boots. She jerked her petticoats off, knowing that their encumbrance could get in the way of riding a horse. It was bad enough that she was dressed in a flimsy cotton dress with a low-swept bodice, let alone frilly petticoats lined with yards and yards of lace!

And then she hid her hair inside a sombrero and knew that no more time could be wasted. She got a glance of herself in the mirror as she hurried to the door. Laughing at her comical reflection of sombrero, dress, belted pistol, and ugly boots, having never seen a combination worn together before, she hurried onward.

Reaching the back door, she knew the challenge then began. But she knew the side streets and alleys well. Perhaps better than the soldiers, who had just been ordered into the town. That was surely to her advantage.

And fully believing this, she began ducking from one building to the next, stopping to get her breath after each fresh attempt at escaping. She looked up at the sun. It was hot in its reflections this morning, the sea breeze welcomed against her flaming cheeks.

Then her eyes once more became directed straight ahead as she lifted her skirt and began running from the main street to a street lined with houses. The houses were quiet. The only signs that led one to believe that anyone lived there were the slow spirals of smoke drifting up from the chimneys and the aroma of spicy food cooking from somewhere off in the distance.

She knew that if she required help now, other than that of José, she would get none, for those left in the town of Rufino were only Mexican. She had been singled out to be left alone, and she feared the true reason why. What did General Rufino truly have planned for her now that she was virtually isolated . . . the only American . . . ?

But she smiled to herself. She wouldn't be around to find out. She would, hopefully, be with Brandon. And if she didn't get to him soon enough, she would then go on to the mansion and stay there until he returned. . . .

But if he didn't . . . ? What *then* would she do? He had promised her a future with him. Surely the only thing that could dissuade him of this decision was Cyril and his influence over him . . . or perhaps, even the sea! In a sense the sea was a lady, a seducer of men, in its loveliness.

Leana knew well enough the enchantment of the water as it changed colors from light turquoises to pale blues. When one came under the spell of the sea when it was showing such a lovely side to itself, one could so easily forget its darker, more treacherous side . . . a side shown as a jealous, scorned wench might behave, becoming stormful, whipping ships about as though a tiny mouse being smacked about by a cat's paw. . . .

Blocking all thoughts from her mind at this moment except for total escape from Rufino, Leana ran to hide from house to house until, thankfully, she finally reached the outer edges of town. A soft neigh welcomed her from the brush, only a few footsteps away, across the narrow path of road. And Leana knew that José had been as successful as she and was patiently awaiting her arrival.

And now to get across the road, on the horse, and safely away. To her the rest would be simple. By daylight she knew the Big Thicket well enough. She had traveled it enough to almost have it memorized. It was the night travels that she would never get used to. By night, the thicket changed. Though just as menacing by daylight, it was the night that made it become a reality!

Holding her breath, Leana leaned out away from the tree which she was hiding behind and glanced up the road one way, and then another. When seeing no signs of anyone traveling this stretch of road, she rushed across the road and searched through the brush until she suddenly came face-to-face with José, who was also looking for her, having heard her light approach.

"José," Leana said, puffing hard as she clasped onto his arms. "You hid almost *too* well." She laughed nervously, then saw a horse's tail swaying gently from where the animal was hidden behind the widespread trunk of a live oak.

"If you hadn't found me, I would've soon found *you*. I knew you should be along about now," he said thickly.

Leana gave him an eager hug, then hurried to the horse, an already saddled brown gelding, one quite dependable for her escape. She placed a foot in the stirrup and swung herself up into the saddle.

"I must hurry," she said, grabbing the horse's reins. "José, please be careful. If the soldiers knew you helped me—"

"*Sí*," José said, smiling widely up at her, nodding his head. "José is *always* careful." He placed a hand to his throat. "José likes to feel his head still attached to his neck."

Laughing throatily, Leana swung the horse around and led it from the brush and to the road, knowing she must travel by way of the road for at least a little while, though the dangers were many. But to wind her way through the brush and trees would take too long. She knew just the exact spot to enter into the Big Thicket for her travels to be cut in half. Chances were good that she would make it. All the soldiers seemed to already be in Rufino. Surely she was safe!

Turning her head, she waved at José as he stood behind, watching. And then she ducked low over the horse and led him into a gallop. She cursed her dress as the wind caught at its hem and whipped it up about her thighs. She cursed the heat of the sun as it beat down upon her bare shoulders and arms. She *blessed* the air as it washed across her face in her hasty flight.

Thrusting the heels of her boots in the horse's flanks, she urged him on faster . . . faster . . . and then her heart lurched when she heard the sudden, quick sound of an approaching horse and buggy behind her. She dared not look back! She must go onward. She didn't have that much farther to go until she would be safely hidden in the denseness of the Big Thicket. Oh, who could be following along behind her, to spoil her plans . . . ?

Her gut twisted, knowing of only one person who might have been out for a leisurely ride in a buggy this

449

time of day. General Rufino! And once on the road, he had surely seen *her!* And surely having to find out what she was up to, he was pursuing her, for questioning!

"Giddyap!" she shouted to the horse, thrusting her boots harder into him. She clung to the reins, riding lower, but then she grew stone-cold inside when the horse and buggy that had been following her suddenly whipped on around her and just as quickly blocked her way by turning crossways in the road.

Leana almost fell from the horse as it came to a clumsy, shuddering halt. It raised up on its hind legs, whinnying and snorting. It shook its head and strained at the bit. And then it settled back down, only now pawing at the dirt of the road.

With wavering eyes, Leana met General Rufino's questioning stare. "Señorita, where do you go in such a rush?" he snarled as he rose from his seat to step from the buggy.

But when he stumbled and laughed crookedly at his clumsiness and looked up at her with his bloodshot eyes, she knew that he was in another world. He had been enjoying his opium supply again! Would this work in her favor . . . or against it . . . ?

"I was just out for . . . some . . . fresh air," she stammered, knowing just how ridiculous that had to sound, with her having so very obviously been riding hard to get where she was headed. She felt his gaze move over her and saw his eyebrows lift quizzically as he moved closer to her horse, teetering with each step.

"You have finally chosen to wear a dress, *sí?*" he chuckled. Again his eyes studied her attire. He scratched his brow. "But you still wear a sombrero for which to hide your lovely hair? And you wear . . . men's . . .

boots . . . ?" He frowned darkly as his gaze stopped at her pistol. "And also a pistol?" he growled.

"Each of these things you mention are much . . . more . . . comfortable for horseback riding," Leana said shallowly. She laughed nervously. "Except for the pistol. It's . . . for . . . protection." She flinched when he reached a pudgy hand toward her.

"Get off the horse, Señorita," General Rufino snarled. When she didn't comply with his request, he looked up at her with narrowed eyes. "You do not hear so well this morning, sí?"

"Please let me go on my way," Leana said dryly. "I'm doing you no harm by just riding my horse. Now, am I? I soon will return . . . to . . . Rufino. I needed to only get away for a while. Please understand it is hard to feel imprisoned, even in one's own establishment."

"Get off the horse," General Rufino growled, grabbing her by an ankle, jerking on her. "Beautiful señorita, I think the time has come to teach you many lessons. First, how to kiss?" He laughed and smiled crookedly up at Leana. "Do as I say. Dismount."

Leana watched his left hand move to his saber and rest on it. Then she looked directly into his eyes, daring him with a set stare. "I refuse to do as you say," she said, yet swallowing hard from mounting fear. "Sir, you are quite drunk."

General Rufino's smile faded. His jaw tightened. "I've waited a long time to get a taste of you," he growled. "I will wait no longer. My heightened euphoric state created by my opium will only enhance my time with you. Come. Let's go back to my villa. You will be treated queenly, Señorita."

Leana stumbled from the saddle as he now yanked on

her wrist. She fell to the ground and then was forced to stand before General Rufino while his hands began moving over her. She cringed and bit her lower lip as he cupped her breasts through her dress, a flush appearing on his cheeks.

"You've only been playing games with me all along," Leana hissed. "You knew that one day you would take advantage of my being a woman. The fact that you left me to my business was only because the waiting made the excitement greater for you. Am I right, General?"

"I always did say you were a smart americano lady," he chuckled. "You are right about so many things. But the time has come for me to say what will or won't be. And I say you are going to be totally mine."

He knocked the sombrero from her head and grabbed her by the hair, forcing her lips down to meet his, while his other hand held her forcefully in place. Leana gagged as his tongue plunged inside her mouth. And as he led her backward, beneath the shade of a tree, she knew that he wasn't going to wait until he reached his villa to take her sexually. He was going to rape her now!

Remembering her holstered pistol, she tried to reach for it, but he was too quick for her. She couldn't even reach for her manchette! Though quite in a heady state from the opium, he was alert enough to know exactly what he was doing. He had had enough practice with his harem of women. . . .

Holding her hands behind her back, General Rufino forced Leana to the ground. "Do I have to tie you to secure your hands?" he growled. "Or will you co-operate?"

"I can . . . never . . . agree to anything you ask of me," Leana cried. "You are vile! How can you do this to

452

me? I've done nothing to deserve such treatment."

He leaned into her face. "You are americano," he snarled. "That is reason enough. Gringos are now all being treated the same by the Mexicans. Be they man or woman. They must be taught that Mexicans are the supreme race! The americanos must either be killed, or forced back to America!"

"And . . . you . . . will also kill me . . . ?" Leana asked, shivering as he released one of her wrists to let his hand wander up the skirt of her dress. "You will rape . . . then kill me . . . ?" She tensed, wondering when his fingers would discover the manchette.

He shrugged. "I will have no further need of you," he laughed. "So, *sí*, either I kill you, or if you prove to excite me enough, I might take you and hold you hostage at my villa to use whenever I see fit to."

Leana's eyes widened when she heard a snapping twig close by. When she saw Brandon moving closer and she emitted a low gasp and the Mexican saw the knowing in her eyes, it was enough for General Rufino to know they were no longer alone. . . .

He moved sluggishly as he jumped to his feet. His hand was on his saber, trying to draw it from its sheath, when Brandon plunged a knife into the Mexican's shoulder. He dropped his saber and began running toward the waiting horse and buggy, holding his wound, yelping.

Brandon dropped his knife and hurried to Leana and leaned down over her to draw her into his arms. She sobbed against his shoulder. "Brandon, a moment longer and—"

Brandon placed a finger to her lips, sealing them of further words. "Shhh," he encouraged. "I *am* here. Thank God I decided to come back for you."

453

"Then you and Cyril . . . ?"

"Neither of us thought it was the best time to leave."

"He . . . didn't . . . either . . . ?"

"He has only recently found his daughter. He didn't want to travel far from her. He said his travels on the *Erebus* could come later, after he got to know Darla a little better."

"Would you have gone with Cyril . . . had . . . he decided—"

"No, darling. I had already decided to come for you. You have no business being in Rufino. Not now. Not with all the trouble the Mexicans are brewing."

"Oh, Brandon . . ." Leana sighed, clinging.

"Leana, we'd best get the hell out of here," he said, casting a look over his shoulder. The horse and buggy were no longer there. He had to believe that General Rufino would go for help. Brandon had made a mistake in not killing the bastard. And he had been too concerned about Leana to go on after him! Brandon hadn't been sure if the Mexican had hurt her . . . raped . . . her. . . .

One look at how her clothes were still intact except for a partially upswept dress, he knew that, yes, he had been in time. . . .

"Where shall we go?" she asked, shaky as Brandon helped her up from the ground.

"Where else? To the mansion," Brandon said. "I reined my horse back aways. I saw your horse wandering close by. Come on. Let's hurry. The farther and quicker we can get into the thicket, the better."

Brandon rounded up her horse, then rode with her until he reached his own, then mounted his own steed, and together they began racing through the thicket, fighting low, gnarled limbs of live oaks, swaying Spanish moss, and weeds higher than their horses' heads.

But now skilled in their knowledge of the Big Thicket, they soon felt hidden enough to slow their pace and get their breaths, as well as rest their horses as they moved at an easy gait.

"He'll be out for blood," Brandon growled, looking over his shoulder. "You now know how impossible it will be for you to ever return to Rufino."

"As long as General Rufino is there, yes, I see the problem," Leana nodded. "But, hopefully, Sam Houston and his men can change things. After the Alamo, the *Americans* will be out for blood. *Mexicans*'."

"Until then you will remain with me at the hideout," Brandon said flatly. "I even think it would be best to persuade Matthew and Darla to go there until all the trouble with the Mexicans is over. And then there is still the threat of the Indians. . . ."

Brandon drew his steed to a sudden halt. He wheeled it around to face Leana. "God almighty, Leana," he said shallowly. "We may have just signed death warrants for both Darla *and* Matthew. Surely the Mexican general will be determined to find us, and one place he will surely look will be . . . the . . . Seton ranch. If Darla and Matthew don't tell the general where we can be found, who . . . is . . . to know what will happen to them . . . ?"

Leana blanched. "Brandon, surely not . . ." she gasped.

"It may already be too late!" Brandon shouted. He flung a hand into the air. "You hurry on to the mansion. I'll go and warn Matthew and Darla!"

"I'll go with you," Leana said stubbornly.

"No. You must go where you'll be safe," Brandon argued. "Leana, will you listen to reason for a change?

Do as you're told. Go on to the mansion!"

"Brandon, nothing could keep me from going with you," she said dryly. "You can order me until hell freezes over, and by damn, I will be riding at your side. Now, time's wasting. We'd best hurry on. Don't you think?"

Brandon shook his head and groaned, yet wheeled his horse around and rode back in the direction from which they had just traveled, Leana quite boldly at his side, her hair flying in the wind like streamers of black satin. . . .

Chapter Thirty-Two

The smell of smoke grew stronger the closer Leana and Brandon rode to the outer edge of the Big Thicket. And as they traveled into the open, the brilliant orange cast to the sky and the puffs of black smoke fading the orange cast to a sort of smeared gray, Leana's heart skipped a beat and her throat went dry, constricted so, she couldn't speak.

Brandon's gaze shifted upward. He uttered a few low curse words, then looked toward Leana, his face lined into a dark frown. "Leana, I think we may be too late," he grumbled. He looked across his shoulder, then back in the direction of the smoke-filled sky.

He urged his horse to stop, then wheeled around and faced Leana as her horse drew up beside his. "And I don't think you ought to go any farther with me. It's too dangerous. I'm sure whoever goes near that place will be ambushed."

"Do you think the Mexicans . . . ?"

"Whether it's the Mexicans or the Indians, I don't want you going with me to check out the damage done."

"And you think I'd be safer alone, in the Big Thicket?" she argued. "You know the Mexicans are out for the both of us, Brandon. I prefer being with you once they catch up with us."

Brandon kneaded his brow. "Damn if you're not right," he said, turning his horse around, again studying the sky. "But I hate to think of what might be awaiting us at the Seton ranch. It might not be . . . all . . . that pretty. . . ."

Blanching, Leana circled the reins more tightly about her fingers. "You're not saying . . . ?"

"Damn right. We might find my brother *and* Darla, but not alive," he said solemnly. Then he straightened himself in his saddle. "We've got to get to them. Fast. Perhaps they're not harmed at all, but in need of assistance."

Leana's horse fell into step beside Brandon's, and then into a full gallop. "Matthew has many men at the ranch," she shouted at Brandon over the noise of the horses' thundering hooves. "Surely they fought the Mexicans or . . . the . . . Indians off. Maybe only the houses sitting beyond the protective gate were burned."

"Yeah. Maybe," Brandon shouted back at her. "Just keep that thought, Leana. That's our only hope as I see it."

The smoke became thicker, a wall to travel through, burning Leana's throat and eyes. Fear mounted inside her the closer they drew to the ranch, then her mouth dropped open when finally in eye range. All of the out-buildings lay in smoldering ash, the fence that outlined the ranch house was still in flames, and as Leana and Brandon rode through the burning gate, they saw the ranch house afire and men lying about on the ground, dead.

Leana grimaced and looked quickly away from the gruesome scene of death and destruction, swallowing hard. She now knew to not find Darla *or* Matthew alive. The silence was oppressive, the only sounds coming from the crackling of the flames and the splintering of wood as walls began collapsing.

"God . . ." Brandon gasped, holding his reins as his horse began neighing and jerking its head. His gut twisted as he saw the death scene. His gaze went to the house, knowing that no one could be alive in its roaring inferno.

He again looked at the bodies. There were no signs of arrows. The men had been shot. Brandon could only surmise from this that the ones responsible must be the Mexicans . . . not Indians. And hadn't he thought to expect it? The Mexicans were the initial reason for his having come back to the ranch in the first place.

Anger raged through him, knowing who must have led the Mexicans into this act of vengeance. General Rufino. He must have patched up his wound and was well enough to lead his men to the ranch. After not finding Brandon or Leana, he had taken his anger out on those he *had* found, no matter how innocent those were whom had been slaughtered.

Leana guided her horse beside Brandon's. "Brandon, what are . . . we . . . to do . . . ?" she said shallowly, her heart breaking from the discovery. "Darla? Matthew . . . ?" Her gaze went to the burning house. "They surely are dead."

"We must take a look around," Brandon said, quickly dismounting. "Perhaps they escaped somehow."

459

Leana swung herself out of the saddle. She went to Brandon and clung to an arm, her eyes searching around as they walked from body to body. "I feel responsible," she murmured. "Surely General Rufino ordered this done because . . . because . . ."

"Now, you just stop thinking that way," Brandon growled. When Leana began crying, he turned and clasped his hands onto her shoulders and slightly shook her. "Get hold of yourself," he said firmly. "If even *we're* to get out of this mess alive, you and I must have a level head."

He looked over his shoulder, toward the entrance gate. Then he implored Leana with the darkness of his eyes. "The Mexicans could've been waiting in the brush, just waiting for us to come. Hon, our lives might not be worth a plugged nickel now. Let's take a quick look around and then get the hell out of here."

Leana wiped tears from her eyes with the back of a hand. "I know you're right," she murmured. "It's just . . . just that I'm thinking of Darla and Matthew. They seemed . . . seemed so sincerely happy with one another. And now . . . ? To . . . be . . . dead . . . ?"

"Darling, maybe they're *not*," Brandon said, then began guiding her onward with a firm grip on her elbow. "Perhaps we'll find them. . . ."

The smoke was thick; the heat from the fire as it still engulfed the house was intensely hot against Leana's face as she leaned closer to Brandon. And then her heart seemed to stop when she heard a soft murmur surfacing from somewhere close by. She looked up at Brandon, his eyes meeting hers in a questioning.

"You heard it too?" he said thickly.

"Yes. Oh, Brandon, what if it—"

460

The soft whimper became a scream. Leana jumped as though shot, then she began running alongside Brandon until a cedar tree was reached, its wide back hiding a frail, quivering body behind it.

Leana emitted a soft gasp. "Oh, Lord," she cried. "Darla. Oh, Darla . . ."

She then ran to Darla. She dropped to her knees and lifted Darla's head onto her lap. Leana's gaze moved quickly over Darla, seeing how the skirt of her dress had been ripped half-off. Her lips were swollen with blood dried on them; her eyes were blackening, almost swollen shut. It was apparent that someone had beat her. She only looked . . . half . . . alive. . . .

Darla's limp hand reached out for Leana. "Leana, thank God . . ." she whispered. "Is . . . Brandon . . . ?"

Leana took Darla's hand in hers. She gently squeezed it. "Yes. Brandon is here with me," she said, biting her lower lip, trying to keep from crying. It was so hard not to, seeing Darla in such a condition. Who could have done this . . . ? How *could* anyone have done this . . . ?

"Matthew . . ." Darla said in a choked whisper. "Leana, the Mexicans killed Matthew." She tried to look in the direction of the house, yet only seeing a hazy sort of orange through the slit of her swollen eyes. "He's . . . in . . . there. They left him in there, then set fire to the house."

Leana's stomach churned. She looked away from Darla and closed her eyes, fighting a bitterness rising up into her throat, feeling the need to retch. She now knew there was no hope, whatsoever, for Matthew. Though she had never cared for him, she felt his loss, as though he had been . . . her . . . true . . . brother. . . .

Brandon knelt down to one knee and took Darla's

other hand. "Darla, I'm so . . . damn . . . sorry. . . ." he said, tears stinging his eyes. He looked toward the house. The only thing now remaining was a long chimney standing ominously from the burning rubble.

After all these years of waiting, Brandon had returned to his family to find them all dead but his brother . . . and now even his brother was taken away from him. Though no love had been exchanged between them, he felt the loss. . . .

"Who did this? Which Mexican?" Leana asked, smoothing perspiration-dampened hair back from Darla's battered face. "Did you recognize anyone?" She waited to hear the one name she suspected, though it was hard to believe this particular Mexican general could be capable of such violence. He had been quite congenial to Leana . . . until . . . today. The fact that she was American only seemed to matter this day. Before he had somehow looked to her as an equal, unless he had only been playing a dangerous game with her from the very beginning and she hadn't been aware of it. . . .

"General . . . Rufino . . ." Darla whispered, wincing in pain as she tried to turn her body. "He gave . . . all . . . the orders except one. . . ."

"What do you mean, except for one . . . ?" Brandon asked, leaning closer to Darla.

"He didn't give . . . orders . . . for his men . . . to rape me," she sobbed, turning her head away.

"Raped . . . ?" Leana gasped, the sick feeling inside her becoming stronger.

"More . . . than one . . ." Darla said, then she grew limp, moving mercifully into unconsciousness.

"The son of a bitches!" Brandon roared, rising to his feet. He doubled his fists and glared at the house rubble, yet then turned his eyes quickly away, knowing that in that rubble lay his brother.

Leana softly touched Darla's face. She could no longer hold the tears back. One, then two splashed onto Darla's cheeks. "Brandon, surely Darla isn't dying. . . ." she sobbed. "Do you think . . . she . . . is? She's suddenly so quiet."

"After all she's been through, I can't say," he grumbled. "I'd like to get my hands on those who did this."

"Brandon, hadn't we best get away from here?" Leana asked, looking up at Brandon through wet lashes. "How can we . . . even . . . move Darla?"

Brandon bent to a knee and gently scooped Darla up into his arms. "I'll carry her on my horse," he said thickly. "You hurry and get on yours. We'll take Darla to our hideout. We'll do what we can for her, and if that isn't enough, we just may have to take her by ship to the States, to get proper medical treatment."

Leana wiped tears from her eyes as she rushed toward her horse. "It's hard for me to imagine General Rufino commanding his men to do all of this," she said, swinging herself into her saddle. "Why, he never so much as attempted anything with me until . . . until today."

"Today is one time too many," Brandon growled. He positioned Darla on his lap and held her with one hand while holding the reins and wheeling his horse around with the other. "He had planned all along to have you, Leana. He had only used you up to today. You ran a grand establishment. Did you see any others that grand in Rufino? So you see, in you he had an investment. That's the only thing that kept him from pawing you, until today."

"I guess he thought he might lose his town *and* me if Sam Houston's army came through with their threats to have vengeance because of what happened at the Alamo," Leana said, galloping on her horse beside Brandon. Her jaw tightened, her eyes became inflamed with rage. "I hope Sam Houston runs all of the Mexicans out of Texas. From what I've seen today, the Mexicans deserve no less!"

"Just keep watch for any sudden movement alongside the road," Brandon said dryly, frowning toward Leana. "I don't think we've seen the last of the Mexicans ourselves. They surely haven't given up the search for us only because they had some fun at the Seton ranch."

Leana glanced over at Darla. "How's Darla?" she asked, seeing how Darla's head bounced lifelessly as Brandon's horse's hooves made contact with the ground. "Is she going to be all right?"

"Only time will tell," he said, holding more tightly about Darla's waist. "The Mexicans must've thought she was dead or they wouldn't have left her like that."

Leana threw her head back in a disgusted groan. "It's so horrible!" she cried. "Poor Darla. If she does survive, will she be able to forget?"

"Leana! Watch out!" Brandon shouted as he drew his horse to a sudden halt as Mexicans on horseback suddenly emerged from the brush.

Leana's eyes froze when seeing the Mexicans. She let Brandon take her reins as she drew her horse to a shuddering halt. And then her gaze began moving slowly about her, seeing that she, Brandon, and Darla were now fully surrounded by Mexicans.

General Rufino rode up next to Leana, his arm in a sling. He smiled crookedly at Leana, then his smile faded

464

as his gaze moved onward, to stop at Brandon, and then downward, where Darla lay against Brandon, her eyes swollen shut.

"So. My men did not complete their pleasure, *si*?" General Rufino laughed, nodding toward Darla. "They left much undone with that little señorita." He frowned at Leana. "You should have seen to it that your pirate friend's knife moved closer to my heart, *si*? Beautiful señorita, soon you will join your friend in such misery as my men left her after enjoying her body. I will teach you to say no to me, one of Mexico's greatest generals!"

Knowing what this man had just done to the Seton ranch, Matthew, and Darla made Leana gain the courage to lash out at him. "You call yourself a great general?" she mocked. She let her gaze move icily over him, then challenged him with a set stare. "Most of the time you're so drugged with opium you don't even know what time of day it is. I would call you disgusting."

Brandon began to reach out for Leana, to urge her to silence, but his eyes were directed elsewhere. When he saw Indians on horseback suddenly appear on the road just ahead with their lances upraised in an aggressive position, and some with arrows notched to their bows, his mouth dropped open and his eyes widened. . . .

Leana's insides froze when gunfire broke out as some of the soldiers turned and fired upon the Indians, and then were slain by lances themselves. Knowing they were outnumbered, the remaining Mexicans quickly dropped their firearms.

A stout, dignified Indian rode up on a great black stallion, stopping before General Rufino while the other Indians made a wide circle about the Mexicans, Leana and Brandon included. He wore a breechclout and

465

buckskin leggings decorated with beadwork of porcupine quills and glass baubles. He carried a quiver of feathered arrows slung across his back, and a lance.

His thick, coarse braids fell below the waist, decorated with feathers, silver ornaments, and beads. His horse's neck and haunches were painted vermilion, and eagle feathers were woven into its mane and tail.

But it was the coldness of his fathomless eyes that held one's attention. And even when he began speaking in broken English, it was the eyes that seemed to be saying the most.

"Ugly Mexican, I warned you against inflaming my Indians against the white man," he grumbled. "Many of my warriors have been killed because of you. You will now be killed. But slowly, ugly Mexican. Slowly."

Brandon's back stiffened, knowing that he, Leana, and Darla had just been thrust in the midst of a personal vendetta, understanding quite well that this was a tribe of southern Comanches, the Pehnahterkul, some of whom had joined the Mexicans to rape and kill the white men, with the blessings of Mexico City.

This Indian now facing the Mexican general must be the chief of a band of the Pehnahterkuls, a band of Indians who had not willingly participated in this plan to frighten Americans back to the States. And he had probably been planning a raid on the city of Rufino.

But it hadn't been necessary. Wouldn't it be much simpler to disarm the soldiers while they were together, basking in their own sort of glory after a successful raid on an American's ranch?

But now that they had surrounded them, what would the Indians now do? If the Indian chief wanted to slowly kill the Mexican general, that must mean it was going to be done . . . in . . . an . . . Indian village. . . .

Leana was trembling so, she found it hard to sit in her saddle. Yet she forced her hands to be still as she clung to the pommel, staring wide-eyed at the Indian who showed such hatred for the Mexicans. What would he do with these three *Americans?* It was obvious what the fate of the Mexicans would be. . . .

The Indian chief moved his gaze from General Rufino, who was stone-silent with fear, to Brandon, then to Leana, then to Darla.

Then he sat square-shouldered and challenged Brandon with a set stare before speaking. "Chief Running Bear did not come from village to hunt for white man and woman," he growled. A slow smile lifted his lips as he gave Leana a half glance. "But you will accompany my warriors along with the Mexicans to my village anyway. You must watch how I treat my enemies."

Brandon reached a hand out toward Chief Running Bear, but the chief had already wheeled his horse around and was working his way through the circle of his Indians.

Brandon instead reached a comforting hand to Leana. "Seems we have no choice but to tag along," he said, chuckling low, trying to make a more relaxed atmosphere for Leana at this time of danger.

"Brandon, how can you joke at a time like this?" Leana said, then whipped her hair across her shoulders and thrust the heels of her boots in the flanks of her horse and followed alongside Brandon as they were ordered to make a wide turn in the road, to begin following the Indians.

"Darling, we'll get out of this," Brandon reassured as he leaned close to Leana to speak quietly beneath his breath.

Leana looked woefully down at Darla. "But will *she?*"

she murmured. "Can she truthfully survive an attack by the Mexicans *and* Indians in one day?"

"Darling, *we* have, haven't we?"

"As unbelievable as it is, yes, I guess you could say we have."

"Then so shall Darla. I'll protect her with my life, Leana."

Leana gave him a wavering look, then stared straight ahead, numb. . . .

Chapter Thirty-Three

The thumping of the drums outside the tepee and the shrieks of the Indian squaws made Leana wince. She could see enough through the raised entrance flap to know that General Rufino was still being tortured, though two days had now passed since the Comanches had taken the prisoners to their camp.

Looking away, Leana didn't want to see the squaws inflict any more wounds to the Mexican leader, not understanding how he could still be alive after the squaws had now beat and slashed him for two full days and nights. His nude body was now hanging limply from the stake, yet his dark eyes were still open, silently begging for mercy. . . .

Feeling the bindings at her wrists and ankles cutting into the flesh, Leana emitted a soft cry, yet still tried to work herself free as she sat on one side of the tepee while Darla lay unconscious on the other, now dressed in a dainty buckskin dress with a buckskin blanket drawn over her tiny body.

Darla hadn't appeared to be any threat to the Indians,

still unconscious from her assaults by the Mexicans, so her hands and legs had been left free of bonds. The Indians had thought she was too injured and weak to fear her, even had shown some signs of humility when seeing her so tiny and helpless. Chief Running Bear had given the orders to make her comfortable. He had said something to the effect that she would soon be traveling the road to the happy hunting grounds. . . .

Leana's wrists stung and burned as she worked with them, then paused, breathless, as she began scooting herself across the floor of the tepee, having the need to again see if Brandon was all right. And as she got within viewing range of where he was also staked, she breathed a sigh of relief when seeing that thus far he had been unharmed except by the burning rays of the sun. His body was aflame with sunburn, yet Leana was so thankful that most attentions were being paid to the Mexicans.

But she expected the time would come soon enough for the white man to also get the same treatment as the Mexicans. The Indians might even think it more cruel to make Brandon look on, making him worry and dread that the same might happen to him. That was a sort of cruel punishment in itself. . . .

Leana's eyes filled with tears as she looked more closely at Brandon, feeling their futures were never meant to include each other. Now the Indians were going to see to that.

Her gaze moved slowly from Brandon to General Rufino, at least grateful for space between where they had been staked. Brandon was alone, closer to the cluster of tepees.

Hope rose inside Leana. If she could somehow manage to get free, she could sneak from behind one tepee and then another, and finally reach Brandon. If she could at least get him freed of his bonds . . .

Leana's gaze then went to the Comanche Indian squaws prancing about, wreaking their own sort of havoc on the other Mexican soldiers staked farther away from Brandon and General Rufino, themselves naked, staked spread-legged to the ground.

The squaws' coal-black, coarse hair was *shorn,* or rather hacked off, their ears had been painted red, and their cheeks were orange with rouge.

Attired in buckskin dresses and fancily beaded moccasins, they looked beautiful, yet seemed to be more fierce in their means of torturing than even the warriors. Their anatomical knowledge of the most sensitive portions of the human frame were too exact. It was as though the squaws had developed torture into an act and practiced it well, knowing even how to prolong it. Their victims now yowled and begged for mercy, and the more they cried out, the more attention was given to them.

Leana glanced from Brandon back to the men spread out on the ground. Brandon was for now at least being ignored, the squaws too intent in their games with the Mexicans, who were some even half-dead from torture.

But Leana *couldn't* expect this to last much longer. Then the squaws' attentions would *most surely* turn to the *American.* Though Chief Running Bear had given orders that the American was to only watch, to then be set free to later spread the word to the other Americans of Texas of what awaited those who caused the Comanches any more problems with land and buffalo, Leana only had to look at Brandon and see him staked nude to the pole to know how quickly things could change. Should Chief Running Bear decide to, Brandon could quickly be turned on by the squaws. . . .

"I've got to get loose," Leana whispered. "I've got to get *Brandon* loose."

Wriggling, positioning herself so she could crawl, she inched her way around the fire space in the center of the tepee floor, her eyes intensely studying Darla. Darla's hands were free. She could free Leana of *her* bonds. If only Leana could get Darla to awaken from her unconscious state.

Yet surely she couldn't. The Indian chief was surely right to not worry about Darla. She surely was even dying. . . .

Biting her lower lip in frustration, trying to not believe that all of this was hopeless, Leana now knelt over Darla, seeing Darla's utter paleness and the contusions of her face. Darla's eyes were still swollen shut, her lips purple with bruises.

But Leana had to at least try to awaken Darla. Darla was her only chance. . . .

Bending her lips to Darla's ear, Leana began talking low, saying anything and everything that could reach Darla, to stir her back to consciousness. And when nothing she said seemed to help, Leana became desperate. Her body shook with sobs, her heart ached with sadness over her dear friend, the worry of Brandon, and over not being able to do anything about *any* of this.

Leaning lower, Leana nudged Darla with her shoulder. "Darla, you've *got* to wake up," she softly cried. "All of our lives depend on it. *Please* wake up. Brandon is staked to a pole. The Indians will surely kill him."

Not seeing any response, Leana shook her head sadly. She turned around and sat down with her back to Darla, again watching the squaws as they laughed and danced

472

around the naked men.

"It surely won't be long now," Leana whispered. "Lord, I've never felt so helpless. . . ."

She tensed and her breathing slowed when she felt icy hands touch her wrists, which were tied behind her back. She turned her head with a start and saw tears rolling down Darla's cheeks while she lifted her shaky hands to the leather bindings at Leana's wrists and began working clumsily with them.

"Oh, Darla, you *heard*," Leana whispered. "You're going to be all right."

"Leana, I . . . can't see," Darla whispered back. "My eyes. They're so swollen. But I can *feel*. I'll try my best to untie you."

"I thought you were dying," Leana sobbed. "You were unconscious . . . for . . . so long."

"I've drifted in and out of consciousness," Darla said softly. "I wasn't aware where I was until only moments ago. Your voice . . . it reached me . . . like a lifeline."

"The Comanches. They brought us here to their village," Leana said, feeling the bonds weakening at her wrists. "They've also brought General Rufino and his soldiers here. The Indians have ways of torturing you wouldn't believe. . . ."

"Brandon? How is . . . ?"

"So far he hasn't been touched."

"But he's being held captive?"

"Darla, he's tied to a stake. He might be next to be tortured. That's why I've got to get *free*. I have to find a way to free *him*."

Her hands fell awkwardly away from the leather bindings as they became undone. Leana's heart began beating faster. She hurriedly untied her legs, then turned

473

and fell to her knees beside Darla, gently lifting Darla's head, to cradle it in her arms.

"Darla, sweet Darla," Leana crooned, rocking her. "Thank you. Oh, thank you. We're going to get out of this mess. Somehow."

"Hurry. Go to Brandon," Darla said, her lips quivering as tears sprang from her swollen eyes.

"Hopefully I'll return soon," Leana murmured. "But first I've got to find a way to *get* to Brandon without being caught."

Darla searched with a shaking hand until she found Leana's face. She cupped a cheek in her palm. "Be careful," she whispered.

"I *must* be," Leana said, then eased Darla's head back to the blanket.

With weak knees, Leana rose slowly to her feet, her eyes moving in jerks as she searched the tepee for anything that might serve as a disguise for her escape.

Her gaze stopped at a stack of clothes and rolled-up blankets. Among these clothes she could make out buckskin dresses. Moccasins were even placed beside these. And to hide her hair and face, she could use . . . a . . . blanket. . . .

Her hand went to the sheathed manchette at the calf of her leg. She smiled to herself. The Indians had taken her pistol but hadn't searched and found the manchette. Brandon had given it to her for her protection. Ironically, it was not going to be used to assure him of his *own*. . . .

Hurrying out of her own clothes and into the buckskin dress, Leana slipped the soft moccasins onto her feet. And once her heart began beating more regularly and she could breathe easier, she placed the bright striped Indian blanket about her head and shoulders and began moving stealthily toward the entranceway.

But she stopped to take one more lingering look at Darla before stepping from the tepee. Chances were this could be the last. . . .

"Are you going now?" Darla asked. "I heard you moving about and then become so quiet."

"I'll be back. *Soon,*" Leana whispered, then edged from the tepee, her eyes wild with fear. Now that she was out in the open, she could see that the Indian warriors were nowhere to be seen, having seemingly left the torturous deeds to the women of the village.

The air was heavy with the smell of tobacco. Leana surmised that the warriors were in council with their chief, gloating over this victory, while passing the pipe from man to man.

Leana smiled smugly, glad for the Indians' retreat into the wigwams. And dressed as she was, she didn't have to walk so cautiously about. And how convenient that a wigwam stood so close to Brandon! She could stand in its shadow while cutting through the leather bindings on his wrists and legs.

Moving in a steady gait, Leana passed several wigwams. Out of the corners of her eyes she was watching the squaws and their continued games with the Mexicans. The squaws were still too caught up in this to notice *this* squaw who chose to be away from the others, and who hid her face from the sun beneath the protective layer of blanket. . . .

Leana moved on to Brandon. And once there, she stood directly before him. Scooting the blanket back enough for him to see her face, she smiled coyly up at him, then stepped into the shadow of the wigwam and reached her hands beneath the buckskin dress for her manchette. With trembling fingers she placed the weapon to the leather bindings at Brandon's wrists and cut them smoothly away. She then stooped and freed his legs.

Leana straightened her back, almost choked up with happiness to see him free. Then her gaze swept over him, once again aware of his nudity as he turned to fully face her. "Take the blanket," she said, jerking it away from herself. "Hurry, Brandon. We must find a way to get out of here."

"Darla?" he said, stepping quickly to Leana's side, wrapping the blanket around him.

"She's going to be all right," Leana said, reaching to touch Brandon's cheek, reassuring herself that he wasn't a figment of her imagination. He was real. And he was at least free from the *stake*.

"But truly *is* she?" she quickly added. "How can we all escape, Brandon?"

Brandon's gaze traveled across the land, seeing horses grazing close by. And luck was with him. He saw rifles in some of the leather sheaths on some of the horses.

His gaze moved to Leana. "The Comanche warriors must be in council with the chief," he said thickly. "Let's hurry while we have at least a chance."

"But *how?*" Leana asked, now not feeling so hopeful. Though she and Brandon were now free of their bonds, were they truly? Surely they couldn't escape from the Indian village. . . .

"We'll escape on horses. And as we ride away we'll scatter the remaining horses. That could give us at least a little time."

Leana wanted to rush into Brandon's arms, to cling to

him. But instead she began moving alongside him until they were finally back inside the tepee, where Darla still lay.

"Darla, Brandon is here. He's going to carry you to a horse," Leana reassured as Brandon swept Darla up into his arms. Leana replaced her manchette in its scabbard. "Hopefully we can get away before the warriors leave the chief's tent. And the squaws are too busy to notice anything but the Mexicans."

"Just go without me," Darla softly cried. "Surely taking me will only slow your escape."

"You're going with us," Brandon said flatly. "Now, just save your breath. You'll need all your energy to stay on the horse as we ride quickly away from this place."

Leana eyed the pile of clothes and then Brandon and his scanty attire of blanket. It couldn't stay secured around his shoulders while he attempted to catch a horse. He must have something more substantial! She rushed to the clothes and found men's leggings. She hurried back to Brandon and jerked the blanket from his shoulders.

"I'll hold the leggings steady as you step into them," she whispered. "Hurry, Brandon. But don't *stumble* in your haste."

She wanted to giggle at his awkwardness at placing his legs into the leggings. But she knew this was not the time for giggling. This was, perhaps, the most serious moment of her *life*.

She instead drew the leggings on up and over Brandon's hips, fitting him well at the waist.

"Let's go. . . ." Brandon said, nodding toward the entranceway. "If we're lucky, we'll reach the Big Thicket by at least nightfall."

Once outside, Leana and Brandon moved stealthily

from one tepee's shadow to another. The cries of pain from the Mexicans filled the air, a warning of what could happen if Leana and Brandon were caught while escaping.

Brandon stopped and placed an arm in front of Leana, stopping her, eyeing the horses now so temptingly close. "When I begin running, tear the hell out of the ground with your feet, Leana," he growled. "Run as you've never run before. Get on a horse and ride it hard. I'm not sure just how much I can scatter the horses. Could be the Indians will be right on our tails."

Leana sucked in her breath, her heart pounding so hard it threatened to cause her to faint. She blinked her eyes wildly, steadying herself, then ran fast after Brandon as he headed toward the horses.

"Get on a horse and leave quick!" Brandon said, giving Leana a dark frown as he placed Darla on a spotted mare. He swung himself onto the horse, waiting for Leana to leave, and then began riding around through the grazing horses, scattering them.

Clinging to Darla with one hand and reins with another, he then urged his horse into a fast gallop, fearing the horse's hooves would draw the attention of the Indians, which Brandon so wanted to avoid.

Shivers ran up and down his spine when hearing the sudden shouts of Indians behind him. He turned his head just enough to see the Indians chasing the horses and then held on to Darla for dear life as he sank the heels of his boots into the flanks of his horse and rode harder until he was riding alongside Leana.

"The Indians . . . ?" Leana shouted, her hair flying in the wind. "I hear them. They know!"

"Hell, yes, they know!" Brandon shouted back. "Ride

478

hard, Leana. If we can find some sort of cover—"

Brandon's words were cut short when he saw many approaching men on horseback. And then his breath caught in his throat when recognizing the lead rider. It . . . was . . . *Cyril.* . . .

Laughing boisterously, Brandon wheeled his horse to a halt. "Leana! Stop! I'm going to place Darla on your horse with you," Brandon shouted. "Seems Cyril and I are going to fight side by side again, but *this* time on *land.*"

Tears of relief flooded Leana's eyes as she watched Cyril and his rustic-looking pirate crew coming closer. Their raised sabers caught the shine of the sun in them, the bright colors of their clothes a sight to behold!

Leana wheeled her horse around and went back to rescue Darla. As Brandon placed Darla on Leana's horse, he and Leana exchanged lingering admiring glances, and then Cyril and his men were there.

"Came in the nick of time, eh?" Cyril barked, his eyes wavering when he saw Darla and the condition she was in. "The bastards! Let me at them Indians!" he shouted, grabbing his rifle from its leather sheath.

Brandon saw Cyril's pained expression. "The Indians aren't responsible for Darla's disfigurement," he said, mounting his horse. "It was the damn *Mexicans!*"

"But you're runnin' from Indians," Cyril said, forking an eyebrow. "I went to the Seton ranch to visit me daughter. I found the ranch burned to the *ground.* That's how I knew to come searchin' for you at the *Indian* village. The Indians are known for burnin'. Not Mexicans."

Brandon chuckled. "I'm glad you've made this sort of mistake," he said.

"But if the Mexicans . . . ?"

"It's a long story, Cyril," Brandon said, removing the rifle from the leather sheath on his borrowed horse. "One I'd rather tell later. For now? Let's go show the Comanches a thing or two."

"Aye, aye, so we shall!" Cyril laughed, winking at Brandon. "It makes no difference, lad, whether we fight on land or sea. It's just damn good to be by yer *side* again. . . ."

Chapter Thirty-Four

One year later

The sun was waning in the sky, an orange disk lowering toward the horizon, casting orange shadows onto the distant mountains, and closer still, onto grazing longhorns and horses. Leana leaned into Brandon's embrace, looking from their parlor window, content, finally at peace with herself and the world. After Sam Houston's victory at San Jacinto, with the Mexican General Santa Anna offering Texas its independence in exchange for his freedom, all Americans who chose to, remained in the new republic of Texas.

Leana and Brandon had been among those who stayed. They had married, built a new ranch on the site of the ravaged Seton ranch, and their cattle and horses were thriving on the rich Texas grasses. The mansion in the Big Thicket was Leana and Brandon's private getaway, while there they were filled with many memories, always so missing Cyril and Darla. . . .

"Do you think Darla and Cyril are truly happy in

Scotland?" Leana sighed, resting her head against Brandon's arm about her shoulders. Her hair hung long and free down her back, soft, shining, and black. She wore a low-swept blue silk dress which clung to her voluptuous figure, revealing all that was important to Brandon's feasting eyes.

Brandon smiled down at her, seeing how her face was still so young and gentle despite the battles fought against the Mexicans and Indians. Her skin was the color of ivory, her body was supple and slender. Her eyes were lustrously blue, wide as she looked trustingly up at him.

"I'm sure they are," he said, now nestling his chin into the depths of her jasmine-scented hair. "It was a wise decision for them to return to Scotland. It was good for Darla to be introduced to her heritage. Her grandparents and her great-aunt Maudie surely were in awe of her."

"And now she has met a man and is going to be married," Leana said, her smile fading when remembering Matthew and how he had died. "I'm glad she has been able to place the tragedy of Matthew's death behind her. I truly had doubted she would."

"I miss Cyril," Brandon said thickly. "It was hard to say goodbye after all the years of being at his side. But it was a break that was sorely needed. I know that. Most sons *do* have to bid their fathers farewell when they have to chart their own future." His eyelids grew heavy. "He was the same as my father, you know."

"Yes. I know. Are you happy with your decision to put your sea adventuring days behind you?" Leana asked, giving him an almost timid sideways glance.

She knew he still dreamed of being on the *Erebus*. He whispered about it in his sleep. She had to wonder if he *would* be able to place his restless nature behind him. It

482

was as though the sea beckoned to him like a lover. Leana even dreaded riding into Rufino with Brandon for supplies, always watching Brandon's eyes silently studying the ships moored at the quay. . . .

"How could I be anything but happy, darling?" Brandon whispered into her ear, the warmth sending a wave of rapture through Leana. "I have you, don't I? You're all I need, darling. Always remember that."

Leana snuggled more closely to him, twining her fingers into his hair as his arms circled her waist. She sighed contentedly, again looking from the window. It was springtime. The grounds surrounding the ranch house were a symmetry of dusty pink oleanders and sky, possessing the clarity of a painting.

In the distance she could see pleasantly rolling country on one side, and roads knifing through the tall, cool trees like winding snakes on the other. And if she looked farther, she could see where the Big Thicket stretched out in its mysterious shroud of green, towering trees.

But her thoughts once again returned to the town of Rufino, and now even its namesake. "José says General Rufino's condition has worsened," she said, coldness entering her heart at the mere mention of his name. "He surely will die this time."

"Yeah, the bastard," Brandon growled, slipping away from Leana. He went and poured a glass of port in a tall-stemmed wineglass, silently offering it to Leana as she settled down into a velvet wing chair. "He should've died long ago. But he's hung on to life, just like a leech does to skin."

"If it wasn't General Rufino we were talking about, I would feel sorry for the man," Leana said, taking a sip of wine to warm her insides, still cold from remembering so much about the cruel Mexican general. "But as it is, he deserved no less than what fate has handed him."

Brandon settled down into a chair opposite Leana, twirling the wineglass around in his hand, looking into the blaze of the fire on the hearth. "Yes, he is a pitiful sight," he sighed. "The Indians' torture left him as though only a vegetable. He doesn't hear or see, nor feel. He is fed by others, as though a baby." Brandon visibly shuddered. "Yes, I would pity the man if it wasn't the damned Mexican. He's already dead, though, you know."

"Yes, I guess you could say that," Leana said, then directed her thoughts elsewhere. "Isn't José doing such a fine job of running *Leana's?* I'm so proud of that young man."

Brandon chuckled low, his eyes gleaming as he looked over at Leana. "You just wouldn't give up that part of your life, would you, hon?" he said. "I should even be jealous, don't you think?"

Leana's eyes widened. "Jealous? Of what, Brandon?" she said incredulously.

"Of your damn business," he said, laughing lightly. "But, truly, I'm proud of you, hon. You don't see too many women successful in an honest living. It's not as though you were running a whorehouse."

Leana's eyes sparkled. She giggled. "Lord, what a thing to say," she said. She set her wineglass on a table and rose to go to Brandon, her eyes filled with him as she looked him over, even now finding it hard to realize that he was hers . . . totally hers.

Tall, lean, and powerfully built, his features clean-cut, dangerously handsome, oh, so bronzed by the sun, he still made her heart race.

She eased onto his lap and twined her fingers through his reddish-golden shoulder-length hair and drew his lips close to hers.

"I sometimes feel so guilty," she whispered, brushing a kiss across his perfectly straight nose.

Brandon placed his glass on a table, then wove his arms about her. "Why should you feel guilty about anything?" he asked, smiling up at her as she peered down into his eyes.

"You gave up the sea," she murmured, curving her lips down into a pout. "What did *I* give up? I have everything, Brandon. Everything."

"And that's the way it should be," he said huskily, easing his hands around to cup her breasts. "I wouldn't have it any other way. You see, I also have everything. I . . . have . . . you. . . ."

His lips found hers. He gently kissed her, yet it caused a deep burning fire to plunge into her soul. She fervently returned his kiss, easing her hands to his chest and inside his cotton shirt, to coil her fingers through his tendrils of chest hair.

"Darling, it isn't yet bedtime," Leana whispered as Brandon lifted her into his arms and moved from the chair toward the staircase. "Why . . . are . . . you carrying me toward the staircase? There are only bedrooms on the second story of our house."

"Exactly," Brandon chuckled.

As he swept her up the stairs in his arms, Leana looked about her, seeing another reason for her deep contentment. The house was exactly what she wanted, two-storied, large and airy rooms with protruding ceiling beams adding massive elegance to its interior.

The house was filled with the rich mélange of Mexican

and American furniture. Kerosene lamps with bright tin reflectors shone in their wall brackets on each side of the grand stone fireplace. Tables of oak sat about the room beside chairs; the wood floors were bare, highly polished, with only an occasional woven, brightly designed Mexican rug thrown neatly about.

An Indian blanket lay folded at the end of the sofa, a reminder of the Comanches and the threat they had once been. But Leana and Brandon now slept peacefully at night, no longer worrying of Indian raids. The Indian chief Running Bear had accepted defeat at the hands of the pirates, respect shining in his eyes as he had then shared his peace pipe with Cyril and Brandon, confessing how he respected those who stood up to him. . . .

Reaching the second-floor landing, lighted by candles shimmering in wall sconces, Leana looked toward a bedroom door when hearing low gurgles surfacing from the room.

"Tommie isn't yet asleep," she softly laughed. "He's going to be as restless as you, Brandon. Like father, like son? Yes, I believe so."

"But he's only three months old," Brandon chuckled. "Wouldn't you say it's too early to tell?"

Leana snuggled against Brandon, savoring the scent of him, that of the outdoors and after-shave. "Darling, he's your son," she murmured. "He can be nothing but one who loves adventure. I only hope I haven't stifled you too much."

"I'm about to have the adventure of my life," Brandon said, stepping into a room adjoining the nursery. "Darling, *you* are my adventure."

Leana laughed softly, easing from his arms to her feet. She stood on tiptoe and placed her arms about his neck.

"I only hope I continue to be enough," she said, her eyes showing an intense worry in their depths. "Tell me again that I am, Brandon."

"Yes, yes . . ." he chuckled. "You are enough." He nodded toward the nursery. "And also my son, Leana." He began loosening the buttons of her dress. "But having a daughter could be another incentive for quelling my adventurous nature, don't you think? Let's see if we can make us a daughter this evening, darling."

"That would make life perfect, wouldn't it?" she sighed, letting her dress slip down away from her to the floor. She stepped from it, then quivered in ecstasy as Brandon slipped the straps of her undergarment down from her shoulders, revealing the taut tips of her breasts, which he now possessed with his lips, moving from one to the other, worshipfully.

"If anything got any more perfect, I don't know if I could handle it," Brandon laughed softly. He drew her into his arms and kissed her with a fever, searing her lips with the heat. His hands cupped her breasts, his thumbs circling her nipples, causing them to pulse against his flesh.

"Love me, fully love me, darling," Leana said, easing her lips from his. "Another moment longer and I might melt right into the carpet."

Brandon unbuttoned his shirt, his eyes hazed over with his own building passion as Leana released herself of the rest of her clothing and slunk onto the massive four-poster bed, patiently waiting. The brass lamp suspended from the ceiling beside the bed, its wick turned up, spread its glow along her lovely limbs and ripe breasts. Her eyes were a deeper blue with her building intensity of feelings, her lips seductively parted as she smiled ravishingly up at him.

"You're so slow," she said, climbing from the bed to assist him. She slipped his shirt from his shoulders and tossed it aside, then crept her fingers to the waist of his jeans and unfastened them. She watched his eyes take on a pained expression as her fingers lowered his jeans and then touched him where he so unmercifully throbbed.

"Darling, I feel as though I might explode if you so much as move your hand on me," he said thickly, guiding her hands away from his hardness. He sat down on the edge of the bed and struggled, then tossed his boots and socks aside.

Leana eased on the bed beside him. He spread out on his back and drew her up, over him. His lips reached up and caught the nipple of a breast between them. His tongue flicked, causing Leana to take a sharp intake of breath, the pleasure was so intense.

She wanted to touch him all over. Her hands traveled along his powerful shoulders, downward, circling his nipples, then lower over his narrow hips, and then around where she again dared a touch of the part of him that would soon cause her to spin in ecstasy.

Brandon's eyes twinkled as he felt her hand encircle his hardness. "I don't believe you heard my warning," he chuckled.

"Yes, I did," she teased. She lay atop him and urged him around, to straddle her, then guided his manhood inside her. "Now. Is that better?"

Brandon's eyes closed, he lay his head on her chest as he began his gentle strokes inside her. "It's better each time," he murmured. "Darling, how did I ever exist without you?"

Leana's face was flushed, her pulse raced. "How did I,

without *you?*" Leana whispered. "Had you not boarded the ship *Jasmine* that day, Lord, what I would have missed. Even if it *was* for all the wrong reasons that you *did* board her."

Brandon rose partially away from her, his body now still. He framed her face between his hands and spoke softly to her. "It's time that you should know that the capture of the *Jasmine* was a mistake," he said hoarsely. "It was thought to be a Mexican ship, carrying *firearms.* That alone was our reason for firing upon her and boarding her."

Leana's mouth went agape, stunned by the confession. "Why didn't you tell me earlier?" she gasped. "I always thought—"

He softly kissed her. "That I was a rogue?" he laughed.

"Why *didn't* you tell me, Brandon?"

"It is not my nature to confess to mistakes," he chuckled. "Not unless it benefits me to do so."

"And it benefits you now?"

"Aye, it does," he said, his eyelids heavy. "I wouldn't want my wife mistaking me for a *rogue,* now, would I?"

Leana moaned as his lips crushed down upon hers, savagely kissing her, fully possessing her, making her forget the wonder of his confession.

Brandon's hands moved over her; he was delighted that having the baby had not stolen her loveliness, her suppleness. Her body trembled at his touch; her flesh seemed to be begging for more. Lifting her hips about his waist, she urged him more fully into her, her hands now at his buttocks, pressing him closer . . . closer. . . .

Setting small fires, Brandon's lips rained kisses along the slender taper of her neck, the firm globes of her breasts, her liquid curves; he then ran his tongue along her cleavage.

Leana emitted a shaky moan. "Brandon, you're making me become . . . almost . . . mindless. . . ." she whispered, her body seemingly overheating. "But I always do, when with you."

He swept her up into a torrid embrace, closing his mouth over hers. Kissing her hotly . . . passionately . . . he thrust more strongly inside her, savoring the tightness, the wetness about his manhood. Sparks ignited in his loins. He uttered a husky groan as together their bodies quaked in an extreme, joyous climax.

And then they lay in an embrace long and sweet. "I so love you," Brandon said, tracing the outline of her breast with a forefinger. "Always love me as much as you do at this moment, Leana?"

"Always . . ." she sighed, tingling all over with aliveness as Brandon again kissed her.

But their moment of private loveplay was suddenly disturbed when Tommie began softly crying from his crib. "Ah, but the true master of the household beckons," Brandon said, easing up, away from Leana. He climbed from the bed and slipped his jeans on. "I'll go to him. I'll rock him for a while, Leana. Just you stay in bed and relax. You see to Tommie all day. The evening hours are reserved for *my* attentions."

"If you wish," Leana purred, fluffing a pillow beneath her head.

Brandon winked at her, then went to the nursery. Leana closed her eyes, smiling drunkenly from the total peace she was experiencing. Her right hand dropped limply from the side of the bed; then she rested it on the outline of the springs. Without even meaning to, her hand strayed beneath the mattress. Her eyes flew widely open when discovering something there.

Jumping from the bed, she knelt and lifted the mattress and discovered a folded piece of paper tucked away there. With a forked eyebrow from puzzlement, she removed the paper and dropped the mattress back in place. Going to where the light from the lamp was more intense, she unfolded the paper; her heart skipped a beat when seeing that she had just discovered a hidden map. It was a map of the Pacific Ocean, and with a large, bold X drawn over what appeared to be an island.

She stared openly at the map, then toward the nursery door, then back down at the map. This could only be Brandon's. He would only have hidden it to keep her from seeing it! Did this mean . . . that . . . he hadn't been able to completely place the lure of the sea behind him? Was he planning to go in search of some hidden treasure on this . . . this . . . island . . . ?

Refolding the map and placing it back beneath the mattress, Leana went to a drawer and withdrew the manchette. She held it momentarily in the palm of her hand, recalling when Brandon had given it to her, and why. At the time she hadn't known the importance of the manchette to him. If she had, she would have known then just how much he already cared for her. She had to believe that he still cared as much, even more now that they had become so close as man and wife, and wouldn't leave her to return to the sea.

She returned the manchette to the drawer and crept to the door of the nursery. She looked into the room. Her insides turned to a warm mushiness when seeing Brandon sitting in the rocker with Tommie in his arms. Brandon couldn't look more at peace, more content than now. And as he rocked, he smiled down at the small bundle in his arms, Tommie's tiny face peeking from beneath a blanket wrapped snugly about him.

Leana's breath caught in her throat when she listened to Brandon talking softly to Tommie. . . .

"Son, did I ever tell you of my exciting adventures at sea, of buried treasures, of baubles and beads?" he murmured, his eyes gleaming. "I had the time of my life, I did."

Brandon paused and got a faraway look in his eyes as he looked away from Tommie. Then he once again spoke to his son, looking down at Tommie's soft blue eyes, and skin as pink and soft as a rose petal.

"But, son, pirating is now out of fashion," he murmured. "It's now only things dreams are made of. It's no longer for me. As it will never be for you. But I've a map hidden that I plan to present to you when you are older. It will be a sort of, uh, memento of the life your father had, before settling down."

He eased Tommie to his shoulder and patted his back through the blanket. "Ah, but what a life I now have," he said hoarsely. "Nothing could compare with what I now have. . . ."

Tears scalded Leana's cheeks as they crept from her eyes. She smiled, radiant in her happiness. . . .

SWEET MEDICINE'S PROPHECY
by Karen A. Bale

#1: SUNDANCER'S PASSION   (1778, $3.95)

Stalking Horse was the strongest and most desirable of the tribe, and Sun Dancer surrounded him with her spell-binding radiance. But the innocence of their love gave way to passion — and passion, to betrayal. Would their relationship ever survive the ultimate sin?

#2: LITTLE FLOWER'S DESIRE   (1779, $3.95)

Taken captive by savage Crows, Little Flower fell in love with the enemy, handsome brave Young Eagle. Though their hearts spoke what they could not say, they could only dream of what could never be. . . .

#3: WINTER'S LOVE SONG   (1780, $3.95)

The dark, willowy Anaeva had always desired just one man: the half-breed Trenton Hawkins. But Trenton belonged to two worlds — and was torn between two women. She had never failed on the fields of war; now she was determined to win on the battleground of love!

#4: SAVAGE FURY   (1768, $3.95)

Aeneva's rage knew no bounds when her handsome mate Trent commanded her to tend their tepee as he rode into danger. But under cover of night, she stole away to be with Trent and share whatever perils fate dealt them.

#5: SUN DANCER'S LEGACY   (1878, $3.95)

Aeneva's and Trenton's adopted daughter Anna becomes the light of their lives. As she grows into womanhood, she falls in love with blond Steven Randall. Together they discover the secrets of their passion, the bitterness of betrayal — and fight to fulfill the prophecy that is Anna's birthright.